Praise for

Kudos to Kimberley and Kayla Woodhouse for their spine-tingling novel *Race Against Time*. This mother-daughter team has proven once again that they've got the goods when it comes to action-packed stories. Highly recommended!

—Janice Hanna Thompson, author of *Hello Hollywood!*

Kimberley and Kayla Woodhouse rocket out of the gate with another winner. Laden with compelling characters and an intense plot, *Race Against Time* pulls the reader through rapid-fire encounters with intrigue, danger, and deadly trails. There is also a beautiful innocence in the Woodhouse's craft that is unlike any other. *Race Against Time* is a solid read—one you can't afford to miss!

—Ronie Kendig, author of *Nightshade*, *Digitalis*, and *Wolfsbane*

Kimberley and Kayla Woodhouse are a potent combination, delivering riveting storytelling and poignant insights into the human condition. Exhilarating, heart-felt, and well written, *Race Against Time* takes readers on a journey long remembered after the last page is turned.

—James L. Rubart Bestselling author of *Rooms*, *Book of Days*, and *The Chair*

Kim and Kayla Woodhouse make an amazing team as co-writers. Their love of God and writing shines in their work, and I can't wait to read their next novel. I highly recommend their books to readers of all ages who enjoy intrigue, family interaction and heart-warming fiction.

—Tracie Peterson, best-selling, award-winning author of more than ninety-five books, including the Striking a Match and Song of Alaska series

Praise for *No Safe Haven*

Non-stop action from an unforgettable mother/daughter team.

Brandilyn and Amberly Collins, coauthors of the award-winning Rayne Tour Series

No Safe Haven is a page-turner on several levels—adventure, excitement, and compelling characters. But I'm fascinated that it was written by a mother and her teenage daughter, and that the young character in the book suffers with the same disorders that Kayla Woodhouse has. That gave it more texture and urgency and made it difficult to put down. I look forward to seeing more from these authors.

—Terri Blackstock, author of *Intervention* and *Predator*

No Safe Haven is a nail-biting delight of a romantic suspense novel. I loved the Alaskan setting and characters. The Woodhouse writing duo is dynamite!

—Colleen Coble, author of *The Lightkeeper's Ball* and the Rock Harbor series

No Safe Haven is a remarkable book that grips you from page one and doesn't let go. Romance, suspense, intrigue—Kimberley and Kayla Woodhouse have crafted a book that has it all. You won't be able to put this one down!

—Jenny B. Jones, award-winning author of *Save the Date* and A Charmed Life series

No Safe Haven explodes onto the suspense scene with an intensity and energy that only Kimberley and Kayla Woodhouse can create. What a compelling look into daily lives—with a burst of excitement and adrenaline—of these powerhouse ladies. *No Safe Haven* is a page-turner you don't want to miss. I'm so impressed—and a huge fan!!

—Ronie Kendig, author of *Nightshade* and *Digitalis*

To Grace - I hope you enjoy!°° God bless!°° - Kayla R. Woodhouse

RACE AGAINST TIME

With Abundant Joy!! Kimberley

KIMBERLEY
AND KAYLA R.
WOODHOUSE

B&H
PUBLISHING GROUP

NASHVILLE, TENNESSEE

Published by B&H Publishing Group,
Nashville, Tennessee

Dewey Decimal Classification: F
Subject Heading: MYSTERY FICTION \ ALASKA—
FICTION \ SLED DOG RACING—FICTION

Authors represented by the literary agency
of Alive Communications, Inc., 7680 Goddard Street,
Suite 200, Colorado Springs, Colorado, 80920,
www.alivecommunications.com.

1 2 3 4 5 6 7 8 • 15 14 13 12 11

DEDICATION

From Kim:

To Deanna Chang, for hitting me over the head. Literally.
I deserved it.

You were right. Yes, you heard me. And without you, I never
would've tried.

Thank you, friend.

And to Kayla, precious girl. Sure do love you. I love how
much God is teaching me through you. What an honor and privilege to write with you. Love you more.

From Kayla:

To God be the glory. Now and always.

To Daddy, thanks for being the most awesome-est dad ever.
I love you mostest. Plus infinity and beyond.

I win.

ACKNOWLEDGMENTS

First and foremost, we'd like to thank our Lord and Savior Jesus Christ. Because of Your love and sacrifice, we have the hope and joy of eternity with You. Thank You. We want to glorify God in all that we do.

Jeremy—husband to Kim and dad to Kayla. You are the best. Thanks for your support, encouragement, love, and prayers. We love you so much.

Josh—son to Kim and brother to Kayla. Often the quiet and unsung hero, we wouldn't be able to do all this without you. We love you!

Karen Ball—again, we can't express how brilliant you are and how blessed we are to have you as an editor and, more important, friend. Thank you for suggesting we write together. We love it. Thank you for challenging us, teaching us, and bringing out the very best in our writing. You're amazing. Just sayin'.

Ronie Kendig—fellow author, dear friend, and crit partner. We praise God for bringing you into our lives. Here's to many more years (and books!) of phone calls, visits, book signings, brainstorming, Bible study, and blessed friendship.

Julie Gwinn—what a blessing to work with you. You always have such great ideas! Thank you. Especially for all your understanding when times are crazy.

Diana Lawrence—for your beautiful covers. Thank you so much for listening to all our opinions and ideas and bringing forth a great design.

Karen Vincler—for allowing us to use you as Anesia on the cover. It's beautiful.

Lydia Vincler—for taking the wonderful picture of Karen. Thank you so much for sharing!

Greg Pope—the book trailers for *No Safe Haven* and *Race Against Time* are amazing. We've heard from so many people who are captivated because they watch one of the trailers. Well done. You are a master.

Our B&H Family—thank you. You've poured a lot into us and we know there are so many behind the scenes at work. Thank you. Thank you.

Callis Family—The Naltsiine Kennels would not have come to life on the page without you. Thank you for taking the time to teach us all about sprint racing and for answering all our crazy phone calls. We can't wait to see you all again! Give the dogs some love from us. (And thanks for allowing us to use some of your unique dog names.)

Tammy and Katie Vachris and Holly Morookian—we love you all so very much. Thanks for extra Alaska expertise and for being part of the fam. We treasure you.

The Country Café in North Pole—wish we lived closer so we could eat there all the time! Thank you for being so generous with us and treating us like family.

Terri Nelson at North Pole Police Department—Thank you for taking the time to answer our questions. I know time is precious with the important, life-saving work that you all do. And to all at the North Pole Police Department. Thank you.

Brigadier General (Ret.) Lane Killen—Wow. Thanks for help once again with all the military "stuff"—and thanks for all the years of prayer and support. We'll never forget OCF Bible study and Colonel Freimark and y'all teaching us the ranks all those years ago.

And to our other two military sources who have to remain anonymous for security reasons—thank you. Your input was invaluable.

Wanda Uballe and Melissa Conatser at Hotel North Pole—we had the greatest experience with you all at the hotel. Thank you for taking great care of us, helping us with research, and allowing us to use it all in *Race Against Time*. It's been a privilege to get to know you both. Thank you.

Carrie Kintz—crazy friend extraordinaire. Thanks for writing discussion questions (for ALL my books so far!), helping with marketing, reading, critting, and most of all, thanks for your precious, precious friendship. Love you much!

Lori Healy—friend, assistant, PR person, encourager, and much, much more. Thank you for sticking with us all these years. You've learned how to keep up and jump in to just about every insane experience we have and help us with it all. You are wonderful and we love you dearly.

Darcie Gudger, Becca Whitham, Sally McPherson, Shelly Ring—critters. Thanks for taking the time to read! Especially in the crunch times. Whew. We're blessed to have you with us. Darcie, thanks for helping with the discussion questions as well.

The Ahtna Heritage Foundation and Dr. John Smelcer— Thank you for all you do to preserve the Ahtna language.

David and Lori Phelps and family—you all are precious to us. Thank you.

The amazing people at *Extreme Makeover: Home Edition*. You all rock. Thanks again.

And last, but definitely not least, you, our wonderful readers. Thank you for investing a part of your lives in our story and in this book. We love to hear from you!

WORD GLOSSARY

These are the Ahtna words used in *Race Against Time,* with the pronunciation (in the brackets) and their definition. Enjoy!

Anesia [A-knee-shuh]
C'gaaya [Kay-Guy-ah]—Bear cub
Deltlaagi [dell-tlaw-gee]—Clock, watch
Kon' [kon] (C,L)—Fire
łic'ae [thick-a]—Dog
Naltsiine [Nall-chee-neh]—Down from the sky clan
Natsagga [nat-sag-ga] (M)—Smoked salmon strips
Sabiile' [sa-beel-eh]—Rainbow
Saeł [sath]—Box
Syats'ea [soo-yats-eh]—Niece
Ts'ede' [ched-ah](C,U)—Blanket
Udzih [yoo-jee]—Caribou
-yats'e'e [oo-yats-eh]—Daughter (woman's daughter)
Yanlaey [yan-lay]—Clouds; overcast

ANESIA
Eve of World Championships
Sprint Dog Racing
Anchorage, Alaska
4:26 p.m.

The word *lose* didn't exist in Anesia Naltsiine's vocabulary.

Liquid sloshed over the rim of Thunder's bowl and, in seconds, turned to ice. Anesia leaned down to her prized racing dog and checked his paws, then broke a piece of frozen water off the edge.

How appropriate. The chill in the air matched the one in her heart.

For thirteen years she'd raised her daughter, Zoya. For thirteen years she'd raced her heart out over the snow and built her kennel up to the prestige it held today. For thirteen years . . .

She'd been alone.

If only Dan—

Her braid whipped against her face as she shook her head. Cut it out. World Championships were tomorrow. And she'd keep her thoughts on that if it killed her.

Every major championship the past five years had her name at the top. She owned this race. She owned a good and decent legacy to pass down to her daughter.

Rubbing the heads of her dogs as she passed each one, Anesia visualized the race. The snow. Her dogs. The sled. When she closed her eyes, she could feel the wind freezing her face as the dogs flew over the snow. She could hear them yip and yap and feel the runners under her feet. She lived and breathed racing. Other than Zoya, it was the one thing that made her feel alive.

Anesia popped another Atomic Fireball into her mouth and checked the gear for tomorrow. The hot and spicy cinnamon burned her tongue. Over the years she'd tried to break the habit of sucking on the red jawbreakers as she raced. Far too often she almost choked on one when her sled hit a bump. Or when one of the curves jolted her. Then there was the time her best friend's husband, Marc, threatened to take a picture and send it to the paper.

But she wouldn't give them up. The spicy balls of fire were her good luck charm.

The press loved the shot Marc took of her flying down the trail on her sled. Her dogs all appeared to be in midair, her hood and hair whipped back by the wind. An exultant expression filled her face.

And red drool streaked down her chin from both corners of her mouth.

The shot ran on the front page. In full color. Marc and Jenna never let her live it down, and yet she continued the crazy ritual.

Marc and Jenna. How many times had Anesia longed for that same kind of love? Even felt jealousy over the relationship they shared?

Guilt flooded her heart as she pictured Jenna.

Alone.

Marc died almost a year ago.

Anesia wanted to be there for Jenna. She did. But her heart often betrayed her and still longed for a companion—a husband— of her own.

A tidal wave of loneliness washed over her. Might as well be honest with herself. She longed to be loved again. Longed to find someone special.

A sharp, stabbing pain to her midsection made her catch her breath. She pushed it, and her morose thoughts, away. She had no right to feel sorry for herself. She had Zoya. Her beautiful, bright daughter.

She had her kennel. And all her dogs.

She had Jenna and her daughter, Andie.

The ache intensified. Maybe she'd pushed too hard. She must be tired.

Needed to focus.

Win the race.

Then she'd take a break.

She and Zoya could take some time off from home school and enjoy the spring. Besides, Andie's one-year anniversary of her brain surgery was coming up. As soon as the Tikaani-Grays returned from the one-year checkup with the neurosurgeon, they'd celebrate. Maybe planning would help take her mind off the conflict and desire churning inside her.

She nodded to confirm her decision. No more selfish thoughts. Zoya needed her. Her dogs needed her. Jenna and Andie needed her.

Her life was full.

And it was going great. No time for loneliness. Besides, she'd made a vow. Never, ever repeating past mistakes.

Squashing down the yearning inside, she gathered a few dogs in her arms and closed her eyes again. Pictured herself racing tomorrow . . .

Cheers from fans cascade over her like a warm blanket as she passes the marker at the mid-way turnaround and her body turns with the sled . . . The race passes by in a blur . . . A smile splits her lips as she crosses the finish line and raises her fist in the air in answer to the roaring crowd. Once again the champion.

And desperately alone.

CHAPTER ONE

ZOYA _____
Ten Months Later
January 2
Outside North Pole, Alaska
1:12 p.m.

Trees and the soft blanket of pure white snow zoomed past. I took a deep breath and caught the smell of fresh forest wilderness. The trees, the snow, the breeze.

Everything seemed so . . . perfect. As always.

The Painkiller Litter ran with everything in them. We flew down the trail. I could hear the harnesses rattle, the dogs panting, birds chirping.

I smiled. My sled slithered and slid across the pristine paleness, my hands gripping the fiberglass handle.

Out here I was free. Free from school, free from anything that stressed me. In this beautiful escape I was free to fly. Fly like the wind, and not worry about anything.

Thank You, God. I smiled and giggled at the dogs' antics. Silly *łic'ae.* "Stop clowning around or you'll get tangled."

Morphine looked back at me, mischief in his eyes.

I rotated my shoulders.

Sore. How could I be sore when the Junior Championships were still weeks away?

Would we win?

Just thinking about the upcoming events sent a thrilled shiver down my spine. Yes, we would. Mom was a champion. Dad was a champion. I would be a champion. The dogs were champs already. Everybody knew we could do it.

Newspaper articles and TV interviews flashed in my mind . . .

"Thirteen-year-old, Zoya Naltsiine, wins Junior North American Championships . . ."

"Thirteen-year-old, Zoya Naltsiine, wins Junior World Championships . . ."

What would the reporters say then? And all those people who gossiped about Mom and Dad? Who disapproved of them?

Like the terrain flying passed, my imagination went wild. I could see myself racing across the professional trails that only the best of the best got to traverse. I could feel the excitement of finally winning the race I'd always dreamed of winning. I could almost hear the cheers as I won . . .

First place.

The dogs whined, bringing my attention back to the present. Ibuprofen and Aspirin panted. Morphine barked. We approached a clearing. My eyes widened.

BANG!

The sound echoed through the trees. Slow-motion pictures sailed by . . .

An old man fell to the ground. His head surrounded by a pool of blood.

Three men turned to me. One of them grabbed something out of the victim's pocket. Another reached for a gun. Pointed it at me.

Another gunshot.

Sharp pain shot through my neck and up into my head. I gasped and grabbed my shoulder, holding back a scream. *"All right!"* My command sent the dogs into full-speed. They barked and growled, looking over their shoulders.

"Morphine, RUN!" I blinked. Fog closed in. No . . . Unconsciousness? "All right! *All right!"* I turned to face the front of the sled. I could hear the men shouting behind me.

The dogs gained speed.

I grasped the sled handle and steadied my weight onto one of the runners, kicking the snow behind with one foot. We couldn't go fast enough.

The fog lifted. Then returned.

Pain. As if a thousand arrows had been stabbed into my neck, shoulder, back . . .

Blurry shapes . . .

I blinked. Tears streamed down my cheeks.

God, help us!

Another bullet *zinged* passed.

I screamed and ducked. Then everything from my neck down my spine went numb. I winced and tried to stay upright.

We rounded a corner. Keep going, keep going! Oh, please, keep going!

I sucked in short gasps. Air . . . the pain . . . My eyes squeezed shut. *Don't pass out!*

Adrenaline pumped throughout my veins. Dizziness took over.

No! I couldn't pass out. Needed to keep going. My heart beat faster. Faster. Faster. I thought it might explode.

I needed to keep going . . .

Reality wasn't listening.

Zoya, stay focused!

We rounded another corner. Then another. Then another.

Had we lost them?

My knees almost gave out. I straightened my elbows, trying to hold myself up. "Whoa!"

The Painkiller Litter stopped. Glanced back at me as if I were crazy.

My entire body shook. Fuzzy, spinning images floated around me. I staggered over to the front of the sled and fell. Morphine whined and walked over to me. Licked my face.

Would those men come after me? Could I get to safety before they caught up?

Spots danced in front of me. Trees swirled above. The cold wind filled my lungs.

The scene replayed . . .

An old man fell to the ground. His head surrounded by a pool of blood.

Three men turned to me. One grabbed something out of the victim's pocket.

Another reached for a gun. Pointed it at me . . .

My eyes popped open. Blue sky, white fluffy clouds . . .

The blood sliding down my shoulder and the thumping of my pulse made me sit up with determination.

I blinked. Stood.

We had to get out.

Now.

ANESIA
January 2
Naltsiine Kennels
North Pole, Alaska
1:56 p.m.

Dog feces flew through the air as Anesia cleaned the kennel and prepared it for fresh straw. Dozens of champion sprint racers sure could make a mess.

Not that she was much better. Why did she want to go and mess up her life?

Because she was lonely. That's why.

Watching Jenna and Cole the past few months had fanned the loneliness embers inside her into flames. Her best friends loved her. She knew that. They wanted what was best for her. She knew

4

that too. But did they know how much the ache inside grew every time she saw them together?

Man, she was a bad friend. She should be rejoicing in the fact that Jenna had found love again after Marc's murder. So how was she supposed to know it would open old wounds and make her desire someone for herself?

Anesia thrust the shovel into another snow-crusted pile of poo. On a normal day she loved mucking the kennel. Hard labor invigorated her. Today?

It gave her too much time to think.

Jenna's words after church yesterday forced their way into the forefront of her mind. "Anesia, you are amazing. You deserve to be loved. Why won't you even give yourself the chance?"

Sure, Jenna meant well. But Anesia couldn't help it. She'd bristled. Crossed her arms over her chest. But Jenna wasn't deterred. She just stuck her finger in Anesia's frowning face.

"I'm not saying you're not independent and fully capable of taking care of yourself, so don't go getting yourself riled up. But you know as well as I do that Zoya could use a dad. And you could use someone to walk this journey of life with you. You have a beautiful heart. Now open it up."

Mint and Basil from the Herb Litter nosed up to her leg and cocked their heads. Could her dogs be in on the conspiracy as well?

Her laughter filled the frozen air as she loved on the dogs. Funny, how open and loving she was with them. Why couldn't she be like that with people? *God, could You please help me? I want to be open to loving someone again, but I don't want to mess up. Like the last time . . .*

Even so she couldn't stop the longing. So. Time to face the music. It scared her spitless. No doubt about it.

Maybe she should spill her guts to Jenna and get it all out in the open. There'd be no turning back once her best friend heard the words from her lips. That was the best part of their friendship—accountability. They'd promised each other decades ago that they'd hold each other's toes to the fire.

Decision made, Anesia put her tools away and pulled a small bag of smoked and dried salmon from her pocket. Popping a few strips of the *natsagga* into her mouth, she savored the flavor and headed to the house.

She rehearsed her words for Jenna as she walked—

"Anesia!" Beth, one of her employees, ran toward her from the house. "Anesia! The hospital is on the phone."

The urgency in Beth's voice and her complete abandon of coat and shoes set Anesia's pulse racing. Could something have happened to Jenna and Andie again? *Oh God, please no!*

Her heart raced in rhythm to her feet as she barreled into the kitchen and grabbed the phone. "Hello? This is Anesia Naltsiine."

"Ms. Naltsiine, we need you to come to the emergency room as quickly as possible—"

"What's happened?"

"Ms. Naltsiine, your daughter, Zoya, is being treated. It isn't life-threatening, but she's been shot . . ."

The woman's words slurred into random noise in her ear. Zoya? Shot? How could this happen? Anesia's knees collapsed and she sank to the floor. Her baby—

"Ms. Naltsiine? Ms. Naltsiine? Are you there?"

The voice brought her attention back to the phone in her hands. "Yes, yes, I'm here. Is she okay? Who shot her?"

"I don't know the details, it was relayed to me that her injuries are not life-threatening. Ma'am, how soon can you be here? Your daughter is asking for you."

She grabbed the counter, pulled herself up, and stiffened her spine. Zoya needed her. "I'm on my way."

COLE

January 2
North Pole, Alaska
2:23 p.m.

Cole Maddox swiped chocolate chips from the bag on the counter as his stepdaughter, Andie Tikaani-Gray, stirred cookie dough.

Without blinking an eye, she swatted him with the wooden spoon. "No cookies for you, Cole, unless you stop stealing all the chocolate." She turned to him, wiping her other hand on her apron and planted her feet in a fencing position. "*En garde!*" The spoon slashed through the air.

"So that's how it's going to be!" He shot her his best scowl.

"You don't fool me, Echo."

He grinned. The kid loved using the nickname she'd given him when they were trapped on the side of Sultana.

He loved it too.

With lightning reflexes, he reached for a spatula. "You ready to get trounced again?"

"Not a chance, old man. You're losing your touch." She smacked the back of his hand with the spoon. "See?" She hopped around the kitchen wielding the spoon like a sword. "Gotcha again."

"Old man? Seriously? You're not living up to your call name, Einstein, with all that trash talk." He approached her with the spatula, settling into his own fencing stance. "It's time for the student to learn from the master." Family could heal a world of hurt. His first wife, Amanda, and their three-year-old daughter, Chloe, had been killed in a tragic accident more than a decade ago. Nine long years he'd hardened himself. His heart. His mind. Then he met Jenna and Andie. And they introduced him to God. The same God his Amanda had believed. The one true God.

Spoon and spatula clacked together in rhythm as they fenced their way around the giant granite-topped island. The stress on his shoulders eased as his stepdaughter took his mind off the AMI facility and test coming up.

Andie lunged, smearing sticky dough on the side of his face. "Oh really? I think you're goin' down—"

Jenna appeared out of nowhere and plucked the spoon from Andie's hand. "No one will be going down today, I'm afraid." She grabbed his spatula. In one swift move, the utensils clattered into the sink where Jenna tossed them and she wiped her hands together in the air. "That's that, you two."

"Awww, Mom!"

"Awww, hon!"

Cole erupted into laughter at the whine duet he and Andie produced.

Andie waggled her brows at him. "You should thank her." She snitched a piece of cookie dough out of the bowl and popped it into her mouth. "'Cause you would've lost."

As if anticipating his next move, Andie shot out of the kitchen.

He was in full chase mode and already around the island when Jenna caught the back of his T-shirt.

"Honestly, babe. It's like having two toddlers."

"And you love it." He winked at his bride of four months.

The twinkle in her eyes gave him all the encouragement he needed. Wrapping his arms around her, he nuzzled her neck.

Andie appeared and swiped another chunk of cookie dough.

"Nope, no way. Think you can just worm your way back into my good graces with—" Jenna glanced at her teenager then pulled back and crossed her arms over her chest. Trying to look all stern.

Too bad it didn't fool him.

She took another step back. "You"—she pointed a finger in Cole's chest—"are a stinker."

Andie hopped up to sit on the counter. "Or a very tall toddler." She chucked a chocolate chip at him, laughing.

"And you"—Jenna continued, her gaze fixed on Andie's blue eyes—"need to clean up this mess. Have you seen my red duct tape? All I can find is purple, teal, and plaid . . ."

The ringing of the phone saved them from Jenna's scolding and search for the tape. As she headed to answer it, Cole reached over and flicked Andie's nose.

Giggles permeated the air around him as Andie defended herself with flying chocolate chips.

"So you think you can distract me with the chocolate, huh?"

Andie climbed off the counter. "Yep. It worked, too!" She darted back around the island, challenge in her eyes.

"As much as I want to win this war, you heard your mom, we need to clean it up." He could hear Jenna's reprimand that someone needed to be the adult. Too bad that someone had to be him.

"You're right. Would you put those cookies in the oven for me? You know how well hot ovens and I go together."

Good ol' Andie. Always finding a way to laugh her way through her rare disorder. "No problem, Squirt." Even at thirteen years old, the intelligent, independent, young lady still had to be careful. Cole learned more each day about things to watch out for, and how he could protect this precious kid without smothering her. Jenna was gifted at protecting and guiding. Giving Andie her space to grow into an adult, yet always cautious and vigilant about Andie's surroundings. Showed him how inadequate he was at this whole father thing. But he was learning. He often tried to put himself into Andie's shoes. Being unable to feel pain and unable to regulate your own body temperature could be a real bummer. Not to mention life threatening.

After sliding the pans into the convection oven, Cole spotted Jenna as she barreled into the kitchen. Her face a pasty-white, eyes brimming with tears.

She chewed on her bottom lip. Jenna's eyes darted to their daughter and then back to his face. "We need to get to the hospital."

Andie nestled up against his side. "What—"

"It's Zoya. She's been shot."

CHAPTER TWO

SEAN _____
January 2
North Pole, Alaska
3:25 p.m.

The black of the sky at such an hour in the afternoon amazed him. Sean Connolly had been in Alaska since the day before Christmas, but the lack of daylight for the majority of the day still mesmerized him. What would it be like when it was reversed in the summer? His brain wasn't quite sure he could fathom it.

After working his way across the country on foot, he'd reached Canada, then the ALCAN highway. The lone weeks of trudging through the wilderness in freezing temperatures had given him plenty of time to think. And plan.

For the first time in his life, he was living by _his_ rules.

He'd left Fairbanks that morning and headed southeast down the highway toward North Pole. Why he chose North Pole, Alaska, as his final destination could only be explained by his desperate need to get as far away as possible from—

Sean shook his head. No. He wouldn't let his mind dwell on it. He did the right thing.

An exit ramp veered off the highway. A Carr's grocery store and the Hotel North Pole were to his right. Without another thought, his feet took the exit and he headed into the small town he hoped would become his home.

A sigh left his lips as he walked along the roundabout and headed for the hotel. Interesting. The streetlights were decorated as giant candy canes. Christmas decorations covered each post, sign, and window. The decorations appeared permanent. Giant light posts on the main street were painted red and white. The short posts on either side of a fire hydrant were painted the same. Surely they didn't repaint after the holiday season. Well, with a name like North Pole, maybe that was the city's calling card. Christmas year-round in North Pole, Alaska?

A quirky little town to be sure for this Eastern city boy. His family would've looked down their noses at everyone here.

All the more reason to like the place.

He dropped his pack in the parking lot and worked the aches out of his muscles. He'd walked more than 6,000 miles the last seven months. Part in anger, part in stubbornness, but mostly to disappear.

Time to find a place to stay. Soon he'd find a job he loved, learn all about it, and then live his days out in joy and solitude. His past would fade away. He no longer lived under his father's thumb. At thirty-seven years old, he was finally his own man.

About time.

Sean picked up his pack and with a lightness in his heart that he hadn't felt since he was a child, he headed to the front door of Hotel North Pole.

DETECTIVE SHELDON

January 2
North Pole Police Department
3:34 p.m.

Detective Dave Sheldon shut the door to the office he shared with the three sergeants and took a deep breath. Who would shoot at a little girl?

A murderer. That's who. One who knew that child was a witness.

He gathered what little information they had so far and scanned his notes. They'd need to interview the teen as soon as the doctor called him. Didn't give him much time to piece together more than the bare facts: a murder of an alleged homeless man, and the attempted murder of a thirteen-year-old sprint racer.

A knock at the door brought his attention up.

"Detective Sheldon, I'm Agent Philips with the FBI."

Dave tried not to bristle as he shook the man's hand. Were the feds stepping in?

Agent Philips held up a hand. "Don't worry, I'm not here to take over. But there is some sensitive information you need to be aware of."

"Have a seat."

"As you know, your office was exemplary in helping the FBI with the Gray case last year."

"Thank you. We were happy to assist."

"Well, the young girl who witnessed the murder this afternoon is Zoya Naltsiine."

Dave looked at his watch and back at the papers in his hand. "How did you find that out so quick?"

"The Naltsiines are close to Jenna and Andie Tikaani-Gray Maddox."

Great. His stress level increased by a hundred percent. "So you think it's related somehow to the technology Gray invented?"

"We're not sure. That's why I asked to come talk to you. The Maddoxes are sure to be at the hospital by now."

"What is it you're not saying, Agent Philips?"

The agent turned and looked back to him. "Be forewarned. The Naltsiines and Maddoxes stick together like glue. They already know too much about Gray's invention. Major Maddox is read-on for SCI."

"Run that by me one more time?"

"Sensitive Compartmented Information. Top Secret Clearance. TS."

"And you're telling me this because you think they may suspect something? Worry it's connected in some way?"

Agent Philips shook his head. "No. Not at all. But Zoya Naltsiine witnessed a murder. Her best friend was almost killed last year by the men who killed Marcus Gray. Gray was special ops. Maddox was special ops. Jenna and Andie and I'm sure Anesia and Zoya are already well versed in the secrets that brought them to this point."

"Gray's technology."

"Yes. I'm here to offer assistance if you need it. Of course, we'd also like to be kept apprised of the situation, in case there *is* any connection."

Of course.

The phone rang. Dave nodded to the agent and picked up the receiver. "Detective Sheldon."

"Detective, this is Doctor Graham, the doctor in charge of Zoya Naltsiine. You asked to be notified when she was moved to a room and awake. Both happened a few moments ago."

"Thank you, Doctor. I'm on my way." Dave grabbed his jacket off the chair and hung up the phone.

Agent Philips held out his hand. "Thanks for taking the time to see me. We appreciate your cooperation." He smirked on his way out the door. "And by the way, Gray's daughter, Andie, is quite the spitfire. Good luck with that."

ZOYA

January 2
Fairbanks Memorial Hospital
6:22 p.m.

Mom talked in the corner with Auntie Jenna.

Andie sat by my side. Not saying a word.

I didn't want her to.

Did I?

No. Then I would have to reply. And that took way too much energy.

The strong scent of disinfectant filled the room. My nose wrinkled with the foul-smelling sensation. Sounds, voices, the squeaks of rolling wheelchairs from the hospital hallway drifted in. Spots danced in front of my eyes. Noises rang throughout my head . . .

BANG!

The sound echoed through the trees.

An old man fell to the ground. His head surrounded by a pool of blood.

Three men turned to me.

I blinked. Shook my head, sending sharp pain down my spine.

Stop it!

Why couldn't I get those scenes out of my head? I swallowed, then leaned back to rest on my pillow. Shivers crawled up and down my back. Like icy fingers . . .

Don't think about it, Zoya. Think about something else.

But what good would it do?

Why couldn't I have lost my memory? Or gone into a coma? Maybe then I wouldn't have to think about—

BANG! . . .

An old man fell to the ground . . .

Tears formed and threatened to slip down my cheeks.

I closed my eyes.

Beeping from the machines, voices floating from far away, clinking and clanking.

It was pitch black outside. Like the man's eyes as he turned to me and pulled the trigger . . .

Stop it!

I clamped my jaw shut.

With the dim hospital lights everything still seemed dark and foreboding. No matter what I tried to think of, the memories still invaded. Took over my entire being.

My body went rigid.

An old man fell to the ground. His head surrounded by a pool of blood . . .

Stop thinking about it!

I reached over and grabbed Andie's cold hand. At least I wasn't alone anymore . . What did I do? How did I move on?

Even the white sheets and *ts'ede'* seemed to hold a threat. Every noise scared me. Each footstep outside the door. Each time someone sneezed. Each time someone talked to me. Why? What was wrong with me?

What if they came and found me? What would they do? Strangle me? Shoot me? Kidnap me?

I glanced up as the doctor walked over to Mom and Auntie. No doubt telling them the extent of my condition. They said I had been very lucky.

Lucky? Sure.

Mom's hands shook as she nodded her head and bit her bottom lip.

Why couldn't I just go to sleep and stay asleep? Maybe then I wouldn't have to think about . . .

Do. Not. Think. About. It.

"I'm sorry, Zoya." Andie glanced at me, tears streaming down her cheeks.

Why was she crying? She had nothing to cry about. I was the one who had witnessed—

Chills raced up and down my spine. Why was I so cold? Inside and out. *Maybe I just need to pray harder.* Yeah. Pray. And maybe talk to Andie about it. But would that help?

No. I wanted to talk. But couldn't. What was there to say?

I looked up to the popcorn ceiling. The shapes. The different clusters of texture. A monkey shape. An owl shape. A *c'gaaya* shape. A lady with a large pitcher of water on her head. A gun . . .

I swallowed. *Stop it!*

My throat itched. I needed water. But what was the point of drinking anything? It wouldn't do any good. The memories would remain. The fear would remain. Those murderers were still out there.

I again swallowed. Nothing helped.

"I wish I could make things better, Zoya. I wish I could help."

But she couldn't. No one could erase what I had seen. Never. They'd stay with me. Haunt me. Forever more.

What was God doing? Why was He tormenting me? Those visuals, terrifying moments . . .

I closed my eyes.

BANG . . . *Three men turned to me* . . .

My spine stiffened. *Was this my fault?*

No, how could it be? It wasn't like I had done the murdering. But I should have done someth—

No. It wasn't my fault.

Yes. It was.

Mom glanced over. "Girls, we're going to get some coffee, we'll be right back, okay? If you need anything, the officer is outside the door."

"Okay, Mom." Andie nodded and turned back to me.

Our gazes locked. She looked down and fiddled with the edge of the sheets.

What's going on, God? My eyes closed. I turned my head away from her. No sense in letting her see my tears. *Why didn't You stop those men? Where are You, God?*

I stared up at the ceiling, avoiding the gun-shaped pattern—

Whatever.

My head hurt. Neck hurt. Heart hurt. Like the ember of my will to live was dying. Did I want it to? How was I supposed to light the ashes and turn them back to flames?

No energy . . .

My body relaxed.

Just think about happy things.

Nothing but the drab colors.

Nothing but the darkness.

CHAPTER THREE

ANESIA _____

January 2
Fairbanks Memorial Hospital
Fairbanks, Alaska
6:35 p.m.

Anesia couldn't breathe. Her tight chest ached, and the fog wouldn't clear from her brain. Standing in the hospital room, seeing her daughter in that bed, hearing her heartbeat on the monitor . . .

Air. She needed air. Why was it so thick and dense in here? Pushing toward the door, she sought release from the nightmare.

She closed her eyes. She'd almost lost it in there. Barely made it out to the hallway before the shaking set in. *God . . . please . . .*

"Anesia." Jenna's voice penetrated the cloud swirling through her mind. Her friend's small hand closed on her arm. "Anesia."

A hard blink. Another. She swiped a hand across her bleary eyes. She had to focus. Had to. For Zoya. "I'm sorry. I don't know what's wrong with me."

"You're probably in shock." Jenna hooked arms with her as she pulled her the last few steps toward the coffee machine and a few chairs. "Now. Sit. Talk."

Anesia glanced down at her hands. Rough and calloused from years of work with her kennel of dogs. Strong. She'd always prided herself on her strength. Her ability to take care of herself and her daughter. How had she let this happen? Why couldn't she protect her own daughter from the horror she witnessed today?

"Spit it out, girl." Jenna reached over and rubbed her arm. "I can see those wheels turning."

"I don't know what to do next." Helpless. That's how she sounded.

And how she felt.

"I know. It's an uncomfortable feeling to be out of control."

Anesia drew a breath. Yes. Jenna understood. Probably better than anyone else. With Andie's disorder, Jenna had to do everything she could to control every environment her daughter was ever in. Or Andie could die.

But this? How was she supposed to protect her daughter from something like this? "I should have been there. How could I let this happen? And there's not anything I can do to take those horrible images away."

Jenna gripped her hand and nodded. Understanding. Sorrow. Compassion. It was all conveyed in that simple gesture.

Anesia looked away. What right did she have to wallow in self-pity? Jenna was the one who'd gone through so much. Her daughter fought a rare nerve disorder every day of her life . . . her husband had been murdered and their home destroyed by men out to steal the military technology her husband developed . . .

No, she didn't have any right to wallow. She'd only faced this kind of thing for a few hours. Jenna had spent a lifetime trying to protect her daughter.

Anesia straightened. She needed to be strong. Like Jenna. But how? When all she wanted to do was curl up into a ball and cry herself to sleep?

"Anesia Naltsiine." Jenna tugged on her hand. "Don't you *dare* start comparing."

Anesia met her friend's eyes—and felt the tension melt away. Jenna knew her too well.

Her friend's tone was low, soothing. "Zoya will be all right. Physically she will heal fast, and we'll have to rally around her for emotional healing. She's a tough kid. You've raised her well."

Had she? What if she'd messed things up along the way? What if—?

No. She wouldn't allow herself to finish that train of thought. "I had no idea I could fall apart like this."

"Hey, you've been there with me every time I've fallen apart."

"Yeah, that's the problem." Anesia attempted a smile at her friend. "It's easy for me to be the stoic, strong friend. I'm good at that. The proverbial sidekick. Your backup. I like being there for you and being your support. But I haven't had to deal with anything like this myself since . . ." Tears pricked her eyes. No, she would not give way to them. She couldn't cry. Wouldn't. Not now.

"Since Dan died?"

All she could do was nod.

Jenna walked around the table and wrapped her arms around Anesia. "Girl, you are the strongest person I know. I don't know what I would've done without you all these years. God blessed us with each other." Jenna pulled back and wiped tears from her eyes. "Now it's time you let me be there for you. Let us help carry this load. It'll be all right. You'll see."

Anesia allowed herself the comfort of her friend's arms. Let herself lean on Jenna. Just for a moment. But then she needed to stand. Be strong. For Zoya—

Her gut clenched. Zoya was all she had left. If anything had happened to her—"I can't let Zoya race."

"Well, of course you can't." Jenna smiled and dragged her back toward the coffee machine. "The doctors aren't going to let her race for a while. Not until she heals."

"No, that's not what I meant." She fidgeted with her hands. "I can't protect her while she's out there. What if somebody comes after her while she's on the trail, while she's racing? What if—"

"Stop it. You really think you're gonna hide from all this? That you'll be able to stop racing? That you'll be doing the best thing for Zoya by keeping *her* from racing?"

Anesia opened her mouth to argue, but words were useless against Jenna's truth.

Cole appeared in the entryway to the lounge. "Hey. Sorry to barge in, but the police are waiting to ask some more questions. They'd like to talk to Zoya."

Anesia felt Jenna's grip tighten. She straightened her shoulders, set her teeth. She could do this. She had good friends. Zoya was a strong kid and they would make it through. The police would catch the shooter, and they could relax.

All they needed to do was catch the shooter and everything would be fine.

With a glance to Cole, she nodded and stood. "Let's go."

When they reached Zoya's room, two officers stood outside the door. They nodded toward her. One stepped forward. "Mrs. Naltseen."

Steady. One breath at a time. "It's Naltsiine—*nall-chee-neh.* And it's Miss."

"I'm sorry, Miss Naltsiine. We need to ask your daughter a few more questions."

Cole's arm wrapped around her shoulders. Her friend's husband oozed with strength. If only some of that would rub off on her right now.

"Of course." The sooner they caught the shooter, the better. She pushed the door open and steeled herself. "Andie, the officers need to ask Zoya some questions."

"Okay, Auntie." Nervous blue eyes looked up at her. "Can I stay?"

Anesia shot a look at the officers.

The one clearly in charge shook his head. "I'm Detective Sheldon, this is Sergeant Roberts. I'm afraid that's not allowed. Not in a murder investigation."

Anesia watched Zoya retreat into herself and shrink into the mattress. Andie shot up from Zoya's side, hands on her hips. "Sir, I don't mean any disrespect, but Zoya is my best friend. She already told me everything she saw, she needs me—"

"Andie." Jenna's soft voice silenced her daughter.

The detective glanced at Zoya. "I know this is really difficult for you. But could we ask you a few questions with only your mom present? Are you okay with that?"

Anesia watched a tear slide down Zoya's too-pale face. Andie leaned down and wrapped her arms around her friend while Zoya clung to Andie in return.

"It'll only take a few minutes, I promise."

Andie pulled back and gave the detective a look. Had the situation not been so serious, Anesia would've laughed at the protectiveness and spunk of her *syats'ae.*

The door closing behind her precious friends sounded like a vault. Its thud resounded in her heart.

Zoya needed her to be strong. Anesia reached for her hand.

Sergeant Roberts smiled at her daughter. "How are you feeling?"

Zoya reached a hand up to push the hair out of her eyes. "Okay, I guess." Her voice sounded so small. So childlike. "The doctors said I'm really lucky the bullet just grazed me."

The reminder sent prickles through Anesia's mind. She couldn't even fathom the pain of losing her precious daughter.

"We are glad of that as well. You'll be better in no time." The officer turned serious. "Zoya, we have your preliminary eyewitness account, but we're wondering if you can remember anything else?"

Anesia sat on the bed next to her daughter. Why did Zoya have to be the one to witness the murder? *Why not me, Lord? Why her? She's just a child!*

"I don't think so, sir." Zoya wouldn't look at any of them. Her small hands fidgeted with the blanket. "There were three of them.

22

All in dark heavy coats, dark hats, dark boots . . ." Zoya sucked in a breath. "Wait a minute. The one with the gun. The one who shot him? He had a hunter's orange skull cap underneath his baseball hat. I remember seeing the bright orange."

The detective took over. "Good job, Zoya. Very good. That will help. Anything else? Do you remember any birthmarks, tattoos, jewelry?" The detective scribbled on his pad.

"No. Just the orange sticking out."

"What about the kind of gun? Do you remember the size or shape? Any distinguishing characteristics?"

Anesia watched as her daughter leaned over and eyed the holster on the man.

"It looked a lot like the one you have. But we were moving pretty fast, so I don't know."

"That's okay." He scribbled some more. "What about after the shot? Do you remember anything else?"

"Like I said before, they spotted me, grabbed something out of the guy's coat, and then shot at me. I ran for my life. I thought they would kill me." Tears streaked down her cheeks.

Anesia closed her eyes. *No. Stop.* She opened her eyes. Willed her mouth to say the words.

"Understandable." He finished writing and looked at Anesia before speaking to her daughter again. "Would you be able to identify the shooter—or any of the men—if you saw them again?"

Her daughter ducked her head and began to shake. Anesia couldn't bear it any longer. "Stop! Please. This is too much."

The detective nodded. "I understand your concern, Miss Naltsiine, but we need to know if your daughter can identify them."

"No." Zoya squeaked between sniffs. "No, I'm sorry. I don't think I could."

"Thank you, Zoya. I'm sorry for all this. But I'm going to leave you and your mom my cell phone number. If you think of anything else, anything at all, you let me know, okay?"

Zoya wiped tears from her face with the back of her hand then took the extended card. "Yes, sir."

The other officer extended his hand toward her daughter. "You've done well, young lady. Now you get better, all right?"

Zoya nodded and buried her face in Anesia's shoulder.

"Miss Naltsiine?" The two men were by the door. "Can we speak with you outside?"

Anesia kissed the top of her daughter's head and held her close for several seconds. She whispered into her hair. "I'll get Jenna and Andie to come back in."

Zoya's soft sobs tore her heart to pieces as Anesia headed out with the officers. Jenna spotted her, rushed over, and wrapped her in a hug.

"Could you guys stay with Zoya a few minutes? I don't think she wants to be alone." Her words came out stronger than she'd thought she could muster, but her heart was a jumble of emotions. The intensity of them scared her. The desire to melt into a puddle and cry warred with the intense urge to hunt down the shooter and kill him with her bare hands.

The door clicked shut behind her. She wrapped her arms around herself. "What do you need?"

"The evidence at this time is pointing to the fact that the man your daughter saw murdered was a homeless man." The two men's expressions confused her already scattered mind. She couldn't read either one. She needed answers. Not more questions.

"But?"

"We're not convinced. The fact that they fired at your daughter and pulled something from the man's coat tells us there is more to the story. We will be digging deeper."

Chills skittered through her limbs. She swallowed and nodded at them to continue.

"And in light of that, we suggest you be careful. We'll be posting an officer here at the hospital. Until we finish checking it out, we ask that you don't return home. We'll bring you anything you need. We may be a small town, but we won't let the shooter get away."

She blinked at them. Was this really happening? Banned from her own home? "Wait a minute. What about my kennel? My dogs? They need to be fed and cared for—"

"Our men are there right now, checking it out. It shouldn't take long."

"But—"

"We're taking a precaution, ma'am. Making sure no one is there that shouldn't be. It's not every day that a minor witnesses a murder like this." The detective's eyes held compassion. Concern.

"As soon as we're done, we'll let you know." The sergeant handed her two cards. "Please don't hesitate to call if Zoya remembers anything else, or if you need anything."

The men nodded and walked away. The walls around her seemed to shrink before her very eyes. Sergeant Robert's words rang in her ears.

If you need anything . . .

What she needed was to protect her daughter.

What she needed was to turn back time.

What she needed . . . was for the killer to pay.

CHAPTER FOUR

SLIM
January 3
Naltsiine Kennels, North Pole, Alaska
6:30 a.m.

The dog moved in his arms. "Steady, boy. I'm not gonna hurt you." He tightened his grip. He should be telling himself to be steady. Sweat broke out on his upper lip even though the temperatures in this frozen land were well below zero.

He flipped the magnifying lens down over his night goggles and made the tiniest of incisions. One more deep breath and he'd be done.

A vibration in his pocket sent the dog into furious barking as he barely managed to slip the macrochip under the skin of the wiggling beast. A drop of liquid bandage, and he was done.

Releasing the dog, he exhaled his pent-up breath. He reached into his pocket and pulled out his cell. The phone's screen glowed in the deep dark of an Alaskan winter morning. With a sigh, he touched the screen and hissed into the phone. *"What?"*

"Well?"

"Well, what?"

"How many?"

"Over thirty."

"Are you sure it's working?"

"Of course, it's working. I've told you for weeks this plan is brilliant. Now leave me alone, so I can get outta here."

"Cool it, hot shot. Yes, your plan is brilliant. We've all attested to that fact, but the stakes are high, and we need to know that it's going to work. That all the chips are safe and no one's the wiser. There's too much money involved for you to screw this up."

"Whatever. I'm doing my end, now shut up." He ended the call. They would all pay soon enough. He was tired of being treated like an idiot. This was his job. The one he'd been waiting for. Nobody would ever think he was a screw-up after this. They'd all respect him.

And if they didn't?

They'd find out soon enough that he was a force to be reckoned with. He'd been waiting for this for years. No more watching from the outside.

He straightened his shoulders. Maybe he'd just kill them all.

ZOYA
January 3
Fairbanks Memorial Hospital
10:57 a.m.

An orange ray of morning sun peeked through a slit in the hospital curtains. Through the slit I could see the dark outline of the mountains against a blur of red, orange, pink, yellow . . . Dust fragments danced in the sun's rays as if they had nothing in the world to worry about.

No guns. No murderers. No pain.

Just a Swiffer Sweeper that would pick them up and carry them off somewhere else.

If I could be a speck of dust, maybe then I could get out of this hospital dungeon.

I sighed and tried to roll over. Thanks to the IVs that was impossible without setting off some kind of alarm.

My eyes slid shut against my will. My spine stiffened. I knew what came next.

Try as I might to stop them, the images invaded.

I saw the man. I heard the gunshot. I felt the blood.

And the pain wouldn't go away.

My body ached. My hands were cold as ice. My knees shook, I couldn't stop the tense movements. The familiar sound of grunts, cursing, and my sled sliding along the fresh snow echoed, as if in some giant chasm. They echoed. And echoed. And echoed. On and on.

Why?

My ears starting ringing. Were they protesting to the memories as well? Then why wouldn't my mind listen?

I failed Him.

Like a knife being jabbed into my heart, those words flooded over me. As if I hadn't had enough pain already.

Was that true? Did I fail Him?

My gaze jerked over to the corner. Shadows shifted. What? A man?

I swallowed. *Stay calm!*

The shadow moved. Sunlight streamed in.

I sighed. My shoulders relaxed.

Just the curtain. *You're fine, Zoya.*

The memories, so powerful and profound, seemed to hack a deep gash into my heart. How could one experience change me so much? My eyes shut.

Was I supposed to save that man?

No. *God, I couldn't have done that! This isn't my fault!*

Tears slid down my cheeks. It couldn't have been my fault . . .

If You had been there, God, this wouldn't have happened. I wouldn't have been shot, I wouldn't have these visuals, I wouldn't have this terrible feeling inside of me.

The rebellious thoughts hurt.

But they also felt good. Almost too good.

I let out a sigh. *Zoya Sabille' Naltsiine, stop thinking like that!*

I couldn't stop it.

But I had to.

My shoulders slumped.

Just calm down. Zoya. You'll be fine.

Just take a nap. Yeah. Take a nap.

This wasn't His fault. It couldn't be. He loved me. He wouldn't make me suffer like this . . .

Would He?

Why was everything so confusing?

I turned my face into my pillow and squeezed my eyes shut. But nothing could stop the tears from running down my face.

CHAPTER FIVE

SLIM

January 4
Fairbanks Memorial Hospital
4:40 p.m.

His shoe squeaked.

Turning on his heel, he straightened the white lab coat he'd stolen out of a locker and walked away from the police guard at the door of room 326.

Great. Now the cop knew he was there. No chance he'd get to her now.

An expletive shouted in his brain. The kid hadn't been alone for one second all day. And he was running out of time.

Two more uniformed officers and a guy in a suit coat rounded the corner. Headed straight for the kid's room.

If only he could get a little closer.

The men nodded at the guard and entered the room. He needed to hear what they were saying! How much did the kid know?

He glanced around, then ducked into the closest room and grabbed a chart from the bed. Chart in hand, he strolled by the door to 326, scribbling as he went.

Through a crack in the door, he heard muffled words, then footsteps. He continued down the hallway but stopped in his tracks as he recognized two words from the guy in the jacket.

Sketch artist.

He threw the chart into the nearest trash can and raced down the stairwell, stripping off the white coat as he went.

The little brown car waited for him in the parking lot. He jumped in and slammed the door, punching numbers into his cell.

"Well?"

"You've got a problem." He cranked the engine. "The kid knows something."

"How do you know—?"

"'Cause she's guarded around the clock and I heard the police say they're bringin' in a sketch artist."

Silence. Then a frustrated grunt. "So, we know what we have to do."

He knew. All too well.

RICK

January 6
Anchorage, Alaska
3:37 p.m.

"She's that good?"

Rick leaned back in his leather and mahogany chair, unable to keep the smile from his face. The leather had turned soft and buttery over the years of use, the wheels and wood squeaked each time he moved. But he wouldn't change it. The feel, the smells, the sounds. They were comforting in his fast-paced, high-stress life.

"Yeah. She's placed in the top three her past eight runs. She's not just good, she's great." The beautiful young woman balanced on her scary high heels and pointed to the page in front of him.

He scanned the text. "I had no idea. Guess I should've paid closer attention over the years."

His assistant smiled at him. "Like you've had any time what-soever. To do *anything.*"

He chuckled. Would life ever slow down? Would he ever get the chance to retire like he dreamed? He turned to stare out the window. And what about family? His didn't even know he existed. But maybe it was better that way. He didn't want to bog anyone down with his business.

"Mr. Kon'? Rick?"

"Sorry, Christy, I was lost in my thoughts."

"I'll bring in your coffee, you can look over all the news, and then you can dictate your notes on the new project." She pointed to the file she laid on his desk and walked toward the massive, cherry double doors to his office. "If you need anything else, just let me know."

"You're a gem."

"I know."

The doors shut behind her with a soft click. Closing him into his silent, high-priced prison. He'd have a few minutes while she prepared his favorite French press coffee.

The chair turned with ease back to his desk. The file in front of him. Everything he needed to know about his niece and her mother. The other file could wait. For now.

The manila folder opened with a flick of his wrist. Pages of notes, stacks of pictures. So many years that he'd missed. Oh, he'd always had someone give him an annual report, but that was it. Now, there was more at stake. He wanted to know more about this niece that would be an adult before he knew it.

Lots of dogs. Dogs filled every picture. Running the dogs. Taking care of the dogs. Playing with the dogs. She seemed to be completely at ease with twenty or more canines surrounding her.

Just like her dad.

An ache filled the empty spot in his heart. Why had he stayed away so long?

ANESIA
January 8
Naltsiine Kennels
11:50 a.m.

"It's good to be home, huh, sweetie?" Anesia pasted on her best smile, hoping to bring Zoya out of the quiet cocoon she occupied. The dogs in the kennel raised a ruckus as they walked up to the door.

The past few days had passed in a blur, but Anesia couldn't wait to get back to her dogs. And some sense of normalcy. Routine was a good thing.

Sasha, their faithful husky and Zoya's loyal companion, barked and stuck to her girl's side. Anesia's key turned in the lock and she pushed the door open. Funny. The alarm wasn't chiming for it to be disarmed. Sasha barked again and took Zoya's coat in her teeth, pulling Anesia's daughter backward.

Sasha let go and let out a round of rapid-fire, ferocious barks.

Anesia's stomach flip-flopped.

No. Stay calm. It's nothing.

No. It wasn't nothing. Sasha's instincts were always correct.

Anesia entered her home and rounded the corner to the alarm's control pad and came to an abrupt halt. Zoya walked right into the back of her and then came to her side and gasped. Sasha growled.

A chill raced up Anesia's torso. "Don't touch anything. I'm calling the police." Heart pounding, she punched in the number for Detective Sheldon.

"Hello?"

"Detective? This is Anesia Naltsiine." Her gaze drifted to the disaster that used to be her living room. "Someone broke into our home."

"Don't touch anything. Lock yourselves in your vehicle. We'll be there as fast as we can."

Her limbs wouldn't move. Her feet weighed a thousand pounds. She dropped the phone and took in the chaos around her.

This couldn't be happening. Sasha ran to her and pushed on her legs.

Zoya crossed to the bulletin board in the kitchen where everything had been ripped off and thrown onto the floor. All that remained on the board was a single note, nailed into the middle.

We can get to you whenever we want. Keep your mouth shut.

Anesia took a deep breath. Who would do such a thing? Her breaths came faster. Heartbeat drumming in her ears, black spots danced before her eyes. No. She needed to stay calm. Focus. Protect Zoya. She grabbed her daughter by the shoulders and wrapped her in a hug.

This was her home. How dare they? Anger bubbled up and drowned her fear. Whoever these people were, they'd chosen the wrong lady to mess with. She would not allow—

"Mom?" Zoya's grip tightened around her waist.

"Yeah?"

"I'm scared." Her teen's chin quivered. "I don't want to talk to the detective anymore."

DETECTIVE SHELDON
January 8
Naltsiine Kennels
12:32 p.m.

"Sergeant, make sure they dust everything." Dave Sheldon walked through the house watching his team at work. The case kept getting more complicated. Would someone go to all this trouble over a homeless man? He didn't think so. And he *would* crack this case. North Pole might be a small town, but they took pride in being top notch. The state troopers always lent their support and expertise when they needed it, but Dave knew his team could handle it.

He walked out to the porch, where Anesia and Zoya sat huddled under a blanket. "Are you sure you don't want to go to your friends' house now?"

A muscle ticked in the side of Ms. Naltsiine's face. "No. Not yet. I'm sure you'll find something to help you catch this guy."

He could tell she didn't feel near as confident as her words. "Ma'am, it's going to take a while, and it's freezing out here."

"I know. But we're used to the cold."

Stubborn woman. "All right. I'd like to discuss plans with you."

Her angry eyes bore into his.

"We'll keep an officer posted here each night when your employees leave. I don't think there's anything to worry about, this is probably just a scare tactic. We need you to continue on as normal. Don't let them know they spooked you."

"Normal? Seriously, Detective. My life will never be normal again. But you can bet your life that we'll carry on. I won't be threatened and harassed. I've got buyers coming for dogs, and we've got major races coming up."

Zoya's head snapped up. Was she excited . . . or terrified? Her mother went on.

"I can trust Beth and Joe and Derek. I've already decided to hire someone full-time and let him live on the property. I'll get to work on a job description and posting. Hopefully, I'll be able to find a reliable man right away."

He nodded but noted the fear behind her eyes. Anesia Naltsiine might put up a strong front, but she was scared. "That would be great, ma'am. Until then, why don't you stay a couple days at the Maddox home. Joe promised to tend to your kennels, and we'll finish up as soon as possible." *C'mon, lady. It's sound advice. Take it.*

Her friends rounded the corner of the house and glanced at him. Perfect timing. He looked from them to her. "What do you think?"

Anesia Naltsiine sat a little straighter and pulled her daughter close. "Is it okay to take some clothes with us?" She shook her head. "Never mind. We'll pick up what we need. When can we clean the place up?"

"I'll call you. Possibly tomorrow. Most likely the next day."

Anesia and her daughter headed toward the Maddoxes' vehicle. Score one for the good guys. At least he didn't have to worry about them for a few nights. Now, on to the next step. "Major Maddox, can I have a word?"

The man looked at his wife. "Jenna, you all get in the truck, I'll be right there." He turned back to Dave. "Detective?"

Once the others were out of earshot, he continued. "Agent Philips paid me a visit."

The military stance of the man was unmistakable. "Good man."

"He had some concerns."

"About?"

"Gray's technology." Dave waited. Watched the man's eyes narrow. "Any chance this is related to AMI?"

SEAN

January 14
North Pole, Alaska
9:31 a.m.

The deep midnight of morning greeted Sean as he opened the blinds in his room. It had been a restful and rejuvenating several days. Even after staying up late last night to watch the aurora borealis, he awakened refreshed.

Today he would look for a job. His first week in North Pole had been spent eating and sleeping and relishing the abundance of hot showers. After he finally felt full and clean, he ventured out into his new community. His new home. The town wasn't large, but he'd found after a short cab ride to Fairbanks, that between the two towns he could buy anything he needed.

His second week he settled in. The same cab driver hauled him the few short miles into Fairbanks where he purchased a new Nissan Titan truck, a Mac laptop, a Nikon D7000 camera, and enough clothes to last him through the next few months.

Sean grabbed his coat, wallet, and keys and headed out of his room. Jogging down the wide staircase, he savored the excitement, the thrill of life after so long. How had he not seen the chains that bound him? Why hadn't he stopped it sooner?

He shook the thoughts away and smiled at the woman manning the front desk. "Good morning, Wanda. Lovely day, isn't it?"

"Why, good morning, Mr. Connolly. And um, yes, it is. Even though the sun won't be up for a while yet." Her smile always made him feel at home.

"So it *is* morning?"

She laughed. "I guess we're so used to the dark up here that we don't think twice about it. And yes, it's definitely morning." She pointed at him. "Wait right there, Mr. Connolly. I'm about to take some cookies out of the oven." Wanda scurried away and returned in a few minutes with a plate of warm cookies. "Here you go. Nice and gooey."

Sean hesitated, then gave in and grabbed a napkin and two cookies. He stepped aside as another guest commandeered Wanda's attention. No hurry.

He took his time munching on the warm, sweet snack. Now . . . how to find a job in a town as small as North Pole? Probably best to find out from a local.

The guest left the desk, and Sean stepped up to get Wanda's attention.

"Do you need more cookies?" She pointed at her chin with a wiping motion.

He pulled out a handkerchief and wiped his chin. "No, ma'am. As you can see, I've had enough. But I do need your assistance in finding a job."

She stepped back and lowered her eyebrows. "A job? Here?"

"Yes."

"Really? You need a job?" She covered her mouth with her hand. "I'm sorry, Mr. Connolly. I shouldn't have reacted that way. I thought you were another tourist passing through." Wanda pulled her cell phone out of her pocket. "What can I do to help you?"

"I'm looking for something long-term."

"That's wonderful, Mr. Connolly! I know you will love it here." She flipped open the phone and he watched her scroll through the contact list. "Now, what kind of job are you looking for? There's not a lot in North Pole, but I'm sure we can find somebody who knows something."

He furrowed his brow. What *did* he want to do? He loved photography but wasn't sure he even wanted to try to make a living that way. Being outside was always good. Even in the bitter cold. "Something outdoors."

"Okay." She giggled at him. "Do you have anything else? Other than being outdoors?"

Sean leaned over the desk and scratched his head. "Seems a little on the ridiculous side, huh?"

"No." She smothered another laugh. "Not at all. You just seem very . . . well, very educated, and well . . . established."

Sean straightened again. It was true. Her honesty made him comfortable in his own skin, even if he wasn't sure he liked who he was anymore. "I'm starting over."

Her fingernails tapped on the counter as she looked lost in thought. Then, with a grin, she pointed at him. "You know, I have a friend who owns a large kennel."

"Kennel?"

"As in dog kennel. She breeds and trains dogs for sprint racing. She's won a lot of races. And her daughter. Wow. Her daughter is definitely an up-and-coming star."

"She?"

"Yes." Wanda peered over her glasses at him. "She's one of the top breeders and racers in the country and told me the other day she was looking for a new hand to help with the upkeep and training." She continued to scroll through numbers on her phone.

"Sprint racing? Like the Iditarod?"

She grinned at him again eyeing him over her glasses. "No. Iditarod is long-distance. It's like runners—you have long-distance runners and sprinters."

Dog sprint racing. Never heard of it. Well, it was outdoors. And there were dogs. Maybe it wouldn't be so bad to learn something new. Maybe he'd want to invest in it after he learned all about it.

Wanda waited, fingers hovering over the land line phone. "So, you want me to give her a call?"

Sean was ready to take the plunge. "Yes. I'd like that very much."

Fifteen minutes later he was on his way. Anesia Nal-something-he-couldn't-pronounce was looking for a full-time employee and wanted him to come for an interview immediately. He hadn't even had time to change before Wanda shoved a Coke and napkin full of cookies into his hands and scurried him out the door. Small towns did things a tad different. In the city an appointment would have been made for at least two weeks out, then he would've had time to research all about sprint racing and this kennel.

But now, as he drove into the sticks with Wanda's handwritten directions, he was unprepared. Thankful for four-wheel-drive, he bounced along a semi-gravel, semi-ice-and-snow-covered road.

The top of a red painted barrel on the side of the road was barely visible above all the snow. That was his last landmark and only signal to turn onto the unmarked dirt road. As he bounced along, a sign about 100 feet in front caught his eye.

Naltsiine Kennels.

Sean slowed and stopped. Was that the place? Were there other kennels in the same area? That name didn't look anything like the way Wanda pronounced it. He tried to sound it out, but everything his tongue spit out sounded even further from the name he'd heard less than an hour prior.

Not wanting to be late, he drove on up to the main house. Hands slick with perspiration. His first real job interview. All on his own. Without a soul knowing who he was or what family he came from.

It thrilled him. A glance down to the seat beside him brought his new camera to mind. Maybe he could take pictures of her dogs. He reached for it, but then thought better of the impulse. He was here for a job interview.

As he parked his new truck, a tiny lady hopped off the porch and approached him. Her jet black hair pulled back in a thick braid swung like a pendulum, her parka and boots seemed to swallow her whole.

And she was the most beautiful woman he'd ever seen.

CHAPTER SIX

ANESIA
January 14
Naltsiine Kennels
North Pole, Alaska
10:20 a.m.

The door slammed behind her. No doubt Detective Sheldon wanted to hover again. She was appreciative of the concern, but she needed to stand on her own. Anesia stopped and waited for the detective to catch up. Sasha followed on his heels.

"And you said Wanda recommended this guy?"

"Yep. She called me earlier. Said she liked him. That he was new to town and had been staying at the hotel. You know Wanda. She gets to know all of her guests and spoils them rotten." She watched the object of their attention open his door.

Detective Sheldon grunted. "You're right. And you know what? I recognize the truck. I ran plates on him the other day. Looked like a tourist with a cup of coffee in one hand and rubbernecking when he spotted a moose. Thought I was going to have to confiscate his camera to keep the guy safe."

So the good detective had run plates. "Did you find anything?"

"Nope. Seemed clean. Nice guy. A bit stiff. But a nice guy."

41

Anesia couldn't help but feel a slight sense of relief. But trusting anyone at this point just didn't seem possible.

"How many interviews have you done?"

She laughed as her next interviewee approached. "Too many."

Sasha darted ahead, barking. The husky stopped in front of the newcomer and sniffed. Barked. Sniffed again. Then her tail kicked into high gear. *Well, score one for you, Mr. Connolly.*

She wasn't sure what she expected in Sean Connolly, but this wasn't it.

Tall and lean, he exuded an air of sophistication she hadn't seen in this neck of the woods since . . . well, *ever.* His short, thick blond hair stuck out in every direction as he removed his hat to greet her. Green eyes held a depth—and a hint of a twinkle. Was he laughing at her? Better not be.

Not if he wanted a job.

Anesia narrowed her eyes to examine him closer. No, it wasn't laughter in his eyes, it was more like a sense of wonder. Even delight. Like a child exploring for the first time.

And yet, there was nothing childish about him. He wore confidence like most men wore baseball hats. Easy. Comfortable. Add to that his good looks . . . make that his very good looks . . .

No. Mr. Connolly wasn't what she'd expected. And she wasn't exactly thrilled. That a man like this was here, asking her for a job at her kennel—it was strange. At least he didn't fit Zoya's description of the shooter.

She held her hand out to him. "I'm Anesia. And you must be Sean Connolly." *That's it. Try to be nice.*

"Yes." His grip was strong, assured.

"This is Detective Sheldon." *Keep him on his toes.*

"Sir. Yes, I believe we've met."

"Good to see you again, Connolly."

"Yes, Detective. You too." He cleared his throat. "I have since refrained from taking pictures while driving."

Detective Sheldon smiled. "Good to hear."

Anesia needed control of the situation and soon. The detective was only doing his job, but she needed them to know *she* was in charge at Naltsiine Kennels. That threats and murderers didn't scare her. At least she wanted them to think that. "So, I appreciate you coming on such short notice, Sean. I hear you're looking for a job?"

"Yes." He stared at her.

"Nervous?" Or, more to the point . . . "On the run? Eluding the law, perhaps?"

Something flickered in those eyes, and a small smile tugged at his lips. "None of the above."

Detective Sheldon laughed and patted Anesia on the shoulder. "I need to get back to the station." He turned to Sean. "Good luck."

Anesia slid her hands in her pockets as Sheldon drove away. "Didn't mean to get personal. It's . . . well, I don't normally get an older—I mean a full-grown—I mean—"

"Someone my age?"

"Well, to be blunt, yes. My usual applicants are a bunch of teenagers looking for jobs. Sometimes a college kid who wants to work their way through." Was she sure she wanted to hire this man? No, but life had to return to some semblance of normal. For Zoya. "Do you mind me asking your age, Sean?"

"Not at all. I'm thirty-seven."

She scanned him again. He looked strong. But could he protect them if they needed it? "And you realize I'm looking for someone full-time?"

"Yes."

"But I don't think I can pay you what you're looking for."

He lowered his eyebrows. "And what do you think I'm looking for?"

No beating around the bush. That was good. "I'm sure you've probably got a family to support, and I don't think I pay enough for that."

"No. It's just me."

"Really?" That surprised her. And, for some odd reason, pleased her.

"Really. Just me."

This was getting more interesting all the time. "Welcome to Naltsiine Kennels. Shall we get on with the interview?"

"Yes."

Not bad. Maybe this guy would work out after all. Anesia turned to lead him up the steps.

"Ma'am?"

She looked back at him. "Please, call me Anesia."

"Anesia." He angled a look at her. "Would you mind saying your last name again? I haven't grasped the pronunciation yet."

Nice that he addressed it right up front. Too many people kept trying, only to butcher her name until it was unrecognizable. "Nall-chee-neh."

His lips moved as if attempting the name but shook his head. "Once more, please."

"Nall. Chee. Neh."

"Nalcheeneh." He nodded. "Different. Unlike any other language I've studied. Thanks for the help. I like to be accurate when I pronounce people's names."

"I appreciate that, Sean." How many languages had this guy studied? She led him through the front door and they removed boots and coats in the mudroom. She opened another door and led him toward her office at the front of the house. "Thank you for asking. It's Ahtna-Athabaskan. And not many people speak the traditional language anymore."

"So you're Native Alaskan?"

"Yes, I am." She walked into the office and offered him a chair. "And very proud of my heritage." She nodded toward artifacts lining the west wall. "Would you like some tea or coffee?"

"No, thank you."

Another rarity in this area: impeccable manners. His speech had a lilt that suggested . . . what? Obviously from the lower forty-eight . . . maybe a city-boy? Whatever it was, he was way out of her league. Way out of Alaska's league, for that matter. Here, people were down to earth and helped one another survive. So what on earth was he doing in this place?

"All right then. How about we get down to the nitty gritty?"

He sat back and lifted an ankle to rest on his knee. In control. Comfortable with the business of the situation.

"I need someone full-time, probably more than forty hours a week. Since you're single, if you're hired, I can offer you the one-bedroom cabin at the back of the property to live in. I need someone to live here to help keep an eye on things. We won't take advantage of you being there, but it would add to your"—she made quote signs in the air—"'benefit package.'" She looked into his eyes to see if he caught her joke, but he just seemed to be listening. With serious intent.

"Anyway, as you can tell, we have extensive property. One hundred and fifty acres total, with plenty of trail space to run the dogs. The kennel"—she pointed out the window—"the fenced-in area over there, takes up a good acre. We have seventy-five dogs at the present time, but that will be decreasing soon since two of the new litters are already sold."

"Excuse me." He cleared his throat. "Did you say seventy-five dogs?"

"Yes." She watched the proverbial wheels turn.

"Wow."

"Cleanup and feeding alone is a huge task."

"An enormous undertaking, yes." The first hint of uncertainty touched his features. "Would I handle cleanup and feeding?"

He was quick too. Seemingly unafraid of hard work. Not bad. Now to see if pretty boy passed the background check. "You would help me. You'd also watch over the kennel and dogs if I need to leave, help us train and run them, and assist at races. It would also be your responsibility to oversee the property and keep the trails in shape. A lot of it is trees and along the river, but we still keep the trails clear and watch out for anything that could potentially hurt us or the dogs."

"Do you have other help?"

"I do. My daughter, Zoya, and I run the kennel together, and I normally have two or three part-timers who help out. Right now we have Joe, Beth, and Derek. Beth will be returning to the lower forty-eight soon, her grandmother is ill. That's why I decided to bring on someone full-time again."

"So you've had a full-time employee before?"

"Yes." Anesia stood up and walked over to the window. She hadn't anticipated this. She should have thought it through.

"Would you mind if I spoke to him or her to get a feel for the job? I'd like to be as prepared as possible."

She turned to face him. No way around it now. "I'm sorry. But that's impossible. Peter was killed last year."

ZOYA
11:03 a.m.

My Bible sat open on my lap.

Nothing seemed to make any sense. No heavenly words of wisdom popped out on the page. No trumpet sounded.

No magnificent instruction came.

Nothing.

I swallowed and focused on the words in front of me.

"Many, O LORD my God, are the wonders which You have done."

Wonders? Like a murder was wonderful.

"You, O LORD, will not withhold Your compassion from me; Your lovingkindness and Your truth will continually preserve me."

Lovingkindness? Preserve me?

A little voice in the back of my mind started talking . . .

"He hasn't done anything for you. He's abandoned you. He didn't protect you from those murderers. He didn't help that man."

My eyes shut. *No . . .* I would not let those thoughts take over. And yet, everything in me said to let the anger burn. To let God have a piece of my mind.

But why? The Bible said He was watching over me . . .

Why couldn't I believe that?

I frowned down at the thick book. *And I thought you were supposed to be full of the truth . . .*

I slammed it shut. Then walked over to the window.

Lovingkindness?

If You loved me, then why did You let this happen? If You're a kind God, then why was that man murdered?

I tried to hold back the tears. Blinked.

What was I thinking? He was there.

Wasn't He?

My squeezed eyelids did little to stop the flow of tears from escaping. One by one they fell.

Like bodies on a battlefield.

I may have failed Him, but *He* had abandoned me. *He* was the one that left, took off without warning. Left me behind to fend for myself. Couldn't He see that I'd needed Him most right then and there? Did He know what kind of suffering I was going through?

Did He *want* me to go through this?

My brow furrowed. No, how could He? He was loving, kind, caring, devoted . . .

Or was I supposed to be the devoted one?

No! A strong shake of my head sent pain shooting through my shoulder, reminding me once again of the murder, of the images. Of the scars. Mute proof that God hadn't watched out for me.

Or had He? I mean, I wasn't killed, was I?

Ugh!

I flopped back onto my bed. Grabbed the blanket and held it against me. I needed to feel something . . . anything. Even if it was a soft *ts'ede'*. Or anger.

The bandage on my neck itched, hurt, was too tight. My wound hurt, burned. Just another reminder of the murder. Of that man . . .

Would those murderers come after me? Did they know who I was?

Of course not. How could they?

Stop it. Just focus. Everything would be fine, I just needed to get back to normal.

If I even had a normal.

Stop it! Focus. Focus. Focus.

It's January 14. That gives me about two months until the big race. You can do it, Zoya.

But the more I did, the more questions rose within me.

God? Why did You take my dad away? Why did you let all those things happen to Andie and Auntie Jenna? Why haven't You come again to take the sin out of the world?

Where was He?

My stomach knotted. Thoughts came flooding in. Memories. Emotions. Pain.

Andie in Uncle Marc's arms. Andie playing with Uncle Marc.

Andie hugging Cole. Andie teasing Cole. Andie and Cole doing a craft. Andie and Cole laughing together.

Why did she get all the good stuff?

She had the faith. She had the dad. *Two* dads. How come she got two when I didn't even have one?

I'd always believed God was my heavenly Father . . . but He was supposed to take care of me. Right?

It wasn't fair. The tears kept building up. But I couldn't let them escape . . . Mom didn't need another thing to worry about.

It just isn't fair!

I sniffed. I *would not* cry. Mom would hear. Try to talk me into spilling my guts. But she wouldn't understand. She didn't need more stress.

No. No crying.

I swallowed. *Why aren't You here? I can't feel You.*

I stared at the Bible. Waiting. Searching.

Nothing.

I picked it up and threw it. Its thud against the wall made me wince.

But it felt good.

I did it again. Over and over. The spine tore. A chunk of 1 Timothy fell to the floor beside a few pages of Matthew and Job.

I let the tears fall. Bit my bottom lip, trying to hold back the sobs.

My Bible lay on the floor. Pathetic . . .

"Zoya? Are you all right?" Mom's voice echoed up the stairs.

I poked my head out the door. "I'm fine." Sasha sat like a sentinel and cocked her head at me. Blue eyes searching.

"I heard a bunch of thuds?"

She sounded worried.

Great. *Way to go, Zoya.*

Whatever. "Yeah, that was um . . . just Sasha." I dragged Sasha in and shut the door. Would Mom figure out my lie? Did it even matter?

My shoulders slumped. Why was I so angry?

I fell onto the bed and let every emotion simmer. Every tear fall.

God, what's going on with me?

Sasha jumped onto the bed and whimpered. I wrapped my arms around her neck and buried my face in her fur.

The voice in the back of my head ranted: *"Don't listen to Him!"*

I jerked upward. Then picked up the tattered Bible and shoved it onto the top shelf of my closet.

Sasha barked. I sniffed and wiped my nose on my sleeve. *See if I care what that book of lies says.*

Lovingkindness . . .

See if I care.

CHAPTER SEVEN

SEAN
January 14
Naltsiine Kennels
11:09 a.m.

"Okay, Sean, I'm ready for you again."

Sean turned to follow Anesia back into the office. He'd been pacing the hallway since she received a phone call that interrupted her explanation of how her previous full-time employee was killed.

"Sean, I'm so sorry for that interruption. It was my daughter's doctor. If I hire you, I promise to explain everything in detail, but right now, well, it's enough to say we've had some major things to deal with the last couple weeks."

Sean sat down and leaned forward, resting his elbows on his knees. "Forgive me for asking, but is it financial?"

She waved a hand at him. "Heavens, no! Don't worry about it." She sat back in her chair. "Now, let's get back to the interview."

"Yes, Ms. Naltsiine." He couldn't blame her for brushing his question aside. He'd asked out of concern, but she probably thought he was worried she couldn't afford to hire him.

"Anesia, remember? Now, what is your educational background?" She pulled out a pen and paper.

This could be awkward. He cleared his throat.

"Mr. Connolly, we don't stand on ceremony here. There's no need to be ashamed. Please, just be honest."

Ashamed? Yes. But not for the reasons she thought. "I attended Harvard."

Her gaze shot up at him, eyebrows raised. She stared him down for a moment and then wrote it down on her paper. "For how long?"

"Ten years. Bachelors, Masters, and Ph. D."

She dropped her pen as her mouth fell open. Several seconds passed. Her mouth closed. And then opened again. "You mean to tell me that you have a Ph. D. and you're asking *me* for a job?"

"Yes."

Long dark lashes swept down on her cheeks in rapid succession as she blinked. But her eyes gave no hint to what she was thinking. "That's interesting, Mr. Connolly. You do understand I will be doing a background check?"

"Of course."

She blinked again. Several times. Then looked back down at her paper and wrote some more. "All right, then. What about work experience?"

"I've only worked for one company."

"And that would be?" She continued writing.

"CROM, Incorporated."

There went her eyebrows again. "*The* CROM? The multi-billion-dollar manufacturer?"

"That's correct."

She licked her lips and looked back down at her paper. "Interesting. What exactly did you do for them?"

"Do?" He stalled. Complicated didn't even begin to describe the direction of this conversation.

"Yes, what was your title, your position with them?"

He straightened his shoulders. *Here goes nothing.* "I was a vice president, Miss Naltsiine."

Anesia's mouth closed again and her lips formed a thin, straight line. The pen in her hand made a slow journey down to settle on the desk as she tidied up in front of her. Each movement exact. Forced.

The chair rolled back and she pushed herself up to a standing position and leaned over, resting on her steepled fingers. "I know I asked you this before, but this time I'm serious. Are you running away from something, Mr. Connolly? In trouble with the law?" Her narrowed eyes were pure steel.

Sean didn't flinch. "No. But I *am* starting over."

"Might I ask why?"

"God wanted my attention, and He got it." No need to say his family had taken a turn for the illegal. That would come out soon enough. He met her eyes. "I discovered I was being used for purposes that went against everything I believe in. So I left. What I want now is to find a job I love and work hard at it."

Something flashed across her expression. Skepticism? Acceptance? He wasn't sure.

"Mr. Connolly . . . Sean. I appreciate you sharing that with me. I don't want you to think that I don't believe you, but your story is a little uh . . . shall we say incredible? Do you understand what I'm saying?"

"Not entirely, Ms. Naltsiine."

"I'm sorry. That wasn't very clear." She sat down with a sigh folding her hands in front of her on the desk. "Your background is interesting, and your statement about your faith was refreshing to me. But please, understand that I can't hire just anyone. I will not put my daughter at risk, or anyone else I welcome on my property."

"I understand perfectly."

"You do?"

"Yes, I do."

"And you don't want to change your story?"

"No, Ms. Naltsiine. It's the truth."

She hesitated a moment and narrowed her eyes. "Okay then. Well, maybe there is a solution to this problem."

"Go ahead, I'm listening."

"I have a friend with the FBI." She shuffled a few papers and eyed him from the corner of her slit lids. "I'll still need you to sign this form for a regular background check." A paper and pen slid in front of him.

"I'm a bit confused. What exactly are you proposing?"

"I'm going to call him and check into your story." A pause rested between them.

Was she waiting for him to tell her something different?

"Do you mind?"

Was she trying to scare him? Threaten him?

"Not at all. I have nothing to hide." He hoped his quick response would portray he was unafraid of her finding anything. But deep down, he knew there was plenty he kept hidden.

"Good." She stood. "Thank you for your time today. I'll give you a call."

And with that, he was dismissed.

ANESIA
January 14
8:00 p.m.

The living room floor took the ferocious pounding of Anesia's feet with not a creak or a groan. "I just don't get it. Why would someone like that come looking for a job here?"

Cole and Jenna sat on the couch saying nothing and watching her pace in front of them. As if it would be dangerous to their health at this point to interject anything. She cringed. Was she that bad? "Come on, guys. I need your input."

Jenna leaned forward. "Are you sure you really want it?"

"Of course! That's why I asked you to come over." Ridiculous. Why wouldn't she want their advice? She crossed her arms around her middle.

"Anesia." Cole's steady voice calmed her a tad. "We've been listening to you rant for thirty minutes now—"

"I am *not* ranting!"

Cole laughed. "Yeah. You are."

She huffed. Could feel the knots tightening in her stomach.

"Cool it and sit down."

At Jenna's raised voice, Anesia stilled. Jenna never raised her voice to Anesia unless she wasn't listening. Which she hadn't been.

She sat down.

Cole leaned toward her. "Well, I think you've already figured out that this Sean guy was telling the truth. Sounds like Agent Philips didn't have any problems with him. When will the official background check come in?"

"In a day or two."

"Good. I'm glad he's handling it. After everything that happened with Marc and AMI, I agree you need to be careful. The FBI has promised to help us, but if you're going to be paranoid, that's going a bit overboard."

She stood up and planted her hands on her hips. "Cole Maddox, you think I'm paranoid?"

"No. We completely understand"—Jenna stood next to her and wrapped an arm around her shoulders, patting her in a no-we-don't-think-you're-crazy-please-calm-down-before-we-get-the-straight-jacket kind of way—"but I do think there's something you're not telling us."

"Yeah, she's paranoid." Cole ducked to avoid the pillow Anesia chucked at him.

Jenna shot a look at her husband. "I'm gonna have to separate you two." Her best friend turned back to stare into her eyes. "Spill it. What's really going through that head of yours?"

The leather couch squeaked around her as Anesia settled back into it. "God and I had been wrestling over a matter and then all this blew up in my face." She fiddled with the ivory carvings on the coffee table.

"Now we're getting to the heart of things." Jenna sat beside her.

"I need someone here. Someone strong and trustworthy. Someone to live on the property. I still can't believe that Zoya witnessed a murder. That she was shot at. But no matter how hard it is, I have to admit that I *need* someone here. Does that make sense?" Her fidgeting hands moved to the wooden *udzih* carved by her great-grandfather.

Jenna nodded. Cole stared.

"Ugh!" She threw another pillow at Cole. "You just don't get it. Men!"

Jenna laughed, patted her knee, and removed the caribou from her.

Anesia tried again. "I've been strong on my own all these years. Taken care of myself. Sheltered my heart and my mind. Haven't needed anyone. Good grief! I built this kennel with my own two hands, with my sweat and tears." She stood again, walked around the coffee table once, and collapsed back into the sofa. "And yet"—Anesia choked back a sob—"when things got hard, when my world fell apart around me . . . I found out I wasn't that strong after all. This has shaken everything—"

She looked away from her friends. From the weaknesses she'd denied for so long but could ignore no longer.

Weaknesses she hated. Because they meant one thing. One terrible, unavoidable thing.

She was going to have to trust someone besides herself.

RICK

January 14
Anchorage, AK
8:18 p.m.

The slight pain in his chest turned into a hot searing. Shallow breaths. One. Two. That's it. Nice and slow.

Rick popped four Tums in his mouth, knowing full well heartburn wasn't the problem. But he could pretend, couldn't he? Trick his mind into believing that was his problem, instead of a heart on its last leg.

The phone call this morning with his boss had not gone well. The man was a control freak. A tyrant. As hard as they came.

If he didn't watch it, he'd turn into the same thing.

Dark thoughts urged him to unlock and open his middle desk drawer. He did so, then pulled out the file on his niece. Time to focus on something positive.

Family.

He thumbed through the pictures, finding the one of her with her prize winning sled team. The blue eyes of the lead mutt were fixed on the young girl's sweet face. Her lopsided grin was why he loved this picture. An exact replica of her dad's smile.

Maybe he should go check out one of her races. That might ease some of his guilt. That was it. He'd go. Just be another fan on the trail. Another race lover.

And maybe, just maybe he'd figure out how on earth to get out of the mess he'd gotten himself into.

CHAPTER EIGHT

COLE

January 15
Fort Greely, Alaska
10:45 a.m.

"Cell phone, sir?" The young MP secured Cole's other belongings in a locker as Cole reached into his pocket and pulled out his phone. He dropped it into a bag and the young man sent it through the scanner.

"Clear."

Another soldier at the security checkpoint picked up the bag and placed it in the locker with the other items.

"Here's your badge and M9, Major Maddox. Captain Lewis will escort you down to AMI ops."

Cole nodded and returned the young man's salute. He followed Captain Lewis down a long corridor and into a waiting elevator. They entered the elevator and the captain slid his card into a security slot on one side while Cole slid his into one on the other side. At the green light, the doors closed. Cole and Captain Lewis placed their thumbs on the opposite touch screens.

"Verified match." The monotone, computerized voice echoed in the tiny compartment. "Captain Richard Lewis. Major Cole Maddox. State your code for voice recognition."

"Captain Lewis. Charlie Bravo Victor Two-Eight-Seven-Six Tango Alpha."

"Major Maddox. Alpha Golf November Three-Niner-Seven-Four Kilo Zulu."

The elevator began its descent. "Access granted."

Funny, the elevator sounded as stiff as some of his superiors.

Captain Lewis turned to Cole in an at-ease position as the elevator stopped. "Sir, let me know if I can be of further assistance."

"Thanks, Lewis. I believe that'll be all for now."

"Hooah, sir."

Both men slid their cards one more time and the doors opened. Cole stepped out and shared a parting salute with the captain.

Turning on his heel, he faced the immense security entrance to AMI.

Advanced Missile Interceptor.

His long-time friend and spec ops boss, Marcus Gray, had invented the technology, prototype, and the guidance system for this defense weapon. Marcus almost let greed take over—he'd almost sold it all on the black market—when Cole found out and confronted him. Marcus came to his senses, assured Cole he'd return AMI to the U.S., but was murdered before he could.

Car bomb.

Cole had been with him, in his car, only moments before. He'd promised to take care of Marc's family if anything happened to him. To help retrieve AMI and get it back into the correct hands.

He had no idea how that promise would change his life forever.

Marc's wife, Jenna, and daughter, Andie, were almost killed when another operative was sent to sabotage their plane a year after Marc's death. Their home was destroyed by a group of rogue black ops soldiers who would stop at nothing to gain this revolutionary technology. In the midst of it all, Cole found the Lord.

And fell in love with Jenna.

Now, almost nine months later, the Army had built one of the highest security facilities in the nation to house AMI, he'd married Jenna, and the military was getting ready to test their first prototypes of Marc's invention.

"Good morning, Major."

Cole pulled himself from his memories and focused on the general walking toward him at a brisk clip.

"Morning, General." Cole offered a salute as they were both armed.

"After months of preparation, I believe we're ready. Gray's notes were intricately detailed. Let's hope it all goes smoothly."

"Yes, sir."

The general walked him into the ops/mainframe area, down the steps, and up to the podium at the front. Everyone stood at attention. "Ladies and gentlemen. This is our first trial run of AMI. Several tests have taken place, but not with every facet engaged. We will begin the countdown at 1100 sharp. Please run final diagnostics."

Feet shuffled and chairs squeaked as everyone took their places. A thrill raced through Cole. To know he had snatched this back from enemy hands, and that Marc's dying wishes would be fulfilled, that the United States would be protected . . .

That's what it was about.

"Major Maddox!" A wiry man ran from an upper deck waved papers in the air as he attempted to keep his feet and take three stairs at a time down to the command level.

Cole stiffened. This didn't look good.

"General! Major Maddox!" The slight officer came to a halt in front of Cole and shoved his glasses higher on his nose. "We have a problem, sir." He handed Cole a still-warm printout.

The general's brow furrowed as he approached. "What seems to be the trouble?"

Cole speed-read the data on the papers. The last paragraph clenched his gut.

"Major?"

He gritted his teeth, and a muscle popped in his cheek. "General, sir. We have to abort. Apparently Gray embedded an encryption for the final sequence. It was undetectable until the sequence started. From what this report says, once all the pieces are in place, a code must be entered or the program self-destructs."

The general spun and yelled across the gallery. "Shut it down!"

Everyone scrambled to stop the procedure before the countdown started.

"We have less than sixty seconds, people! Shut. It. Down!"

Cole examined the printout again. What had he missed? They'd spent months poring over Marc's data. They'd followed everything to the smallest detail.

The general interrupted his thoughts. "Major. This is beyond serious. The congressional committee is convening in four weeks, and we are supposed to present our findings then. If the public finds out that millions of tax-payer dollars were used to develop this weapon, and we failed?" His mouth clamped into a hard line. He jabbed a finger in Cole's face. "If you can't figure this out, heads are gonna roll."

The man clasped his hands behind his back and turned to stalk away. As he did so, he threw one more comment over his shoulder: "And son? Mine will be second. Right after yours."

SEAN

January 15
Naltsiine Kennels
12:00 p.m.

He could hardly believe Anesia had called him back.

Sean nodded at Beth, another employee, who guided him back into Ms. Naltsiine's—no, Anesia's—office.

Of course, calling him back didn't mean he got the job. It might mean she just wanted the chance to ream him in person. His family was too high profile. No way she hadn't gotten the facts.

All of them.

No matter. He wanted a fresh start. He'd done nothing illegal. She was an intelligent woman. Certainly she'd understand why he didn't disclose the full truth about his identity.

She summoned him to sit with a wiggle of her fingers as she finished up a phone call. Her quiet tone relaxed him and without his consent, his mind wandered, taking in all the pictures, trophies, and Alaskan culture. Carvings lined the walls. Ivory, wood, and several sets of the little Russian nesting dolls.

Anesia tapped her pen on the desk as she spoke into the phone bringing Sean back to the present. "Thank you, I appreciate it." With a press of a button, she ended the call and turned to him. "Well, apparently"—she folded her hands in front of her—"your background is clean as a whistle."

"I couldn't imagine they'd find anything." Liar. Other than his identity.

"And your record at Harvard is very impressive." She rose from her desk. "I'm sorry I doubted you. Your background sounded a bit too unbelievable. Which brings me to my point. There's still the question of why you want to work here. I need someone stable. Someone I can rely on. How do I know you'll stay? Your education and experience could take you anywhere."

Sean looked straight into her eyes. "I'll make a commitment to you." He wasn't sure why, but he wanted this job.

Her brow furrowed. "But you don't even know what the job is like. How do you know it's a good fit for you?"

"Instinct."

She studied him for several moments. No telling what thoughts raced through her head.

"No offense, Sean, but you're thirty-seven years old."

He held up a hand. "In other words, am I having a mid-life crisis because I left a vice-presidency and hiked to Alaska?" He stood, hating himself for letting his anger take hold, but he was not about to let this tiny woman insult him. "I can assure you, that is *not* the case."

She crossed her arms and stared him down. The hand-carved clock in the corner ticked off the seconds. "All right. How about I make you a deal?"

"A deal?"

"Yes. Let me show you around, give you a feel for what the job will be. Then we can discuss everything else."

The relief that swept him was as profound as it was surprising. He drew a steadying breath and nodded. "That's an excellent idea. Thank you."

"Let's go." She led the way out the door. "Normally, you'd need coveralls, XtraTufs boots in the summer and bunny boots in the winter—the dog yard can be disgusting—and if we come to an agreement, I'll provide those for you. But for today, be careful, because the dogs will get excited to meet you." Anesia looked up and down his frame. "You might get dirty."

"I'm not afraid of a little dirt."

"Good." She slid on a pair of worn coveralls. They pulled on coats and boots and headed out the door.

The air was crisp and clean. Unlike anything he'd ever breathed. He could get used to this.

"If you don't mind, we'll walk over to the kennel. We try to keep this path plowed of snow, and that will probably be a job I will delegate to you. I hate clearing snow."

"Not a problem."

She led him down a long, snowy path toward the fenced-in kennel area. It didn't take long before the dogs knew they were coming. Yips and barks started in staccato rhythm until the chorus grew and swelled on the wind. If she hadn't already told him the numbers, he would've thought there were hundreds of them waiting at the kennel.

"They're excited that we're coming." Her steps picked up speed.

Her braid swayed back and forth in time to the spring in her step as they approached her animals. She loved this. How long had it been since he loved what he did? Could he ever have that same passion? A long moment passed as Anesia punched in a code, opened the gate—and the yearning in his soul grew.

She ushered him in and closed the gate. "You might want to stay here and watch for a few minutes. They need to get used to your smell. Otherwise, they'll be all over you."

"Okay." He heeded her words. The sight in front of him was overwhelming, to say the least.

Dogs as far as the eye could see. Jumping, running in circles, and barking in glee at their master. The doghouses were all lined up in rows—one house for each dog. A steel pole stood beside each house, and the dogs were attached to their pole by a long chain. Long enough to give them a wide circle of running room around their houses, but short enough to keep them out of each other's domain.

Sean couldn't help but chuckle at the antics of these prized animals. Some circled their house over and over, while others jumped in the air, onto their doghouses, or attempted flips to get Anesia's attention. The cacophony of barking would have driven any of his Boston friends mad and sent them reaching for their earplugs.

Working her way up and down the rows, she spent time with each dog, loving on them, talking to them, rubbing their ears. And they adored her. They licked and barked, and nuzzled up to her.

He allowed his gaze to roam over the acre of enclosed property and understood the job with a clarity he hadn't anticipated. These dogs were her livelihood. But they weren't just dogs. They were family. Several times she stopped and knelt beside one, checking paws, feeling limbs, looking over their coat. Each one needed care and attention.

He looked to the far end of the kennel and noticed smaller, separate fenced-in areas. He walked toward them to check them out.

"Those are the isolation kennels." Anesia fell into step beside him.

"Isolation?"

"Yes. For the dogs in heat that we don't want to breed at the time, for an injured dog, or for a misbehaving dog that might be bullying or hurting others."

"So, in a way, it's like what some parents call a time-out?"

"Very astute, Mr. Connolly." Anesia laughed. "Exactly like that, yes."

"In essence, you have another seventy-five children."

She leaned her head back and laughed louder. A beautiful sound. "Sean, you crack me up." She smacked him on the arm. "I think you'll fit in fine."

Her acceptance warmed but unsettled him all at the same time.

"Come. Meet the dogs." Anesia took hold of his arm and tugged him toward the yapping masses.

Stopping just beyond the reach of the nearest dog, Anesia held out her arms. "Well, here they are." Her face absolutely glowed. This was her love. Her life. "The chains have colors on them, do you see?"

Very interesting. "I do now. Why are they colored?"

"Helps us keep track of the different litters. All the dogs from a litter are given a color. The blue chains are the Bible Litter. The green are the Glacier Litter. The pink, the Painkiller Litter—"

He frowned. "Painkiller?"

Her dark eyes twinkled. "Yep. Zoya names all the dogs. That particular litter was born after a friend was in the hospital."

"So what are their names?"

"Morphine, Aspirin, Ibuprofen, Percocet, Codeine, and Caffeine."

"Caffeine?" He furrowed his brow. "I didn't know that was a painkiller."

"In Alaska, Sean, you'll find out that caffeine can cure just about anything."

He couldn't help it. He grinned.

Anesia continued down the rows. He followed. Just like a puppy himself.

"The red are the Sweets Litter, yellow is the Weather Litter. Over here, in orange, is the Flower Litter, purple is the Wildlife Litter, white is the Herb Litter, black is the Ice Cream Litter, and the multicolored chains are the Alaska Litter."

"What about those two rows over there?"

"Those are the two that are sold to a man from Iceland. He won't be here for another month or so to pick them up, but he wants to start breeding his own and he likes ours because they've proven to be fast."

"Fascinating." Sean took another long look around the kennel. "They're beautiful. But not what I expected. What breed are they?"

"German short-haired pointer and Alaskan Husky mix."

He nodded. "Anesia, forgive me. But this is a lot of information to take in all at once. I'm still processing." His fingers itched to grab his camera out of the truck. The dogs would be great subjects.

She smacked his arm. Again. "Don't worry about it, and don't be so serious. You can lighten up, you know. You don't have to be all 'professional' out here, but I do need you to care and do your best."

What a change! In the office she'd seemed so serious, all business. Out here? She was vibrant. Totally in her element. Even . . .

Joyous.

"Uh, thank you. I will. I had no idea." This job wasn't about manual labor. He would be caretaking. All these beautiful animals. And it mattered.

"It's all right. Let's head back to the house. I'll show you some more after lunch."

He couldn't hold back the request any longer. "Would you mind if I took some pictures out here sometime? Your dogs are handsome animals."

A smile lit her face. Pride shining from head to toe. "They are gorgeous, aren't they? Sure, you can take pictures. Are you a photography buff?"

"I am. Have always enjoyed being behind the camera, peering at the world through a lens." An uncomfortable feeling filled his stomach. Time to change the subject. "I took the liberty of doing some research last night. Sounds like you and Zoya are quite the champions."

She kept walking toward the house.

"I know this is racing season, so might I inquire about when your next race will be?"

She spun to face him. No trace of her brilliant smile remained. "We won't be doing any racing for a while, Mr. Connolly."

CHAPTER NINE

ANDIE
January 15
Naltsiine Kennels
12:26 p.m.

"I think Auntie Anesia's outside." I pushed the soft silky curtains out of the way. Then peeked out the window.

Sure enough, Auntie and Mom were talking to a man.

A strange man. A really strange man.

Who is he and what's he doing here?

I squinted. Nope. Never seen him before . . . I shrugged off the questions and turned back to Zoya.

Would Auntie and Mom let us go? *I hope so!* This had to work. If it didn't, I should give up and retire.

Zoya stood and headed for the door. It was the most of a smile I'd seen in days. Even though it wasn't very big. Wasn't even a smile.

God, what's wrong with her? She's acting strange . . .

It hurt to see her so upset. And yet she kept saying nothing was wrong. It hurt more knowing that she wasn't telling me something. She had just closed up. Acted like a robot—stiff. Forced movements.

Something was really wrong.

67

We grabbed our coats and walked outside. The cold air hit my face with a big *swoosh*. Hopefully it wouldn't start snowing. I tugged my coat closer. *Just be thankful you're not too hot, Andie.*

Thanks, God.

Zoya didn't seem to notice the cold. Like she was in another world, far away from everything. And everyone.

I had no idea how to get her back.

We walked on in silence. The dogs barked and jumped around their doghouses. Birds chirped and sang their joyful melodies.

Zoya didn't say a word.

I was sick and tired of the quiet. *Sick and tired! Girl, you need to suck it up and get back to normal. Wallowing isn't going to help. Just try not to think about it.*

"Mom?"

So she spoke. Improvement. I raised my eyebrows. If I could just get her to keep it up . . .

Auntie and Mom turned and smiled at us. "Hey girls."

I waved. If only they could read my expression. I dropped my eyes. Then looked to Zoya.

Auntie turned to the man standing beside her. "This is Sean Connolly. He might help us with the dogs."

I tried to smile, but how could I when my friend wasn't being herself? She didn't even say hello to the man. Urgh. Maybe she just needed someone to hit her over the head with a two-by-four.

Auntie must have seen my expression. She gave a slight nod.

"Hello, Mr. Connolly." I cleared my throat and looked at the stranger from head to toe, which was pretty hard to do since he was taller than Cole. Impressive.

He was muscular, not like Cole, but muscular just the same. He had green eyes and blond hair and his clothes were clean as a whistle. Had they been any cleaner, they might have shone like one.

Nice jeans. Too bad they wouldn't stay clean for very long. I smiled. Not with Zoya's dogs. *No, sir! You might as well kiss those pants goodbye. You'll need somethin' a lot sturdier than those high-dollar jeans if ya wanna work here.* I scanned him again.

The shirt! The shirt was just plain, good ol' fashioned *wrong*. What man in his right mind would wear a button down Oxford to work in a dog kennel?

All in all, this guy was weird.

Where on earth was he from anyway? The White House? Buckingham Palace? Mars?

"You can call me Sean, if you would prefer."

I nodded. Hmmm . . . So he didn't speak Martian. No British accent.

Must've been from the White House.

Zoya said nothing. Just stood there. And stood there some more.

I sighed.

Time for action.

"Auntie, we were wondering, if we could take the dogs out for a run?"

I saw the worry flash in her eyes. "I don't—"

"Maybe have a picnic?" Was I pushing too much? My "pathetic look" took over my face. I couldn't stop it. We *really* wanted to go. And besides, maybe it would help Zoya.

Come on, please say yes . . . it's not that hard. You just sound it out, like so: Ye-eh-sssss . . .

She glanced from me to Zoya.

This didn't look good.

"We'd be careful. And I'd make sure Zoya didn't overdo it." I pleaded with my eyes. That always worked with Cole.

But then again, Auntie's smarter than he is. I tried not to smile. *No offense.*

Mom looked to Auntie Anesia's pale face and shook her head. "Andie, I don't think—"

"Pleeeeeease?" Time for the puppy-dog pout. I stuck out my bottom lip as far as it would go. It almost hurt. Almost.

At least that brought a smile. From the stranger.

Guilt swirled in my stomach. We weren't allowed to beg . . .

But desperate times call for desperate measures, right?

Right!

"We'd take it easy, plus if we had a picnic we wouldn't go very far and would sit down for awhile." I looked to Zoya. She nodded back.

It was working. *Yes!*

"Please, Mom?" Zoya shoved a hand into her pocket and looked up.

Bingo. Two against one. This *had* to work.

"I don't know." No missing that being-way-too-careful-for-my-own-good deep breath.

She was worried, but I was too. S*omething* had to get Zoya back to her old self. And—as far as I could see—this was the way to do it.

Auntie's face changed. I'd never seen that expression before.

Mom held up a hand as she and Auntie exchanged one of those mom looks. "What if I go with you? I think that's the only way you—"

"Yay!" I clapped. Excitement bubbled up inside. *God, please let this do the trick! I want my friend back.*

"But!"

Uh-oh. The excitement bubble popped. *"Buts"* were never good.

"We're not going farther than the Chena River."

Auntie nodded. "And make sure you're back by three o'clock."

"So we can have a picnic too?" I raised my eyebrows.

"You can make PB&Js. And there are some small bags of potato chips in the pantry." Auntie sighed. "Just, be careful. Okay?"

We were making progress. "Yes!" I couldn't help the happiness, it decided to overflow. I jumped up and down on my toes. Maybe for Zoya's sake. Maybe to warm up. It didn't matter, we got to go. Good enough for me!

"Come on, let's go water the dogs so we can get going before our time runs out."

Zoya nodded and grabbed my hand, pulling me over to the shed.

I hope this works.

An hour and forty minutes later, we had our lunches packed, the dogs watered, and were checking the harnesses. I petted M&M's head and looked to Auntie Anesia. She stood by the kennels with The Stranger—Sean—telling him all the dogs' names.

I think he was confuzzled.

Zoya stood and looked toward the kennels. "Let's get the dogs set up."

"Okey dokey." I smiled and walked over to the dogs. *This has to do the trick. But what if it didn't? It has to!*

Zoya hooked up Percocet, Ibuprofen, and Aspirin to her Bewe sled while I hooked up Licorice, Candy Corn, and Snickers to my Danler. We made sure the harnesses were secure, the dogs weren't tangled—much to Candy Corn's dismay—and waited for Mom.

Lupine, Moose, and Susitna pulled at their harnesses as Mom fastened the picnic basket to her sled.

The dogs kicked their legs behind them as if saying, "Come on, let's get going already!"

Snow flew everywhere. I giggled until a chunk of ice slid inside my shirt and down my back. *Eeek! Cold!*

I jumped and slapped a hand onto my back. "Cold ice! Cold ice!"

Zoya gave a small smile. "Having problems?"

"No kidding!" I tried to get the ice off my back. *Ick!*

Our lead dogs barked. Morphine jumped and twirled, his tail wagging as fast as a hummingbird's wings.

I sighed and walked over to M&M, my faithful, excited, eager lead dog. The ice melted leaving a cold, wet spot on my back.

Oh. Perfect! I rolled my eyes. *Nothing I can do about it anyway.*

We hooked up the lead dogs. Within milliseconds of stepping onto the sled and saying "All right!" the dogs were flying down the path.

Amazing . . .

They all barked. Their excitement seemed to rush out of every pore as they sailed along the path. My heart beat in a steady rhythm as we slid and glided around one turn and another. *It's so beautiful out here.* I smiled. *Thanks, God.*

We neared the frozen Chena River. If only time would stand still, so I could take a picture and place it in my heart's scrapbook. This was a moment to cherish.

Even though there were still murderers out there.

I whistled three short tweets as we reached a small clearing. *Perfect spot for a picnic.*

"Whoa." I flipped the mat down and put pressure onto it with my foot and the dogs slowed to a stop. "This place look good to you?"

Zoya pulled up beside me and nodded. "Perfect."

Mom brought up the rear of the party.

"My thoughts exactly." I hopped off the sled, set my hook so the dogs wouldn't go racing forward, and went to grab the basket. Food would be welcome. "Let's eat. I'm starving!"

"Same here. I haven't eaten very much lately, and PB&Js sound great." Zoya plopped a thick blanket down on the snow and sat on top of it.

I glanced up at her and smiled. "You know, that's the most you've spoken in the past week."

"Andie, I'm fine. Just tired." She looked down at the blanket and started fiddling with a loose end. "Really tired."

I should've known she would shrink back inside herself, but I didn't want to believe it.

I sighed. My best friend was turning into someone I didn't even know. And she denied it. Denied it with everything in her! *Zoya, talk to me, please . . .*

Mom grabbed the picnic basket and passed out food.

Again I sighed. *God, please give me the right words. I just want to be a good friend. Please, help me to say what she needs to hear.*

"Zoya, why won't you talk to me? I'm your BFF, remember? You can tell me if something's on your mind." The sandwiches were passed out and Zoya repositioned so she sat criss-cross-apple-sauce. But she didn't look me in the eye.

"I'm fine. Just tired."

"You are *not* fine." I crossed my arms. "Zoya Sabiile' Naltsiine, something is wrong and you're going to tell me what it is right now." I reached for her gloved hand. Maybe the closeness of a friend would break down the growing walls. Maybe. "Tell me what's going on."

Mom stood and patted Zoya on the head. "I think I'm going to walk to the edge of the river so you two can chat."

"Thanks, Mom." I waited for Mom to get out of earshot. "So? We're alone, and you can always tell me anything. You know that."

She sighed and shrugged. "Andie, I don't want to talk about it."

"Zoya, please." I squeezed her hand. *You're as stubborn as a mule!* "You're scaring me. I feel like I've lost my best friend. You're turning into some closed-in creature I don't even know!" Tears sprang in my eyes. *Stinkin' tears. These are the times I hate being a girl . . .* I sniffed. "Please talk to me. I miss you, Zoya. I know it's hard, but please . . ."

"No. You wouldn't understand." She looked up and stared into my eyes.

How could she think that? "I can try, Zoya. If you'd just give me the—"

"No." She stood and walked over to her sled. "I'm not hungry, I'll meet you back at the house."

"What? Zoya!" I jumped up and followed her to the sled. "Come on. I know you better than that."

She stopped. Jaw clamped together.

73

Oops. She was mad. At me.

God? Please . . .

She stepped onto the sled and yelled "all right." The dogs took off running at full speed.

"Zoya, wait!"

My shoulders slumped and I shivered.

What on earth was wrong with her?

CHAPTER TEN

ANESIA
Naltsiine Kennels
2:48 p.m.

Sean didn't deserve the remnant of her anger, but she didn't want him constantly asking about racing either. She stiffened. It still riled her that some sicko had stolen her joy, her racing. Sean would get over the way she'd responded to him. Her job was to protect Zoya. Period.

Time to get back to business. "The barn over here houses more gear and sleds. We do a lot of work in here in the winter because it's warmer than being out in the wind. You'll need to help make sure that things are kept clean and straight. We often bring dogs in here and don't want them to get injured on any of the equipment. The lawnmower is over there as well as several snow machines."

"Snow machines?"

"I think people in the lower forty-eight call them snowmo-biles. But they are snow machines." She brought him over to the far wall. "This table, as you can see, runs the length of the barn. We use it to work on harnesses. This way we can stretch the lines all the way out and look for any problems, knots, fraying, etc."

Anesia demonstrated the equipment, showing him all the intricacies. He appeared eager to start, but she wanted to be honest with him. "Sean, I'm not going to guarantee anything right now." She paused to gather her words. "Please don't misunderstand. Agent Philips gave me a glowing report, and I'd like to hire you. But there is so much you don't understand yet, and I won't hire you officially until the full background check comes back."

His green eyes softened. "I understand."

"However, if you are willing, I'd like you to come back on Monday. I can continue to teach you the ropes around here and you can tell me what you think."

"What I think?"

"If you think the job would be a good fit."

"Oh. Sure." Eagerness sparked in his eyes. "I'll be here."

"Good." The man was entirely too handsome for his own good. But he didn't even seem aware of it. She stuck out her hand. "Sean, thank you for coming. I know it was a long day. And a little overwhelming."

"The pleasure was all mine, I assure you, Anesia. Thank *you* for the opportunity."

She watched him walk back to his truck. He was perfect. Whoa. For the job. And only the job.

If he truly was who he said he was and his background check came back clear, she could hire him in an official capacity and protect her daughter.

But that still didn't stop the frustration building inside.

How long would she be able to carry the load without crumbling beneath it?

SLIM

Near the Chena River
2:53 p.m.

His breath turned to crystals in the air as he walked through the woods. Tree limbs moaned in the wind that bit into any exposed skin. Snow crunched under his boots.

He hated snow.

Hated winter.

Hated Alaska.

The sooner he got outta here, the better. Some place warm. With lots of sunshine, girls in bikinis, sand, and plenty of sunscreen. Someplace he'd get the respect he deserved. No more peon jobs for the big boys.

He would *be* the big boy. He would unleash all his brilliant schemes and have peons working for him. Ma had always said he'd make it. She'd supported him, listened to his ideas, helped the desires inside him grow. She'd been his best friend. The only one he'd ever had. The only one who truly understood him. And his genius.

It'd been her idea for the double-cross. Oh, he'd come up with the plan of hiding the chips, knowing that such a massive program could only be stolen piece by piece, but she knew how to go for the jugular. And that's exactly what he planned to do. He had what they were so desperate for, and he planned to make them all pay. They thought he was stupid. That he didn't know what they were hiding. But he'd show them. He'd take their money. And then sell the stolen chips to someone else. Someone bigger. With more money. And less conscience.

Ma'd be proud then. Real proud.

ZOYA

2:57 p.m.

"Why are You doing this to me?" I clasped the sled's handle. *God, why?*

He made me lose everything. My freedom, my sanity, my best friend . . . why couldn't He just leave my life alone?

Tears sprang in my eyes. I sniffed.

If He wasn't a kind God to me, then let Him be no God to me.

That little voice pushed at me again, whispering, and with everything in me I wanted to listen to it. But something fought back.

I hated this! Why couldn't I be master of my own mind?

"Haw." The dogs turned left and sped toward the house. I swiped at the frozen tears covering my cheeks and hopped off, opened the gate, rode through, then closed it.

"Whoa." I flipped the mat down stopping the dogs.

Mom was still talking to the new guy.

I huffed and stormed over to Morphine. "Come on."

Why do we have company at a time like this? We don't need another hand to help us. I can take care of the dogs . . . always have.

"Zoya?" Mom left the new guy and walked over. "Where's Andie and Jenna?"

Morphine's chain gave a sharp click, telling me it had closed around his collar. I stood and walked over to the other sled.

"Zoya, where's Andie?" Worry etched her face. Again. It seemed it was becoming a permanent feature.

Whatever.

"She should be here any minute." Next it was Ibuprofen's turn. *Just keep busy, Zoya, that's all you need to do.*

"If His eye is on the sparrow . . ."

Stop it! Do not think like that. He wasn't there. So just leave it be. He's isn't here, Zoya. He's never been there for you . . .

"Did you two race home? Why isn't Jenna with you?"

Why was she so concerned? I could take care of myself, she didn't have to go and rub it in that they weren't with me. "Not exactly." I frowned and stroked Ibuprofen's back. Distraction . . .

"Zoya!"

Just then, Andie's sled came within sight. She brought the dogs through the unlocked gate and was soon beside me.

I was sure I saw steam rolling out of her ears. *See if I care what you say, Andie. I don't want to hear it. Just go away.*

When she saw Mom, her mouth opened. Then closed without a word.

Mom nodded as if she and Andie had shared a silent conversation, then walked back toward the visitor, peeking at us over her shoulder as she went.

Boy, was I in for it now.

"Zoya, why did you leave like that? We were supposed to stay together. Mom is gonna kill us that we took off like that and left the mess for her to clean up!"

Just keep your mouth shut or you'll say something you regret.

"Zoya, talk to me!"

Aspirin whined as I dragged her over to her doghouse. Why couldn't everybody just leave me alone?

The anger burned. Growing. Gnawing at everything I'd ever known. Ever believed. "I'll take care of your sled." Distraction. That's what I needed.

"Zoya, I can take care of my own sled." She grabbed my arm.

I jerked away. No way was I gonna spill my guts. And that was exactly what she wanted me to do.

"Just tell me what's wrong." She plopped down on one of the porch steps and looked up at me.

"Let me take care of your sled. You go on inside." I stalked toward her Danler. *Leave. Me. Alone.*

"No." She reached for my arm again.

My chest constricted. Everything became a blur.

BANG!

The sound echoed through the trees. Slow-motion pictures sailed by . . .

"Zoya?"

I blinked. *What?*

I shook my head, trying to bring myself back to the present. It was as if the scene was echoing, if that were even possible. It replayed. And replayed.

Stay in reality, Zoya!

Our gazes collided.

Go away, go away, go away . . .

Andie couldn't help me. She couldn't feel what I was feeling, see what I saw, or hear what I'd heard. She wouldn't understand. Nobody would.

Not ever.

My eyes closed. "Leave me alone." I could feel my heart beating.

Pump-pump. Pump-pump. Pump-pump.

"Zoya, plea—"

"Just go away, Andie!"

I was losing my best friend. And it was my fault.

No. It was God's.

My eyes popped open.

I could see Andie's jaw tightening. She stormed inside.

The door slammed.

Like a hammer on a nail. And like that nail, I was stuck in a stud.

With no hope of ever getting out.

━ ━

The dogs were soon taken care of and the harnesses put away. I moved around snail-like. Not wanting anyone to notice me.

Thoughts of my dad came rushing in. His picture, the only one I'd ever seen, flashed in my mind. Why couldn't I have known him? Why did he have to die? Why was God doing this to me? My shoulders slumped as I sat down on a log bench in the shed.

My Bewe and Andie's Danler stood side by side. Hadn't we done that not more than two weeks ago? We stood side by side for pictures, stood side by side in a line waiting for dinner, sat side by side on the couch watching a movie . . .

Then God had to go and ruin everything.

I glanced around at all of our equipment. Not a soul in sight. Good. Maybe the quiet would help me sort out my jumbled thoughts and gain some sanity.

If that was possible.

I doubted it. Just like I doubted everything. I rubbed my temple. When had I started doubting?

When God destroyed my life.

Or was I the one that destroyed it?

My brow furrowed. *No. It was His fault.* He could have prevented that murder. And I was the one paying for it.

"Thanks a lot." Sarcasm oozed out of the words, but I didn't care. I wanted to strangle someone. Even if it was me.

This is all His fault . . .

"Zoya?" Auntie Jenna opened the creaky door and walked in. "There you are. Mind if I sit with you?"

I looked down and shook my head. I knew what was coming. The lecture. Like always. *Oh, great. Not you too . . . please. Just go away.*

"Is something wrong?"

Wow. Wasn't *she* the observant one.

"No." I looked up and stared at the wall. She could talk if she wanted. But I wasn't going to listen.

"Yes, there is."

"Nope." I was not going to spill my feelings. Lay them down for everyone to see. They were mine, and they belonged inside. Just like always. No one had ever seen how I felt about my dad's death, no one had seen how I was angry at God for that. And I wasn't going to let them start seeing now.

"Zoya, look at me."

I shook my head, then regretted it. *Now she'll know something's wrong.* But I looked at her anyway. Her face showed concern.

I didn't need to be worried over. Just left alone so I could collect my thoughts.

"Auntie Jenna, I'm fine. Just a little tired." That wasn't a lie. I was exhausted. Maybe I should take a nap.

"So you and Andie had a fight because you were tired? That doesn't sound like you. Andie's the grumpy one." She laughed. "And I know where it comes from."

So true . . .

"So why did you guys fight?"

I frowned again. Pushy. "Just 'cause." I fiddled with my hands. This conversation was getting tiresome.

"And what's that supposed to mean?" She sat down and patted my knee.

Sympathy. I didn't need sympathy. I needed quiet.

"Zoya, ever since the shooting you haven't been yourself. What's going on? You can talk to Andie, me, Cole, or your mom. You should know that."

I did.

But I didn't *want* to. Why couldn't they see that? I didn't want to do anything. Just sit and not feel a thing. Sit and not have to talk to anyone. Sit and be alone. Sit and not relive that scene . . .

"Andie said you blamed yourself for what happened."

"Whatever."

"Does that mean you do or don't?"

"That means I don't want to talk about it."

I didn't mean to hurt her, just wanted to get off that subject. But that was all anyone wanted to talk about. I blinked back the tears. It was a wonder I had any tears left to shed. "Sorry. I want to be left alone." I stood.

She looked like she wanted to say something, anything, to make me feel better.

I walked out the door.

It was too late for comfort.

I was on a sinking ship.

And I hoped it went down soon.

CHAPTER ELEVEN

RICK

January 15
Anchorage, Alaska
7:14 p.m.

Quiet ruled his enormous house. He'd long since sent Margaret, his housekeeper, home. Sometimes he preferred being alone.

The sky had been dark for hours. That's what happened in winter in Alaska. Dark late into the morning. Dark early in the afternoon. But he didn't mind. Gotten used to it after all these years.

Winter did hold something on him, though. It always made him think. A little too much.

Walking through the living room, he pondered the situation with Zoya. He'd never been there for her. And in that, he'd failed his brother. But hadn't he kept watch from afar? That had to count for something.

He flicked a switch for one of the gas fireplaces. Flames flickered to life and warmth began to fill the area around the hearth.

His grandfather had been an elder for his tribe. And very superstitious. The man lived to the ripe old age of 102 and had groused at him every minute of those last years. Warned him of the great spirits of his ancestors and what they would do to him if he didn't protect his family. Rick gave those superstitions no weight, but still . . . what if they were true?

His grandfather had been livid with him most of his life. For ignoring his heritage. Ignoring his instruction. Ignoring his family.

As he gripped the photo of Zoya, he contemplated the outcome of his actions. Could it be his fault? She never should have been there. Never should have seen that murder. And now . . .

Now they were after her.

His gaze rested on the fire licking at the permanent logs behind the glass. Shapes took form in the flames, and his grandfather's voice echoed through him . . .

"You will burn . . ."

COLE
January 15
Fort Greely, Alaska
7:34 p.m.

The frigid air froze Cole's lungs as he drew a long breath in through his nose. But he didn't care. At least he was finally out of the secure facility. Days like this made him long to leave military service behind. Days of no windows. No fresh air. And too many problems.

Problems that risked national security.

What had he missed? Marc's notes spelled out everything to the letter. No detail hidden. So how could he figure out the encryption? Obviously Marc added it as an extra security measure against Viper, but wouldn't Marc have left Cole a clue? Somewhere? Or maybe Marc would rather his invention be destroyed. So no one could use it.

The numbing cold forced him to move forward and pull on his gloves. He yanked keys out of his pocket and headed to his truck. The drive home would be long enough. Maybe he'd come up with something after he talked it over with Jenna.

But there was no mistaking the frustration in AMI ops. They needed answers. And soon.

A shadow moved by his truck, and he tensed—then recognition eased the rigid set of his jaw. "Grant?"

"Major Maddox." They shook hands. "Good to see you."

Cole nodded. "So, Agent Philips"—Grant arched a brow at the formal address—"seeing as it's thirty below, I'm assuming you're not here on a social call."

The FBI agent crossed his arms over his chest. "Correct. Let's talk in the truck."

Cole pressed the automatic starter on his key chain and unlocked the doors. His lungs burned from inhaling the arctic air, so he took short breaths through his mouth.

Grant locked the doors and checked behind the seats. "We've got a problem."

"Oh?"

"Involving AMI."

Not good. The FBI had handed control of AMI back over to the military once their investigation finished. "All right. I'm listening."

"It's being stolen."

"That's impossible."

"Actually, no it's not. And there's more. We've had a guy on the case for weeks . . ." Grant rubbed his head. Lack of sleep showed around his eyes. In that moment he looked ten years Cole's senior. And they were the same age.

"The goal was . . . *is* to bring down an arms dealer ring we've had on our radar for years. The opportunity finally presented itself. An opportunity involving AMI."

"Why wasn't I told about this? Don't you think I needed to know this kind of information?"

Grant held up a hand. "Sorry, Cole. My hands were tied."

Cole banged his fist on the steering wheel. "Great. Just great." He turned to his friend. His expression went blank. Something was off. "What aren't you telling me?"

"We need someone on the inside."

"What about your guy?"

"Missing."

Cole closed his eyes. It was much worse. His gut told him. "And?"

Grant hesitated. "You know—better than anyone—the security measures surrounding AMI's programming. No more than eight megabytes of any given file can be copied at one time in that facility. The program is more than three thousand gigabytes. We thought we had plenty of time to find out the top guy's identity."

"Cut to the chase, Grant!" Cole slammed his hand on the dashboard. Couldn't believe his ears.

"Our guy . . . we're pretty certain he's dead." Grant pulled in a deep breath. "But the buyers needed proof that they were getting the real thing . . . we allowed part of AMI's programming to be stolen. Eight megabytes at a time. On macrochips. But only part of it. Our man assured us that the rest of it was dummy files."

"*What?*"

"It was the one way to reel them in. But now we've lost all contact. We don't know how much they have, or where they have it." He leveled a grim look at Cole. "Basically, we don't know much of anything."

ZOYA
January 16
Naltsiine Kennels
2:37 a.m.

My body shuddered. Sickening clashes of lightning flashed across the sky. Bolts jumped from cloud to cloud with unimaginable speed.

Everything went pitch black.

Something like icy fingers crept up my back. Then down again.

The mountains trembled and rumbled. Trees shook, snow fell. The wind whipped across my face, crashing thick slates of ice against my cold skin.

I took a weak step forward. Then another. My hands stayed out in front of me, feeling for something. Anything. My calves burned, my cheeks stung. The bare skin on my arms tingled, then lost all feeling.

Someone called out my name.

No, I couldn't answer.

"Zoya!" Andie stood in front of me. "Why won't you talk to me?"

Over and over again those words repeated. Like malicious vultures they encircled my mind, grabbing it. They wouldn't let go. Or was it the anger that wouldn't let go?

I wouldn't let her stop me. I needed to do this . . .

"Zoya, please. You're worrying me."

Agitated screams tore out from the depths of my soul.

What had God done to me?

"Zoya, look out!"

Tears that froze on my cheeks seemed to disappear as I looked up. The sun shone through as the clouds parted . . .

A click.

A scream.

Andie's body collided with mine, pushing me to the ground.

A gunshot . . .

I screamed and toppled off my bed onto the floor. Rasping wheezes came between sobs as I clutched the side table until my knuckles turned white. I stared at my hands.

No. No. No!

I could hear Mom running to my room. The handle rattled.

"Zoya! Zoya, let me in! What's going on?"

I wanted to get up. To unlock the door. But my legs wouldn't let me. I wanted her to hold me. But it wouldn't help.

I gritted my teeth. Eyes closed.

No. It couldn't be true.

The end of the dream replayed . . .
A gunshot.
Andie's body lay motionless on the ground.
Blood spilled forth from a wound.
A bullet wound.

CHAPTER TWELVE

SEAN _____
January 16
North Pole, Alaska
6:21 a.m.

Ringing. Somewhere.

Another ring.

Sean jolted awake and sat up in bed. The hotel phone. He reached for it. "Hello?"

"Sean."

Any cobwebs left in his brain disappeared. He knew that voice. All too well.

"What? Nothing to say to your old man?"

Plenty. He simply chose not to say it. "How did you find me?"

The condescending laugh was all too familiar . . . "You should know by now that you can't escape my reach." The tone turned to steel. "Ever."

"What do you want?"

Curses poured through the phone wires. "You know what I want. Your place is here. Get back here. Now."

Sean leaned back against the headboard. "No."

"What exactly do you expect to accomplish with this? Your money will run out soon enough, and you'll have to come crawling back."

Typical. All his father cared about was money. And control.

"Ah, the silent treatment. Aren't you a little old for that, son?"

Sean kept his tone level, calm. "I've left. It's permanent. Please, just let it go."

"Let it go?"

He could picture his father, roaring into the phone, an enraged lion putting an upstart in its place.

"You are my son, you insolent, ungrateful—"

"Father—"

"Don't '*Father*' me, Sean! I've invested my life in you—"

"I'm hanging up now." The soft click of the receiver in the cradle might as well have been the slamming of a door.

He was done. With his father. With that life.

Sean slid from the bed and walked to the window gazing into the black night. "God, show me Your will."

Honor your father and mother, Scripture said. He'd done his best. All his life. But what his father had become . . . what he'd wanted Sean to become . . .

That he *couldn't* honor.

A ribbon of green caught his attention. He stared through the right-hand corner of his window as the ribbon was soon joined by a yellow gold streak, and then, in the seconds that passed, the two intertwined and shot across the sky. The Northern Lights. They took his breath away.

As he watched the lights move and sway in their ribbons of magic, the stark reality hit him square in the face. It would never be over. He'd defied his father, and now he'd have to fight the battle for the rest of his life. It didn't matter. It was the right thing. Even if it was the hardest thing he'd ever done.

If only his mother and baby brother had lived. But would it have made any difference?

His life would never be the same, but the correct path couldn't be clearer. Every fiber of his being knew it.

God never said this life on earth would be easy, but that He'd walk the path beside His children. Sean had his heavenly Father. And God's words in Scripture. And other believers . . .

Sean smacked his palm on his thigh. That's what he needed. Church. Fellowship. He'd need them more than ever if he wanted to resist the pull of power and money. And his father.

Heading to the shower, he whistled an old hymn. The hot water invigorated him as he wondered how long it would take him to find a church he liked. He'd better get moving. Needed time to shave and dress, make coffee, research churches and their locations on the Internet, and then—

All thought left him and time stood still as he glanced at the steamed mirror. Someone had left him a message on the glass:

Go home, Sean. No one wants you here.

DETECTIVE SHELDON

January 16
North Pole, Alaska
10:15 a.m.

"Sir? What do you make of this?"

Dave looked up from the forensics report. "What exactly is it?"

One of the new officers handed him a torn-up blue plastic bag. "Macrochips. One of the dogs dug it up about 100 yards from the murder site."

"Macrochips?"

"Yeah, really small ones. Each one has a casing. Pretty high tech."

"I'm assuming you've already checked for prints?"

"Yes, sir."

"And?"

"The prints match the victim." The officer smirked. "Captain knew you'd want to see it."

His captain was a great man, but he knew how much Dave hated technology. "Bring 'em over."

"We haven't been able to decipher what's on them yet, sir. But the guys said to tell you they were working on it."

"Thanks, Riley." He studied the bag. Macrochips. How much information could be on one of those things anyway? They looked similar to the micro SD card that was in his phone for the camera. Amazed him that the little thing could hold so many pics and was a help during investigations.

One of his sergeants leaned halfway in the door and tapped the wall. "We've got a problem. Those chips hold some top secret encrypted military intelligence. Captain wants you to call the FBI that worked on the Gray case. He's on the horn with the state troopers."

The Gray case? That meant . . .

He blew out a big breath and dialed. "Agent Philips? Seems we are in need of your assistance . . ."

ZOYA

January 16
North Pole Community Church
11:10 a.m.

"Paul said in the book of Philippians, 'Not that I have already obtained it or have already become perfect, but I press on so that I may lay hold of that for which also I was laid hold of by Christ Jesus. Brethren, I do not regard myself as having laid hold of it yet; but one thing I do: forgetting what lies behind and reaching forward to what lies ahead, I press on toward the goal to win the prize of the upward call of God in Christ Jesus.'"

The new pastor, Brian Jamison, stood at the pulpit preaching. More like yelling.

His sermon was long. Too long. I couldn't stand listening to him say over and over that God was love, that God was waiting for me to return to Him, that God had given me gifts, that God wanted me to run the race. God, God, God.

It was as if he was trying to tell me, and only me, that I was doing something wrong.

Well, I wasn't. It wasn't my fault. It was His.

Wasn't it?

Yeah.

He abandoned me, not the other way around.

I turned my head to look out the window, letting the little voice argue away in my mind.

Why had Mom made me come anyway? I told her I didn't feel very good. It wasn't a lie. Not exactly.

My Bible sat open on my lap. I turned and glared at the tiny book. *And I thought I'd never have to look into you again.* Andie coughed from where she sat with Auntie Jenna and Cole a few pews in front of us. I hoped I wouldn't have to talk to them. Maybe Andie was getting smart and knew I wouldn't want to see her. At least, I didn't want to *talk* to her . . .

Mom grabbed my hand.

I pulled away.

Hurt touched her face, and she looked back to the preacher.

I don't care. I just want to be alone.

The congregation stood and we started singing "Victory in Jesus."

Yeah, right. Whatever.

As soon as the pastor dismissed us, a loud murmur of voices filled the room. My ears rang with all the noise, however little it may have been.

Finally, we could get out of there.

"Zoya, how nice it is to see you up and around. We all prayed for you after the accident, and it looks like God has answered our prayers abundantly, no?" Mrs. What's-her-name smiled down at me as her head bobbed.

Please, just go away. The tears were about ready to spill. I held them back. Held my emotions in the bottle . . . the bottle that wanted to break so I could lash these things out.

The voice grew louder. *"Don't listen to that preacher . . . don't let them see your anger . . . this is God's fault . . . don't believe what they tell you . . ."*

"Yes. Thank you for your prayers, Mrs. Appuglies." Mom grabbed my hand and dragged me toward Auntie Jenna and Andie.

I'd rather listen to Mrs. Apple-whatever gab for hours than talk to Andie. She was my best friend. She knew. I shook my head and tried to swallow back the urge to yell. *Just let me die and get it over with.* "Mom, can I go to the car?"

"No, we're gonna go see Andie and Jenna."

"But Mom—"

"Jenna, Andie, Cole." Mom nodded to the three of them and pulled me up to her side.

Andie's and my gazes locked for a split second—

No, I wouldn't let her read me like a book. I turned away.

The voice . . .

Act natural . . . Act natural . . .

"Hey, girl." Auntie Jenna smiled. "How're you guys doin' today?"

I stood there as Mom and Auntie talked of the new guy, of the dogs, of blah, blah, blah. *For goodness sake, stop talking and let's go!*

"How's it going with Sean?" Auntie dug for something in her purse.

"Well, he'll certainly take some getting used to."

Out of the corner of my eye, I could see Andie staring at me. I couldn't engage in conversation . . . I knew what would happen. I'd blow my top. And that was the last thing I wanted to do. Especially in church.

I turned my head away.

Mr. Howe smiled down at his two-year-old daughter, Emma, then with one swift movement placed her on his shoulders. Even from where I stood, I could hear her giggles and see her smiles.

Familiar feelings somewhere deep inside me cried out.

Why couldn't my dad be here for me? Nobody ever lifted me onto their shoulders . . . everybody knew that was a father thing.

But I had no father.

I blinked.

End of story.

Why did he have to die? The anger boiled. My eyes scrunched. Head started to hurt. But I couldn't let the anger explode. Not here. Not now.

I let them open. Again Emma's giggles invaded my mind.

Andie stared at me.

I looked away. Blinked. The tears hurt, wanting to be let out of their bondage. Wanting to fall. And never stop falling.

Why did we have to be here? Why couldn't I just run home and stay locked up in my room forever? There wasn't anything for me to see out here. There wasn't—

The realization hit me.

There was no dad to comfort me.

Was that why I was so angry? Was that what I wanted? At this point, I didn't know.

I didn't want to go down there. Into the black. Into the mire. Into the nothingness. But then again, where else was there to go?

Again the tears threatened. Where were these thoughts coming from and why couldn't I get rid of them?

"Zoya? Zoya, are you okay?"

Mom was staring at me.

Just let me go home, please!

"Let's go home, sweetie. I think you've overdone it today."

I nodded and walked beside her as we headed out the side door.

Leave me alone . . . Leave me alone . . . Leave me alone . . .

Who I was talking to, I didn't know. But I was done.

With church. With murders. With life.

With everything.

    ▬   ▬

I sat in our red Nissan Xterra staring out the window. The drive home was silent. All except the humming of the car's engine. Thoughts flittered back and forth about this and that.

The dark thoughts scared me. But then again, everything did. Why was God putting me through all this torture?

"What's wrong, sweetie?"

Oh, brother. How many times could I hear that in a week? I ignored the obnoxious question. What good would it do to reply?

"Zoya Sabiile' Naltsiine, why aren't you talking? You're not telling me anything. You mope around the house all day and don't do anything but pet the dogs and sit on the couch. You don't want to talk to, or even see, Andie or Jenna. Ever since the accident you've changed. What's going on?"

"Accident." I grunted. *Stop calling it that.* "Why does everybody call it an accident?" *Don't do it Zoya. Don't. Let. Her. See. Your. Anger.*

"What do you mean?"

Whatever!

I turned to Mom and glared. "It wasn't an *accident.*" My heart tensed as the scenes replayed.

Stop it!

"It was a *murder.* Why do people have to assume that if they call it a murder I'll get all wound-up and hysterical? I'm fine! I don't need anybody's sympathy, I don't need anybody's care, I don't need anybody telling me what's wrong with me!"

It wasn't true . . . I wanted somebody to care.

I wanted Dad to care. To be here with me. I wanted to know him. To love him. To have him love me.

But no. He was dead. *Dead.*

Get over it, Zoya!

"Zoya, we do not think—"

My eyes closed again. "And why can't people just leave me alone? All I hear is 'what's wrong' and 'talk to me' and 'you've changed' and 'you haven't been yourself' and—"

Tears started to slide down my cheeks. How long would I have to put up with all this nagging?

"Zoya, stop it!" Mom's stern voice filled the car. If I hadn't known any better, I'd think she was talking to a three-year-old.

My head jerked back to the window and I sniffed.

Mom got quiet again. The silence made me want to squirm in my seat. Mom never yelled at me. Then again, I never yelled at her. I wanted to open up. Wanted her to hold me, comfort me. Wanted it all to go away.

The guilt engulfed me. But it was better than the dark cloud that threatened to squash everything I'd ever known.

God, why do You keep messing everything up?

I tried to swallow back the sobs.

Just get out of my life.

I didn't need Him. Didn't need anyone.

Get out and never come back.

CHAPTER THIRTEEN

ANESIA
11:27 a.m.

The rest of the drive back from church was too quiet. What was it going to take to break through Zoya's shell? It seemed to harden more every day.

Anesia gripped the steering wheel. She couldn't believe she just yelled at her daughter like that. But it was starting to really frighten her. Zoya seemed to be getting lost in the darkness surrounding her. Maybe a little normalcy was in order. "Wanna eat at the Country Café?"

Her daughter shrugged.

That was it. She was tired of the unresponsive shrugs. Some parents might be able to do all the calm-collected-wait-patiently-for-the-kid-to-open-up routine, but not her. Their world contained the two of them. That's all they had. Communication had been the key all these years to their close relationship. And she refused to allow anyone or anything to snatch that away. Her daughter was hurting and she intended to solve the puzzle.

Right now.

She pulled off the road, put the truck in park, and turned to face her daughter. "All right, girlfriend. I've had enough."

Zoya's head snapped up and her eyes widened.

"You know that I don't like to raise my voice to you, but this has *got* to stop. And I'm going to do everything in my power to keep you from disappearing into this black hole that seems to be sucking you in."

Tears pooled in her daughter's eyes. Her bottom lip trembled. Anesia grabbed Zoya's hand. "It's always been you and me. We're family. We're a team. And we promised each other that we would always be open and honest with one another. So I'm going to hold you to that promise."

No response. Anesia could feel the tension oozing out through her teenager's fingers.

"Honey, talk to me. Whatever it is, it's tearing you up, and I would be a horrible mom if I just sat here and allowed it to get worse. I love you too much for that."

"I know." The quiet words tumbled out as tears streamed down her cheeks.

At least she was talking. "Okay, so we've got plenty of time. Why don't you tell me what's going on?"

Zoya grabbed a Kleenex from the console. She sniffed and wiped her face.

A minute passed.

"Zoya?"

"I'm angry."

"At who?"

"God. That's who." The steely voice was so unlike the quiet, sweet one that always came out of Zoya's mouth. Uh oh. Anesia felt like someone dark and raging had swapped places with her daughter. Whatever had hold of her . . .

Deep breath. This was worse than she imagined. "You're angry at God? Why?"

"Because He let it happen, that's why. He let me be on that trail. Allowed those men to be there. Allowed them to shoot that guy. *Allowed* me to get shot. To see the murder. And the images won't go away."

Anesia's jaw dropped. No words would come.

"I think every sound is a gunshot. I keep feeling the numbing zing of that bullet. How I thought I was gonna die. And now, because I'm a witness to a murder, God took my dream away. The one thing I loved to do." Her daughter turned her face away. "I'll lose my best friend. And I'll lose you. I'll never win the championship, and never make Dad proud of me. 'Cause you'll never let me race again!" Zoya flung the door open, jumped out of the vehicle, and ran to the edge of the woods.

"Zoya!" Her scream didn't deter the progress her daughter made across the snow-encrusted terrain. Anesia watched her daughter collapse at the treeline. A knife in the stomach couldn't have hurt worse.

Zoya knew.

Anesia *had* decided it wasn't safe to let her daughter race anymore. At least for a while. She'd wanted to protect her only child. But her kid was smart. They could read each other like books.

Zoya knew her mother would do everything in her power to keep her safe. Anesia hadn't voiced her concerns yet, but there wasn't a need. Zoya *knew*.

As she reached for the driver door, Anesia wrestled in her mind to figure out a solution. The door creaked open, and she jumped out, thoughts tumbling in her head. How could she fix this? Zoya said she was angry at God and if Anesia kept her from racing, would her sweet daughter turn that anger toward her as well?

Each step felt like a mile. *Oh God, give me the words. Give me wisdom. I don't know what to do. And I'm afraid. Afraid for Zoya, afraid to lose her. Afraid of her anger and what this could do to her.*

She reached the balled-up form. "Honey, I'm so sorry."

"You didn't do anything." Zoya's words were muffled by her sleeve. "You're just trying to protect me. I know that. But I don't have to like it."

"No. You don't have to like it."

Zoya finally looked up. "I *hate* it. Hate that one minute everything is fine and then the next freaky minute my whole world is changed. And I didn't want it to change."

Anesia opened her arms. Zoya moved into them. Her once quiet daughter was dealing with more than she'd ever imagined.

"I'm so sorry, honey." She grappled for words. "As your mom, I want to take all the pain away and fix it. But I can't."

"I know, Mom. I hate it. It's eating me up. I've never felt so black and ugly and gross on the inside. I'm so mad, I could spit. I want to bite everyone's head off. I don't want anyone to talk to me. Don't want anyone to care."

"Well, that's where you *can* do something about it. You've got to let go of this anger, Zoya. You've got to give it to God."

"No!" The word was half anger, half wail.

"He could've stopped it from happening, Mom. Could've protected me from it. My life was fine before all this happened. He'll just let me down again. What if He makes *more* junk happen?"

"Zoya Sabiile'! God did not let you down. Those men who committed the crime are the ones who did wrong. Not you. Not God. He loves you. And whether you want to admit it or not, 'junk'—like you put it—happens to all of us. To good people. All the time. And you know good and well that God never promised us an easy life on this earth. Remember what we studied in history? Remember the Roman Empire? Can you imagine what it was like to be a Christian then? To know that you could be crucified at any moment because of your faith? Could be sent to lions in the Coliseum? Or forced into slavery? Are you blaming God for all the bad things in history as well?"

Zoya squeezed harder.

"And what about Andie? Look at all she's been through. Her nerve disorder, all the doctor's appointments, hospital visits, MRIs, CT scans . . . never being considered a 'normal' kid. Brain surgery."

Zoya looked at the ground.

Anesia couldn't give up now. "Well? You think God *made* it happen to her?"

Her daughter shrugged.

"And look at what God has done *through* those circumstances. Look at what He's done in my life and in yours—just because we know them and love them."

A sniff was her only response.

Anesia sighed. Long and hard. "I'm no great theologian. You know that. But"—she held her daughter at arm's length and looked straight into her eyes—"I see a beautiful young woman in front of me who loves the Lord. And I see all the wonderful things He's done in you and through you, and I see that He's got a mighty plan for you. Don't you think that the enemy *wants* you to be angry? He wants to keep you from giving God the glory. He wants to keep you from focusing on the Lord. His goal is to keep you from everyone and everything, and to keep you in this black hole. 'Cause personally, I think he knows your potential. Your potential to live for God and be a shining light through all this darkness. And that scares him."

Zoya's eyes widened again. She walked a few steps away.

Anesia waited. *Oh God, bring her back to me. Please.*

Zoya turned. Her face an unreadable mask. Hands clenching and unclenching.

For a few moments Anesia couldn't breathe. Time stood still as her heart cried out to God. She felt the spiritual battle going on around her. In her desire to break through to Zoya, she'd hit the nail on the head. God had given Zoya incredible gifts. Anesia knew that. And now with a clarity she'd never before had, she saw that what she'd said was so true. Zoya's precious life could touch so many.

The enemy hated that.

Battle lines had been drawn.

Deep within her soul, Anesia knew it was just the beginning. Was she ready for this? *Oh God, give me strength.*

Zoya turned back to her in her pacing. A tortured look on her face.

Lord, help us to put on our armor. I know I've been sorely lacking in that area.

Anesia stood taller, bracing herself.

Her own words to God flitted through her mind . . . she was afraid to lose Zoya. Kept crying out to God to bring her daughter back, to give her strength to make it through.

And yet, what had she been doing?

Relying on her own strength.

Stubborn, independent Anesia. Out to prove to the world that she didn't need anyone or anything. Wanting to show everyone that she wasn't a screw-up. That the unmarried, teen mom grew up to *be* somebody.

She'd been begging God for help all these years—and she believed He blessed her—but hadn't thrown off her own shackles. Hadn't rested in and savored His grace.

With Zoya's back to her, Anesia knelt in the snow. The one way her daughter could truly find healing would be for Anesia to let go.

Give the reins to God and let Him be in control.

ZOYA
11:59 a.m.

"I see a beautiful young woman in front of me who loves the Lord . . . and I see that He's got a mighty plan for you. Don't you think that the enemy wants you to be angry?"

I stood still, staring out at the trees. Not wanting to think about what Mom said. But then again, I had to.

Was she right?

Could she be right? Or was this just some plan to get me back to being myself?

No, Mom wouldn't lie. Never had.

But how could I believe what she said? I couldn't trust Him again. Wouldn't. Could I?

I wanted to scream. To say it wasn't fair. To yell and rant and rave about anything and everything. To give God a piece of my mind. To let Him know how I felt.

But what did I say? That the God of the universe wasn't loving like He promised?

I fell to my knees.

Why? Why have You let all this happen? Why haven't You been here for me? Why can't I feel You?

The little voice began its tirade. It was annoying. But comforting all at the same time. *"Don't trust Him, what has He done for you? What good has He done in your life?"*

No. No, no, no!

The voice kept chanting, over and over again. I couldn't get it to stop. The tears came flooding back. Again.

I wanted to let everything out. To cry out to God. But what if He didn't answer? Was He there like He'd said?

I knew I couldn't be angry anymore. But that didn't mean I had to forgive Him, right?

I knew I needed Him. I knew He loved me. I knew it was wrong of me to blame everything on Him. I knew I needed His forgiveness.

But how did I start? How did I apologize for all I had done, thought, said?

God?

I'm sor—

No!

I turned and slammed my hand into the tree trunk.

He didn't deserve that! If He was God let Him prove it!

God, You're not doing anything! I can't feel You!

My shoulders stiffened.

"Be still. . . wait upon the Lord."

What?

I looked to the sky. My hands shook as I tried to wipe the hair off of my soggy face and searched for a sign. Anything.

God, show me! I don't see You! I swallowed.

The voice . . . *"Don't listen. He would've shown you He was there if He cared."*

He wasn't there.

I was a champion. My mom was a champion. My dad was a champion. I could beat this. Just persevere. Get it over with.

Right?

Yes. I could get through this. But if God wasn't there to give me His strength, I'd do it on my own.

I leaned my head against the tree trunk and let myself cry. *You're not here. Where are You?*

I sniffed.

I'm fine. I can do this on my own. I was strong and determined. I could do anything. I was a champion.

I sat up straight.

"You don't need anyone."

Not a God who says He's there and isn't.

I'm fine. Don't need anyone.

I'm fine . . .

And I could play the part.

ANESIA
12:14 p.m.

Anesia inched closer to her teen.

Zoya.

Always so quiet. Stoic. Steady. Always had a smile handy and an encouraging word.

As she neared, she watched Zoya's expression change. Anger, then indecisiveness, then . . . what?

Had she failed her daughter? Was it too late? Zoya's face seemed cold and hard as the ice underfoot.

"What's going through that head of yours?"

Zoya looked at her. Almost straight through her. Several seconds passed. Anesia held her breath . . . waiting, hoping. She didn't know what to do. Didn't know how to help her daughter. What if she didn't break free of this oppression? What if the murder had done irreparable damage to Zoya's psyche?

Had she lost her daughter?

Tears pricked the corners of Anesia's eyes. Willing them to freeze where they were, she drew in another quick breath. And watched. And prayed.

"Are you worried about the note we found?"

Zoya shook her head, hard.

"Because you know they were just trying to scare us, right?"

A nod.

"Are you worried about me? 'Cause you should know by now that I can handle myself." Moments stretched. Zoya held her gaze. "Oh, honey, talk to me. Please."

Zoya's shoulders crumpled. "Oh, Mom. I'm so sorry." She ran into Anesia's arms.

Anesia held her daughter tight. Relief flooded her body making her knees go weak. "I've been going about this all wrong. We've got a battle to fight."

"I don't want to fight any battles. I'm tired. I don't want to deal with this anymore. I just want to go back to normal."

"Oh, honey, I wish that were possible. I wish I could take it all away, but I can't. We've got to deal with this and try to move on. You can't keep pushing people away."

Her daughter pulled away, looking down. "Maybe that's what my dream meant."

"Wanna finally tell me about it?"

"It was about Andie. I was angry and pushed *her* away. Just like God. But she stayed. And then, when someone tried to kill me, she took the bullet for me."

"Just like Jesus on the cross."

"Yeah. But I'm so terrified the dream is gonna come true. So I thought if I stayed angry at God and pushed everyone away, then no one would get hurt on account of me." Her daughter wouldn't look her in the eyes. Just stared at the ground, toeing the snow with her boot.

"Oh, Zoya." She pulled her daughter back into a hug. "Why didn't you tell me about it? You've always talked to me about your dreams."

"It was too easy to stay angry." Her daughter looked away again.

Anesia nodded. Knew that feeling all too well.

"And just because you dream something doesn't mean it's going to come true."

"It has before."

"I know that. But you need to give it over to God. Don't let fear take over. I'm working on the same thing. Realized that I didn't have the right to be holding onto you so tight. You belong to Him first, not me."

Zoya pulled back and straightened. Determination framed her face as she nodded.

"I'm sorry, Mom," she half-smiled. "Can we still go eat at the Café? I'm dying for some croissant French toast."

"Sure thing, Rainbow. Let's give Jenna and Andie a call and see if they want to meet us there."

They walked arm in arm back to the truck. "Now if only my fingers and toes will thaw out before we get there."

Was it too much to hope that God had given her daughter back? Only time would tell.

CHAPTER FOURTEEN

ANESIA
January 16
235 North Santa Claus Lane, North Pole
2:26 p.m.

Anesia's BlackBerry buzzed as they exited the Country Café in North Pole. "I am so stuffed." She pulled it from her pocket to check the e-mail.

"Me too, Mom. We need to do this more often."

"We most certainly do." It was an e-mail from the service she used. The background check on Sean. Good. It was about time.

As they climbed back into the truck, she took the time to skim the e-mail. A few things caught her eye. Things she'd need to discuss with Sean ASAP. Maybe she should put in another call to Agent Philips.

"Mom?" Zoya's question brought her out of her thought process.

"Hmm?" There was that face again. That forced smile. Maybe this was harder on Zoya than she thought.

"Could we have a girls' night tonight?"

She tucked the BlackBerry back into her pocket. "That's a great idea, honey. Whatcha got in mind?"

"Well, I'm thinking homemade pizza later, popcorn with lots of butter, and . . . *Pride and Prejudice.*"

"Which one? The five-hour or the two-hour?"

"Well, I like the music and cinematography in the two-hour better, and I love Keira Knightley as Elizabeth Bennet, but the five-hour one is more accurate and has some really great scenes in it."

Anesia laughed and stared at Zoya. Was she faking it? "When did you go and grow up on me?"

"I haven't. At least not yet. But I do love a good movie. Especially when it's based on one of the greatest books of all time." There. That half-smile again.

Maybe they all needed some normalcy. She didn't want to pretend nothing was wrong. But maybe if she tried to steer things back to the way they were, then they wouldn't be reminded of it all. "You got that right. The five-hour one it is. And we'll make our pizza halfway through to break it up. How's that?"

"Sounds good." Zoya placed her hand on Anesia's shoulder. "And Mom?"

"Yeah?"

"I'm sorry. Again. I'm glad you had the guts to push me. Thanks."

Normalcy. Yep, that would do the trick. Anesia placed the keys into the ignition and stopped. She turned to face her daughter. "I love you, Zoya. Nothing will ever, ever change that. Just promise to keep talking to me, okay?"

"Okay."

"Even if you're angry, you can always talk to me." She took a deep breath. Might as well go through with it. It might be the only way to get things back to how they were. Before. She knew what she needed to say, but hesitated. It meant placing all her trust in God. There'd be no control on her part. There'd be no guarantees of protection. "And . . . I've also made a decision about something else."

Zoya stared.

"I don't want to take away your dream, Zoya. I know how much racing means to you, how much it means to me, how much it meant to your father. It's in your blood." She took another deep breath. Ugh. This was hard. "So, I want you to keep racing."

Her daughter's eyes lit up. "You do?"

"I do."

"You mean, you're not afraid something awful will happen?"

"Oh, I'm afraid. That's for sure." She grabbed her daughter's hands. "But God doesn't give us a spirit of fear, remember?"

"I remember." Zoya smiled even though she rolled her eyes as she rattled off 2 Timothy 1:7: "'For God has not given us a spirit of fearfulness, but one of power, love, and sound judgment.' You made me memorize it and repeat it for my very first race. I couldn't even see over the handlebar of the sled."

Anesia allowed herself to chuckle at the memory. "And I know I can't always protect you, even though I sure do want to. But I know I need to leave all this in the Lord's hands. We'll get through this together, okay?"

Her daughter squeezed her hands three times—their signal for *I love you*. "You're right, Mom. Thanks."

Zoya was saying all the right things. And yet . . .

Anesia shook her concern away. If she could just let go. Trust God with it all. With her daughter's heart and mind, with her recovery and safety. If only she could be at peace and not worry.

But could she do that when a murderer might still be hunting her child?

SLIM
January 17
Naltsiine Kennels
1:57 a.m.

Green lights lit up the screen of the handheld scanner. So far, so good. All the chips were still in place and protected. Amazing.

Technology created to help find people's precious pets was helping him hide a multi-billion-dollar program.

No one was the wiser.

Three more chips waited in their plastic casings to be implanted. He'd already checked them on the laptop this morning. The information was viable and no longer encrypted. Just wait until he had it all and could put it together.

Technology was impressive. Ten years ago, who woulda thought that 5GB of data could fit on a chip one-tenth the size of his fingernail?

His brittle laugh echoed off the barn walls in the cold air.

Like Ma always said, he was a genius. He just needed to wait for the right plan. The right time. And he had.

Patience would win this game for him.

And he would prove he had patience. Enough to out-wait them all. Then who would be on top?

Him.

He'd hold all the cards.

Then he'd hold the prize.

Leaning over, he stroked the head of another champion. "Good boy."

RICK
January 17
Anchorage, Alaska
3:26 a.m.

Zoya ran through the woods chased by an army of armed soldiers. Her screams pierced the air. "Help me! Someone, please help me!"

He tried to follow, but no matter how fast he ran, he couldn't catch up.

She fell, and the army clothed in black descended upon her like a pack of ravenous wolves. The numbers grew like ants swarming an anthill. More appeared from the trees. More fell from the sky.

"No!" His voice carried on the wind, but no one heard him.

"Uncle! Save me! Please!" The young girl's cries for help were quickly smothered by the mass of humanity piling on top of her—

Rick sat up with a jolt. Sweat drenched his entire body. If he didn't do something, he'd never fulfill his promise. His grandfather had been right. He'd burn forever on this earth, be haunted and never allowed to die. The spirits would curse him if he didn't protect her.

A plan began to form in the back of his mind. He had the resources and the power to do it. Maybe he should find the old tribal elders. Some that believed like his grandfather. They could surely help him find what the spirits required of him to fulfill his promise to his brother and grandfather.

He was the only one left.

He couldn't let Zoya die.

SEAN
January 17
Naltsiine Kennels
10:33 a.m.

His brain threatened to explode with all the information Anesia threw at him, but it fascinated him too.

The air was bitter. Colder than he'd ever thought possible. Colder than he'd ever felt in Boston. But then again, he'd always ridden in warmed Town Cars, and the Connolly Towers had a special entrance for the family to protect them from the elements of a harsh winter and prying eyes. He never had the privilege of shoveling snow at home. Sean tugged off a glove and glanced down at his hand. Definitely broken-in the past months on the road, but still the hand of a spoiled, office-lounged VP.

The glove slid back on as they moved toward another row of dogs. His eyes darted heavenward again. The sky a deep purple-black. So many stars. He shook his head and forced himself to pay attention and not keep looking up at the sky. Ever since he'd caught a glimpse of the aurora borealis, he watched the sky for more.

Anesia continued explaining. She'd been a little stiffer this morning than she'd been the previous week. Maybe she was overwhelmed and needed him to learn fast. "In the winter we water the dogs in the morning. But we mix a little food in the water. Just enough to flavor it."

"Why do you mix food in it? Do they need the extra nourishment?" He jotted down notes with a pencil on the small notebook he carried with him. He learned the hard way that most pens wouldn't write in this kind of cold.

"They won't drink clear water in the winter."

"Really?"

"Yeah, it's just too cold. So it's kinda like bait to get them to drink enough. They need plenty of hydration, especially to run."

"Oh. I see."

"During training season we water them, clean up, and give them an hour and a half of rest before we run them."

His eyes scanned the kennel full of dogs. Just watering them would take a good bit of time.

"And then we feed them in the afternoon."

"How much does it cost to feed this many?"

She inspected the paws of the dog in front of her. "About a dollar a day per dog. So a couple thousand dollars a month."

Quite an investment.

Anesia had already moved to the gate. "Come on. There's still a lot more."

"All right."

The volume of the dogs increased.

She turned to face him but continued to walk backward. "And by the way, you probably don't want to say 'all right' too much in front of the dogs."

"Why is that?"

She gave him a small smile. "That's what most mushers use as their call to go, to get the dogs to run. We release the hooks and yell, 'All right.'" She turned back around.

"Oh." He wrote that down on his pad. Certainly an important piece of information. Several more questions tumbled around in his mind. "How do you practice with them when there's no snow?" He took a few long strides to catch up to her quick pace and so he could hear her.

"We use a four-wheeler instead of a sled."

Sure. Now why didn't he think of that? "Isn't that heavy?"

He watched her shake her head and continue walking. When they reached the barn, she slid a large door open. "We have two dog trucks." She pointed to the odd vehicles parked inside.

The cab of the truck looked normal, but the back was covered with a large enclosed area. Almost like the trucks he'd seen for the humane society. But bigger. Much bigger. There were eight doors on each side. "Do you buy these somewhere or have them built?"

"I had mine built to my specifications. Each compartment will hold two dogs. So we can haul up to sixty-four dogs at a time. Although we usually don't carry that many. Most rides we let them each have their own compartment." She opened one of the doors so he could peer inside. Hay covered the floor of each. "And there will be times I'll need you to drive one of the trucks. Especially when it's a big event."

"All righ—" He jerked his head up from what he was writing. "I mean, yes, I can do that."

She laughed. "Are you comfortable driving a stick?"

"Yes. But I may need practice." When was the last time he'd driven a manual transmission?

"Good." She looked down and fidgeted with her gloves as her smile disappeared. "Sean, I wanted to show you some other things, but there's something bugging me. We need to go inside and have a chat."

He nodded. In silence she closed up the barn and they walked back to the house. She must know. Not that he didn't expect it. But it was sooner than he anticipated.

They didn't speak again until they were seated in her office. She pulled out a file and folded her hands on her desk. "Why didn't you tell me your father owned CROM?"

There it was. The accusation in her voice. "I'm sorry, Anesia—"

"Sean, let's get something straight right now. More than anything, I need someone trustworthy. The work is hard, and I'd like someone who loved what they did, but trust is of utmost importance to me."

"I understand." Disappointment washed over him. He hadn't realized until now how much he wanted this job.

"I'm not sure you really do. There's a lot I haven't told *you* yet, either." She stood and walked to the bookcases lining the east wall. Her fingers traveled along the books. "Our dogs are worth a small fortune, as is the property, kennels, and equipment. But more important than all that is my family and my friends." Her gaze came to rest on him. "Your background check came back clean, Sean. I just couldn't figure out why you wanted to keep the fact of your family away from me."

"My family may be extremely wealthy, Anesia, and they may own CROM, but I don't want anything to do with them. I wanted a fresh start."

She cocked an eyebrow. It hadn't taken her long to put all the pieces together, had it? And she wasn't letting him off the hook now.

"I began to discover things I didn't like about how my father did things. My father is a brilliant man. But he's also a greedy man. It took me many years to decide which path I was going to choose."

"So that's why you continued on with your father's job and expectations of you?" She nodded as she paced. "The education, the VP, the overseeing of exciting projects."

"Unfortunately." Nothing got past this woman. "It took God getting hold of me to rescue me from the muck and mire that dragged me down."

"Your father knows you're here?"

"Yes, he does."

"And he's okay with that?"

"No. He's not. But I couldn't stay in Boston one moment longer."

"Why?" Those intense eyes drilled into him.

"I realized I'd been lukewarm. And in staying, in essence, I was agreeing with everything my father did. I couldn't swallow it anymore. I couldn't let my name be a part of that."

"By lukewarm, I assume you are referencing Revelation 3:16?" The tiniest smile worked at the corner of her mouth.

"Yes." He tilted his head and furrowed his brow. Was she mocking him? Best to get it all out in the open now. "Do you mind if I ask how you feel about God, Anesia?"

She laughed. "Not at all. In fact, I'm glad you opened the door for this discussion. I'm a believer."

Relief flooded through him. His hands relaxed, hadn't realized he'd tightened them into fists during their talk. "I am too. I'm sorry to say it took so many years for me to come to my senses, but I'm thankful I finally put Him first in my life." Sean looked down at the floor. Time to lay it all out on the table. "I didn't come here to hide. But I did come here to start over. I can't promise that my father won't try to make things difficult for me, but I can promise that I will work as hard as I can and to the very best of my ability."

Her eyes creased at their corners as a smile lit her face. "I'm glad to hear that. And since everything else checks out on you, I'd like to offer you the job."

"Thank you." He started to stand.

She held up a hand. "But you might want to hear me out before you take me up on the offer."

Sean sat back in his chair.

"I know this has been a little on the odd side. I kept wondering how the timing of all this worked out, with Wanda sending you my way, you're a man, I mean a real man, I mean . . ." She wiped a hand down her face and laughed. "Let me start over. You're not a college kid."

He laughed along with her wanting to put her at ease.

"And right now. I need someone like you."

Hm. This sounded . . . interesting.

She must have realized how that sounded, because her jaw dropped and then closed. A tinge of pink touched her cheeks as she continued. "Um, to live here on the property, I mean."

"Of course."

"My daughter witnessed a murder recently and it has upset our quiet little world."

He absorbed this information. No wonder she'd been so on edge. And her daughter, the poor kid. No kid should have to go through that. "I'll do everything I can to help."

"It will help to know you're here, on the property."

"Are you afraid the killers will come after her?"

She met his gaze, and he saw the answer—and the fear—in her eyes. Sean nodded. "I understand. And I promise you, Anesia, I'll do whatever I can to keep your daughter safe."

CHAPTER FIFTEEN

ZOYA
January 17
Naltsiine Kennels
11:45 a.m.

Mom and Sean talked near the sleds. No doubt she was telling him how to get the dogs ready. Again.

Auntie Jenna and Cole stood on the porch drinking hot chocolate and chit-chatting.

Andie crouched to the ground and formed a snowball.

I followed suit. Maybe if I pretended to laugh and have fun she would think everything was fine . . . Yes. That would work. It had to.

"Andie, Zoya." Mom caught us.

Andie giggled and we hid the round objects behind our backs. "Yes, ma'am?"

As soon as she turned her back the games began. One ball after another would soar through the air until colliding with the intended target.

"Ah!" Andie ducked as two came flying. "Oh, you're in for it now!"

I tried to give a smile, and almost succeeded. *Come on, pull yourself together. You're supposed to be all better, remember?*

The fight continued for more than ten minutes as Mom showed Sean once again how to attach the dogs to their harnesses.

A niggling feeling passed through me, starting in my stomach and going up. Was I wrong to pretend?

No, it will help everyone.

Mom's words echoed throughout my head . . . "*God did not let you down. Those men who committed the crime are the ones who did wrong. Not you. Not God. He loves you. And whether you want to admit it or not, 'junk'—like you put it—happens to all of us. To good people. All the time.*"

I shook my head. The voice returned.

"*Don't trust Him . . . Don't trust Him . . .*"

Andie's surprise hit brought me back to the present.

"Yikes! That's cold!" A chunk of ice made its way down my jacket and onto my shirt. It melted, leaving a cold, wet spot. "Andie! I don't have time to change!"

"Hey, you did the same thing to me."

"Did not."

"Did too!"

"Oh yeah?"

"Yeaaaah . . ."

And snowballs went airborne again.

"Make sure you don't tell the dogs to go one way and shift your weight to the other, these dogs go so fast you may fly off. This rubbery, mat-like flap right here can be flipped down with your foot, place your heel on it and it will help slow you down. For a turn or whatever. But don't use the foot brake unless it's an emergency. It'll tear up the trail. 'Gee' is right and 'haw' is left. Got that?" Mom pointed to each thing in turn as she explained.

Sean nodded.

"Okay then, time to go." Mom issued the cease-fire. Lunches were packed, Sean's lessons were done.

Finally.

Everyone jumped onto their sled. Cole and Auntie Jenna in the front, me and Andie in the middle, and Mom and Sean in the back.

We rode for awhile, no one saying a word.

I closed my eyes. I'd missed running the dogs. It was good to be back on the sled.

I glanced beside me at Andie. She grinned and motioned for me to look behind.

Loosen up. Stay calm.

"Don't trust Him . . . Don't trust Him . . . Don't trust Him . . ."

A shiver jolted me. I wanted to get rid of the voice. But it seemed to be there to stay.

Were there murderers out there?

Andie giggled. "Look."

I looked behind me to where Andie pointed. Mom was still giving instructions to Sean.

"And shift your weight, like so . . ."

Andie laughed.

I tried to. But the little voice kept speaking. Reminding me . . .

Go away!

"God did not let you down . . . He loves you . . ."

"Please don't think I'm being mean, it's not like he's a bad guy or anything . . ."

I jerked my head over to Andie. Thankfully I hadn't fallen off the sled. I really needed to pay attention.

Andie smiled and looked behind. "But he's *sooooo* weird."

I nodded, trying to bring myself back to the present. *Sean?* "For someone his age you'd think he'd catch on a little quicker." I cleared my throat.

Andie nodded. "And with his *education.* Mom said he went to Harvard."

Harvard?

Cole yelled at us from up front. "How about we stop at the big clearing up ahead?"

"Okay." Andie smiled.

I nodded. *I just hope there aren't any bad men waiting for us.*

No! Zoya, stop thinking like that. I shook my head.

"Gee." One at a time Cole, Auntie Jenna, Andie, and then me yelled for our dogs to turn into the wide clearing.

Mom sped up in front of Sean and turned too. "You're next, Sean."

I hopped off my sled and went to unpack the lunch boxes. Distraction . . .

"Gee!" Sean's shout brought more than one bird out of their nests.

I covered my ears.

"Not so loud, Sea—Look *out!*"

I spun around. *Well, he shifted his weight all right.*

A laugh bubbled up. It felt good to laugh. But did I want it to?

Sean flew through the air and landed smack-dab into the trunk of a full grown tree. Even from where we stood I could hear his loud "UMPH!"

Mom and Cole ran over and yelled for his litter of dogs to stop running.

Auntie Jenna walked up next to us as Mom and Cole helped him out of a pile of snow. "I hope he's not hurt."

Mom nodded. "I think he'll live."

The foursome walked back over to us, Sean dusting snow off himself as he walked.

Andie clapped. "Bravo, Sean. That was an excellent performance."

I couldn't help it. A smile stretched across my face. It felt good. Almost.

A blur in the trees caught my attention.

A man.

Pointing at me.

COLE
1:11 p.m.

Cole lifted his face to the vanishing afternoon sun. The tension of the AMI encryption would send him to an early grave if he didn't watch it. Jenna walked up beside him and slipped her gloved hand into his.

"Hey."

"Hey, babe." He released a long sigh.

"I'm glad you took the afternoon off to spend with us." She pulled him closer. "But I can tell your mind is elsewhere. Wanna talk about it?"

"Wish I could, but I can't. At least not yet. Just issues with the prototype." He wrapped his arms around her. "Sometimes I wish I had retired when I had the chance."

Jenna's arms reached around his neck and tugged him down. "You? Retire? Yeah, right." She pulled a little harder and stood on tiptoe.

As their lips met, he tried to focus on his wife, enjoy the moment.

She laughed and pulled away. "I don't think you'll ever be able to retire. You enjoy the thrill a little too much."

"More like a headache right now."

"Well, if I know you, Cole Maddox, and I do"—she wagged a finger at him—"I know you will figure it all out and save the world in the process."

He grabbed her before she could get away. "Okay, little miss-know-it-all"—he kissed her soundly—"thanks for the boost of confidence."

She sauntered away, a glimmer of triumph in her eyes. "You're welcome. And I expect our date night tonight to be totally focused on you and me. Got it?"

"Yes, ma'am." Cole watched her walk over to Anesia. God sure had blessed him with that one. And she was right. His AMI problems could wait until later. Needed to focus on her now. He glanced over to the sleds. Sean went from dog to dog checking harnesses. Time Cole got to know the new guy. Zoya wasn't herself and they needed to protect her.

"Understand it all yet?" He stuck his hand out. Anesia told him she'd received the background check and had hired Sean that morning. She also informed him that she'd spoken with Agent Philips about Sean. That relieved a lot of his worry, as had the news that Mr. Connolly was a Christian.

"Not remotely." Sean received his handshake with a firm grip.

"Don't worry. It took me months and plenty of eye-rolls from all four of those lovely ladies over there before I caught on."

"Let's hope it doesn't take that long, considering this is now my job and I'm being paid to learn this canine business."

This guy was different. Seemed honest enough, but a little too polished. "So what brought you here, Sean?"

"A fresh start."

"From what?"

"The family business."

"Oh? Something you didn't enjoy?"

The other man glanced at Anesia. "My boss knows the truth, and that's enough."

Truth? What truth? Hadn't Agent Philips cleared this guy? That's all he needed. Another mess to clean up. He must've been scowling because Sean held up his hands.

"It's not what you're thinking."

He stiffened and his jaw clenched. No one messed with his family. "And what exactly am I thinking?"

"Let me start over. My name is Sean Connolly. Of the Boston Connollys. My father owns CROM."

Open mouth. Insert foot.

Sean shook his head. "Sorry, Cole. You have every right to be concerned about your friends."

Cole cleared his throat. "I'm the one who should apologize. I appreciate your honesty."

Sean held his hand out for another shake. "Shall we begin again?"

"Yeah." The grip was hearty and shared mutual respect. "But, we've got to get you to relax in your speech a little."

A laugh was Sean's response. "If you have a cure for thirty-seven years of grooming and breeding, I'd take it. But I'm afraid some things aren't easily achieved."

"You can say that again."

"I was hoping that in my travels here, some of it would be erased, but I guess it's still obvious."

"How did you get here?"

"I walked."

Cole sucked in too big a breath and choked on the icy air. "You what?"

"I walked."

"From Boston?"

"Yes. I had just read in Luke about Jesus challenging His followers to leave everything behind and follow Him. And I'd felt the prodding for some time that I was lukewarm, the only way to be on fire for the Lord was for me to leave that life behind. So I did. I sold everything I owned in Boston, packed a backpack, and set off on my journey."

"Wow." Had to give the guy credit. That was a lot of miles to cover. "You *walked* all the way here? How long did it take?"

"Indeed I did. Plenty of people offered rides, but I declined. It took the better part of seven months. Covered over 6,000 miles."

"Guess you took the long way, huh?"

"In a manner of speaking, yes. I wasn't entirely sure where I'd end up." Sean looked down at his hands. "For many years I've been sequestered among the social elite. The chosen few my father allowed into our 'circle.' Everything was about title, money, speech, and appearance—to be quite blunt—a façade. I hated myself. Didn't even know myself."

"That's intense. To have the guts to just pack up and leave? How'd your family take it?"

"Not well." Sean's green eyes met his. "My father is *not* pleased."

"He knows where you are?"

A sad laugh. "Unfortunately. He has unlimited resources. And likes to know everything."

Cole nodded. "I can imagine." He patted Sean on the shoulder. "Sounds like you did the right thing. And you've got us to help you through it."

"What do you do?"

"Oh, a little of this and a little of that." Cole smiled at him. "I'm in the military. A lot of stuff, I can't talk about."

"Understood. It's good to know you're here though. I would greatly appreciate a solid male friend."

"Man, we've got to work on you. Get you to loosen up. We've got a men's Bible study every other Saturday morning. Sometimes my work keeps me away, but it would be a great opportunity for you to meet with other men. And we hold one another accountable, which is a good thing."

"Sounds exactly like what I've been looking for. And I would love help in 'loosening up' as you put it. You don't have any idea how difficult it is to blend in."

Cole chuckled. "You should've heard Andie the first day. You and your button down Oxford shirt. Leave it to a thirteen-year-old to put you in your place."

"Well, when the majority of the wardrobe you've had for fifteen years is three-piece suits, and you wore them almost around the clock, it's a little difficult to discern what one wears to work at a dog kennel. Believe me, I was afraid Anesia would kick me out in my Oxford."

Cole chuckled. "You don't want to mess with Anesia, that's for sure." Something in the trees caught his attention. "But don't worry. We'll help you figure it all out. I'll get your number from Anesia and call you about Bible study." Hopefully he didn't sound too rushed, but his gut told him something wasn't right.

"Yes. I need to find out what needs to be done next." Sean walked toward Anesia.

As Cole headed to the tree line where he'd seen movement, he scanned the perimeter. He slid a hand inside his down jacket and pulled his sidearm free.

Rustling greeted his ears.

Snow crunched.

Then antlers appeared.

Cole exhaled and, as he holstered his gun, the moose grunted at him. But as he turned to head back to their picnic, something else caught his eye.

Footprints. Of the human kind.

And they were fresh.

SEAN
January 17
1:34 p.m.

Even though he'd been through an information overload, Sean forced his brain to alertness. To watch and learn. These people had deep relationships. They knew each other well. Closer than any other family he'd witnessed.

Yet the undercurrent of fear was tangible. Anesia seemed to tackle the day, almost forcing everything to be . . . what? He wasn't sure. Cole and Jenna appeared like any other newlywed couple. In love, enjoying every minute. But Cole . . . no missing that edge of vigilance. How he never quite let his guard down.

Sean watched Cole as he crouched in the trees. What was he looking for? When he turned and came back to join them, a smile cracked his face. Maybe it was nothing.

Anesia caught his attention. Sharp, attentive, intelligent, independent. She poured her life into her work. His new boss intrigued him.

"Time to eat." She smiled at him before she started tossing bags to everyone.

Cole approached him. "Hey Sean. Let me show you something real quick."

Jenna placed hands on her hips. "Don't take long, babe, we've got a feast waiting."

As Sean followed Cole, he heard Jenna say to the girls, "Men. Gotta love 'em."

Several yards away from the others, Cole turned. A stiff smile on his face. He pointed to his left. But stared at Sean. "Paste on a smile and don't say anything. I saw something in the trees earlier and found footprints. I think we're being watched. Keep your eyes peeled."

"What?"

Cole gripped his shoulder and laughed heartily. "Don't you dare scare them. Keep it light. Pretend, Sean."

Pretend. He'd never been in a situation like this before. And even though Cole appeared to be joking with him about something, it was all an act. The man was protecting his family.

Years of suppressed emotion and desire welled up and shattered the shell surrounding him. Like a cocoon falling away, Sean felt new life surge forth inside him.

More than anything he wanted to be part of a real family. More than anything he wanted a reason to care.

More than anything he wanted to protect Anesia and Zoya.

CHAPTER SIXTEEN

ZOYA
January 17
1:46 p.m.

A breeze floated by.

I blinked. Tried to pull myself out of my thoughts. I needed to stop thinking about the murder. The gun. The blood. But how could I when they wouldn't let go of my mind? That guy I saw pointing at me wasn't real. It was just my imagination.

Auntie Jenna and Cole laughed. At Sean no doubt. Andie tried to lick sticky, half-frozen strawberry jelly off of her hands and face. Mom sat reorganizing the lunch boxes.

Andie giggled. When had she become so happy-go-lucky? Oh, wait. She'd *always* been that way.

I was the one who changed.

"Mom, how much jelly did you put on this thing?"

Auntie Jenna shrugged and pointed to Mom. "Anesia made the ones with strawberry jelly. I made the blackberry."

"Oh, so you're the culprit!" Andie pointed her half-eaten sandwich in Mom's direction.

She winked.

"Having trouble?" I turned and tried to smile. *Just play the part. That's all you have to do.*

"*Me*? No way!" She giggled. "This is normal. My PB&Js always fall apart and slather my hands in goop. What's new with you?"

I glanced at the empty Ziploc bags littering her feet. Peanut butter and jelly stuck to the inside and out. I raised my eyebrows. "How many sandwiches have you eaten?"

"Only four," she smiled, "and a half."

Mom and Auntie Jenna stood.

"We'll be right back, we're gonna put some of these empty lunchboxes on the sleds."

"Okey-dokey." Andie nodded.

When they were out of hearing range, she turned to me. "I'm glad you're okay. What happened?"

"You mean how'd I get out of the depths of despair?" I swallowed. *Play the part* . . . I nodded to Mom. "I was at the end of my rope. Then Mom and I talked. In the back of my head I knew it was wrong of me to think what I did, but I couldn't help it. I guess . . ."

I stared out toward the trees. A clump of snow fell from one of the limbs. Sunlight shone onto it, making it look like a ball of prisms. "I guess I still think some of those things now." *What? You weren't supposed to say that!* "But it's okay. I'm good now, everything will get back to normal." I nodded and kept my gaze on the clump.

So much for playing the part.

She would be able to tell something was missing. I could see just by looking at her face that she didn't believe me.

"Just know that I'm always here for you, okay?" She reached out and grabbed my hand.

"Okay."

Mom and Auntie walked back over and sat down.

"We'll leave these two snack bags where we can get to them, just in case one of you gets hungry, okay?"

"Thanks. But I don't think Andie will be eating any more for awhile." I tried to smile up at them. *I'm just tired. Yeah, tired.*

Okay. You believe it, now just try to get them to believe it.

"I think you're right. I've eaten enough for two people! Ugh." Andie giggled again and patted her stomach.

Cole and Sean walked over. "Ready to go?"

Mom nodded. "Just about. Do one of you want another sandwich?"

Cole grabbed his stomach and winced. "No thanks. I'm *stuffed.*"

"Like an overgrown teddy bear." Andie licked her fingers.

"If your hands weren't covered in sticky stuff—"

"Oh, come on, Echo, you're braver than that!" She smiled and held up her gooey fingers.

"Ah, yes. And don't you forget it!" He crouched down and tickled her sides, somehow avoiding her still icky hands.

A loud screech was her reply.

I closed my eyes. What did it feel like to tease your dad?

"Sean, another sandwich?" Auntie Jenna held up another delicious snack. "Before the PB&J monster snags them all."

"I won't eat them all!" Andie grabbed Cole's hands and tried to pry them from her sides. He tickled harder.

"EEEEK! Stop! Uncle!" Andie laughed and tried to break away from Cole's grasp.

"What's the magic word?"

"Pleeeeeease?"

"Nope!"

Massive arms wrapped around her as he leaned in.

"Not a zerbert!"

He smiled.

Pffbbbttttt!

My head jerked back over to the two noise makers.

"Zoya, help me!"

I gave a small smile. "I'm a little tired, maybe later."

Cole looked to me. He searched my eyes. Probing. And very serious.

I wanted to squirm. Why was he so inquisitive? There was nothing wrong with me. I was fine.

I looked away.

"I think you've got things under control." I stood and walked over to the dogs, escaping Cole's death stare.

The dogs barked and wagged their tails as I covered the ten feet between us. *At least you won't question me all the time.* I focused on the soft feel of their fur coats. Each one had different colors. Each one had a different personality. Each one seemed so excited every time we raced.

Each one looked up to me with those pathetic eyes and stared. As if asking me . . .

Not you too. Will I ever get away from all these questions?

Cole's and Andie's laughter rang in the air.

I blinked. *Don't think about it.*

"Zoya, you wanna take the dogs out for another run?" Mom walked up to my side and smiled.

I nodded. Good idea . . . yeah. Good.

"Cole and I will stay here with the food if you guys want to go." Auntie Jenna smiled and poked Cole's arm. "Maybe a time-out will teach him a lesson on how to be the adult."

"Mom, give it up already. He's a giant toddler, we all know that." Andie smiled and stood, getting just out of his reach.

"Hey!" Cole crossed his large arms. "Sean, are you going along?" Why did he look so stern all of a sudden?

"Can we go now?" I petted Morphine. Not looking any of them in the eye. Better to just get on the trail.

Sean nodded to Cole and hopped on his sled.

Mom gave more instructions.

My stomach churned. Couldn't we just go? Each minute seemed to tick by as if it were traveling through molasses. But soon we were off.

Andie stayed by my side, as we were instructed, with Mom in the back and Sean in the front. We took the long trail. As we picked up speed, my thoughts began to swim.

Mom said I could race. But was I ready? What if something happened?

My heart wanted to trust God again. But could I after what He had done?

No! I would not let Him deceive me again.

I wanted to tell someone about how I was feeling. But no one would understand. Better to keep it to myself.

I glanced at Andie. She smiled and encouraged the dogs as we rode on.

Why was she always so—

Someone stood in the trees. Almost hidden thanks to his camo outfit.

I gasped.

An orange hat that stuck out like a lion among sheep . . .

My head jerked to the front as we zoomed past. He was real.

My mouth dried up. I couldn't scream, but I had to say something. I shivered.

He had stood there. Staring.

At us.

At me.

ANESIA

January 22
Naltsiine Kennels
6:00 a.m.

Incessant beeping broke through her sleep-clouded mind. Anesia reached over and smacked the snooze button. Sleep had been elusive until around four a.m.

Now it was six and she didn't have time to relish the warmth under the covers. A giant yawn caused her to stretch and sit up.

Race day.

On an average race day she loved these mornings. The adrenaline pumping through her system. Anticipation for the race. She lived to race. So had Dan. No wonder their daughter had the same race-driven blood running through her veins.

But today was different.

Today was scary.

Uncertain.

And she had no control.

Anesia rubbed her eyes with her hands. Why did she have to hold on so tight? She wanted to leave it all in God's hands and know that Zoya would be safe and protected. She *wanted* to hand over the reins to Him. She'd made that decision, right?

But she lived in the real world. And knew there were bad people out there. People who might, even now, be after her daughter.

Those thoughts scared her the most.

Anesia stood by the edge of her bed and shivered.

Her conversation with Zoya came zinging back to her:

"But God doesn't give us a spirit of fear, remember?"

"I remember . . . 'For God has not given us a spirit of fearfulness, but one of power, love, and sound judgment' . . ."

It was all fine and good to lecture her daughter to bring her out of her shell, but now here she stood quaking, shivering. And her own words convicted her. She dropped to her knees, her muffled cries of anguish buried in her arms. *God, I need Your power. Please take away this fear. Protect my baby.*

"Mom?" Zoya bounced into the room. "You're usually the one having to drag my rear end out of bed . . ." She walked around the bed. "Mom, you okay?"

Deep breath. Gotta be honest, but don't scare her. "I'm okay. Didn't get a lot of sleep last night."

Zoya quieted. "Because you're excited or because you're scared?"

Smart kid. Anesia hated bursting her bubble. She pulled her thirteen-year-old into a hug. "You know me too well. Yes, I was scared. But I heard your voice quoting 2 Timothy 1:7 this morning and I've prayed. So it's time to pick myself up by my bootstraps and get moving."

"That's my mom." Zoya squeezed tighter.

"That's my girl."

"Well, since I'm ready before you, I'll fix your coffee. Just the way you like it."

"Sounds great, sweetie. Sorry I'm dragging my feet today." She reached for her long underwear. "I better get out there."

"Sean's gotcha covered. He's been out there with the dogs for a good fifteen minutes."

"Really?" Where were those thermal socks?

"Yep." Zoya giggled and threw the socks at her. "You know, Andie and I thought he was pretty weird at first. So prim and proper all the time. But he's actually pretty cool. I think he likes it."

"Yeah, he does fit in well, doesn't he?" For some reason, the thought warmed her.

"And he's nice. He listens. Doesn't treat me like a snotty teenager. Like he respects my opinion and who I am."

Anesia walked back to her daughter and smiled. "That's because you're not a snotty teenager. If you were, I'd invent a device to suck all the snot out. Who wouldn't love you?"

Zoya rolled her eyes. "You're such a *mom*, Mom."

"And proud of it." She patted Zoya on the head. "Now I need that coffee."

"But don't you think he's nice?"

"Of course I think he's nice, I hired him, didn't I?"

"But isn't he around your age?" Zoya bounced on the balls of her feet, a mischievous twinkle in her eye.

"All right, my little rainbow. That's enough for now." She began to shove Zoya out of the room. "Yes. He's nice. Yes. He's around my age. And might I remind you that yes, he *works* for me."

"Okay, okay. I'll leave it alone. For now. But—"

"No buts. I need coffee. Or I'll turn into the Wicked Witch of the West."

Zoya scooted out giggling just as Anesia shut the door. Leaning against it, she wondered if her daughter needed a man in her life. Part of it had to be because of Cole and Jenna.

Jenna's first husband, Marcus, had been the only father figure Zoya'd ever known. As best friends with Jenna and Andie, Anesia and Zoya had spent all their time with the Tikaani-Gray family. But when Marcus was killed, it affected them all in different ways. Zoya grieved Marcus's death as if he were her father as well and not just the dad of her best friend.

Then Cole entered their lives. Jenna and Andie were happier now than the Naltsiine girls had seen them since Marc's death. Maybe that was it. Did Zoya think they could have a fresh start as well if Anesia found a husband?

Anesia moved toward her bathroom to get ready. She couldn't blame her daughter. After watching the overwhelming happiness enter Andie's and Jenna's lives with Cole, Anesia thought for a brief moment that maybe there was a little more to the whole married thing. Like maybe she should give it a little more consideration. But no. She had her daughter. Protecting her had to be the top priority. She had Jenna and Andie. She had her dogs. That was plenty. She made too many mistakes when it came to men.

A quick shower, packing of gear, and two cups of coffee later, Anesia found herself outside the truck loading the dogs with Sean at her side. His aftershave was unlike anything she'd ever smelled before. A little high-class mixed with a lot of masculine. Wow. Or maybe it was the guy wearing it.

No. No. No. Must be the thoughts planted by her instigating little offspring.

She would not go there. Even if he was incredibly good-looking. With that crazy blond hair, and those green eyes that she could get lost in. Especially when he was learning something new. The yearning, the intensity, he was so . . . real.

Whoa, girl. Get a grip. "Not gonna happen."

"What's not going to happen?"

Blood rushed to her face. "Did I say that out loud?"

Sean chuckled. "Are you always this driven, this focused on a race day?"

Maybe she had been attacking the chores this morning with a little more vigor than usual. If he only knew. "Sorry, Sean. I guess I just have a lot on my mind."

"I know. I prayed for you guys this morning. And especially you."

"Really?" Why did her voice have to go and squeak like a schoolgirl's?

"Yes, I did. I know this must be very trying for you. To allow her to race with everything that has happened. For *you* to race."

The words were innocent. His sincerity rang true. She could tell. But it didn't stop her heart from melting into a puddle at her feet. What was *wrong* with her? "Thank you, Sean. That means a lot."

He shrugged, giving her that now familiar smile—the one that made her insides tingle all the way down to her toes—and checked all the doors on the truck.

The man learned fast. She'd have to give him that. And she'd made him jump in with both feet. Not many people could've stood up to the challenge, but so far she'd been nothing but impressed with Sean Connolly.

Anesia straightened. And allowed herself to smile. Zoya was correct. Sean *was* a nice man.

But there just wasn't time for romance. She didn't think her heart could ever take it again.

Ever.

CHAPTER SEVENTEEN

SEAN
January 22
9:00 a.m.

The morning flew by, but he didn't mind. Time spent with Anesia Naltsiine increased in value daily. And the dogs. Loved working with the dogs. For the first time in many years, he had purpose. Honest work. Honest pay. A man. His own man. The scare from their picnic excursion turned out to be nothing, but Sean noticed Cole's ever-watchful gaze. And Cole called him several times. Asking him questions, telling him to keep his eyes open.

As they jostled along in the dog truck, he snuck another glimpse at Anesia. Her native features were elegant. The shine on her hair reminded him of black silk, like his mother's favorite scarf.

Sean pushed the memory of his mother away. All the if-onlys couldn't erase the fact that the last time he'd seen her they'd argued.

Focus on Anesia. She was here. Now.

Even bundled up in her gear, she was breathtaking.

Zoya poked him.

He'd been caught. Again.

There hadn't been a lot of conversation between him and this tiny teen, but every so often he got glimpses of her depth. She had great ideas. Loved racing. And loved her mom. Sean hadn't known many teenagers since he'd been one. But he'd heard horror stories from fellows at work. Thank goodness Anesia's daughter wasn't anything like that.

They shared a conspiratorial wink and he nudged her with his elbow. It felt good to be a part of something bigger than himself. Part of a group of people . . . friends that cared about one another.

Like a family.

The thought struck him an intense blow. Exactly like a family *should* be. The old memories tried to surface. Could he be a part of this family?

"Sean?" Zoya's dark eyes peered up at him.

"Yes?"

"So what do you think of us so far? Are you liking it?"

"I love it. Never knew I could love work so much."

"Even poop-scooping?" Zoya stuck out her tongue. "Blech. That's the part I hate the most."

"Even poop-scooping."

Anesia laughed but her eyes remained glued to the road as she shifted gears.

"Wow. You really must've been desperate."

"Zoya!" Anesia looked at him then, shock and mirth twinkled from her eyes. Her lips pursed and twitched. An unsuccessful frown turned into a smile as a laugh escaped from her lips. "Sorry, Sean."

"Well, you know what, Zoya? I think you're right. I was desperate. Desperate to do what's right. Finally."

The teen crossed her arms and angled toward him. Eyebrows raised. "Scooping poop is 'right'?"

"You bet. If that's what God wants you to do."

"All righty then. It's official. You *are* weird."

"A good weird, I hope." He nudged her again.

"Anyone who enjoys cleaning up the kennel must be out of their mind. But more power to ya, Sean." She elbowed him back with a grin.

"So. Tell me about this race today."

Her face lit up as she talked about the race, which dogs she was running, and the thrill she felt each time her sled flew over the snow. Sean enjoyed watching her animation. Zoya came out of her shell when it was time to race. It seemed to be the only time he had the opportunity to see the real kid.

Of course, it didn't hurt that he caught a glimpse of Anesia every now and then as well.

It was obvious, mother and daughter were in love with the sport. And he would do everything in his power to keep those smiles on their beautiful faces.

Permanently.

ANESIA
January 22
Fairbanks, Alaska
10:00 a.m.

Anesia pulled more gear out of her truck, hinting to the other musher to move on. But no such luck today.

"So, you running the Rondy this year?" The man gripped his travel mug with both hands.

She shook her head and kept working with the harnesses.

"Of course, you are. That was a dumb question. You've won it the past few years, haven't you?" His nervous chuckle hovered in the air.

"Yep." Why wouldn't he just leave? Every race, the man made a beeline for *her*. To make stupid conversation. She had no idea why he even entered any of the races, he was always dead last.

"Looks like your daughter is followin' in your footsteps too."

"Uh huh." She hated making small talk. Especially before a race. What she wouldn't give for Sean to come back about now. She slammed a door on the truck a little too hard, attempting to get rid of some of her frustration.

It didn't work. Ugh. Would they fine her if she just punched the guy in the nose?

"Do you have plans for that weekend?"

"What?"

"Plans. For the Fur Rendezvous?"

"Of course. I just told you, I'm racing."

"Got any time for any social activities?"

"Huh?"

"You know, like—"

"Hey, Anesia." Sean jogged up to her. "Zoya's got you all ready to go."

His timing was perfect. She smiled at him. "Good. Thanks."

Sean reached out a hand to the other musher. "Good morning. I'm Sean Connolly."

"Carl Fagan." A frown now etched the man's face. "I guess I better get back to my dogs."

"Nice to meet you, Carl." Sean's grin stretched even wider as he laid a hand on Anesia's shoulder.

"You too." Carl mumbled and moved away.

Anesia couldn't help the laugh that sprang out of her as she watched the man walk away. She gave Sean a playful swat on the shoulder. "You deserve a raise."

"Whatever for?" Those green eyes twinkled down at her.

"You know perfectly well, Mr. Connolly. And thank you."

"You are most welcome, m'lady." He winked and bowed. "My gift is rescuing damsels in distress."

———

Twenty minutes later Anesia found herself out on the trail. Her draw had been a good one—she'd left first, so there wouldn't be anyone to pass. That meant she could run Tornado as her lead dog. He was by far the best and fastest leader but a horrible passer. Which meant a good majority of the time, she didn't get to race him because she was the fastest and needed to pass. Sometimes several times during a race.

As she blazed down the trail, her thoughts drifted back to Sean. He'd had entirely too much fun teasing her about her admirers. Warmth flooded through her as she remembered how she flirted with him. What had gotten into her? But she'd enjoyed it. Maybe a little too much.

Reaching into her pocket, she searched for another Fireball to suck on. She'd crunched the last one to pieces thinking about Sean. Good grief. She wasn't a teenager anymore.

The fiery hot cinnamon hit her tongue, and she crinkled the wrapper back into her pocket. The thrill of the race and the trail disappearing beneath her sled made her want to go faster.

Anesia whistled to her dogs. Faster. Faster. The sled surged forward as the dogs lunged and picked up speed, their tongues lolling out the sides of their mouths.

She laughed to the wind. The dogs loved speed as much as she did.

Samson's head turned to the right to peer at Goliath as if to say, "Ha ha! Watch this!", and in the process the dog stumbled and got a snout full of snow. The team continued on, but Samson was tangled.

"Whoa." Anesia flipped down the tread-like mat and pressed with her foot to help slow them down. If it weren't the middle of a race, she'd be laughing at her dogs' antics. Sean was right. They *were* just like little kids.

Once they stopped, she grabbed her snow hooks and set them with lightning speed. As she approached her team, she recognized Samson's common dilemma. His leg was over the neckline.

She ran back to the sled as soon as the tangle was undone and pulled up her hooks. "All right!"

Tornado took off and the rest of the team followed. Another great day on the trail. Even with the tangle, she'd make great time. They were flying.

Movement out of the corner of her eye caught her attention. Was that a man behind that tree?

She shook her head. Too much stress the past few weeks. And too many thoughts of criminals. Her imagination must be running wild.

But at the next mile marker, she swallowed her jawbreaker.

Another man.

With a gun.

━ ━

The finish line flew by in a blur. Jenna, Andie, and Sean all ran for her. But the image of the man by the tree haunted her. Had she dreamed it? Maybe her imagination went overboard. No. She'd definitely seen two men. One had glared straight at her.

Threatening.

Anesia glanced all around at the spectators as her dogs came to a halt. Andie rushed to greet her team with lots of petting and rubbing behind the ears. No one in the crowd looked suspicious. They were all happy. Cheering. Smiling. Laughing.

There were no guns.

No harsh expressions.

No stiff forms.

Jenna wrapped her arms around her. "I'm so proud of you! You did it again, my friend. Another great time."

"Thank you." The words felt rubbery as they fell out of her mouth.

Jenna pulled back, kept her hands on Anesia's shoulders, and squinted. "What's wrong?"

Anesia let her gaze roam the crowd again.

"Anesia, what is it? Are you okay?"

All eyes shifted to her. Her anxiety over the men she'd seen landed in her gut like a boulder. Her paranoid mind wanted to protect Zoya at all costs.

"Where's Zoya?"

Andie looked up from the dogs, "Her race started just a minute or so before you came in."

Anesia gasped. *No.*

Jenna grabbed her arm. "It's okay, I know the new rules are different, but we were all there to cheer her on. She had a great start, so let's get you over there to watch her."

Breathe. Just breathe. Her lungs grabbed for air. "Okay." Those men weren't real. Couldn't be. She refused to believe it.

Zoya was already out there. Racing.

Oh, God. Protect my child.

DETECTIVE SHELDON
On the banks of the Chena River
11:01 a.m.

Dave stared at the sight in front of him. Two more bodies. Bloody. Frozen. All in black.

"No IDs, sir. But they're both armed. Heavily." Sergeant Williams shook his head.

"Were their weapons fired?"

"No, sir. Not one shot."

"So they weren't threatened by whoever killed them. Otherwise, they would've defended themselves."

"Nope. Quick and point-blank range." The new sergeant stood with hands on his hips then crouched down beside one of the deceased. "Two shots each. One to the head, one to the chest."

Dave walked around the bodies, viewing all angles. Senseless violence. The murder count in less than a month topped the count from his first year in North Pole. These two were different though. He hated to think what it meant. "Check ballistics against each of those guns. I bet one of them is the murder weapon from a few weeks ago."

He walked away and let his men do their job. Dialing in the now familiar number, he waited for Agent Philips to pick up.

"We've got a development."

ZOYA
11:09 a.m.

"Haw!" We swished to the left and sped on. Cold air burned my cheeks and dried out my eyes. Even with the thick gloves, my hands were as ice.

And I loved it.

It's so good to be back on the tracks. I smiled. "Come on, guys. Just a little faster!"

Trees zoomed by. The snow slid underneath my sled as we raced on. It couldn't get better than this.

But what if something happens? My smiled faded. What if there was someone waiting for me? Waiting to kill the witness? What if I witnessed another murder? What if *I* was murdered?

No! God wouldn't let that happen.

Would He?

Why would He be concerned with me anyway? He hadn't been before . . .

I caught sight of the two racers ahead of me. One had started four minutes before, the other two minutes. If I could pass them, my time would be awesome. The dogs must have sensed it as well. I gained on the two racers in front of me and shook my head. *Do. Not. Get. Distracted.*

"Come on, guys! You can do it!" I leaned in close to my handle as we sped on. All I needed to do was get over to the side and zoom past. Time to call trail.

"Trail!"

The team closest to me pulled to the side and slowed to a stop to follow correct racing rules. I tossed a wave over my shoulder.

One more. One more pass.

KIMBERLEY AND KAYLA WOODHOUSE

The other kid in front of me looked over his shoulder.

"Trail!" I shouted over the dogs.

He had no choice but to pull aside and stop.

But as my team passed, I caught a blur in the trees.

Zoya, stop! Focus!

I raced on by and smiled. My time would be great. Not just great . . . *Awesome!*

"Come on, Morphine! Go, Percocet! Faster, Ibuprofen!" I looked behind. *Just watch, Dad, I'll win this race for you.*

Five, six, seven minutes ticked by. "Come on, guys! Let's win this thing! Come on!" Faster and faster we went. The trees seemed like big white and green blurs as we flew by at twenty miles an hour. Snow fell, but only enough for me to see a haze of tiny white specks here and there.

We gained speed. The dogs panted, but I could tell they were just as happy as me to get back to racing. "Come on, you can do it!"

We passed the five-mile marker.

"Come on! Let's go, come on! One more mile!" Morphine picked up the speed even more.

Within moments I could see the finish line.

"Come on, Morphine, just a little farther!"

People's cheers filled the air.

We crossed the line.

The dogs slowed, and Mom ran over, her face glowing.

I looked to the big digital clock.

Zoya Naltsiine: 22 minutes 58 seconds

I smiled.

My draw had me leave third, so that was four minutes into the clock time, which meant I did the six-mile run in 18:58. An average of about three minutes and ten seconds per mile.

Best time ever.

And no murders.

CHAPTER EIGHTEEN

RICK
Fairbanks, Alaska
11:31 a.m.

Great race. And a record time, too. She *was* as good as her dad.

The crowd continued to press in as more racers crossed the finish line. But he saw what he came to see. Now . . .

Regret. Deep and searing.

After all the years of distance, should he even risk dropping into her world now?

Rick melted into the crowd. Another day, perhaps.

His cell vibrated in his pocket. Digging it out with gloved hands proved to be a trial.

"Hello?"

"Hey, Boss. We've got news from the big man. Looks like another project."

Great, just what he needed right now. "And?"

"I'm sure it can wait until Monday, but knowin' how much of a workaholic you are, I thought you'd want to know."

The kid was right. He *was* a workaholic. He just hoped this new project didn't have to do with what he feared.

"Thanks. Leave it on my desk. I've got a long drive ahead of me, but I'm on my way."

"Sure thing. Does that mean I can take the rest of the day off?"

He sensed the eagerness in the young man's voice. "Go ahead. I'll call Christy in if I need her. I've got it from here."

"Thanks, Boss. See ya Monday."

Rick ended the call and shoved his phone back in his pocket.

As he reached for his keys, the tightness in his chest started up again. He stopped in his tracks and took some deep breaths.

Not now.

With slow steps, he made it to his truck and grabbed his pills out of the console.

ZOYA
11:37 a.m.

"Great job, Zoya!" Andie ran over and we high-fived. "I can't believe you cut that much time off!"

"I can't believe it either! That's my best time ever!"

"You are one special racer." Andie winked and grabbed my hand. "What do you say we celebrate?" We looked over to the moms.

Auntie Jenna and Mom nodded. "Sounds great. What'll we do?"

"Could we watch *Pride and Prejudice*?"

"Yeah!" My smile grew. "Pleeeeeease?"

"Zoya, we just watched the five-hour version." Mom put her hands on her hips.

Andie and I danced around in circles. "Or we could watch *Persuasion*." I threw over my shoulder.

Mom glanced around. Like she was nervous about something.

"Okay, then. *Persuasion* it is." Mom nodded, then turned to talk to Sean. She was way too serious. Wasn't she happy for me?

My thoughts went back to my time. *18:58, I can't believe it!*

"I can't wait for the next race. Did you see how fast the dogs were going?" I stared off into the crowd and felt a smile—a *real* smile—fill my face. "Dad would be proud."

Andie nodded. "I'm sure he would be. Your mom sure is. I haven't seen Auntie smile so big in a long time."

"Yeah, next I'll be on my way to the Junior North American Championships."

"Whoa, girl! You've got awhile until the biggies."

"But I know I can do it. I know I can win. I have to make Dad proud."

"You already have, Zoya." Andie frowned.

"No, not really." I looked down at my shoes and swallowed. Then shook my head. "Just wait until I win."

"Zoy—"

"I will, Andie. I have to make Dad proud." My stomach churned. "I will win."

COLE _____
January 22
Naltsiine Kennels
7:02 p.m.

Happy voices floated across Anesia's house to him, but Cole had trouble joining in. He couldn't even stay in the moment. This encryption mess was eating him up. And he couldn't shake the feeling that someone stalked Zoya. Why couldn't he figure it out? And why hadn't Marc left him a clue about AMI?

"Hey, handsome." Jenna wrapped an arm around his waist. "What's got you so distracted?"

He attempted a smile. "You, of course."

Jenna pulled back and punched him in the arm. "Liar. Nice try, big guy. Spill it."

Thank God for that woman. "You know me too well."

"Don't you forget it. Now, I'm waiting." She cocked an eyebrow and tapped her foot.

"All right, all right. But let's grab the others and gather in the living room. I think this is going to take everyone's help."

Jenna wasted no time with a response. She grabbed his hand and practically dragged him into the other room. What a woman. When she meant business, she *meant business.*

"Anesia? Can everyone come in the living room?"

Her head popped around the corner. "Sure." She turned back to the kitchen. "Come on, girls."

Jenna, Andie, Anesia, and Zoya all sat on the couch. Eyes on him.

He paced in front of them. "I need your help."

They all sat a little straighter.

He took a deep breath before plunging into the rest. "I can't give you any details, but I need to figure out words or phrases, verses, numbers, anything that Marc could've used as an encryption code."

Zoya raised her hand. "This has to do with AMI, doesn't it?"

"I'm not at liberty to say." He raked a hand through his hair.

Andie nodded. "It's got to be. That's what Dad was working on. That's what they've got you working on now."

"Einstein, stop trying to figure out what this is for. I need your help to figure out what he could've used for an encryption code."

"Sorry. We'll help." She scrunched up her forehead.

"Think of anything that was special to your dad. Something he could've hidden. Some kind of clue—like the ones he left for the code on the bunker."

"But he gave us hints for that." Jenna cocked her head. "Do you have any hints for this?"

Cole sighed. Deep and heavy. "Not one." He started to pace again. "This is where it's tricky."

Andie and Zoya glanced at each other, then his stepdaughter raised her hand. "So our national security is at risk?"

"You've been reading too many suspense novels, Einstein. Like I said, stop trying to figure out what it's for and help me figure out a clue or code."

"Could you get in trouble?"

Teenagers. Didn't they listen? "This isn't about me. Right now we need to figure out the encryption."

Jenna planted her elbows on her knees and leaned her chin on her hands—and then covered her face. The devastation of losing Marc had been tough enough, but learning what he did for a living just about destroyed her. With a swipe of her hands, she lifted her face, a new determination in her eyes. "Okay, let's figure this out. What do we know?"

Atta girl. Cole connected gazes with his wife. "Nothing."

"It's gotta have something to do with us." Andie's blue eyes stared up at him.

Made sense. He'd been thinking the same thing. "Go on."

"Well, the passwords to get into the bunker had to do with me. My nickname, medic-alert number, and the dog tags he gave to Mom. Dad was a super-genius. And way too good at impossible riddles. But he'd know you needed to figure this one out, right? So I bet that whatever the code is, it has something to do with us. With family."

Cole's gut told him she was right. Now all they had to do was figure out what it was. Before time ran out.

SLIM

January 22
Fairbanks, Alaska
10:52 p.m.

Only the glow from the laptop lit up his tiny room. As he scrolled through file after file, he found the full description. In full detail he read the military specs on the Advanced Missile Interceptor.

A smile split his face. Just what he was looking for.

He read through the document. Jackpot.

Then found another.

And another.

Plenty of details. Enough for him to show that he'd acquired the program. And could sell it. To whomever he wanted.

Ma had always warned him about playing with fire. But this time, he couldn't get burned.

Because he controlled it. He held the matches. And could fan the flame however he wanted.

Let the whole world burn.

He looked forward to watching.

ZOYA

January 23
The Tikanni-Gray-Maddox Home
9:05 a.m.

Andie jumped off the bed and walked over to the dresser. "My toes are cold. I'm gonna put on some socks." She dug around in the drawer then sighed. "This thing is way too jammed!" She started removing pairs and setting them on the dresser's top.

I tried to hold back a yawn. *I'm so tired . . .* I blinked back the sleepiness and sat up straighter. *Do not fall asleep.*

Andie set one pair of socks after another on the smooth wooden surface of her dresser. A familiar little black box sat next to her hairbrush.

I cocked my head. *Maybe there's something in there.* "Hey Andie, what's in that box? It belonged to your dad, right?"

Andie nodded, reached for it, and tossed it to me. "We found it in the plane after our crash. It has his initials. But I can't figure out how to open it." She took out more socks.

I fiddled with the odd, shiny thing. *I wonder what's inside.* "Looks like it needs a key, but maybe we could pick the lock or something."

"You can if you really want to, I'm gonna find those—ah-ha! Here they are." She pulled out a pair of purple monkey socks, then started jamming the others back into the drawer.

"Andie, you can't wear those crazy socks to church."

She smiled. "Who cares?"

I giggled and went back to studying the small *saeł*. Uncle Marc's initials were carved onto the lid in bold letters. My finger traced them. I squinted.

"Hey Andie?"

"Yup?" She shoved more socks in.

"These initials, there's something wrong with them." Again I traced them with my fingers. It felt funny.

"What do you mean?" Andie walked over and took it, turning it over in her hands.

"See the letters? It looks like there was something underneath them." I stood and peeked over her shoulder.

Andie turned to me and smiled. "Yeah, it does. Almost like—"

"Like someone sandpapered over it."

"Exactly." Andie rubbed it under her thumb. "We may have just found a clue."

"Well, let's go tell—"

"Girls, are you ready? We need to leave!"

"Snap!" Andie huffed and sat down onto the bed.

"Well?" I sat down next to her.

"Girls!" Cole's military-man voice snapped us to attention. "Let's *go*."

"Uh oh, we better 'hut-two.' You know Cole, we have to be on time for everything. We'll have to wait." Disappointment sank into my stomach.

"Andie! Zoya!"

"We'll tell them after church." Andie clutched the small black object to her chest. "The moment we get out those doors, we'll show them."

CHAPTER NINETEEN

ZOYA

January 23
Naltsiine Kennels
11:44 a.m.

"I loved the sermon this week. Especially his joke." Andie giggled, walked over to her backpack and began pulling out everything, throwing it on the floor. "Baby elephants in a bathtub . . ." Her giggles turned into gasps as she snorted and laughed.

"You've got stuff to change into, right? If we want to go out with the dogs you're gonna need to change." I ignored her mirth and sat down on the bed. *Stay focused, Zoya.*

"Yup! Got 'em in here . . . somewhere." Andie smiled and passed me the week's bulletin. "Will you put that in my Bible case?"

"Sure." I nodded. *Don't pay attention to what it says. It won't help.* I tried to smile. *I can't wait to go riding.* Excitement bubbled up.

"Zoya, Andie, come eat!" Auntie Jenna's call for lunch brought another round of giggles from Andie.

"Perfect timing."

I placed the bulletin back inside her Bible's cover where a sheet of paper lay. Andie and my scribbled notes caught my attention. "Oh! We forgot to show Cole the box!"

Andie bounced off the bed and opened the door. "Well? Come on!"

We ran down the stairs and into the kitchen. Mom, Auntie, and Cole stood waiting for us.

"Ready to say the blessing?" Auntie Jenna smiled.

"Not yet!" I smiled back and jumped up and down. *Hurry up, Andie!*

Andie grabbed my hand. "Mom, do you remember when you gave me that little black box with Dad's initials on it?"

"The one I found in the plane? Yes." Auntie Jenna looked from Andie to me, question written on her face.

Andie giggled and reached inside her pocket. "Zoya and I found it this morning and thought it—"

She dug around in her pocket some more.

Cole nodded. "Thought it . . ."

"Well, we think it's a—"

My brow furrowed. "What's wrong, Andie?"

"A what?" Cole took a step forward.

My heart beat quickened. Eyes widened.

Andie looked to me and nodded.

No!

"It's gone!"

ANESIA
11:51 a.m.

"Oh no." Her daughter gripped Andie's hand.

"What's gone?" Cole stepped even closer to the girls. "The box? How did you lose it? What was in it?" Military man just crossed the line.

Tears formed in Andie's eyes and her bottom lip trembled. Then words spilled out. "I'm so sorry. I don't know what happened. I put it in my pocket this morning before church, 'cause I knew we were coming over here for lunch, and we wanted to tell you all about it, and then I lost one of my shoes this morning, and my jeans ripped, and Dasha wanted to play in the snow and didn't want to come in and—"

"Andie"—Jenna wrapped an arm around her daughter's shoulder—"it's okay. Breathe. Just calm down. We're *not* upset about it." Her friend drew out her words and shot Anesia a pleading look that clearly said, *save the day before I kill my over-interrogative husband.*

Time she stepped in. "Andie, Zoya, why don't we sit down at the table. Get some food in us and hash it all out, okay?"

Andie sniffed. "Thanks, Auntie."

"You're welcome, sweetheart." She shot a glare at Cole that he couldn't miss. "No one is going to grill you over a little black box."

Cole frowned.

Go ahead. I dare you. She stared him down. Good thing their relationship had a good foundation. Otherwise, she'd be *really* mad.

Everyone took their seats around the table.

Zoya glanced around. "Where's Sean?"

"He had to make a phone call, so he said to start without him." Each person reached for the hand of the person next to them until they were all joined around the table. Anesia inhaled and absorbed the sweetness of having family. "Cole, would you please say the blessing?"

"Huh?" His furrowed brow relaxed. "I'm sorry. Of course."

After a brief prayer, the platters of food were passed, and quiet settled on everyone. The silence was so thick, she wanted to slash it with a knife. As soon as everyone had food, silverware clattered and they started to eat. "All right then, now what is this about Marc's black box?"

Zoya chewed for a minute. "We were gonna try and figure out what Uncle Marc could've used for the code when we spotted his shiny box on Andie's dresser."

Andie nodded. "Yeah, and I've never been able to open it, so we thought maybe the secret was inside."

"I turned it over and saw Uncle Marc's initials, but the more I rubbed, the more I noticed that it looked different under the light."

"It wasn't as shiny. You know, a little duller." Andie shoveled more roast beef into her mouth.

"And one of the letters was longer than the others. But the closer I looked, I realized the long part wasn't attached."

Anesia felt like an observer of a tennis match. Andie and Zoya volleyed their words back and forth across the table. She shook her head. "Okay, so let me get this straight. You think Uncle Marc's box holds the clue for whatever Cole is looking for?"

"Uh huh."

"Yes."

"All right. But what does the dull part about his initials mean?" Anesia poured herself more tea. "I'm a bit confused."

"Don't know. Just thought it was interesting." Zoya shrugged.

Jenna and Cole set their forks down and stared across the table at each other. Uh oh. What did they know?

"Girls, we need to find that box." Cole wiped his mouth with his napkin.

Anesia had to give him credit. At least he remained calm. For the moment.

"Where did you last see it?" Jenna asked. "Was it at home when you placed it in your pocket?"

Andie shook her head. "I remember rubbing the smooth surface during the sermon. Sorry. I got a little distracted and started thinking about how to open the box and what could be in the box . . . I hadn't thought about it in so long. It was kinda fun. Like a mystery that needed to be solved."

"And we wanted to help solve it." Zoya looked to Cole. "We were hoping you could help us get it open today. Even if we had to break it."

"Well, I will gladly help you with that." Cole raked a hand through his hair. "But we need to find it first."

Andie turned to her stepfather. "Are you mad at me for losing it?"

His face softened. And he sighed. "Sorry, Squirt. I know I seem tense right now, but I'm not mad at you. After your description of the engraving on the back, I'm curious to take a look at it."

A knock sounded at the door, and then Sean called out.

"Come on in, Sean, we're in the dining room." If only Marc had never been involved in the military and its secret technology. How much would they have to endure for the rest of their lives because of it?

"Hello, everyone." Sean sat down and began to fill his plate. He looked around the table at the solemn faces. "What's going on?"

"I lost something important today." Andie looked like she just might cry.

"Well, we'll just have to find it then, won't we?" He shot her *syats'ae* a smile. "Where do we look first?"

Zoya smiled at him. His kindness to her best friend must've earned him some brownie points. "The church. That's the last place she remembers having it."

"All right." Anesia caught her daughter's eyes and winked at her. "Now that we have a plan, why don't we finish eating, and then we'll call Pastor about letting us into the church. Sound good?"

Cole and Jenna shared another glance down the table. Was there some other significance to the box?

ANESIA _____
3:22 p.m.

The troops clomped back into the house without speaking a word. A dark cloud hanging over their heads wouldn't have been more obvious. What happened to the box?

Pastor Brian had helped them search the entire campus. Everywhere the girls had been. Even the snowy parking lot. He'd even pulled out shovels and they dug through all the snow piles.

But no black box.

Andie and Zoya clung to each other and sat side by side on the couch.

The adults stood in her foyer, trying to figure out what to do next.

"Cole," Jenna wrapped an arm around her husband's waist. "We can't do anything about it. Maybe it will turn up."

"I know, hon. I'm more frustrated with myself that I didn't think of it sooner. Hank, Marc, and Lee all had one of those boxes. They had to hold something important."

"But maybe it wasn't anything you actually need."

"Yeah." He smiled down at his wife.

Anesia felt that sense of longing flood her again. There were times watching those two that she thought maybe, just maybe she was missing out by remaining single.

Cole grabbed her by the shoulders. "Thank you for not killing me earlier." He chuckled. "I know you wanted to. You know how thick a skull I have, and well, I needed you to temper me."

"You're welcome." Her best friend had found a prize in that one.

Sean clapped and rubbed his hands together. "Well." He winked conspiratorially at Cole. "Who's up for a game of Phase 10? I hear we have a champ in this house, and a couple of teens who think they can beat me."

The girls perked up on the couch. Anesia could've kissed Sean for his suggestion.

Whoa! Where did that come from? Kiss him? Not likely. Not that the idea was repugnant or anything—

Anesia shook her scrambling thoughts into submission, hoping her face wasn't as red as it felt.

"You okay?"

She jerked a look at Sean. "What? Why?"

"Your cheeks are all pink."

Drat. Time for a distraction. She forced a smile at him. "Let's go back to the dining room and I'll get everyone some ice cream and hot chocolate."

"That would hit the spot."

Sean's warm smile sent her stomach into a little flip. What was *wrong* with her? She wasn't a teenager anymore.

The men followed Andie and Zoya into the dining room.

Jenna came up beside Anesia. "Hit the spot, huh?" She elbowed Anesia in the ribs.

"Oh, stop it."

"No way. After all the razzing you gave me about Cole, you have to give me my turn."

Anesia elbowed her back. "Razzing? I don't ever recall razzing you, my dear friend."

"Whatever." Jenna laughed. "I'll stop. But you're not foolin' me, Anesia Naltsiine. I've known you far too long."

"What is that supposed to mean?"

"Oh, please. You're attracted to him. And that scares you to death."

"Wha—?" Anesia could feel her jaw muscles stretch as it lowered to a definite bug-catching stance. No other words would come. She stood there. With her mouth hanging open.

Her friend wrapped her in a hug. "I've got two eyes."

Anesia pulled back and stiffened. "That's good. Maybe you should open them more often."

"Don't get all bristly with me. Give me a little credit here."

Anesia rolled her eyes. "Fine. Let me have it."

"If you think you're fooling anyone, you're wrong. I'd have to be blind to miss the attraction between you two."

"Who two?"

"You and Sean."

Anesia gasped. Was it that obvious? Could her daughter see it, too? Did Zoya think she flirted with Sean? Is that why Zoya teased her about him? She covered her mouth with her hand.

Jenna grabbed her arm. "Don't worry. I don't think the girls suspect anything. And Sean's just as clueless."

"Hey!" Cole yelled from the other room. "You ladies gonna join us?"

"Be right there." Anesia wanted to melt into the floor then and there. She felt the heat rise to her cheeks yet again.

"Just be yourself. You've put off your own happiness for far too long."

"I'm not sure I appreciate God's sense of humor here."

"Huh?" Jenna started scooping ice cream into bowls.

Anesia slammed her hand onto the counter. "I mean, right before the shooting, I'd finally gotten tired of feeling alone. Finally thought I'd give love another chance. But Jenna, look. I've got to keep Zoya first. Look at what that poor kid has gone through. I've got to protect her."

"Whoa. Hold it right there. Don't you think you should leave Zoya in *God's* hands? And what if God sent Sean so you'd have someone to lean on, someone to *help* you protect her?"

"This coming from my OCD, control freak, best friend." The barb slipped out before she could stop it.

"Yeah, it is. And God had to use a plane crash in Denali National Park to get my attention and show me that *He* could take better care of my daughter and me. I don't think you want to play tough with the Big Man." Jenna continued filling bowls.

Exactly. She knew what she had to do. Knew the struggle within herself. Knew the conversation she'd had with Him in the woods. But letting go was so much harder than she'd imagined.

"So . . . spill it. I'm right, I told you so, and all that jazz. Now the real question is: What are you going to do about it?" Jenna popped a spoon of ice cream into her mouth and smiled around it.

Anesia lifted her thick braid over her shoulder. "I don't know. I noticed him most definitely when he first arrived, but I thought he was too good looking, you know? Like he wouldn't have a brain or have any substance whatsoever. Then I find out the guy's been to Harvard and was a VP for CROM. Then he had to go and love the dogs, the kennel, the job—he's so stinkin' helpful. The attraction started inching its way in. But with everything we've been through . . . first Marc, and then you and Andie, and now the mess with Zoya witnessing that murder . . . I just don't know."

"It's okay to allow yourself to fall in love, Anesia."

"I made a vow, Jenna." Her words sounded harsh to her own ears.

"I know. But the vow was to the Lord, to stay pure until marriage. Not a vow to never allow yourself to love again."

Her friend could never know the truth. That she didn't trust herself. She was too passionate. That couldn't be honoring to God. And she didn't want to lose herself again. Couldn't forgive herself.

Jenna patted her arm and walked toward the dining room. "I hope you all are ready to get trounced, because I aim to win tonight."

Anesia stood there for a moment longer and pulled a long breath into her lungs. Was she that attracted to Sean? She shook her head. There wasn't any room for these thoughts right now. Sean was her employee. And her friend. She wouldn't allow herself to go any farther than that.

Besides, she'd made a vow. One she didn't want to risk breaking.

CHAPTER TWENTY

SEAN
January 24
7:54 a.m.

Loosen up.

As he drove to the kennel, Sean couldn't get Cole's words out of his head. Loosen up, indeed. Cole had no idea what kind of world he'd lived in all these years. On the surface, it looked enviable. Living in a mansion, surrounded by staff. Hosting elegant fundraisers where the tickets sold for $2,500 a head. Attending coveted dinner parties with politicians.

And his office. A nice little 1500-square-foot corner suite at the top of CROM tower, with walls of windows, two full-time secretaries he didn't need, and enough technology to run a small country.

He'd come to hate it all.

Cole was right. He *was* stiff. His whole life had been stiff. Rigid. Trapped in the confines of lies and deceit he hadn't even known were binding him. But he was free now. So why did he still feel . . . imprisoned?

Maybe he should take up watching television. See how the real world lived. Isn't that what most Americans spent their free time doing?

Then again, he'd rather not. The few channels he'd flipped to other than his favorite ESPN were filled with reality shows that seemed about as far removed from reality as the moon was from the earth.

He was stuck.

His father's words raced back into his mind. His gut churned. Then the message in the bathroom mirror drifted into his mind.

The churn turned into a rolling boil.

"Stop!"

He slammed his fist against the dashboard. But the growing fury remained.

All those years he'd worked under his father's thumb, stuffing his frustration. His resentment. It wasn't until he broke free, until he was days into his trek across country, that the rage finally erupted. And kept erupting. Sometimes when he least expected it.

He'd gotten good at holding it all in until he was alone, but that wasn't the answer and he knew it

God, I'm done with that life! Why can't I let the anger go?

No answer. Well, what had he expected? More and more lately, when he prayed, that was the result. Silence. Like God's words to him were somehow being blocked . . .

Not blocked. Deflected.

Sean frowned. Deflected? By what?

But even as he asked the silent question, he knew.

By him.

By his anger.

For months he'd wrestled with this burden. The ever-increasing weight pressed into his shoulders with every mile he'd walked. And now . . . that weight had seemed to turn to brick and mortar and stack into an invisible wall.

One that has come between you and God.

The thought brought him up short. He pulled over onto the side of the road. Shut off the engine. And sat there. Taking in the truth.

His anger—and refusal to let go of it—was getting in the way of his relationship with God. The walls, the distance he felt, were of his own making. The rage inside him toward his earthly father waged a battle against his yearning for a closer relationship with his heavenly Father. Instead of allowing himself to heal after cutting the ties with CROM, with his father, he'd fed the growing infection until it festered. And the pain of that was all he could feel. The raging of that resentment was all he heard.

Sean leaned his head back against the seat.

He needed to throw off his old self. Completely. And that meant forgiving his father—and himself—and letting go of the years of bitterness and resentment. Because he wasn't that person anymore. The person controlled by lies.

The person who hated.

For the first time in his life, he felt real. *This* was the real Sean. Hardworking. Starting over. So maybe he shouldn't worry about what anyone thought. He needed to be himself. Even if he needed loosening up. Certainly a few months with the incredible people at Naltsiine Kennels could help him.

Father . . . help me. Help me let go of the past and savor the present You've given me. I keep struggling with anger and it pushes me away from You. I don't know why I can't conquer this, but You do, Lord. You can help me get past this. Just show me what You would have me do.

He let loose a sigh, then turned the key in the ignition and pulled back onto the road, a fresh peace filling him.

The drive to the property from his hotel would be the last. Over the past few days, Anesia had the cabin cleaned, he'd bought furniture and necessities, and he'd even installed Wi-Fi. The race this weekend wore him out, but the last of his new furniture would be delivered this morning. He would finally settle in.

A basket sat on the seat next to him. Wanda at the hotel sent him off in style with fresh fruit, dozens of cookies, and a couple books about Alaska and racing. What a neat lady. She'd always had a smile for him, sacrificed time and energy to help him. He needed to do something special for her. Maybe he'd ask Anesia to help him come up with a few ideas.

He arrived at the long driveway that would take him to his new home.

Home.

A wonderful word. But more than the word was the feeling it evoked. A feeling he'd never experienced.

He belonged.

Here.

With these wonderful people.

Anesia and Zoya bounced down the front steps, pulling on coats as he pulled in front of the house. More purchases from town loaded down the bed of his truck.

He pressed the button to lower his window. "Hey there. This is a nice welcome."

Anesia beamed. "Well, you deserve it. We want to get you comfortable in your new place." She wrapped an arm around her daughter's shoulder. "What can we do to help?"

"Would you like to hop in the truck and ride with me to the cabin?"

Zoya giggled and covered her mouth.

Sean smiled. Laughter and smiles seemed to come easily here. "What?"

"You said 'hop.'" She snorted and laughed harder. "It's so . . . normal. You're usually so proper, it just made me laugh."

"I did indeed." His laughter joined hers. "Guess I might be learning to be a little more laid-back after all." He opened his door so he could walk around the truck and open the passenger door for the ladies.

Anesia must have anticipated his move because she stopped him with a hand to his arm. "No need. We'll *hop* in."

Girlish giggles permeated his truck as he drove around to the cabin. His cabin. It all made him feel more a part of this family. Moving here also gave him a sense of providing. Protecting. Senses that were innate in men awakened with new strength. New desire. They'd always been stripped from him with his father. As if his own manhood had been taken away. In fact, if he were quite honest, he'd not wanted to admit that he often felt like his father owned him. And no man should ever—*ever*—have to feel that way.

After the incident on the picnic, Sean wanted to protect these two. Cole had been a great example. This is where he belonged. This is what he needed to do.

The whole crew tromped up the steps to his domain. He inserted the key into the dead bolt and opened the door for the ladies with a bow.

"Why thank you, Sir Connolly." Anesia curtsied before entering.

"You're so weird." Zoya giggled.

"Zoya *Sabiile*!" Hands on her hips, Anesia looked ready to pounce on her teen.

Zoya appeared to be trying to squelch her laughter and smile after a glance at her mom who still wore her scolding expression. "Sorry, Sean. I didn't mean it. I'm just not used to all the manners."

Sean laughed. "Didn't you tell me that your daughter was very quiet and shy? Didn't really talk to people?" He winked at Anesia. "So"—he tweaked Zoya's nose—"I'll just take your words as a sincere gesture that you trust me. Perhaps even like me?"

The young girl erupted in laughter that doubled her over as she sat on the couch.

"I'll take that as a yes."

Anesia just smiled at him, her big brown eyes twinkling, and headed back out to the truck for another load.

So beautiful. He shook his head. She was his boss. He couldn't be thinking of her in that way. Well, he *shouldn't*. But she *was* beautiful.

Change the subject. "So, what does Sa–bee–lah mean?"

"Sabiile'?" Anesia grabbed a few more Walmart bags out of the back. "It means rainbow."

"Wow, that's very pretty. And unique." He ordered his mind not to watch the way she walked, the way she flung her braid over her shoulder, or how she scrunched up her nose whenever she lifted anything.

"Thank you. It's Ahtna. Just like our last name. There aren't many of us left, so I wanted to make sure she carried on the heritage of the Athabaskan with her name even if she married and dropped the Naltsiine part. Her first name isn't a native name—has more of a history with the Russian people here—but it means *life* and that meant a lot to me."

"Very nice."

They traipsed up and down the steps several times, carrying on with the small talk.

On the last load Anesia placed the box she carried on the table and winked at Zoya. The younger Naltsiine headed out the door and around the cabin. When she came back in, she held some sort of insulated bag.

Zoya bounced up and down. "Welcome home, Sean!" She held out the bag.

Speechless, he took the proffered gift, but stood stiff, not sure what to do next.

"You're supposed to open it." Anesia just shook her head as she stood in front of him and opened the zippered compartment. "We had Derek hide it over here on the back porch a few minutes before you arrived."

Steam and delicious smells rose to his nostrils.

"It's coffee cake. And Jenna's famous peanut butter bars. And"—she pulled the steaming tray out—"homemade Lumpia."

"Wow." He found his tongue. "I don't know what to say. It all smells so delicious." He looked down into Anesia's eyes. "Thank you. But what's Lumpia?"

"It's Filipino. A friend of mine taught me how to make them. Kinda like an eggroll, but filled with beef and veggies. And I'm the one who should be thanking you. I can't tell you what it means to have you here."

And for just a moment he caught a glimpse of what he thought was attraction, coming from the eyes of the most beautiful woman he'd ever known. His heart soared.

He really was *home*.

COLE
January 24
Richardson Highway
6:47 p.m.

The truck barreled down the highway toward North Pole. What a rotten day. The pressure was on, and he wasn't a millimeter closer to discovering the code. And to top it all off, intel came back on the murder Zoya witnessed. The FBI wouldn't allow him to give the details to Anesia—fearing it might incite panic in the already paranoid mom—but Agent Philips cleared Cole to give Sean enough information to help protect the Naltsiine girls.

He looked down at the speedometer. Once again, he was speeding. A lot. Jenna always harassed him about having a lead foot.

He eased his right foot off the accelerator. Needed to keep his aggravation under control. He wouldn't be any good to anybody if he ended up dead from a careless accident. Especially on the icy roads.

The miles disappeared as he ran over the details in his mind. Anesia and Zoya needed constant protection. But the FBI didn't have anyone to spare, every available man was on the case. They also wanted to prevent panicking the Naltsiines.

When Anesia found out though, she would skin him alive.

Jenna would help.

And Andie.

Wasn't looking forward to *her* finding out. A teenager protective of her best friend? Oh yeah. Dead meat would be his new name.

Too complicated. *Marc, did you ever have any idea what all this would cause?* Cole slammed his palm on the steering wheel. What a mess.

He punched the speed-dial for Anesia's home.

"Hello?"

"Hey, Anesia, it's Cole. I need to talk to Sean, does he have a landline out in the cabin yet?"

"Yep, he sure does. But he's standing right here. Let me put him on."

"That'd be great."

A rustling noise came over the line as the handset was passed. "Hey, Cole. What can I do for you?"

"Hey, Sean. Can you meet me at your cabin in about twenty minutes?"

"Sure—"

"Tell Anesia we want to do some guy stuff."

"All right." Sean's words were hesitant and drawn out.

Cole worked through an idea in his mind. "Do you have the satellite set up yet?"

"Yes, I do."

The guy was so stinkin' proper. "Loosen up, Sean."

The guy cleared his throat. "Sure thing."

Cole laughed. "You're great. Look, tell Anesia that I want to check out your new setup and we're going to watch a game. Which is true. That way she won't get suspicious."

"Okay."

"Thanks, man."

"You got it."

The drive to Anesia's property was uneventful. As he pulled through the drive and around to the cabin, he waved at his wife's best friend peeking out her office window. She returned the wave and bent her head back over her desk. No one could ever accuse her of being lazy. That woman was always on top of everything, and she had so much on her plate. Just like his Jenna.

A porch light on the cabin was new. And it looked like the outside had a fresh coat of stain. How had they managed that in the middle of winter? Or had he just been unobservant?

Sean opened the door to the cabin as Cole shifted to park and ventured from the warmth of his truck. The air was even colder tonight than it had been. He pulled his jacket up over his nose and mouth as he ran into the cabin.

"Hey, Cole."

"Sean." He yanked off his boots and coat. "How'd it go with Anesia?"

"She smiled at me and kept working on the books."

"Good." He walked straight to the couch and sat down. "Go ahead and turn the game on, but mute it. We've got a lot to cover."

Sean raised his eyebrows. "All right."

"Anesia and Zoya need protection."

Sean stiffened and sat in the chair in front of Cole. "Continue."

"We've checked into your background, and the FBI has cleared me to talk to you. But under no circumstances are Anesia and Zoya to find out."

"Find out what?" Sean leaned forward, his face serious. "About the footprints?"

"That's only the tip of the iceberg. You know about the murder Zoya witnessed?"

"Yes."

"Well, the victim wasn't a homeless man like the police and papers said."

"Go on."

Cole took a deep breath. "Sean, how much do you know about AMI?"

He shook his head. "I'm afraid I don't know any Amy."

"Let me back up. AMI isn't a person. It's an acronym. Advanced Missile Interceptor. Anesia didn't say anything to you?"

"No, sir."

"Drop the *sir*, Sean." Cole ran a hand through his hair. "I get enough of that on post." He tried to soften the words with a laugh. "I'm surprised Anesia didn't tell you more. She asked me if she could. I know your being here has helped relieve a lot of her worry."

"I will do whatever I can to help."

"That's good to hear, man." Another deep breath. Where to start? "Marcus Gray was Jenna's first husband."

Sean nodded.

"He and I were in the Army together. In the latter years we were in a black ops group. Marc was a genius. Could do anything with computers and designed things no one else could even imagine. Near the end the leader of our group convinced Marc there was more money to be made outside of the military. They started down a road the rest of us knew nothing about. And when we did find out, we didn't like it."

"Marc worked on a prototype for a new defense weapon. He lived and breathed that program. I found out about what was going on and confronted Marc. I knew the guy. Claimed he was a Christian. But he got wooed by the money. We fought. He came to his senses. And then Andie had brain surgery.

Sean's forehead creased. "Brain surgery?"

"Sorry, I'll back up again. Andie was born with a very rare nerve disorder. Hereditary Sensory Autonomic Neuropathy. She doesn't sweat and doesn't feel pain unless it's twenty to thirty times the intensity you and I would feel."

"That's . . . terrible."

"Yeah, not quite sure what you've signed on for, huh?" A sad chuckle died on his lips. "Anyway, because of her disorder they never discovered she had another condition, because she wasn't symptomatic until a couple years ago. Anyway, Andie had to have brain decompression surgery. That week was awful. Marc and I had it out, and he was desperate to find a way to protect his family once he turned his back on Viper—the leader. A powerful man you'd never want to cross."

Cole looked down at his hands. It hurt every time he thought about Marc.

"What happened?"

"Marc was killed by a car bomb while Andie was still in the hospital."

"Over the program?"

"Yeah. Viper found out Marc had contacted the FBI. But Viper already had a deal with North Korea. He wanted Marc's program and the money."

Sean stood abruptly. His fists clenched. "I am so *sick*"—words came out through his teeth—"of avaricious, and power-hungry men who think they can do whatever they want, whenever they want—"

"Whoa, Sean . . ." Cole held up his hands. What was he supposed to say? This was the first time Sean had ever lost his cool. He seemed so mild-mannered, Cole would never have guessed at the anger under all that. What triggered it? Cole would have to investigate later. But right now . . .

The matter at hand was more urgent. "Sit down. There's more."

Sean sat, eyes blazing.

"That car bomb was meant for both of us. Marc had hidden the program and Viper was desperate for it. After Marc was gone, I disappeared for a little while. Tried to dig for myself to get a step ahead of Viper. But he went after Marc's family."

"A year after Marc's death, I met Jenna and Andie in person. We were all on their plane heading back to North Pole when it was sabotaged and we crashed on Sultana."

"Next to Denali?" Sean's eyes were huge. "I hiked the Parks Highway all the way around the park. Good grief, how did you survive?"

"That's a story for another time." Cole wiped a hand down his face. Keep to the facts. "We all worked together to stop Viper, but it wasn't without its cost. He blew up everything on Jenna's property and tried to kill both of them. But he died in the blasts and we recovered AMI."

"And you and Jenna ended up getting married?"

"Yep. Best thing that ever happened to me. I came to know the Lord through all this mess and found Jenna and Andie."

"Where did you find AMI?"

"In an underground bunker on their property." Cole allowed himself to laugh. "My wife, Jenna, is a little paranoid. Likes to be prepared for everything."

"With a special needs child, I can understand why."

Cole swung his head to Sean. This guy was quick. And paid attention. That would be very useful. "You're right. I've always teased her about it, but I guess it does deserve a little respect. After all she's been through . . ." Cole cleared his throat. "That's beside the point. Let me continue. AMI was recovered and is in government hands. But people are trying to steal it. The guy Zoya saw murdered was an undercover FBI agent."

"So you think they're going to come after Zoya?"

"I hope not. But they probably will."

Sean sat very still for several moments. "What do you need me to do?"

"Keep an eye on everything. Especially Zoya. Anesia too. We don't want them to panic right now."

"You can count on me." A muscle twitched in Sean's jaw. "What exactly does AMI do? You mentioned defense weapon, but a missile interceptor is just in defense."

"Not much gets past you, does it?"

"I wouldn't have survived all these years as a Connolly if anything had, and CROM used to manufacture missile interceptors."

Bound to be more to that story as well. "It's brilliant. Not only is it 99.7 percent accurate in destroying the incoming missile, but it can shoot up to three missiles of its own just before impact to wipe out the point of origin."

"Impressive. Any country with that kind of weapon power would rule the world, wouldn't it?"

He hadn't thought of it in those terms, but Sean was correct. AMI in the wrong hands . . . it gave him chills just to think of it. But what if . . .

Was that the goal of the U.S. government? To rule the world? Or was it just to protect its citizens? Both?

"I see I've made you think."

Cole nodded. "There are some things I haven't considered before. My job's been to follow orders, serve my country. Protect her."

"But you're worried about intentions?"

Cole shook his head. "Right now, I need to stay on task. And that is to protect my family and prevent AMI from being stolen. Anesia and Zoya are family."

"Understood."

"We can't let anything happen to them."

Sean nodded.

"It would help if we could find the killer. But I think we're up against more than we know."

CHAPTER TWENTY-ONE

ZOYA

January 26
Naltsiine Kennels
11:20 a.m.

The house was quiet. Almost too quiet. I hadn't heard one thing but the sound of pages turning in fifteen minutes. If I had been a commentator, I would lose my job.

I squirmed in my seat.

"I'm bored. Let's do something"—I grabbed the book Andie was reading and shoved it on the top of a bookshelf—"besides read."

"But you love to read! And it's good! And I don't know wha—"

"Nope."

"Oh, fine." She crossed her arms again and sighed. "So, what do you want to do?"

Sean came through the front door and shed his coat. "Wow, it's cold out there."

Perfect timing.

"Hey, Sean." Andie waved.

"Hey." I gave a half-hearted smile.

"And what might you two pretty young ladies be doing?" He walked into the living room and sat by me on the couch.

"I want to read, but Zoya won't let me. So here I am, stranded on the couch, having to let my mind wonder what happens next." Andie sighed and stared at the wall.

"Woe is she." I nodded.

"Yes, woe is me." She wiped a hand across her forehead.

Drama queen.

"I shall die with anticipation."

Sean smiled. "So I see."

"Hey, this is a very serious matter!"

I could tell she was trying not to smile.

"Yes, don't you see that this poor girl is suffering?" I stood and patted her head.

"Do I detect sarcasm?" Andie looked up and grinned. "Or is that affection? You love me so much that you'll let me finish reading?"

"No, that was sarcasm."

"I thought you'd say that."

Sean chuckled.

"Why don't we take the dogs out?" Andie giggled and bounced across the room. "That would be fun!"

Something in the pit of my stomach curdled. I tried to smile.

Orange hat . . .

A shiver raced up my spine.

Get over it, Zoya. I blinked.

"Well . . ." Sean looked from Andie to me. "Let's go ask your mom."

"If we do go, will you go with us, Sean? I don't want to go out alone." I let out a sigh. Everything in me screamed no. Another shiver raced up, then down, my spine. I didn't want to be out alone. Not one bit. Not if there were people looking for me out there.

"You bet. I'd be happy to go. Actually, I was about to offer. But we should check with your mom first, just to make sure she doesn't need me here."

"Okay. Thanks."

"Not a problem."

Coats on, we walked outside.

Mom was kneeling next to Eklutna, the lead dog for the Glacier Litter.

"Hey, Auntie Anesia?" Andie waved and jogged the rest of the distance over.

I studied her movements. Something wasn't right. Eklutna whimpered and tried to wiggle out of her grasp.

"Hold on a minute, girls."

"What's wrong?" I knelt beside the two and rubbed the dog's neck.

"I'm not sure. But several of the dogs are acting strange, including Morphine, Chocolate, and Aurora. He"—she pointed to Eklutna—"seems to be the worst." Mom looked worried. In fact, I hadn't seen her this worried about the dogs in awhile.

What's going on?

"Do you need my help taking care of them, Anesia?" Sean took a step forward.

She shook her head. "No, but thank you. I just finished checking all the litters." She sighed and stood. "We'll see if anything happens by tomorrow. What'd you guys need?"

I smiled and patted Eklutna again. *Poor thing. I hope you get better, buddy.*

Andie smiled and scooted closer to me. "Can we go out for a run? It's good weather. And Sean said he'd go with us." She tilted her head and gave a 'charm smile.'

"If you don't need me."

"Well . . ." Mom looked from me to Andie to Sean. "I guess. But be careful."

Andie grabbed my hand. "Yes, ma'am. We will."

It wasn't long before we were on the trail, now that Sean knew what to do with the dogs.

Trail after trail we passed. It was amazing to see all the snow and trees. *Awesome . . .*

Sean took the lead. Making sure there was no one waiting for us, no doubt.

After several miles the dogs panted, making us pull over to the side.

"We should stop here." Sean hopped off his sled and walked over to Percocet, his lead dog. "They need a rest. I guess they're pooped."

I smiled. *Loosening up more and more every day, aren't ya?*

"Okay." Andie sat, more like fell, onto a boulder. "I'm pooped too!"

Sean smiled and sat down next to her. I joined.

We sat in silence. The dogs lay down in the snow, still panting.

I guess we ran them a little too hard. But we hadn't gone that fast. *Why are they so tired?*

White, puffy clouds sailed by. The gentle breeze did little more than cause me to feel a small tickle on my cheeks. Patches of crisp blue sky shone through the cover of trees. I couldn't see the sun beyond the thick foliage, but its glow still showed a little.

"Isn't God wonderful?" Sean leaned back on the large rock and pointed up. "A century ago, only birds could touch the clouds. Now we've got planes and rockets, it's amazing." He chuckled.

"Thank God for technology. However confusing it may get." Andie smiled. "And look at the sky, it's so blue today."

Sean nodded.

I sat there, glancing down at my hands.

"Don't trust Him, don't trust Him, don't trust Him . . ."

My eyes closed.

I wanted to believe He was good . . . Or did I?

Something nagged at the back of my mind. Something in me doubted. Something in me wanted answers to my questions. Like why He let murders happen.

"You know, the other day I was thinking about creation, and how God created the creatures and the plants, and the stars and moon."

Sean's smile made my insides hurt. Why did he have to look so peaceful?

"Then I got to thinking about humans, and how, out of all the creatures He made, we're the only ones He breathed into. He created the planets and stars and such out of nothing. Then He made us out of dust and breathed His breath into us." He gave a small laugh. "We must be pretty special for Him to love us that much. To give us His own breath. Then to send Jesus."

Andie nodded. "Yeah. I was thinking yesterday about how even though I'm a sinner, He died for me. It was like one of those random moments where I felt like crying. I wondered why He loved me. Then I remembered Adam and Eve and how He created us to glorify Him, to love Him. With all our hearts, minds, and souls."

Sean nodded. "I remember one time my friend asked me why I believed in God. Why I wanted to follow Him. I spent that whole night thinking about why I had chosen to follow Him, why He loved me. At first, I didn't know."

"That's a hard question." Andie looked back up into the sky. I could almost see the wheels turning in her head.

Again silence took over.

Did God love me? Why didn't I believe in Him anymore?

I caught my breath. That nagging in the back of my mind turned into more questions.

Why had He dumped me?

I shook my head. I guess He gave me another chance many times before . . .

But could I trust Him again? Why even bother?

Why were they talking about this anyway?

I sighed on the inside. Life was hard.

Too many questions. Too many unanswered questions. Too many unanswered questions that hurt to think about.

"Zoya, you okay?" Sean leaned forward and patted my knee. "You've been quiet this whole time."

I tried to smile. "Guess I'm just tired. But I'm okay." That was it. I was tired. Really tired.

As always.

He nodded. "You've been through a lot lately."

Something about the way he said it made my insides tumble 'round and 'round. Why did my stomach keep doing that? Was my conscience trying to tell me something?

"Andie, why don't you go check on the dogs."

She nodded.

Once she was out of hearing range, Sean spoke. "Something *is* wrong with you, Zoya."

I shrugged and looked at the clouds. I didn't have to talk to him. Didn't want to talk to him.

Did I?

"Come on, I may be new around here but I know you better than that." He smiled and grabbed my hand, which was so small compared to his. "Talk to me. I'm all ears." He shifted so that he was facing more in my direction.

"Nothing's wrong." I nodded and kept looking at the sky.

I could feel him staring at me.

Everything inside me felt discombobulated.

I wanted to cry. But I didn't know why.

I wanted to say I'm sorry. But to who?

"You know, when I was a boy I doubted God quite a lot. I didn't know if He wanted me as His child. I didn't know if I wanted Him as my God, my heavenly Father." He gave a small laugh.

I waited. There had to be a "but then I realized" coming.

But it didn't.

He didn't say anything. No words that were supposed to make everything hunky dunky. Just a small smile. Filled with peace.

I looked down at my hands. "I guess . . ." My throat closed. I didn't want to tell him that I doubted God. And that I didn't know where to turn. Or what to say.

"Zoya, it's okay to doubt at times. Everybody does. But don't keep it bottled up inside. If you ever need to talk, I'm here."

My heartbeat quickened. Why?

He stood, then walked over to Andie. But there was something about Sean. Something that made me want to trust him. To talk to him.

But could I?

Either way, I had to admit . . . As weird as he was, Sean Connolly was a really cool guy.

CHAPTER TWENTY-TWO

ANESIA
January 28
2:36 p.m.

Snow swished under the sled as Anesia ran her team down the trail by the creek.

Another week had flown by, which was good. It didn't give her time to worry and fret over everything. But alone with her thoughts now, she knew they'd invade.

She needed this time out on the trail, the wind whipping at her layers, the dogs running all out. If dogs could laugh, she imagined that's what they'd be doing right now, because they loved to run. Anesia saw their dog smiles and the twinkles in their eyes, but most people couldn't see it. They weren't connected to the animals.

But Anesia was. And with that connection, she knew something wasn't right. Several of the dogs acted off. They were still eating and running, but she sensed something else. They seemed to fidget under the harnesses. But she'd checked, over and over, and she couldn't find a problem.

The value of her dogs couldn't be measured. She bred them with care to make sure they had good temperament and amazing speed. Observed everything. Journaled each detail of each dog's life. That's why people came from places as far away as Iceland to purchase her dogs.

They were the best.

She couldn't afford to make mistakes now. And when there was a problem that she couldn't solve, that's what rang true: somewhere, she'd made a mistake.

"Haw! Thunder, Haw! Haw!" Changing the direction of the dogs helped reinforce their training. They knew these trails well, but they also had to listen to their driver. If any emergency arose, the driver needed to know the dogs would obey and not carry them all to danger.

Today the Weather Litter was in training with the Bible Litter. Samson, Gideon, Goliath, Moses, Thunder, Lightning, Hurricane, Tornado, and Rain all moved with agility and precision. These were the most experienced of all her dogs. Around six years old, they'd been running with her since they were four to five months old, as soon as they fit in the harnesses. The Weather Litter was born a few weeks before the Bible Litter. Anesia knew she'd found the secret to breeding them. And her instinct proved true. The pups were crazy, but from the first time she'd harnessed them, they were ready to race.

She remembered their yearling year with a smile. All the energy of a dozen toddlers in each fourteen-month-old puppy. As they grew and progressed through the year, they settled into a bit of maturity.

But only a bit.

Anesia laughed aloud, causing a couple of the dogs to dart a quick glance back. She loved this. The memories were good. They kept her mind off all that had happened. The danger to Zoya. The murder. The police informed her the murder victim was homeless. No family. No one to mourn his loss. But that didn't take away the ache that men had senselessly taken another man's life. Did that man know God? Was he spending eternity with Jesus?

Hot anger burned through her chest. Another reason to hate the killers. Not only had they taken her sweet child's innocence, given her nightmares, and turned her world upside down, but they might've condemned a man to hell. That thought spurred her on. She wanted to smack them all. Then of course, as a good little Christian, she would witness to them. Yeah, right. Like she wanted to spend eternity in heaven with them! A bunch of dirty, evil killers!

"Whoa . . ."

She slowed the dogs and stopped. Thoughts bounced around in her mind like a pinball machine. Had she really just thought those things? She was no better than them!

God, forgive me. If she didn't get a grip on this anger and hatred soon, it would eat her alive. Then who would be there for Zoya?

Taking a few minutes to check the dogs and give them each some attention, she continued to pray. Would she ever learn? How could she ever be an example to anyone else if she kept losing her temper and hating people?

Zoya. Her precious, sweet child. Until this incident, Zoya had always been very quiet. Reserved. She and Andie inseparable. But the anger and hate that oozed out of her teen after the murder scared the wits out of Anesia. One minute she'd be fine, and the next . . . well, she'd never seen such mood swings.

And it was her own fault.

If only she'd been a better mother.

A better example.

Which she'd better start being right now. Or she might lose her daughter to the same vices that threatened her each and every day. She could never forgive herself.

"All right!" The dogs took off at her command. As they picked up speed, Anesia felt like she was flying. More than anything, she loved this. Loved her dogs. Loved to race.

But the nagging thoughts that tumbled around a few minutes prior came back like a board smacking her in the face.

Forgive.

What? Anesia glanced behind her.

Forgive.

Tears sprang to her eyes. She wanted to. She did.

She just didn't know how.

ZOYA
January 29
6:00 a.m.

My alarm sounded, and I sat up straight resisting the urge to scream. My heart pounded in my chest. I slapped a hand to my racing heart. Then glanced sideways.

It was just the alarm. A sigh escaped as I slid out of bed. *Stop being such a scaredy-cat, Zoya.*

Racing day. I blinked, then stretched and yawned.

The feeling I got every morning there was a race calmed my heart and energized me, in some odd way. And I loved it.

Where did it come from? The little niggling feeling in the back of my mind came.

Whatever.

I got dressed. Hopefully Mom was up and about, unlike last time. But she'd been tired. *I could go get breakfast ready for her. Yeah, good idea. She's been working hard. Plus she'd have to make a whole lot if Sean's going to eat with us.*

As I exited my room, I saw light from Mom's room shining underneath the door. *Good! She's up.*

I bounded down the stairs toward the kitchen. *What to eat, what to eat . . .* A box of pancake mix sat on the counter, as if waiting to be opened.

I smiled and began the wonderful process of dirtying up the kitchen. *I'll clean it up after we eat.*

Ten minutes, and a gigantic mess, later, Mom came down stairs and smiled. "Well you're up and at 'em early. Excited?"

"Yes, ma'am!" I beamed. "Can't you tell?" My arm swept across the kitchen's space.

"Oh, yeah. Messes galore."

"I'll clean it up, don't worry."

"Okay."

I smiled and went back to flipping pancakes.

"Did you get Sean?"

"Not yet, but if I know him, he'll be here soon enough."

Mom nodded and kissed the top of my head. "Well, since you seem to have things under control around here, I'll go check on the dogs."

"Okey dokes."

I heard the door close. *I hope the dogs are as excited as I am.*

A few minutes later Sean knocked on the back door.

"Come on in, Sean!"

He entered. "Good morning. How are you this morning, Sunshine?" With much difficulty he unzipped and took off his coat.

I smiled. *Sunshine?* "I'm fit as a fiddle. How're you?" Again, the niggling . . . *stop it! Focus . . .*

"Fine and dandy." He peeked over my shoulder at the last batch of pancakes. "Are those blueberry?"

"And chocolate chip."

"Yum." He winked and sat down.

"Mom should be back in a minute."

He nodded.

The last pancake came out of the pan just as Mom entered the kitchen. Sean smiled.

"Well, well. Looks like I got here just in time."

Sean nodded. "Yep, but I have a feeling little miss racer here will want to be going ASAP."

I smiled. "Pancakes anyone?"

The drive to the race trail was long. I couldn't help fidgeting as we rode along. Everything in me yelled to get on the tracks. *Pick it up, pick it up!*

"Have patience, Zoya. We're almost there."

"I know." I sighed. "But I'm just so excited."

Mom smiled back. "I know."

Sean drove his big truck and honked as he passed us up. Mom honked back as we turned into the racing parking lot. I bounced in my seat.

"Calm down, Zoya." She turned and smiled at me.

"Sorry." I glanced out the window. Cars . . . dogs . . . sleds . . .

The images came again—the shot . . . the old man falling—

Zoya, focus! I blinked. *Just think about the race. That's all you have to do.*

"Come on, Zoya. Let's go get the dogs." Mom hopped out of the car. I followed.

Stay focused!

Sean helped me get the dogs ready. We got the Painkiller Litter out of their compartments in the dog truck and attached them to the harnesses.

"Thanks, Sean."

He smiled and winked. "Good luck, Sunshine."

"Thanks. But that's totally not fair."

"What?" He stood upright and cocked his head.

"You have a nickname for me but I don't have one for you." I secured the last harness. And glanced up to him. What name suited Sean?

"Hmm . . . well that is a problem." He scratched his chin.

Let's see . . . What fits?

"Zoya, are you ready? It's about time to get up there."

"Coming!" I smiled at Sean. "You think about it, and I'll see you after the race."

"Okay." He winked again. "Godspeed."

My smile faded. "Yeah. I'll see ya after." The dogs and I rode up to the starting line.

Godspeed. Why would God care about how fast I went?

I shook my head. No. He didn't care.

"Zoya, it's okay to doubt at times. Everybody does. But don't keep it bottled up inside. If you ever need to talk, I'm here."

No! I just needed to stay focused.

This time, I'd drawn sixth to start. That meant I'd have to wait a whole twelve minutes. But soon we were off. The Painkiller Litter flew down the path as we passed one racer after another.

The wind blew my hair behind me, sending a chill down my spine. It was glorious. We sped down the tracks faster than I'd ever gone.

"Come on! You can do it, guys. Come on!" And still we gained speed. "Haw!" We turned left and rode on. Just a little bit further . . .

A small crowd cheered up ahead. *Cool, our very own cheerleaders.*

We were passing by. I waved to some people, smiled at others. *I wonder how many people came this—*

An orange hat.

Our gazes locked.

I jerked my head back to look at the dogs.

The murderer!

CHAPTER TWENTY-THREE

ZOYA
1:47 p.m.

No, it couldn't have been.

Morphine still led the other dogs down the track. We were almost to the finish line.

That orange hat . . .

Something inside of me yelled that that man was the murderer. That he was there for a reason.

Me.

His face . . .

Even though we had flashed by I could see his eyes. Dark and evil. Filled with vengeance and a deep, menacing sense of power.

Was I imagining things?

We crossed the finish line. Cheers rang in the air.

My heart hammered. My legs were weak. Could it really have been him?

Yes. It had to have been. I wouldn't feel that kind of—

The dogs barked and stopped. A crowd surrounded me. I couldn't talk, couldn't pay attention.

I had to get to Mom. Tell her what I saw.

Sean, a whopper of a smile on his face, walked up. But the smile soon vanished. His brow creased. "Sunshine?"

"Mom?" I squeaked out the word. He looked in her direction.

I followed his gaze and stumbled over. Somewhere in the back of my mind I heard him say he'd take care of the dogs. But it didn't register right away.

I wanted to stay next to Sean, to know he could protect me. But I walked on anyway. My legs felt like Jell-O and everything spun around me. Yet the fear of getting shot kept me going. Mom was close enough that I would still be in Sean's range of protection, right?

My arm jerked as I collided with a man. Something hard pressed against my ribs.

My back stiffened.

Gun!

My head jerked up.

Orange hat . . .

Spasms shot throughout my body. I pulled. Yanked. Kicked. Spots danced around me. I wanted to scream but couldn't. My throat closed. Hard to breathe . . .

And he was gone.

His face . . . Eyes, so dark . . .

My thoughts seemed to swirl. Everything started to go blurry. But the note he shoved in my hand felt as heavy as bricks.

I lifted the paper to read the words. My knees shook, banging into one another . . .

Tell anyone that you saw me and you'll never see your mom alive again.

I shoved the note in my pocket. My fist balled around it.

No. . . No, no, no!

The tears came. I could feel the scar from my bullet wound. It screamed at me. As if I had gotten shot again. Had I been? Was I hurt?

He'd been that close . . . To killing me. Why didn't he?

God, help me!

RICK

January 29
Fairbanks, Alaska
1:52 p.m.

Another great race. Dan would be proud.

But today . . . today Rick would introduce himself to his niece and her mother. He wasn't sure how much time he had left. And with all the stress of his job, he needed this. Who cared about the rest? It would all work out in the end.

As the immediate crowd dispersed around Zoya, he headed in her direction. Anesia spotted him first. She cocked her head at him. And stared.

The last few steps brought him to her side. "Anesia?"

"Yes? Do I know you?"

"No. I'm sorry to say. I'm Rick."

"Hello, Rick." She stuck out a hand in greeting. "Are you here to congratulate Zoya?"

"I am."

She smiled and looked to be searching for her daughter. A proud mother if he ever saw one. Dan told him she was incredible and strong, but he'd never had the chance to see her up close. Breathtaking was a good word. Her brow furrowed as she watched her daughter. Better make this quick.

"And there's another reason I'm here."

Anesia turned back to face him. "Oh?"

"You see, I'm Rick Kon'. Dan's brother."

SEAN
1:55 p.m.

All the well-wishers and small children asking for autographs must have finished up while he loaded the dogs into the truck, because Zoya hurried to her mom and another man. In a split-second Anesia's face turned to stone, Zoya's paled.

Sean quickened his steps to intervene. But before he reached them, Zoya's eyes rolled back into her head and the small girl collapsed in the snow. A horrible crunch sounded as her head struck something hard beneath the powdery surface.

"Zoya!" Anesia fell beside her daughter.

In an instant Sean knelt beside her. Lifting Zoya's head, he checked for blood. "She's got quite a lump already, and it's growing." His heart pounded. He needed control, but his heart felt the keen attachment to this mother and daughter.

With deft movements, he and Anesia worked together as he assessed the rest of Zoya's head. "Zoya, can you hear me?" He touched her face. "Zoya?" Turning to Anesia, he kept his voice calm. She needed that. "At least the swelling is on the outside."

"What do you mean?"

"In a head injury without a laceration, if a lump doesn't form on the outside, it could mean that it is swelling toward the brain. That wouldn't be good."

Anesia's eyes met his. The pleading unmistakable. She looked toward the small crowd still over by the judges. "We need some help over here!" Her gaze darted around. "Where'd he go?"

"Where'd who go?"

"Rick. The man . . . the man who was just here . . ." She mumbled something under her breath that he couldn't understand. "It doesn't matter. We just need to get her to the hospital as soon as possible."

"Agreed."

A couple paramedics rushed toward them.

A single tear dripped off the end of Anesia's nose. Strong, capable, beautiful Anesia. How much had this slight woman endured all these years? And from what he'd learned, she'd done it alone. With tenacity and grace.

While the paramedics loaded Zoya onto a gurney, he grabbed Anesia's hand. "I'll be here for whatever you need."

She never tore her gaze from her daughter. But she nodded.

"Ma'am?" The larger paramedic approached. "Are you riding along?"

"Yes."

The man turned to him. "There won't be room—"

"Not a problem. I will follow." Sean turned to Anesia. "I'll be there." He wrapped an arm around her shoulder as they walked to the ambulance.

A brief turn, and she was in his arms, hugging him with the power of ten men. She jerked away and jumped into the waiting vehicle. But not before he saw more tears streaming down her face.

Sean ran full-speed toward the truck. Cole and his girls had left moments before as they planned another celebration for Zoya on her journey to the championships. Pulling the cell from his coat pocket as he ran, he speed-dialed Cole.

It rang once. "Hey, man."

"Cole, I need your help. Zoya fell a few minutes ago and hit her head. She's unconscious with quite a bump. Anesia is in the ambulance with her en route to the hospital."

"We'll meet you there—"

"Wait, I need you guys to come in two vehicles. I'm driving the dog truck, and since we don't know how long we'll be there, it may be advantageous to have another vehicle in case we need to get the dogs back to the kennel at some point."

"Good thinking. We're almost to the house, so we'll just grab another vehicle and meet you there. I assume they headed to Memorial?"

"Yes. I thought it was the only one."

"Pretty much. We'll call the prayer chain at church, too."

"Thanks."

With a snap, he closed the cell phone. His heart hammered in his chest. He'd been afraid of getting attached, but the truth blared at him.

His heart belonged to the Naltsiine girls.

ZOYA
January 29
Fairbanks Memorial Hospital
5:13 p.m.

Beeping. Talking. Coughing.

What was going on?

I couldn't open my eyes. They felt as if they'd been superglued shut. Why couldn't I open them?

Voices floated around me, lifting the cloud of nothingness.

"It's been awhile."

"She'll wake up soon. If not I'll wake her."

"Andie, you need to eat something." Cole. His voice seemed strained. What was he doing here? Where was I?

"I can last until she wakes up."

"Go on, Andie, I'll call Jenna if she does." Mom's voice. Relief flooded over me. She was alive and well.

Mom, Andie, and Cole. The voices comforted me, yet brought dread.

I had to tell them. But I couldn't. Those men would find and kill Mom if I said anything.

But what if I didn't tell anyone about the note? Who else would get hurt? Would I harm more people by *not* telling?

Cole could protect Mom. He could get the FBI.

But would the bad men know? Would they harm her before the FBI got to us?

Something rustled around me. Blankets?

I couldn't open my eyes. Didn't want to. Anger clung to my heart. It wouldn't let go. Tears sprung in my eyes. But they wouldn't fall. I couldn't fall back asleep.

What was wrong with me?

God, what are You doing? What's going on? Why are You doing this to me? I wanted to love Him. Wanted to trust Him. Wanted to feel Him there. But I just couldn't. I couldn't feel His presence. He wasn't there. Hadn't been.

Had He?

I was abandoned. Alone.

Terrified.

"Don't trust Him, don't trust Him, don't trust Him . . ."

I couldn't do this on my own. But there was no one. If God was there, shouldn't I feel Him? Shouldn't He reassure me of His presence?

I waited, letting the tears slip past my still closed eyelids.

"Zoya?"

I waited. Nothing came. No comfort. No wisdom. I was at the end of my rope. Fear tightened its grasp. Every ounce of strength left my body as the tears came flooding in.

Too many things to worry about. It was too much.

Just let me die!

I needed to sleep. I needed the rest. But why? I would have to wake up at some point. But the anger would remain. The pain would remain. The fear would remain.

Would it be there for the rest of my life?

Yes. I knew it would.

So why couldn't I just die?

There was nothing left for me in this life. People wanted me dead anyway. I couldn't tell anyone what I had seen. I couldn't warn anyone about those men.

I was useless.

I tried to swallow back all the fear. All the anger. All the contradictory feelings. Nothing helped.

God, if You're there, show me! I needed to cry. But I couldn't. Couldn't tell Mom. Couldn't let them kill her.

Anger sizzled inside.

Fine. If You're not going to help me, then I'll do it myself. I'll save Mom. And I'll make sure those murderers get behind bars.

And have a miserable rest of their lives.

CHAPTER TWENTY-FOUR

SLIM
January 29
Fairbanks, Alaska
8:21 p.m.

He dialed the number and hit speakerphone. His notes sat on the coffee table in front of him. Time to play his hand.

"Hello, Slim. To what do I owe the pleasure of you interrupting me on a Saturday evening?" A tapping sounded in the background. Like a letter opener beating an impatient rhythm on a wooden surface.

"Please don't use your sarcasm and condescension on me, sir."

"Well, well. Our young, little helper is offended. My sincerest apologies."

Sincerest apologies. Yeah, right. Let's just see how he responded to the news. "We only have one more chip before the program is complete."

"Excellent. The money will be wired to you and I'll contact the buyer. I expect delivery immediately after the buyer arrives."

"Wait just a minute. I think we've got a little change in plans." Make him squirm. Just a little.

"What do you mean, Slim?" Gone was the cooperative tone of the comment before.

"*I* have all the chips."

Silence stretched for several seconds. "And?"

"I also have my *own* buyer lined up, so the price has just gone up."

A harsh laugh echoed through the phone line. "You don't know how to decode the information, you idiot—"

"It's already decoded"—he let that info sink in before he tacked on—"sir."

Another long pause. "So you've decided to branch out on your own, have you? Well, that's fine. But you're going to pay me for what it took to get the program in the first place. I arranged it. I paid for it."

"And I hid it for you."

"That's beside the point."

"I don't think so." The power he now held gave him more confidence. "All of your guys were peons. And they were all under scrutiny. No one had the capability to keep it hidden but me. When you brought me in on this deal, you even told me how brilliant my plan was. That no matter how many guys the feds brought in on this, and no matter how many guys they busted on this, they'd never find the program until we had it all. And you were right. It *is* brilliant. The feds are so stupid, they're barkin' up all the wrong trees."

"Why you little—"

"So to put it simply, *sir,* I have the program. You don't. And now I want my cut."

ANESIA

January 29
Naltsiine Kennels
10:42 p.m.

It's okay. She's going to be okay.

Breathe. Just breathe.

Cole, Jenna, and Andie had left. Zoya lay on the couch, staring at the ceiling. Sean made coffee in the kitchen.

Anesia sat.

Her knee bounced.

She could do nothing to erase the events of the day. Once again she'd failed to protect her daughter.

Who was Rick? Dan never mentioned a brother. And why had Zoya looked so upset right before Rick arrived?

The questions tumbled around in her brain. This couldn't be happening. She hated hospitals. Twice in a matter of weeks they'd been there. And not for visiting. How had Jenna managed all these years? Her heart broke into a million pieces every time she saw her daughter lying in a hospital bed.

Her perfect-ordered and controlled world had collapsed around her. And she was powerless to do anything about it. The reality of the situation hit home.

Jenna had the special needs child. Not her.

Jenna could handle this kind of thing. She couldn't.

Anesia was better at being the stoic friend. The strong one who held her friend up. Everyone thought she was so strong and stable. But that wasn't true. She loved Jenna, yes. But she preferred being the friend.

Not the one to go through the hardships day in and day out.

Without permission from her, the tears flowed from her eyes. *God, why? Why am I so weak?*

Dan had been gone so long, the memories faded over time. Losing her beloved before they married had speared her heart. The ache settled in to stay.

She hung her head. Just be honest. It wasn't *just* his death—his loss—that devastated her. It was also the fact that she suddenly found herself an unmarried pregnant girl with no hope for her future. And when it all came down to it?

Pride. It stung her pride that everyone knew she'd gotten pregnant out of wedlock.

It stung her pride that she wouldn't ever be Dan's wife. Dan, who'd been on his way to winning every major sprint racing championship. Dan, who'd been so proud to have her on his arm.

It stung her pride that she'd been left alone. To fend for herself. And her baby. With no money, no name, and no education.

Just another native Alaskan girl, who blended into the background.

Zoya turned and looked at her. Really looked at her. Anesia attempted a smile through her tears. But the fear and anger in Zoya's eyes turned her insides out.

Get control. Zoya didn't need to see her blathering. "Hi, sweetie. Do you need anything?"

"No." The words were hard. Stiff.

"Does your head hurt?"

"A little."

"Did you hear the doctor explain everything?"

"Not really."

Wow. What a conversation. But at least she was talking. "You have a concussion. They think you'll be fine. But they do want me to wake you every hour tonight just to be safe."

"Okay."

"So I need you to talk to me, when I wake you up, all right?"

"Okay." Her daughter went back to staring at the ceiling.

"Anything you want to talk about?"

"Not really." Now her words were lifeless. Dull.

What was happening to her sweet kid? Had Rick said something to her? Did Zoya know who he was? "Zoya, I love you."

Her teen reached out to take her hand. "I love you too, Mom. Always." Emotion filled Zoya's eyes until she blinked and the blank stare gained control of her features. The ceiling once again held her attention.

More tears. Thankfully Sean chose that moment to bring Anesia a cup of coffee.

"How are you holding up?" His gentle voice soothed the weary places in her heart.

She smiled up at him. "I'm doing okay." Brushing away the tears, she stood next to him. "You know, you're sounding more and more like a relaxed Alaskan every day."

"I shall take that as a compliment." Sean touched Zoya's shoulder. "How's my favorite girl?"

Zoya reached up and held the hand resting on her shoulder. "I've been better."

Anesia's heart did a little flip. Wow. A whole three-word sentence. How did he manage that?

"Well, I *hope* you've been better. If you tried to convince me you were fine right now, I'd take you right back to the hospital and have them examine your head again." Sean leaned down and placed a kiss on Zoya's forehead.

A giggle—if you could even call that miniscule sound one—escaped her daughter's lips. But she'd take it. Anything. Just to know she wouldn't disappear down that black hole again.

Sean's gaze came back to her. "Anesia, would you like me to stay? It's quite an undertaking waking every hour. We could take shifts."

Her body yearned for her bed. Yet her mother-heart wanted to smack anyone who stood in the way of her taking care of Zoya. It would be good to have an extra set of hands. And to have a little uninterrupted sleep. But no. She couldn't allow him to do that. *She* was Zoya's mom. "I appreciate that, Sean. I really do. But I think Zoya would be more comfortable if I were the one to wake her."

Sean nodded.

"Mom?" Zoya's voice squeaked. "Can Sean stay?"

Anesia raised her eyebrows and looked at her daughter. Words tripped over each other in her mind. Was her daughter afraid? "Sure, honey. If you would feel more comfortable."

"I would." She closed her eyes.

Anesia tore her gaze from her daughter and glanced at Sean. "The guest bedroom is down the hall, Sean. Do you mind staying?"

"Not at all. After all, I did offer."

"Thank you. I still think I'll stay in here to wake her each hour, but it's comforting to know you're here."

Expressive green eyes held hers. This man was such a mystery. The silence stretched as she couldn't look away.

"Well, I think I will turn in. But don't hesitate to let me know if you need me." Sean turned and headed down the hall.

Butterflies danced around in her stomach as she watched him walk away. Exhaustion must be making her delirious. Yeah, that was it.

Pure exhaustion.

RICK
January 29
Hotel North Pole
11:04 p.m.

Well, that didn't go well.

He'd spent all evening chewing on what he said to Anesia, reflecting on what he could've done differently. Rick even sent a man to the hospital and found out Zoya was okay, but it didn't ease his conscience.

Would he anger the spirits more if he didn't fulfill the promise he'd made to Dan? The ancient tribal elder he'd gone to for advice had given him more doubts and superstition. But the answers weren't easy to come by. The fear in his gut grew. As a young boy, he'd thrown off the teaching of his father in a fit of rebellion. Didn't think it mattered. And then odd things kept happening. Bad things. That Dan received warnings for.

Then Dan died.

It all had to be true. That meant the fault lay at his feet.

The ringing of his phone made him jump. He glanced at the caller ID. Great. Just what he needed.

"Yeah?"

"It's time to get rid of the girl."

Not now. Please. "What are you talking about? I thought we agreed—"

"Kon', shut up. She's the only one who can help the FBI discover my identity. And that's not gonna happen. She's the only one who saw my men. We've worked too long and too hard to let some little brat ruin everything by opening her mouth. I've got a plan in motion for tomorrow. Your job is to make sure it gets done."

"But—she doesn't know anything, she just witnessed the shooting. It will only draw more attention—"

"*I don't care!* I don't know what your problem is, but you work for me. I've dealt with enough imbeciles. Do your job."

Rick couldn't catch his breath. The pain in his chest intensified. He knew the implication. The boss had gotten rid of everyone but the shooter. And he'd only let him live because he needed him. At least for a little while.

"Understood?"

"Sir." The one word was all he could get out.

Click.

CHAPTER TWENTY-FIVE

ANESIA
January 30
4:00 a.m.

The BlackBerry beeped and vibrated. Anesia opened her eyes and reset the alarm for the next hour. Four a.m. wasn't pretty on any day as far as she was concerned, but especially not today. Muscles ached all over her body as she stood and stretched. Shuffling over to Zoya, she ran a few fingers through her hair. What a sight she must be.

"Zoya, honey, wake up and talk to me."

"Ugh." The word wasn't much more than a moan. More groaning followed.

She poked her daughter.

"I'm awake, I'm awake." Zoya glanced at the clock. "It's four in the morning, and you're standing over me. Your hair's a mess, and I'm coherent. See?"

Anesia laughed. So far so good. Zoya seemed fine. She talked more in the middle of the night than before.

"Can I go back to sleep now?"

"Yes." She bent to kiss her daughter on the top of her head.

"Love you, Mom."

"Love you, too."

Covers shifted and moved, a fist hit the pillow, fluffed it, and Zoya shifted into a position only a teenager could find comfortable.

Darkness surrounded her, but the nightlight from the hallway illuminated half of her daughter's face. What a precious gift this child would always be.

Anesia had endured ridicule and gossip for so many years. All those "good" Christians who looked down their noses at her for the sin she committed. She'd known right from wrong. But she'd loved Dan so very much. They'd planned to marry after the baby was born, but Dan died in the middle of her pregnancy. Shame surrounded her like a cloak as grief choked her almost to the point of death.

But then Jenna wrapped her arms around her in love. She defended Anesia. Gave the gossiping old biddies what-for when they started their destructive missions time and again. And Jenna showed Anesia God's love through it all.

Yes, God did a wonderful thing through her mistakes. She shook her head. Anesia would *never* think of her daughter as a mistake. Zoya blessed her every day. That blessing was from God. Her mind hummed the tune to the doxology. *Praise God from Whom all blessings flow . . .* That's right. He took her shattered and disappointing life and molded it into something beautiful. It took Dan's death to get her attention. And it made her stronger.

A verse from James stuck out in her mind, *Every good and perfect gift is from above . . .*

She looked at her daughter again. Yes, God had given her so much.

God who loved her more than anyone ever had. God who forgave her and accepted her and gave her a fresh start each morning. God who turned her sorrow into joy.

The God of heaven and earth.

Feet shuffled down the hall. Anesia gasped—then remembered.

Sean.

He appeared in the dim light, blond hair all spiked around his head. "Anesia, are you doing okay? Need anything?" His words a hushed whisper.

What a heart. She'd never met anyone like him. Dare she risk it? "I could use a little company for a while, if you're up for it."

He shuffled the rest of the way into the room and sat on the floor. "Do you need talking company or silent company?"

His thoughtfulness made her chuckle. "Talking would be good."

"All right. What do you want to talk about?"

She sat on the floor next to him, peering at her daughter on the couch. What would get her mind off all the horrific events of late? "What are your dreams, Sean?"

He rubbed his eyes like a little boy then leaned back on his hands, his long legs stretched out in front of him. "Well, to tell you the truth, I wouldn't have been able to answer that question a few weeks ago. Other than starting over, I didn't have a clue." He closed his eyes for a moment. "But now, and please don't misconstrue this as the proverbial kissing up, I believe you've given me a dream. I love this kennel. Love the dogs. Love the racing. Love . . ."

His words were filled with such passion. Passion that matched hers.

Back to the topic. Focus. "Go on . . . love what?"

He shifted his weight to one hand and scratched his forehead with the other. "Oh, just about everything around here. That's basically what I was saying."

She'd made him uncomfortable. Oops. "Well, I have to say, that makes me happy. We like having you around." *Don't do it. Don't say anymore. Glue those lips shut.*

"Thank you."

"And I've got to tell you, you fascinate me."

Really? Was she dreaming? Or was her tongue betraying her?

"Your history, your education, your travels. Even though you don't think you were *you* during all those years, I do believe that all of it shaped you into who you are now."

He took a slow, deep breath and pulled his knees up. "That's a valid point. And in my quest to leave the past behind, I've forgotten that important piece. Thank you for reminding me."

"You're welcome." *Now zip it. Don't say anything else.*

"What are *your* dreams, Anesia?"

Too late. It was like she'd taken some evil truth serum. She couldn't stop the words from oozing out if she tried. "That's an easy question. I want to be the very best mom on the planet. I want to see Zoya grow up into a strong, God-loving, God-fearing woman. And of course I want to be known around the globe for the very best racing dogs. And it wouldn't hurt if I could win the championship every year."

He nodded. The lines in his forehead portraying that he took her words to heart, mulled them over. "Those are all awesome things. But it sounds a little lonely. What about love?"

SEAN
4:13 a.m.

He did *not* just ask that.

Idiot. Just tell her she's pathetic next time.

The most spectacular woman he'd ever known, and he had to open his big mouth.

Then insert his foot.

It would probably take surgery to undo the damage.

Brain transplant surgery.

She'd fire him for sure. But he loved his job. Working at the dog kennel made him feel alive. He needed to beg her for forgiveness.

His horror must've been visible on his face, because Anesia just stared at him. Then she laughed. "Don't look so upset, Sean. You're right."

"I'm sorry. I had no place to say any of that. Maybe I should return to bed now."

"Oh, stop. I'm not mad at you. Just shocked that you were bold enough to be blunt with me. To be quite honest, it's been a sore subject for me, and poor Jenna has had to avoid it like the plague for fear I'll bite her head off."

"I'm still sorry. Maybe I should rephrase—"

"Nonsense. It's an honest question." Her gaze met his. Held it. "And it deserves an honest answer."

COLE
January 30
Tikaani-Gray-Maddox Home
4:15 a.m.

His phone vibrated and buzzed itself toward the edge of his nightstand. Cole caught the phone just as it plunged off the side. He propped himself up on the bed with one arm and answered the call. "Maddox."

"Cole, sorry to call so early, but I need to ask you some questions."

He lay back. The FBI wouldn't be calling unless it was urgent. "Go ahead."

"How well do you know Anesia Naltsiine?"

Anesia? What kind of harebrained idea were they following this time? "I know her well. I'd trust that woman with my life."

"Cole, we know that you have close ties with her, but we need you to be unbiased."

"My answer remains the same." His jaw began to ache from clenching it.

"All right. But we're getting some interesting info."

"Just spit it out."

"We've been tracking a guy named Rick Kon'. Turns out he's the brother of a certain Dan Kon'. Recognize the name?"

Zoya's dad. "You know I do."

"He was seen speaking to Anesia yesterday after the race. Right before Zoya was injured. Then he disappeared. And not ten minutes ago, we followed him to the Naltsiine property."

"And?"

"We think he's the link."

"To what?"

"The arms ring."

"So what does that have to do with Anesia?"

"We think she's helping him."

His temper couldn't be contained any longer. "*What?*"

"And hiding the program on her property. The payment she'd get would fund her kennel for a long time."

"You can't be serious. Anesia has worked her tail off—"

"Exactly the motivation she'd need to go along with the plan." The agent's voice was clipped. He'd already bought into the lie.

"There's no way Anesia is involved in this."

"Believe what you want, Maddox, but you need to be prepared for the possibility."

Cole hung up the phone. No, he didn't. Because Anesia was innocent.

And he would put everything on the line to prove it.

ANESIA
Naltsiine Kennels
4:17 a.m.

She could do this. Maybe the weight that had been sitting on her chest all these years would lift. She might even be able to acknowledge to Sean the fact that he had captured her attention. And maybe, just maybe her heart. "I had dreams of marriage a long time ago."

One of Sean's eyebrows shot up.

"His name was Dan. Zoya's father. We were so in love, and we knew full well that God wanted us to wait until marriage, but . . ."

"You were young."

She nodded. "Too young. I got pregnant with Zoya." Suck it up. Spit it out. "The wedding was planned for after the birth of our baby. Everyone knew, and even though we messed up in the order of things, we wanted to do things right. So we went to premarital counseling, made a promise to be abstinent until our wedding night, and anticipated the arrival of our little bundle of joy.

"Dan loved racing as much as I did. We had the plans for this kennel and purchased the property, saving each and every penny we could—" The last words choked her.

"I'm sorry. You don't have to continue if you don't want to."

"No, it's okay. I need to talk about it." Another deep breath. "Anyway, Dan was killed a few months before Zoya was born. It's one of my deepest regrets, that she never knew him. And there are certain people who won't let her—or me—forget that her dad and I weren't married."

"What happened? To Dan, I mean."

His eyes were so kind, so concerned. "A training accident. He fell through the ice."

"I'm sorry."

"The grief almost won, but Jenna was there for me." She allowed a small smile as the memories came back for the second time that night. "Talk about a mother hen. She protected me and challenged me to break through. But I still allowed the guilt to hover.

"Zoya was born, and then Jenna and Marc had Andie a couple months later. By this time, I was so smitten with my daughter that I decided then and there that I would prove to everyone what a blessing she was. Beauty from ashes, you know? So I put on my little armor of independence and determined to never allow another man close."

It felt good to let it all spill out, but Sean was so quiet. What was he thinking? Was he disappointed in her? Did he think she was—

"Anesia, I had no idea of the journey you've faced. It gives me a better perspective on your drive and tenacity."

Well. Wasn't that nice and . . . formal. "Thanks. I don't want you to feel sorry for me. As you can tell, we've done very well by ourselves." She hated the edge that tinged her voice. Where did this anger come from? It didn't roll in like a tsunami but erupted in an instant. Did she want to prove to him and everyone else that they'd done just fine, in fact, *incredibly* fine all on her own? That she and Zoya didn't need anyone? That *she* didn't need a man?

He leaned forward and placed a gentle hand on her knee. The heat radiated up to her shoulders and helped her relax. If one touch could do that, how could she guard her heart from this man?

"I don't feel sorry for you at all. In fact, to be quite honest, you amaze me. And scare me. All at the same time." He removed his hand.

She wanted it back. "I scare you?"

His smile broke through the dimness of the room. "Not in the way you're thinking."

"Well, by all means, please explain." There went her anger again.

"I don't think you really want to know that."

Like a volcano. "And just how are you supposed to know *what* I want, Mr. Connolly?"

He chuckled.

How dare he laugh at her?

His hands shot up, signaling surrender, as though he could read her mind. "I'm just saying that it is intimidating for a man to be attracted to a beautiful woman, for that same woman to be his boss, and again for that same woman to be so strong and independent and in no need of anyone to come alongside her on the journey of life."

Oh.

Her heart raced.

He sat. Waiting for a response.

But she couldn't make her brain or her mouth work.

The silence stretched.

"I'm sorry. I went too far. Forgive me, please." He hopped to his feet. "It's the middle of the night. I think I'll head back to bed. Let me know if you need anything."

He was attracted to her? A door clicked, shaking her from her thoughts. Wait!

But he was already gone.

CHAPTER TWENTY-SIX

SEAN
January 30
Naltsiine Kennels
9:12 a.m.

The cold penetrated his bones this morning. Unlike all the other days when the excitement and love for the job, for this place, for its people, warmed him from the inside out. How could he have been so stupid?

Anesia didn't speak to him—didn't even look him in the eye—when she awoke and disabled the alarm. She headed to her bedroom and waved at him when he said he'd water the dogs. Not a word. Not a glance. Just a complete dismissal.

Of his words. Of him.

Sean went from dog to dog. Maybe the work would help him forget his stupidity.

"Hi." Zoya's small, bundled-up form stood at the gate.

"Hi, yourself." He forced a smile. "How does your head feel?"

"I've got a headache, but it's not so bad." She walked around petting dogs.

"That's good. I'm glad you're feeling better."

"Yeah. Mom says we'll go to the late service at church and if I'm up to it, we'll eat at the Café for lunch."

"Sounds like fun."

"Will you come with us?"

"I'll be at church."

"That's not what I asked." She stood beside him now.

"I know." *God, now would be a good time to intervene.*

"I heard you and Mom talking last night."

He looked up to the sky. *That wasn't quite the intervention I was hoping for, Lord.*

"I'm sorry I eavesdropped, but it wasn't like you guys didn't know I was in the room."

"But we thought you were asleep." It wasn't his place to scold her.

"I know. And I'm sorry."

"Zoya, you're forgiven. I should be apologizing to you. It was completely inappropriate of me to talk to your mother that way." Heat climbed up his neck. When did he become a bumbling fool?

"She likes you."

"I embarrassed her."

"You need to talk to her."

"She won't even look me in the eye."

Zoya sighed. One of the teenage are-you-really-that-stupid kind of sighs. "Will you come with us, please?"

He turned to face her. Studied her features. The kid was hurting. "All right."

"Yes—"

"On one condition."

"What?"

"You sit down right now and talk to me about what's *really* bugging you. I won't tell your mom and I won't betray your confidence. But you need to talk, don't you?"

"How did you know that?"

"That doesn't matter. Do we have a deal?" He stuck out his hand.

She chewed on her lip. Then squinted. Then stuck out her own hand and they shook on it. "Deal."

He couldn't stop the smile. "Good. Now let's get into the barn where it's warmer."

"Good idea."

They walked the distance to the barn in silence. Boots crunched the snow beneath them. Tree branches swayed in the wind. Dogs yapped. Wood smoke drifted to his nose from fireplaces. Their breath turned to ice crystals in the air, tinkling like microscopic bells. Sean would never tire of this unique land.

As they entered the barn, he dove in. "Okay, Sunshine. Let's hear it."

She plopped down on a bale of hay, lowered her scarf, and shoved her gloved hands into her pockets. "I'm mad at God."

"Okay."

"What? You're not upset with me?"

"No. Go on."

"Well, I thought you'd get onto me and lecture me and all that."

"Then I wouldn't be a very good listener or friend, now would I?"

She considered that, then nodded. "Oh. Right. Well, I'm upset because of all the things He's allowed to happen. And I keep praying, and it's like He's not listening."

The inner prodding was clear. *Listen. Keep her talking.*

"I'm so . . . *angry*. My whole world is messed up. And I'm just a kid. I don't control anything. And I don't want anything to happen to my mom."

What wasn't she saying?

"Anyway, that's it. My brain's a jumbled mix. Trying to figure out what to do."

His instinct told him the story didn't end there. *God, I could use some guidance.*

Listen.

"Sean, I love my mom. She's amazing. I want her to be happy."

"She loves you too."

The first hint of a smile. "I know. She's always been there for me. Even more than Andie." She whispered behind her hand. "But don't tell Andie I said that."

"My lips are sealed."

She hugged herself, and words came pouring out. "Why do people do bad things? And why does God allow the bad junk to happen? Why did my dad have to die? Why does Andie get *two* dads, and I've got no one but my mom. I don't understand why God let that murder happen. He could have stopped it. Why didn't He? And did *I* have to see it?" She stood up and paced. "And I don't understand why He'd let me be so mad at Him, ya know? I don't *want* to be mad at God. I know better than that. I know He loves me. But it hurts. And I'm wondering if He's even real any more. There's too many voices in my head. Angry voices. The only voice that isn't there is His. Why isn't He talking to me? Why don't I feel Him any more?" Tears coursing down her face, she ran over to him, burying her face in his stomach.

He hugged her back. *God, help. I have no idea what to say.* He patted her back and waited. The words would come when God wanted him to speak.

"Are you mad at me?" She sniffed and wiped her nose with her hand. At that moment she sounded more like a small child than the blossoming teen she was.

"Not at all."

"Good. 'Cause I don't think I could handle you being mad at me."

He patted her back again.

Several seconds passed then she pulled back. His coat bore the evidence of her rampaging tears. "Thanks for listening, Sean."

"You're welcome."

"I'm angry and I'm scared. And I don't know what to do." She swiped at her face and headed toward the door. "I need to go. But thanks for not giving me any advice. Or trying to fix me."

Thank heaven he kept his mouth shut.

"I'm glad you're here. And I'm really glad you like my mom." And with that, she ventured out the door.

Sean sat back down on a bale of hay, exhausted—and haunted by one question:

Did he do the right thing?

ANDIE
January 30
235 North Santa Claus Lane, North Pole
2:47 p.m.

As we walked into the Country Café, the wonderful aroma of croissant French toast drifted over to me.

Yum.

"Where do you guys want to sit?" Cole looked around the crowded area and frowned.

I glanced around. There weren't many large tables available. Zoya stood beside me, fiddling with her gloves.

"How 'bout there?" I pointed off to a dirty table in the corner. "We could get someone to clean it off."

Cole nodded. "Looks like someone already is."

A tall lady came and carried away a large stack of dishes, then disappeared into the kitchen.

Auntie Anesia, Sean, Zoya, Cole, Mom and I walked over to the round table.

My nice clothes began to bug me. Why didn't I bring a change of clothing?

"How did you like the sermon, Sean?" Mom sat down and smiled.

"It was very pleasurable, to say the least." He smiled in return. Cole sat down between me and Mom. "Who wants to pray?"

"Cole, we haven't even ordered yet." Mom poked his arm.

"Well!" He crossed his arms. "Aren't we the slow group. Let's order so I can eat!"

All morning he had been complaining that he was hungry. What a man. No patience whatsoever.

Everyone laughed. Except Zoya. She sat still beside me and fiddled with her gloves again.

"Oh, what a surprise to see you all here!" I looked up to find Mrs. Howe from church standing there, her little boy, Jonny, at her side.

"Hello, Laura." Mom stood and hugged her.

She smiled. "I saw you at the service this morning but didn't get a chance to say hi. I found something that I think belongs to you. Jonny picked it up in the church parking lot last week—"

"It shiny," the three-year-old piped up.

"At first I couldn't tell who it belonged to, but it has what I think are Marc's initials on it."

I turned in my seat as she pulled the little black box out of her pocket. "Mom!" I jumped up and started doing the happy dance. How on earth had Jonny found it?

"Thank you, we've been looking for it." Mom smiled and handed it to me.

"Cole, see?" I almost threw it into his hands as Jonny and Mrs. Howe said good-bye and left.

"I see. But what about it?"

"Look at it!" I bounced up and down on my toes. He was such a man! Didn't notice anything!

Zoya just stared at the box. Not saying a word. How was she not as excited as I was? What was wrong with her? I stopped bouncing. *God?*

Cole leaned over the table and placed the box on its surface. His brow scrunched. "Andie, why do you think this could be a clue?"

My heart pounded. Was he that unobservant?

"Look," I pointed, wanting to hit him on top of the head. And hit him hard. *You know, Jesus said many, many times, "he who has ears to hear, let him hear." I think that goes for eyes as well . . .*

"It seems a little duller under the inscription like something was erased, or like sandpapered over, and Dad's initials were etched over it."

He flipped the box to the side the initials were on.

"I'm not sure." He tampered with the lid, then sighed. "I'll have to break it open. Is that okay?" He turned to me.

I didn't want to ruin it. Not since it was Dad's. But it was for the good of our country. I nodded. Then sat back down as Cole got out his nifty tool thing-a-majigger and started working on it. Sean leaned in close from the other side of the table and helped hold it still.

Zoya slipped a piece of paper into my hand.

If I tell you something, you have to promise you won't tell a single soul.

I looked into her eyes. *There has been something wrong, it wasn't just me!* "I promise," I whispered.

She slipped a folded-up letter into my hand. Again I looked into her eyes. She looked . . . sad. And angry.

I stood up. Best to read it in private. "Mom, can I go to the restroom?"

Without even looking at me she nodded. Everyone's attention seemed to be on the little black box. I could feel the tension in the room thicken as Cole worked on it. No one noticed that something was wrong with my friend.

I walked to the bathroom, slipped into a stall, and opened the note:

Andie,

I know you want to be there for me, you always have. But you can't help me with this. Please don't get mad at me, I love you very much. But God and I aren't seeing eye to eye. And I know that your words couldn't help. You've been a great friend and I love you. Thanks for sticking with me, but I need to go on alone.

Love,
Zoya

What was she saying? Go on alone? Go where? She was still mad at God . . . why? I thought she was over that. I had promised, but we had to talk. And I needed Mom's help.

I rushed out the door, slamming it into the wall, and over to the table. Zoya didn't look me in the eye.

Everyone else stared at the box. Mom's hand covered her mouth.

Cole looked up to me and stood. "Andie, this box isn't Marc's."

I blinked. What?

Zoya needed me. Why was he—

Cole stood.

Something was wrong.

He leaned in close, hand clasping my elbow in a tight squeeze. "This box belonged to Viper."

SEAN
3:45 p.m.

Cole's grip on his shoulder intensified. The tension and urgency flowed through his heavy jacket. Whoever this Viper fellow was, Sean knew the stakes had just been raised.

"Anesia, can you spare Sean for a little bit?"

She studied Cole's face, then nodded. "All right, but we all rode together today, you'll need to get him back to the cabin."

He glanced from Anesia to Jenna. Suspicion filled both their eyes. Zoya sat, gaze down, hands clasped in her lap. And Andie looked pale, like the news about her father's precious memento had pushed her over the edge.

As they headed out the door to their vehicles, Sean had the feeling things were about to get worse.

"We need to talk."

It was a barked command. Sean angled a look at Cole. "That's obvious."

Cole's shoulders dropped a bit. "Sorry. You're not one of my soldiers. I shouldn't treat you like one."

"I do understand. But orders being bellowed at me are not a pleasant reminder." In fact, it made him want to punch someone. Like his father.

They climbed into Cole's truck. "I'm sorry, Sean. I need your help."

"Go on."

"Andie and Zoya were correct. I don't know why he did it, but Viper switched boxes with Marcus. There were three that I know of. The leaders from our ops group each had one. Maybe he thought Marc's held the secret to obtaining AMI, I don't know. But this goes back farther than I thought. I'll have to contact the FBI to see about getting Viper's box out of evidence. Because that one, I hope, is Marc's."

"So how did you know the other one wasn't Marc's?"

"The girls were correct. The etching on the bottom had been changed. It was planted." Cole sighed. "Why, I don't know. But I plan to find out." A tic in his jaw showed Sean the tightly-wound anger.

"What do you need me to do?" Cole might be used to all this stuff, but Sean's brain was spinning. National security. Secret defense weapons. Treason . . .

"I received another call this morning. Someone is either trying to hurt Zoya and Anesia, or trying to frame Anesia for something."

"What was the call?"

"I'm not at liberty to say, but Anesia is family and I've got my guard up. I'm not clear what's going on—the pieces are too scattered. But something is happening. On Anesia's property." Cole stared him down. "Don't let anyone near them, you understand?"

Sean gave a terse nod and a fierce protective instinct kicked into high gear. "I'll keep my eyes peeled." His cell phone rang, cutting off the rest of his thought process. He looked at the screen.

Great. Just what he needed. He flipped open his phone, letting his anger singe his words. "What do you need, Father?"

Cole snapped his head to look at him and then looked back to the road.

"Well, is that any way to greet your dear ol' dad?"

His father's syrupy sweet tone didn't bode well. "Why are you calling?"

"I'm sending the jet up there for you. It's time you came back." His dad sounded almost jovial.

Sean's anger heated up a notch, but he worked to keep his tone respectful. "That's not going to happen, Father. I've stated my intentions."

"Don't toy with me"—his father hissed—"You will listen to what you are told and get back here immediately!"

"No."

"What did you say?"

"I said, no. Disown me, disinherit me, whatever you want to do. I'm not taking orders from you any more, not when the road you're choosing goes against what I know is right."

Silence. Had he hung up? Sean hoped so.

"We'll discuss this later."

"No, we won't, Father."

"Yes. We will."

Sean pressed END.

Cole shifted in the seat beside him.

"I'm sorry you had to hear that."

"You've got guts, man. I've heard the senior Connolly is quite a hothead."

"He's always gotten what he wanted. Always. And no one has ever told him no."

"Well, there's a first time for everything, now isn't there?" Cole flashed him a grin.

"Yeah. I guess you're right." Sean sat a little straighter in his seat. "Let's get back to more important matters. What do I need to do to protect Anesia and Zoya?"

DETECTIVE SHELDON

North Pole Police Department
3:49 p.m.

They'd ID'd the two dead men. One of the guns proved to be the murder weapon. That left one of three—probably the shooter—still alive.

What was he missing?

Was it this Rick Kon'? He picked up a profile. Too many holes.

Dave's gut told him that Anesia didn't know anything, but the FBI were sure barking up her tree. Why weren't they more concerned with protecting her and her daughter? So much at stake, and a kid stuck in the middle . . . and Dave was afraid the Naltsiines were in greater danger than any of them realized.

Of course, the FBI wanted him to share information from his investigation, but the more he gave, the more they kept to themselves.

Something just didn't add up.

Dave had no choice. If he wanted answers, he'd have to find them on his own.

CHAPTER TWENTY-SEVEN

ZOYA
January 30
3:50 p.m.

Mom and I hopped in the car. I buckled up, thoughts tumbling over one another. Mom didn't say a word.

What was she thinking? Was I in trouble? I wanted to cry, but I couldn't figure out why. Was it because I was worried or angry? I didn't know. Didn't know anything really.

Mom pulled out of the parking lot. She didn't say a word. She knew me too well. But I couldn't let her see what was going on. I had to protect her. But how? Did she notice something was wrong? I wanted to talk to her. But then again, I didn't.

As we drove onto the roundabout something caught my eye.

I squinted. A man turned around.

Orange hat.

I gasped.

He stared at me. Then smirked.

They were following me?

No! This couldn't be happening.

Did Mom see him?

"We're gonna have a talk. And you're going to tell me what's going on, is that understood?"

My heartbeat quickened. *Not now! God, if You're there, help me!* "Why should we talk? It won't do any good." Try to keep her off the subject . . . yeah. Keep her off the subject. I swallowed.

"Excuse me? *I'm* the one who will determine that, young lady."

We drove on in silence.

After about fifteen minutes Mom pulled onto our road. Soon we'd be to the house. If I could keep her sidetracked until then . . .

Minutes passed by. Each moment my anxiousness grew. Was the man following us? Would he hurt Mom? Did I need to do something?

Mom still said nothing. As if she were waiting for me.

We pulled up to the house. "Go to your room. I'll be up in a minute, and we'll talk."

Before she could scold me again, I opened the door and hopped out. I couldn't let her find out about the note. About those men . . . They would kill her.

I ran into the house, glancing around. Was the man here?

Sasha jumped up and ran over to me, tail wagging.

"At least I don't have to worry about you questioning me all the time." I patted her head. Somehow that comforted me. Eased my shaking. Would she protect Mom? Of course she would. But Sasha couldn't stop a gun . . .

Mom came through the front door and walked into the office, then shut the door behind her.

A walk. I'd go on a walk. Maybe for a day or two.

"Stay, Sasha." I walked over to the back door. She whined.

"No, girl. Not this time."

She obeyed. But I could see the worry in her eyes.

Once again I glanced around, then slipped out the back door.

Tiny plate-like discs of ice scattered here and there crunched and crackled underneath my feet as I walked. I neared the end of our property. Thoughts and emotions wouldn't stop swirling within me.

Where was I going? I couldn't trespass on other people's land, and if I took the road Mom or Auntie would find me.

I should have taken Sasha. She could have comforted me, kept me company. But then again she would have made noise and Mom would've known what I was doing.

It's cold out here. I wonder if there are any wild animals watching me. What's Andie doing right now?

Andie? Why was I thinking about Andie?

Thinking of my best friend brought on the tears.

No. I wouldn't cry. Couldn't. Had to be strong.

I wrapped my arms around my middle and kept walking.

A twig snapped behind me. My back stiffened.

What was that?

I jerked and turned around. I couldn't see anything through the heavy foliage.

A click.

No. A gun.

I gasped. I could hear my heart hammering. Everything went into slow motion.

A man stepped out from the cover of trees. His smile chilled me.

I stared as his arm raised and a gun pointed at me—

Something growled and attacked his arm.

The man screamed and fell, smashing his head into a fallen log. Blood dripped and pooled into the clean white snow.

Sasha turned to me and barked. She walked over and licked my hand, easing my speeding pulse.

The gun lay a few feet away. I should take it. But what if he woke up?

"We need to get Mom!" No sooner had the words left my mouth than we started running back the way I had come.

"Mom!"

We were at least a mile away, she couldn't hear me. But yelling for her helped anyway. Maybe Sean was out and would hear.

Oh, God help me!

I wasn't getting enough air, but I couldn't stop. I ran. Sasha nudged my leg, as if prodding me to go faster.

Couldn't. But had to.

"Mom!" Air stopped filling my lungs. *Out of breath . . .*

Sasha ran ahead and barked. Soon the house came within view. Derek ran out from the barn.

I couldn't focus. Everything was a blur. A man had just pointed a gun at me! I couldn't believe it. Didn't want to. I gasped for air.

I could hear myself wheezing. Had to keep running. Almost to the house. My legs gave out and I fell. My gloved hands picked up a handful of snow.

No. No! The tears fell.

Had to get up, get to Mom . . . I pushed up and continued running. Almost there.

Nothing would stop those murderers from killing the only witness.

Me.

ANESIA

January 30
Naltsiine Kennels
4:19 p.m.

Zoya's scream split the air, and the hair on the back of Anesia's neck rose. She jumped up from her desk and flew out the front door. No shoes, no coat. Didn't matter.

Zoya was in trouble.

Barreling around the house, she heard her daughter scream again and ran in the direction of the soul-piercing sound. There. She spotted her daughter rounding the corner past the barn. Sasha barked at Anesia and just about toppled her over as she ran full-force into her legs. Then the dog ran straight back to Zoya.

"Mom!" The seconds stretched into hours as they ran for each other.

Anesia caught and wrapped her precious baby in her arms.

"Mom!" She gasped for air. "Mom . . ." Another gasp and a shiver.

But as Anesia tightened her hold, she realized Zoya wasn't shivering. She was shaking.

"Zoya, talk to me. What happened?"

Glassy eyes gazed past her shoulder. "Mom . . ."

Anesia knelt in front of her only child, pushing her an arm's length away so she could check her over. "What?"

Zoya looked her in the eyes. "A man. With a gun."

"What? Where?"

"Tried to kill me. Sasha . . . knocked him down . . . hit his head . . . blood everywhere . . ." Her daughter's tiny frame collapsed in the snow at Anesia's feet. Zoya sucked in air.

Oh God, no!

She spotted Derek standing by the barn. Once again, God was looking out for them. "Derek! Get over here!"

"Yes, ma'am?"

"Help me get her in the house, please." Not until that moment did Anesia feel the cold seeping into her own bones. Her socks were drenched, and her feet were burning. Frostbite happened all too fast at these temps.

As her stocky employee helped them into the mudroom, Anesia realized Zoya was shaking harder. Was she in shock?

"Derek, go check the perimeters of the house and barn."

"Yes, ma'am." He started to head out the door.

"And Derek? Just so you know, Zoya said there's someone out there. I'm calling the police. Please make sure no one else approaches the house."

His dark eyes flashed at her. "Yes, ma'am."

Anesia locked the door behind him and ran through the house, checking all the doors and windows, and setting the alarm system. Back in the mudroom Zoya lay unconscious. As Anesia pulled all the wet outer gear off her daughter, she also stripped off her own wet socks and jeans. She yanked on a pair of dry sweats and socks from the mudroom shelf and ran to the phone. All the while talking to Zoya.

"Wake up, honey. You've got to tell me what happened."

The cordless handset beeped as she dialed 911. Anesia ran her hand down Zoya's face. "Honey! Wake up!"

The operator came on. As she explained that someone had attacked her daughter, Zoya began to moan and flail around.

"-*Yats'e'e*?" Her daughter wouldn't respond.

The calm voice on the other end assured her that someone would be there as soon as possible. Did she want them to stay on the line with her? No. She just wanted them here. Now.

"Mom . . ." Dark eyelashes fluttered.

She pulled Zoya into her arms. "Oh, hon, you had me worried."

"It was awful, Mom. I was so scared." Her daughter jerked away from her. "Is he still here? What if he's in the house?"

"No one's in the house. It's locked up tight and the alarm is set. Now just calm down and tell me what happened."

Fat tears rolled down her cheeks. "I'm so sorry, Mom. I should've listened to you, but . . . I . . . I can't seem to think straight. I snuck out the back door and went into the woods on the west side of the property."

Not a time to scold her daughter. But oh, the consequences. This would cause even more guilt to heap onto Zoya's already burdened shoulders. "It's okay, baby." She wiped tears. "Shh. It's okay. Just tell me the rest."

"I was standing there trying not to think about all this junk when I heard a twig snap and then . . . I heard a gun cock." More tears streamed in tiny rivers and dripped off Zoya's chin. "There was this man. He was going to shoot me, Mom! He was going to shoot me!" Sobs wracked her small frame.

Icy fingers clutched Anesia's heart. Someone tried to kill her daughter.

Again.

"And then Sasha came out of nowhere, growling and snapping. She knocked him off his feet. He hit his head on a fallen log and started bleeding all over the place. That's when I ran. As fast as I could. I couldn't stop screaming for you. I just wanted to be home." The tears stopped then, but as Zoya climbed into Anesia's lap, she saw the anguish and terror in her daughter's eyes. Small arms wrapped around her waist and squeezed with a force so strong she thought she might snap in two.

And then the anger came. Filling her gut with a searing hot flame. Whoever did this better not live to see tomorrow. Because if he did, Anesia would kill him.

SEAN
4:29 p.m.

He banged on the door and jiggled the doorknob. The echo of Zoya's screams still ringing in his head. He'd heard them from the entrance to the Naltsiine property. The terrifying screams of someone in pain. In trouble. "Anesia! It's Sean. *Anesia!*"

What could've happened? He continued to bang as loud as he could on the door. He tried the knob again. Locked. Anesia never locked the doors during the day. Something was terribly wrong.

"Anesia! Zoya!" He pounded until his fist throbbed from the pain.

The dead bolt clicked and Anesia opened the door an inch, keeping the chain intact. Her eyes were filled with fear and skittered about until she recognized him. "Oh, Sean. I'm so glad you're here." She lifted the chain and opened the door.

Before it could register, she was in his arms. Holding onto him with a fierceness he'd never known. "Anesia. I was so worried. I heard the screams. What happened?"

Sobs shook her frame and she held on tighter. As tiny as she was compared to him, he loved the feel and fit of her against him. "It's Zoya. Someone tried to shoot her in the woods."

He stiffened. He should have been there! Should have protected them! "Have you called the police?"

She nodded against his chest. "They're on their way. I called Jenna too."

Sean's arms tightened around her and he kissed the top of her head. "It's okay. I'm so glad I got home when I did." Even the anger he held against his father couldn't compare with what he felt toward the shooter at this moment. Every instinct screamed at him to search and destroy. How dare anyone attack his girls? He squeezed Anesia one last time, then eased her away. "You go on inside and lock everything back up. I'm going to see what I can find."

Fresh tears streamed down her face and she shook her head. "Sean, be careful. I wouldn't want anything to happen to you." She grabbed the front of his coat.

He took her hands in his and squeezed. "I'll be back. I promise."

She hesitated, but then went back inside. He didn't leave the porch until he heard the lock and chain.

Taking the steps in one long leap, Sean headed out to search the property. If it took him the rest of his life, he would help bring the shooter to justice.

For Anesia.

COLE
4:34 p.m.

The Expedition ate up the distance between the Naltsiine property and their own in short order.

Jenna touched his arm. "Cole. Babe, slow down."

A glance at the speedometer told him he'd doubled the speed limit. With snow and ice, that was plain stupid. He let his foot off the accelerator. Andie's eyes met his in the rearview mirror. This wasn't a military operation. This was family. *Careful, Maddox.*

Almost there. "I'm sorry, girls." He let out his breath. "It's just—"

"We know, Cole." Andie blurted, crossing her arms across her chest. Anger dripped from her words. "I want to hurt whoever's doing this."

Jenna whipped around in her seat. "We're all upset about this, young lady, but that is no way to talk."

Andie's face turned beet red as tears streamed. "They've stolen my best friend, Mom! Stolen her spirit, her faith, her trust, her laughter! We've been connected since we were babies, you said so yourself—"

"Squirt—"

"I feel like I've been torn in half, and I don't know if I'll ever get the other half back." She sobbed into her hands.

Cole and Jenna exchanged a look.

"I'm sorry." With heavy sniffs, Andie wiped the tears from her face. "I'm sorry. I'm just so stinkin' worried about Zoya. She hasn't been herself since this whole thing started."

Cole pulled into Anesia's driveway as Jenna reached back to their daughter. He shifted the truck to park. "It's all right, Squirt. We're all a little tense."

Jenna nodded. "But we need to be strong and find out what's going on, okay? This is tough junk for you guys to have to handle, but please remember that you can always talk to us. Always."

Andie's blue eyes lifted to stare at Sean. Sadness etched lines into her forehead. "I know. But if Zoya keeps stuffing everything inside and doesn't talk to me, we're going to have a bigger problem."

The wisdom in their daughter's words struck his gut like a physical blow. He searched Jenna's face. Her mouth set in a grim line. As they all exited the vehicle, Cole watched his girls head up the front steps to Anesia's home. His gut tightened.

If his suspicions were correct?

God help them all.

CHAPTER TWENTY-EIGHT

COLE
January 30
Naltsiine Kennels
5:34 p.m.

Sergeant Roberts walked in the door. "There's no one there."

Cole watched Zoya for a reaction.

Her eyes widened and she shook her head. "But . . . he was there . . . and all that blood . . ." She clamped her mouth shut and shook her head again.

Detective Sheldon turned to the other officer. "I've got a statement, let's get back out there and do a full sweep."

"Yes, sir."

The detective turned to Cole. "Keep the door locked behind us and it would be a good idea to set the alarm again." The man's intense gaze swept the room. "Is there anything else you need, Ms. Naltsiine?"

Anesia looked at Cole. "The dogs need to be checked on, but that can wait 'til you get back."

The officers took their leave. Cole locked the dead bolt and went to the alarm key pad.

"Just hit STAY," Anesia rubbed her neck and held onto Jenna's hand. "Thanks for coming, guys."

Jenna wrapped her arm around her long-time friend. "Not a problem. I'm so glad you called."

Cole pulled a chair up beside the couch and touched Zoya's knee. "How're you doing, kiddo?"

No response. Just a few silent tears rolled down her cheeks. Zoya's knuckles were white where she gripped her mother's arm. The kid was in shock.

He turned to Anesia. "Did she recognize the guy who shot at her?"

"No. And if Sasha hadn't gone out the dog door behind her, he probably would've succeeded."

Jenna gasped. "Anesia, maybe you shouldn't say things like that in front of—"

Anesia's gaze snapped to Jenna, then Cole, then back to Jenna. "I'm not going to coddle anyone, Jenna. We've always been honest and open about everything. This terrified my daughter, yes, but she *saw* what happened. I can't change that. Can't take it away." She wrapped Zoya in a fierce hug as tears pooled in her eyes. "First, Zoya witnessed a murder. A murder, Jenna. And I can't do anything about that. Can't take those horrible images away. And now? Now someone has tried to murder *her*! Again! You might not think I'm handling this correctly, but let's face it." The tears were streaming down her face now as the volume of her voice grew. "This is our reality."

Jenna's jaw dropped. And then snapped shut. She looked to Cole.

He shook his head. Hoping she'd get the hint.

But she spoke anyway. "Anesia, I'm sorry. I didn't mean that you weren't handling this right, I was just—"

"Trying to help. I know." Anesia stood, Zoya attached to her arm like glue. "Let's just drop it. I never should've snapped at you."

"Ladies, emotions are running a little high right now, and we've neglected the most important thing."

Anesia's fiery gaze focused on him.

"We need to pray." He grabbed Andie's and Jenna's hands. "You guys know I'm still new at this. But—"

Andie squeezed his hand bringing his gaze down to hers. Tears brimmed her eyes. In a sudden rush of emotion, Cole was back on the side of Sultana, a treacherous mountain in the Alaskan Range. Stranded. With nowhere to go. And two injured women to care for. No matter how hard he'd tried, he couldn't do it on his own then, and he couldn't handle *this* on his own now. They needed to turn it over to the only One who could help them through.

He gave Andie a slight nod and closed his eyes. "Father, we don't understand what's going on. But we come to You seeking wisdom and guidance and protection. We can't do this alone. Please protect Anesia and Zoya, help us not to fear, but to trust in You. And Father, help us to forgive, just as You have forgiven us. In Jesus' name, Amen."

As he opened his eyes, his gaze was drawn to Zoya first. Her face was bland. No expression. One hand clung to her mom, the other methodically stroked her dog's back.

Sasha stood by the edge of the couch like a sentinel, protecting her girl. Her ears on alert. Eyes darting around the room at each little noise. This animal had saved Zoya's life. How many people would've risked everything to do the same?

"Thanks, Cole." His wife wrapped an arm around his waist. "Maybe I should fix something hot to drink for everyone." When no response came from Anesia or Zoya, Jenna glanced at Cole— fear and hurt evident in her eyes—before heading into the kitchen.

Andie went and sat beside Zoya's stiff form. Didn't say anything. Just sat there.

"Zoya?" She'd already been through enough, but he needed answers. "I need to ask you some questions."

A nod. But she wouldn't look him in the eyes.

"Can you tell me what the guy looked like?"

"Tall. Like a stick. Ugly. Mean face."

"Did you see what he was wearing?"

"All black."

"Color of his eyes, or hair?"

"Black. Awful black."

Cole ran a hand across his jaw. Not a lot to go on. Poor kid. "Anything else you noticed?"

She stared at Sasha. "I didn't have time. Didn't even know he was there. Just heard that sound, like he was getting ready to shoot, and I looked up." A tear slid down her face. "I don't want to talk about it anymore."

And like that, an invisible wall shot up. Gone was the sweet girl who loved to talk to him about Jesus. Gone was the face that so easily offered a smile. Gone was the soft-spoken encourager . . .

Andie was right. The experiences were ripping Zoya apart. *God, we could really use Your help.*

He nodded at Anesia and left the room. Right now, all he wanted to do was punch somebody. And worse. He wanted to mete out punishment—to serve vengeance on whoever stole the innocence and life out of that precious kid. And the FBI. He knew they were busy, desperate to bring the ring down, but Cole felt more pressure from them to keep everyone safe. He was only one man. And these people meant everything to him.

A knock on the door broke through his anger. He walked back to the front. Checked through the peephole. Detective Sheldon stood on the porch. More official vehicles were parked along the driveway.

"Anesia, I need to disarm the system and talk to the detective."

She gave him the code.

After the detective entered, several seconds passed before he spoke. "We found blood. Hastily covered up with snow. But there nonetheless. Footprints seem to have been brushed away, so we haven't found enough to get a cast yet, but we'll keep searching. Appears to be at least two men."

"Anything else?" Cole eyed the shocked pair on the couch. "Zoya said she only saw one."

"Not yet. But the team is out there looking. We'll keep a car here with surveillance around the clock. Apparently the second man came to help the shooter. That's all we can guess at right now." The detective turned to Anesia. "Please let me know if your daughter remembers anything else."

"Thank you, Detective."

They headed out the door.

Cole stood on the threshold, watching the men leave. How could he protect them and find what he needed for AMI at the same time? The pressure built in his head.

Sean raced toward them and took all the porch steps in one. He nodded to the detective. "You might want to hear this." He bent at the waist to catch his breath.

Cole closed the door behind him so they could talk on the porch. "What?"

"I went around the perimeter of the property. And I found this"—he lifted a tiny, plastic-encased macrochip—"next to some Snickers wrappers."

"Did you touch anything else? Were there any footprints?" The detective crossed his arms.

"No, I tried to leave it all untouched, and yes." Sean straightened. "Appeared to be at least two sets." He zeroed in on Cole. "How are they?"

"Not good." He shook his head. Sean was a good man. His concern was evident. And his anger.

The detective sighed and turned to Sergeant Roberts. "Go with Sean and check it out, collect all the evidence."

"Mind if I have a look at that?" Cole lifted the chip up to the light. "Detective, I think you need to come back inside."

"Major Maddox, there's something you need to know. That's not the first one we've found."

"Excuse me?" His anger burned. "And you didn't think it was important enough to mention? Do you even know what this is? Because I can tell you right now, sir, that this isn't just a murder investigation." He glared at the detective. "It's a matter of national security."

RICK
January 30
Anchorage, Alaska
7:11 p.m.

An elephant sat on his chest. The pills weren't working. Neither was the amber liquid in the shot glass in front of him.

The spirits had cursed him. And now there was nothing he could do about it.

The phone rang.

"Yeah?"

"We have a mess that needs to be cleaned up."

Please, don't let it be Zoya. "What?"

"Our man was unsuccessful today."

He let out the breath he'd been holding. So Zoya was still alive.

"You need to dispose of him. And I'm putting you in charge of eliminating our problem."

"Sir?"

"The girl. She's too skittish. And from the way she's reacted when he makes himself known, she definitely recognizes him. You need to get rid of the witness. No questions. No buts. Just do it."

Maybe the spirits hadn't cursed him after all. Was this the way out? "I'll take care of it."

"Good. The sooner the better."

"Yes, sir."

"And Rick?"

Here it comes. His chest tightened to the point he didn't think he'd ever be able to take another breath. "I'm listening."

"You're my best man. My second-in-command."

"Thank you."

"Don't make me kill you too."

The vise around his heart squeezed harder.

"Get the job done."

ANESIA
January 30
Naltsiine Kennels
9:31 p.m.

The nightmare just wouldn't end. After Cole spoke with the FBI, another set of armed and uniformed people came to her house. With more questions. Always the questions. New ones, and the old ones. Over and over and over.

If Anesia didn't know any better, she'd think they suspected *her* of stealing AMI. The only thing going for her was the fact that all the boot prints they collected were from men's boots.

Andie and Zoya sat side by side in a big overstuffed chair. Legs all tucked up under them, their heads leaning together. Neither one speaking. Would the trauma to these two never end?

Cole's voice echoed off the wood floors. "Thank you for coming. I'll be in touch." He closed the door on the last batch of FBI personnel and walked toward her.

Jenna wrapped an arm around Anesia's shoulders. "They've cleared you for now, Anesia. But this doesn't look good. Somehow Dan's brother, your property, and tiny macrochips . . . it's all connected to stealing AMI."

Anesia placed her hands on her hips in exasperation. "I'm a mother for crying out loud! And I own a dog kennel! Why on earth would I steal Marc's stupid program?"

Jenna squeezed her shoulder and went to sit on the couch.

Great. Now she'd hurt Jenna. The one person who'd always stood beside her. "I'm sorry."

Her friend looked up at her. "I understand. It feels like a fresh stab wound every time AMI is brought up. I'm thankful Marc turned around in the end, but the consequences keep following us. Such destructive power." Jenna shook her head. "I should be apologizing. Here we are facing an unknown enemy and I'm feeling sorry for myself."

Andie stood up and joined her mom. "Daddy wouldn't want us focusing on all the negative stuff. God's brought us so much good from all this mess." Her spunky *syats'ea* eyed each person in the room. "Cole and Sean for starters."

"You can't argue with her there." Cole smiled and patted Sean on the back.

Anesia's heart beat a little faster. Sean. The complexity of the man unnerved her at times. As she learned about him in layers, the more she trusted him. Liked him. As their gazes collided, he frowned. She'd embarrassed him by not responding last night. Maybe even hurt him. Would she ever get the chance to let him know how much she respected him? How drawn she was to him?

"Mom?" Zoya rested her head in her hands on the arm of the chair.

She walked over and knelt in front of her daughter. "You okay, sweetie?"

"My head hurts. And I'm really tired."

"Let me get you some medicine. It's been too long of a day and you just had a concussion." Was that only yesterday?

"I don't want to be alone."

"Okay. I'm not going anywhere."

"No. I don't want to be alone when I sleep."

"Would you like to sleep in my room?" Her heart broke at the forlorn look on Zoya's face.

"Yeah." Zoya lifted her face. "Auntie Jenna?"

"Yeah, Punkin?" Jenna walked closer.

"Can Andie stay for a few days?"

"Sure thing. Cole and I already decided that we were going to stay here for a while. And when you're feeling better, you can come stay at our house too, okay?"

Zoya nodded. Exhaustion and grief and fear all mixed in her eyes.

"Let's get you two settled and then us adults are going to talk for a while, all right?" Anesia lifted her daughter's limp hand and tugged. The poor kid had no energy. "Hey Cole, would you mind carrying Zoya for me? I don't think she's got any strength left."

Cole was at her side in an instant and lifted her precious child into his arms. Sean stood watching. His hands flexed at his sides. The muscle in his jaw twitched. If only she could read what was going on in that head of his. She turned to the stairs.

Not a sound came from Zoya. It was like she'd given up. Once they made it to Anesia's room, Cole laid her on the bed.

"I don't want to be alone." Zoya's words were hollow. Full of fear and dread.

"I'll stay with you." Andie slid onto the bed next to her. "Don't worry. I won't leave. Not even to go to the bathroom. Not until your mom is here, okay?"

Zoya nodded and clutched Andie's hand.

Anesia kissed the tops of both of their heads. "I love you. We'll be downstairs."

As Anesia left the room, the anguish in her daughter's eyes wrapped her heart in a tight squeeze. Would they ever get Zoya back?

She grabbed the rail and started to descend the stairs, but stopped on the second step. *God, I don't know what You're doing, but it sure would be nice to have a little help. Forgive me for my doubts, Lord. But I'm so afraid.*

Tears clogged her throat, but they wouldn't come. And for once, she really *needed* to have a good cry. Lowering herself to sit, she released a long breath.

A shadow rounded the corner.

Sean.

He looked up into her eyes. No words were exchanged, but he got the message. As he approached, he took time with each step. Reaching her, he lowered himself to the step below her in silence.

The ball was in her court.

Her fingers fidgeted.

He sat. Patience and something undefined written all over his face.

Maybe it was time to just let it all out. "Sean, I need to apologize. I couldn't collect my thoughts last night and everything overwhelmed me. I never wanted to hurt you. And . . . hopefully you see now how much I . . . need you."

"Don't worry about it. It was entirely my fault." His words were too stiff. Even for him.

On impulse, she reached out and grabbed his hand. Their fingers intertwined.

"Anesia—"

"Sean, let me talk before I lose my nerve, okay?" Heart racing, she tried to find the words in her brain to express what she was thinking. Feeling. But the more she sat, the more her tongue tied itself into knots. "Oh, good heavens, you'd think I'd be better at this."

"It's all right. You don't have to say anything else." He tugged on his hand to pull it free, but she refused to let go. "Too much trauma has encapsulated your family."

"No. I *do* have to." She tightened her grip until she thought for sure she'd lose all feeling in her fingers. "You and I . . . what I mean is . . . I haven't been attracted to anyone . . ." Ugh. She beat her forehead against the wall. The memory of his arms around her urged her on. She needed him. Wanted him in her life. Now more than ever.

Start over. One word at a time.

But she couldn't. The words just wouldn't come. She looked to Sean for help.

He squeezed her hand. His face softened. "When no one is trying to kill you and there's some semblance of order around here again, we'll talk. As much as I'd like to have this conversation right now, I'm more focused on keeping you and Zoya safe."

She leaned against him. Even on different steps, their heads were at the same level. "Thank you. That means more than you'll probably ever know. I don't know how much more of this stress I can take. But I want you to know my feelings are . . . well . . . they're real. And I wanted to tell you."

"Well, it's about time!" Jenna's voice drifted from down the hall. "Ow! Cole! Stop it."

"Jenna, you need to keep your little nose out of this. Let Sean handle it." Cole appeared around the corner. "Go ahead, Sean. We'll just wait for you in the kitchen." He looked back toward his wife. "Where we can't eavesdrop."

Anesia pulled a Kleenex out of her pocket, wadded it up, and threw it at Cole.

Sean pulled her in for a hug and kissed her forehead.

And, if only for a moment, that tender action eased her fear.

CHAPTER TWENTY-NINE

SEAN
January 30
Naltsiine Kennels
9:50 p.m.

They entered the kitchen hand in hand. The change between him and Anesia all but electrified the air around him. But he felt her stiffen and attempt to withdraw. What held her back? Dan's death? Or was it something else?

Women had chased him for years because he was wealthy. He'd enjoyed the attention in college, but after learning their intentions, their greed, his broken heart decided to wall itself off. There'd been plenty of rich socialites to hang off his arm for big events—his father made sure of that, had to impress the media with pictures—but he never allowed himself to discover if any of them had anything besides fluff and greed inside their head.

This new Sean—the real Sean—living in North Pole, Alaska, opened up his mind and heart. Anesia captured it. Almost from their first meeting. Intelligent, beautiful, independent. She was the epitome of a Proverbs 31 woman to him. And for the first time in years, he allowed himself to dream about a future with a family.

This family.

But the anger returned. And the tension. To have a future, they needed to catch the killer and eliminate the threat to the Naltsiine girls.

"Sean?" Cole's look turned serious again. "Do you mind taking shifts with me?"

"Shifts?" His introspection had made him miss something important. "I'm sorry."

"Not a problem. I was just saying if we took shifts, one of us would stay awake at all times until they catch the shooter."

"Good idea. You know I'll do whatever it takes."

"Thanks. I know the ladies will feel safer that way." Cole glanced at Anesia. "We all will."

Anesia gasped. "The dogs. I completely forgot about the dogs."

"Can it wait until morning?" Cole scratched his chin.

"They haven't been fed today. And by now, the kennel must be a mess. No one has been out there for hours."

Sean raised his eyebrows in question to Cole. "Think it's safe? With all the chaos around here earlier, do you really think he'd come back?"

"I don't know. If he's desperate enough, he might."

Anesia glanced up at Sean. Pleading. Those dogs were her livelihood. Her family. And she probably needed a small sense of normalcy. Some manual labor to get her mind off the horrors of the day.

Sean decided to take the risk. "What if Anesia and I work together? We can finish it pretty quick."

"What about Derek? Wasn't he here earlier?"

Cole's military stance told him the direction of the man's thoughts.

Anesia shook her head. "He only works for me two hours on Sundays. After the police got here, I saw one of them talking to him and I haven't seen him since."

Jenna placed a hand on Cole's arm. "What if I helped as well? That way you'd be here with the girls, protecting them. The three of us could knock out the work in the kennel. Right now a little physical activity would be good."

"Do you have an extra sidearm?" Sean's gaze connected with Cole's again. No words were necessary to convey his intent to protect the women at all costs.

"Let me get it."

No words passed between Anesia and Jenna as they trekked to the mudroom and geared up for the work outside. Sean watched with dismay. So much heartache for these people.

Cole came back with a holster. "I'm gonna set the alarm as soon as you all are out. Anesia's got floodlights out there and I've already turned them on. Got your phone?"

"Right here." Sean patted his pocket. Prayerfully he wouldn't need it or the gun, but it was better to be safe than sorry.

"You know how to use that?" He pointed to the holster.

Unfortunately. "Yeah. My father's always been obsessed with guns. Even have a shooting range in our basement."

"Good."

Sean wished he felt the same sentiment. Coveralls, boots, and coat went on without much thought. Weird how quick routine made a habit. He didn't even mind all the layers anymore. Placing the gun in an accessible pocket, he walked toward the ladies and out the door.

Fear clung to the night air. They'd been walking for a couple minutes and silence surrounded them. Maybe he should start a conversation.

As they entered the gate to the kennel, the dogs welcomed them with yaps and jumping up and down. They moved as quick as they could, going from one dog, one kennel to another.

All in silence.

Time to instigate. Jenna took food to the farthest of the litters. Maybe this would give them a few minutes to talk. Sean's shoulders burned from the constant shoveling, but it seemed easier to talk about difficult things when his body was focused on the task at hand. "You know, Zoya mentioned to me that she wanted to make her dad proud." Maybe, if he and Anesia didn't have to look at one another, she might open up more.

"Really?" She stopped her movement. "I had no idea."

"Yes. She mentioned her dad had been a champion, and she wanted to be a champion just like him. And just like you."

Anesia poured food into another bowl. "Did she . . . did she say anything else?"

He took a deep breath. Looked down at the shovel. "That she wanted to prove her dad's name was a good one. And that you and he not being married shouldn't mar how people think of you. She wanted to show everyone what an amazing mom you are and that your work as a breeder should be renowned."

This time Anesia stopped. She walked closer to Sean. "She really said all that?"

"Yeah. I thought you knew what drove her."

"I just thought she loved it. And loved the dogs . . ."

"She does, but she loves her parents more."

She squatted next to Thyme and Garlic, rubbing the dogs' ears.

He dropped the shovel and did the same. "Anesia. Zoya wants the world to know how much she values you. And how much she values her dad. You're both a part of her. And by showing every-one how precious you are—the pride she has in you—it will also boost her own confidence. Because that's where she came from. It's her heritage. She doesn't want to be known as the girl whose father died. She wants to be known as Anesia Naltsiine's daughter, champion sprint dog racer."

They resumed their work. Had he said too much? Or was she just mulling it all over?

She dumped another measure of food into a bowl. "I guess you understand her better than I do. The whole father thing, huh?" She huffed. "Sorry. I'm not upset with you. Just disappointed that I didn't know the whole story." They worked in companionable silence for several minutes. "Why don't you tell me about *your* father."

"Not much to tell." Scooping poop seemed way too appropriate for this conversation. "My father is powerful, wealthy, and a control freak."

"Wow. So how do you *really* feel?"

"You're quite good at sarcasm, aren't you?"

She laughed, a beautiful sound against the frigid and eerie night.

"But you're right. I guess I have anger issues. And God's been prodding me to forgive him. You'd think walking thousands of miles would cure me of that. But I'm afraid I'm still working on it."

"Forgive, huh?" She shook her head. "Please don't go there."

Could this be the stumbling block for the beautiful lady in front of him? Her tough and independent spirit he admired, but there was always something just under the surface that he'd catch a glimpse of—something he knew needed to be dealt with. He caught a glimpse of the totem standing sentinel in the corner of the kennel. "Okay then, I've been curious about that totem. Where did it come from?"

The tension eased from her face. "My great-grandfather carved it for me when I was little. Naltsiine means 'Down from the sky clan,' so the bottom six carvings represent the generations my great-grandfather knew. The top one is me."

"With the dogs carved into your sides."

She let out a brief laugh. "Yes. He knew my love of dogs and racing before I even understood it myself. He predicted I would be a great champion."

"And look at you now." He rested on the shovel and looked at her. Hoping once again to bring a smile to her face.

She didn't continue. Just shrugged her shoulders. "You have a lot in common with my kid. She thinks you're cool, by the way.

And I'm glad she's got you to talk to if she needs it." The queen of changing the subject was still on the throne.

"Thank you, Anesia. That means a lot." Another shovelful of poop landed in the wheelbarrow. At least it froze pretty quick in these temps. Made it much easier to clean up.

"I still can't believe that someone tried to shoot my baby. And that she witnessed a man murdered in these woods! I can't even protect my own child. What is the world coming to?"

Sean leaned his weight on the shovel for several seconds. "I don't know. You probably weren't even looking for an answer, but I'm glad God brought me here when He did."

She paused in her work and gave him a brief glimpse into her eyes. "Me too, Sean." Before he could respond, she broke the connection and went back to work. "So, I take it you and your dad aren't real close?"

"There's nothing to be close to. He's like a machine."

"Ouch."

"Sad, but true. I got over wanting a relationship with my father a long time ago. I turned my heart toward my heavenly Father, and that helped. Although I must admit, and forewarn you, I have a severe temper. It just takes a lot to get me riled."

"Really?" This brought her head up for a moment with a half-smile before she focused back on the dogs. "You always seem so calm and collected."

"Well, I try. But I am Irish, you know."

She shook her head and laughed. "I've always heard that Irish people and red-headed people and whatever other stereotype you can come up with means they have a bad temper. But frankly, you haven't seen a temper until you've seen an Athabaskan woman in full-force rage."

"Oh really? I guess that means I should watch myself?"

"Be afraid, Sean. Be very afraid."

Their banter died off and the silence of the frozen night surrounded them. Her expression fell as she poured herself back into her work. He imagined where her thoughts were taking her. Keep the conversation going. Get her mind off the events.

"So, what about Peter? He was your last full-time employee, right?"

But instead of bringing a smile back to her face, his words brought a face full of grief. "He was killed during the time Jenna and Andie were in danger. Just an innocent bystander. And they killed him."

Again Sean wished the ground would swallow him up. He wanted to get her mind off all the junk going on, and he brought up another source of pain. "I'm so sorry, Anesia. Were you very close?"

"Our families had been friends for years. We all trusted him. And he loved to work. He protected the girls and the dogs like they were his very own. I miss him."

Was there more to Anesia's relationship with Peter? Is that why she held herself at a distance? Not wanting to engage her heart with the hired help again?

The information sat in his gut like a rock. Jealousy began to rear its ugly green head and squeeze its way around Sean's heart. Did he really care that much?

His phone buzzed and then rang, interrupting his thoughts. He checked the caller ID—it was Cole. Oh no. They didn't need any more bad news. "Hello?"

"Hey, it's Cole." Instead of the terse voice he expected, Cole sounded almost chipper. "The police just called. Tell Anesia that they've caught the shooter."

"Wow. That's great news—"

"Not so much. He's dead."

SLIM
January 31
Fairbanks, Alaska
6:35 p.m.

"So I hear you're having a bit of trouble?"

The man thought he could work him over. They'd soon see who came out on top. "Not a bit. Have you called to tell me you've agreed to my price?"

A dramatic sigh. "You're trying my patience, young man. Although . . . I do respect your entrepreneurialism."

"Whatever."

"Don't get smart with me. I know the police acquired one of the chips!"

One day he'd have the same power this guy possessed. One day soon. "You can't believe everything your little stooges tell you." So one of the copies fell into the snow. Big deal. He had it all under control.

"And I'm just supposed to believe you when you tell me that you have the entire program? Who do you think you're dealing with?"

Checkmate. "An intelligent man who wants to provide the program he promised his wealthy buyer."

The hearty laugh that echoed through the phone sent chills up his spine. No time for fear. His Ma had always said that if you wanted something bad enough, you just needed the courage to take it. He wouldn't be bullied anymore.

"I'll give you seven days. Then I'm selling to someone else."

He slammed the phone down into its cradle. That felt good. Real good.

Now who was the one with the power?

ZOYA
February 2
Naltsiine Kennels
10:02 a.m.

Mom sat at her desk, talking on the phone. I stood outside the doorway, waiting for her to hang up.

You can do this, Zoya. I closed my eyes.

Did I want to do this?

Andie waited upstairs, how would I explain this to her?

No, I wouldn't. Couldn't. Wait until the weekend. That would buy me some time. Time . . . if only I could have more of it.

A sigh that started in the very depths of my soul sprang forth. *Let's just get this over with.*

Mom hung up.

I stepped inside.

"Mom?"

She looked up. "Hey, Zoya. Come on in." She stood from her chair and placed a book on the built-in shelf.

"I—"

She glanced over and frowned. "What's wrong?"

Get it over with.

"I don't want to race this weekend."

I could see the surprise flash across her face.

Please, don't ask questions.

She stared, as if searching my eyes.

What did she see? I looked down to my feet. *Don't let her read your expression.*

She nodded. "Okay. Sit."

I obeyed. But what would I say? I couldn't explain . . .

"What's this about?" She folded her hands and placed them on the desk. Then paused. "Are you scared something will happen?"

"Sort of." I kept my gaze on my sock-covered feet. Best not open the door of conversation.

"What's that mean?"

I sighed. "I'm just worried. That's all." I closed my eyes. "And I don't want to race this weekend."

She kept looking at me. Didn't say a word. I could almost feel her stare burn a hole through me. *Just stay focused.*

"Please, Mom. Don't make me race." My voice cracked. *Get it over with . . .*

"*Make* you race? When did I ever have to make you race?"

I could tell her that it was when I started getting mysterious notes. I could have said that it was since I had witnessed a murder . . .

But I didn't. Couldn't. Not without risking her life. I kept silent. Hoping.

Praying.

God, if You care, show me now . . .

No! You can't give Him another chance.

"Okay. If that's what you really want. I have to admit I was worried, and unsure how to approach the subject. I just don't want to squash your dreams. Not again."

I nodded. Didn't—couldn't—look up. I stood. Then walked toward the door.

Something inside me crushed. Like my heart began collapsing. What had I done?

"Zoya." Mom walked up and touched my shoulder. "You're not doing this because of me, are you?"

I held my breath.

She sighed. And waited. "Is this what *you* want?"

Nod. You have to nod.

I did.

Then walked into the hall.

Why was this so hard? Why was *life* so hard?

Andie met me at the top of the steps. "Hey, wanna check on the dogs?"

Again I nodded. Distraction . . . Distraction . . . Distraction . . .

As we put on coats and boots, I could see Mom watching us.

Don't let her read your expression . . . Keep going . . .

I knew I had to keep going. I knew that was the right thing to do.

But was it?

We walked outside. The air was cold, almost threatening. As was everything now. I pulled my jacket up to cover my nose. Couldn't wait to get into the barn.

Stop it, Zoya. Just keep going . . .

We were soon there. I felt so . . . strange. What was wrong with me? What had happened?

The past couple weeks came flooding back. Was that why Andie seemed so worried all the time? Was it because I had changed for good? Did she think I would stay like this forever?

Did *I* think I would stay like this forever?

The realization hit me like a ton of bricks.

I *had* changed. For the worse.

But how could I fix it? How did I find that peace, that sense of normality, I'd had before?

One answer came.

God.

Could I let Him in? I wanted to . . .

"I'll be right back, I'm gonna go check on Eklutna." Andie walked outside without another word. Had she seen my doubt? Did she know what was going on inside of me? No. How could she?

But couldn't she hear the screaming in my head? *Andie, don't leave me! Don't leave me alone!*

I could do this. I could.

I walked around in the barn, thinking. Something in my boot squished. I took another step. Something was inside it.

My brow furrowed.

I looked down, then bent over to take it off. Once it was off, I held it upside down.

A piece of paper flittered out.

Go away. Run. Or you'll never see your mom again.

I stared at the tiny piece of shriveled up paper.

How . . . ?

They caught the shooter . . . he was gone. Permanently. So how was he still giving me notes?

I clutched it to my chest. Eyes closed. Heart pounding.

God, why? Why are You doing this? I can't handle this!

The little voice inside me screamed. *"Leave. And don't* ever *come back."*

DETECTIVE SHELDON
10:16 a.m.

Another body. The shooter.

Dave paced the office floor. Papers, files, photos cluttered his desk.

What was he missing?

The FBI had already moved passed the murders. Something else—something bigger—took their attention.

He trusted his instincts, and they told him it was all connected.

One big question remained: Who was the mastermind?

CHAPTER THIRTY

SEAN
February 2
Naltsiine Kennels
11:14 a.m.

He'd almost finished cleaning up the kennel when Andie and Zoya arrived, Dasha and Sasha on their heels.

The dogs full of yap and bouncing through the snow. Andie all jabber and animated hand-motions. Zoya . . . quiet and sad.

He placed the shovel inside the tool shed. How could he reach the little girl who'd gripped his heart like no one ever had?

Her face seemed devoid of emotion, but Sean saw past all that. So much sadness. So much fear. All stuffed down.

It broke his heart.

"Hey, Sean!" Andie waved, grabbed Zoya's hand, and dragged her over.

"Well, if it isn't the two prettiest girls in Alaska. How are you two?" He kept his tone light. But every time he tried to catch Zoya's gaze, she stared at the ground.

"We're good. Just a little bored. Wanted to check on the dogs." She leaned in and whispered to Sean behind her hand. "It usually helps cheer her up."

Zoya's eyes darted around the woods.

Sean whispered back. "Good idea." He wrapped an arm around Zoya's shoulder. "How's my Sunshine doing? Looking a bit peaked today, I'd say."

She gave him a weak half grin in return. "A little. Maybe."

"Not sleeping well?"

"Not really."

"Does it help to know they've caught the murderer?"

She shrugged and stared out beyond the fence.

"You know, maybe talking about it will help." He sat on one of the logs they used in the kennel as benches, patting the space beside him. "Andie and I are here to help. We're both great listeners." He winked at Andie.

Andie immediately caught the hint and sat on his other side. She leaned her head toward Sean's and smiled. "See? We're all ears."

He watched Zoya's shoulders slump. Like the weight of the world began to bear down upon her. She paced in front of them, tapping out a rhythm on her leg with her gloved hands. "I don't think you can understand."

"Try us."

She opened her mouth then shut it. Opened it again. And just when Sean thought for sure she was about to spill her guts, she shut it again. Frowned. And he could almost feel the walls come up again.

Lord, help!

That's when it hit him. *This* was the reason he'd struggled so long and hard with anger. It wasn't about him. It was about this. This moment. This place. And this sweet, young girl. *Lord . . . You're amazing.*

He turned to Andie. "Hey, did you know the Bible says it's okay to be angry?"

Andie's eyes widened. "Really?"

"Yep. But it says in your anger don't sin."

"Oh, yeah, like righteous anger, huh? I've heard Pastor say something like that."

Sean nodded. Zoya fiddled with a stick in the snow but stayed close, eyes on the ground. *Lord, please help her hear.*

"So . . . don't sin."

He turned back to Andie. "Right."

"Does that mean we shouldn't let the anger make us hurt someone?"

"Or make us hurt ourselves. Because if we let anger go on too long, dig in too deep, pretty soon that voice is so loud inside us that we can't hear God's still small voice. He's still there, talking to us, speaking truth to our hearts, but we can't hear Him."

"Wow. That'd be awful!"

"It is. I know that because I've been there. I let my anger at my father grow so strong it got between me and God. And God's not going to force His way in where He's not welcome. That's not how He works. But He's always there. Always. Waiting for us to welcome Him in. Gently prodding. Quietly speaking to us."

Andie leaned back, her serious gaze fixed on him. "I hadn't ever thought of it like that. But you're right. Whenever I'm mad, all I can hear is the negative thoughts screaming in my head."

Insightful girl. "Screaming is right. Every time I allow that rage to boil up, it's like screaming, sometimes almost shrieking in my head. How on earth can we hear anything else once we've allowed the angry voice to reign?"

He risked a look to Zoya. She stood still, eyes trained on him. She opened her mouth—

Dasha and Sasha started barking up a storm.

Zoya's attention snapped to the fence around the kennel.

So much for her opening up. Maybe she at least heard his words.

Andie hopped up and went over to the dogs. "It's okay, Zoya. They're not worried about a human. Remember, the shooter's gone." She pointed to their beautiful huskies. "Look. They're sniffing around Morphine's neck and barking."

The fear on Zoya's face disappeared and she turned her attention to Andie and the dogs. "What is it, girl?" She petted Sasha's neck.

Sasha barked and yipped and yapped at Zoya like she was carrying on a conversation.

Sean had never seen anything quite like it. "She's very intelligent, isn't she?"

Andie tried to calm Dasha. "Yeah, and hyper. And protective."

"So why are they barking?"

Andie shook her head. "I'm not quite sure . . ."

They all turned to watch Zoya. She listened to Sasha and watched her movements. Sasha continued to bark and kept pushing her nose onto Morphine's neck.

Zoya talked low and soothing to both dogs as they jumped around. Morphine appeared uncomfortable. Sasha perturbed.

"What is it, Sasha? Show me, girl. What's got you all upset?" Zoya continued her soft words and petted both dogs.

Sasha shoved her snout into Morphine's neck again, pushing Zoya's hand closer.

Zoya probed the spot, leaning in closer. "Sean, come here."

He approached.

"Look. There's something on Morphine's neck. It's really small, but the place looks infected."

As he gazed over Zoya's shoulder, he saw what Sasha had found. "Let me get the first aid kit." He ran over to the shed, grabbed it, and headed back to the dogs. Opening it up, he searched the contents. Then he pulled out a magnifying glass and tweezers.

"Let me take a closer look. Andie, will you hold Dasha and Sasha? Zoya, I need you to hold Morphine still." The girls obeyed and together they worked over the leader of the Painkiller Litter.

The girls' curiosity kept them pressed close as he examined the wound. Sure enough, below the dog's winter coat was a tiny red welt. Fiery red and swollen.

"I'm going to grab an alcohol swab, keep him steady."

"Okay." Zoya tightened her hold.

After wiping down the area, Morphine jerked in his grasp, shaking his head as fast as he could. Sean and Zoya worked to steady him. Clearly the dog was bothered by the tiny area on his neck.

"It's okay, boy. Let me clean this up and we'll be all done." Sean tried to wipe the spot again, when Morphine barked and snapped. The wound popped open and blood and pus oozed out.

"Steady, Morphine." He turned to Andie. "Would you go get Anesia, please?"

"Yes, sir." She dashed away.

"Zoya, I'll straddle his back end, and you hold his head. Looks like something might've gotten under the skin and it's infected."

His young helper nodded.

Maybe he should wait for Anesia, but he couldn't leave the poor dog like this. He might not be all that experienced, but he could at least try. Holding the magnifying glass up to the spot, he wiped down the tiny spot again and applied pressure. When he lifted the gauze, a tiny corner of something poked out of the wound.

Sean leaned in closer with the magnifying glass. It didn't appear to be glass or a splinter. He used the tweezers to pinch the edge. With a gentle tug, he pulled the obstruction loose.

Zoya gasped.

Morphine wiggled out of their grasp and shook his head. He sat on his rear and barked at Zoya seeming content with his circumstances.

Sean turned the tiny piece of plastic back and forth under the magnifying glass. All the puzzle pieces scrambled in his head. It didn't make sense.

But one thing was sure. They'd found another macrochip. Implanted in one of Anesia's prize dogs.

ZOYA
1:23 p.m.

Cole bent over Mint Chocolate Chip and stroked her head. "Good girl. Stay calm." She wiggled and squirmed within his grasp. Her whimpers made me feel like my heart jammed into my throat.

Poor thing. I hoped she was okay. None of the other dogs we'd checked so far had gotten seriously infected in the incision area, but Mint Chocolate Chip looked like she might have.

Who had done this to the poor little things?

I shook my head. People. Nobody had a heart anymore.

I petted Sasha, who stood beside me like a body guard. "Good girl." I couldn't believe it when they had found the chips. Those two were smart.

Anguish twirled in the pit of my stomach.

Go away. Run. Or you'll never see your mom again.

I closed my eyes. A habit now.

Stop thinking about it!

Anger churned in my gut. They had gotten that close. In our barn. To my dogs. How far would they go? Was I putting my family, the dogs, Sean in danger?

The note haunted me. Haunted my thoughts. Haunted my heart. What would they do to Mom if I did stay? Could Sean or Cole save her? Could the FBI save her? No. If they had gotten this close without us even suspecting . . .

But I couldn't tell anyone about the notes . . .

I sighed. Too many "ifs." Too many "maybes." Not enough assurance.

I grabbed onto Sasha's collar.

I had to leave. But when? How could I without anyone finding me? I didn't want to be alone. I could bring the dogs. But someone would hear me. Or see me leaving.

At night?

No. I didn't want to be out in the dark. By myself. With murderers spying on me.

That realization hurt.

I was going to die. No matter what. Those men watched me. Probably all the time. How could I run away without Mom or those men finding out?

I couldn't.

My eyes closed. No. I wouldn't think about it. Just leave and get it over with.

Leave tonight.

Cole smiled as he got the macrochip out from Mint's neck. "Good girl. It's okay."

He passed the chip to Auntie Jenna.

I hoped night would come soon.

If I got murdered, I got murdered.

But I had to save Mom. And I had to do it soon.

ANESIA
2:58 p.m.

The kennel was in an uproar. Cole had pulled more than thirty chips out of her dogs already.

Anesia soothed and petted each of her dogs as they waited for the vet. Who on earth had done this? And why? More than that, why'd they choose *her* dogs?

Since the chip they already found on her property held part of the AMI programming, she could guess what was on the other chips. Would they accuse her of being involved? Was she in danger of being arrested?

What would happen to Zoya?

The stress over the murder and shooting hadn't left her system yet, even though they'd caught the shooter. And now this. What happened to her quiet little world?

Sean jogged over to her. "Cole wanted you to know that the FBI are on their way over."

"Great."

"What?"

"Oh, nothing. I'm sorry, Sean. I'm just a little sick of all this. Who implants sprint racing dogs with chips that have top secret military programming?" She shook her head and walked toward another litter.

Sean followed. "It's ingenious, really."

"What?" She shot a look over her shoulder. Whose side was he on anyway?

"Implanting the chips."

"Sean Connolly"—she thrust her hands onto her hips—"what on earth are you talking about?"

"Whoever did this. I'm not saying what they did was right, but think about it. Placing invaluable information that they don't want anyone else to find on macrochips, encasing them in plastic, and implanting them in your dogs."

She threw another heated look his way.

"They did their research. They knew how well you took care of your dogs. Knew how much they meant to you. What lengths you would go to making sure nothing happened to them."

She whirled on him then. "So you're saying I should take it as a compliment that they chose my kennel of dogs? Is that what you're saying?" She knew she was being ridiculous, but the whole thing burned her up. She had to take out her temper on someone. Sean happened to be the unlucky recipient.

His eyes grew wide. "Hey, I'm sorry."

Her rage evaporated. "No, Sean. I'm sorry." She glanced at his eyes before moving toward another dog. "I just don't get it. First the murder. Then the shooting here. Now this! Has everyone gone insane?"

"Anesia!" Cole's voice came from across the kennel, halting Sean's response.

He followed her over to Cole and the FBI agent who'd arrived. Her friend's calm, quiet presence soothed the edge of her nerves, even though she still wanted to throttle someone.

The agent studied her. "Ms. Naltsiine. Sorry we have to meet again under these circumstances." The man didn't even shake her hand, just started writing on his notepad. "I need to know who has access to your dogs."

"Well, other than Zoya, Jenna, and Andie? No one except my employees. Sean"—she pointed beside her—"Joe, he's over there by Jenna, and Derek. It's his day off today."

"Ever had any trouble from any of them?"

"No. I trust my employees."

"But who else would know the code to your gate?"

"No one, but—"

"Then this is where we'll start—"

"Excuse me"—Anesia tugged on the agent's arm—"are you saying that my employees are all suspects?"

The agent lowered his notepad. Looked through her. "Not suspect, but certainly persons of interest. As is anyone who has contact with these dogs."

She glared back.

"Would you happen to have any veterinary equipment around here, Ms. Naltsiine?" His eyes bore into hers.

"Well, of course, it's a dog ken—"

"Any handheld scanners?"

"Excuse me?"

"The kind that trace those pet-finder chips."

She crossed her arms. Planted her feet for battle. "Exactly what are you implying?"

"Just answer the question, please."

Fine. He wanted to play *that* way. "No."

He scribbled something on his infernal pad and slapped it closed. "That's all for right now." As he turned and walked away, his message was clear.

She was as much a suspect as anyone.

SLIM
February 2
5:00 p.m.

The drop-off was set.

In three day's time, he'd be a rich man.

Money. Control. Power. Everything he'd ever dreamed of.

In three short days.

He hopped up from his computer. Lots to do. He'd need a new suit. He'd need to purchase his ticket.

And he'd need to get all the chips.

He rubbed his hands together. Excitement built up inside him. Ma would be proud.

CHAPTER THIRTY-ONE

ZOYA
February 3
Naltsiine Kennels
2:00 a.m.

Darkness surrounded me as I made my way down the stairs. My hand slid across the wall and my feet felt the shape of each step.

It'd been such a long day. The FBI and police all left, except for one officer posted out in the driveway. Auntie Jenna, Cole, and Andie all went home after the vet left. Andie didn't want to go. She stuck to my side like glue since I gave her the note in the restaurant, but she had a neurologist appointment in the morning.

Good thing, or she might have stayed.

I shivered. *This is the right thing to do . . .*

Mom would sleep like a rock. At least that was in my favor.

I took another step. I couldn't turn on a light. It might wake her. But if I fell down the steps . . .

Thoughts swirled and twirled inside me. What if I was doing the wrong thing? What if those men came after Mom anyway?

I shook my head.

Stop it, Zoya. Just go. Don't even think about Mom, she'll be fine.
Sean will take care of her. Cole will take care of her. The dogs will take
care of her.

I made it to the kitchen. The moon shone through the open
curtains. At least I wasn't in total darkness.

Sasha jumped up and ran over to me, tail wagging.

I patted her head and some of my fear melted away. *This is the*
right thing to do . . .

She nudged my leg as if she understood. But how could she?
She didn't have to worry about murderers. She didn't have to
worry about secret, threatening notes.

My throat closed. Was I sure I wanted to do this?

Yes. Besides, what choice do I have?

I pushed the voice away and slid my backpack off. Then filled
it with the things I'd gathered: Water bottles. Food. An extra pair
of gloves. Four layers already covered my body, but even with a
heavy coat, I knew, in such cold temperatures, it might not be
enough. Would we make it?

"Come on, Sasha." I slipped my arms through the backpack
straps, then crept over to the back door. I disabled the alarm.
Hopefully Mom wouldn't wake up from the beeping. *"Hurry . . .*
Hurry . . ."

The voice was getting irritating.

The door creaked as I eased it open. Sasha whined. Would
someone try to break in while I was gone? The alarm wouldn't
sound . . . would Mom be safe?

Yes. I would be gone, and the men probably knew that. *I don't*
think they'll try to get inside. Will they? "Sasha, we have to do this."

She obeyed. But worry flashed in her eyes. Again.

Who cared what happened? Just so long as Mom was safe. And
Sasha could take of herself, she wouldn't get hurt.

I nodded. Then we slipped out the back door.

More darkness.

Few stars shone in the sky. Very *yanlaey.* Was it going to storm?

My stomach knotted.

This is the right thing to do . . .

A strong breeze swirled among the trees. Snow fell. I shivered and rubbed my arms. Lowering my goggles and raising my neck and face warmer, I prepared for the long night ahead.

I was already feeling the chill, even through the heavy coat I wore. Before I left, the thermometer read sixty below. So cold . . .

A twig snapped.

My head shot up. Was someone watching me? Was that a gun?

I turned to glance at the bushes. Strange sounds echoed around me, stirring an odd feeling in the pit of my stomach.

Was there someone out there?

What if something happened?

Was this the right thing to do?

I could feel my fingers digging into the flesh of my palm. Should I go back into the house?

No. Mom would be safer this way.

I ran over to the barn and grabbed my sled. I hid it on the other side and stretched out the harnesses. The cold kept most of the dogs in their houses, so after entering the code into the gate, it was easy to grab the closest dogs. Moose, Puffin, Bear, and Eagle wagged their tails at my approach.

"We're going on a little trip." *At least you guys haven't raced yet.* But what if the Alaska Wildlife Litter were fast and we didn't even know it? They'd begun their training. Would it be a loss to Mom? Would she be angry that I took the newest litter?

I shook my head. How could I be thinking things like that? It didn't matter who I took. Just so long as I left.

Soon the dogs were in their harnesses, ready to go. Jumping around giving me their barks of excitement. "Shh!" I grabbed the lead dog's harness and walked them to the edge of the trail. A glance back at my home showed no lights. Sean's cabin was all quiet as well.

I hoped he wouldn't wake up. Just a little farther. But Puffin whined. She wanted to run.

"Shhhh! Puffin, be quiet. We can't wake anybody up."

She shied away and whimpered. My heart broke. "I'm sorry. I'm just stressed right now. It'll be okay." *I hope.* I patted her head, then climbed onto the sled.

"All right." Even though I whispered the command, the dogs took off running.

Maybe, by some miracle, Mom wouldn't know I'd left until morning.

I'd need to find a place to stay. A warm place. A place where no one could find me. But where? How far would the dogs be able to go at this time of night? Would they get tired faster?

The dogs ran, wagging their tails. Maybe they thought this was just a practice run.

That was good . . . but then again, if for some odd reason I flew off, they'd go right back to the house. Then I'd get caught.

At least I had Sasha. She ran beside the sled. Soon she'd need to ride on it though. She couldn't run all the way to . . . wherever I was going.

Everything in me wanted to turn back. But I couldn't. I had to keep going. To keep Mom safe. Sean could take care of her.

Keep going . . .

A large cloud passed over head, covering the light of the moon. My gaze shot from one place to another. Everything darkened until it was almost pitch black.

I shivered. Would it snow? That would cover up our tracks, but how far could we get before the storm hit? Or before it got so bad that we wouldn't be able to go farther? What would I do then? What if we froze to death? Was I endangering the dogs? And if those murderers came, would they harm them?

Stop it. I just had to keep going. No matter what.

I focused on the dogs, on the ground in front of them, but I couldn't keep out other thoughts. Words drifted through my memory. The things Sean had said to Andie. . .

God, is that true? Is that why I haven't felt You close? Was I just so angry that I couldn't hear Him? Was I not listening?

"Be still and know that I am God."

But what if He wasn't there? Why was all this stuff happening to me?

Lord, are You here?

"He will never leave you nor forsake you." Was that true? The Bible was supposed to be right . . . most of the time it was.

No . . . all the time.

But what if He let me get murdered? What if He didn't watch over me?

"When he falls, he will not be hurled headlong, for the LORD *is the One who holds his hand."*

God, is that You talking to me? Or is it just the words I've memorized for so long?

Did He hold my hand? Had He been there the entire time?

No. How could He?

I just needed to keep going . . .

"Don't listen to Him. You don't need Him."

My fingers and toes lost all feeling.

Keep going . . .

The dogs panted. They couldn't be tired already, could they?

Snowflakes started to fall.

Keep going . . . keep going . . .

Please, keep going.

RICK
February 3
Anchorage, Alaska
4:30 a.m.

He dialed the number into his cell and hit SEND.

The receiver was lifted and then dropped. Probably on the floor. A muffled curse. "Yeah?"

"I've got a job for you."

Shuffling and more rustling. "Target?"

"Teen girl."

"Fifty thousand."

"Understood. But let's get a few things clear."

"I'm listening."

"We've already had a failure. So, before you even make a move, I have to approve the plan. Every detail."

"Then it's up to sixty."

"Fine. But let me remind you. Every. Detail. You cannot make a move without the go-ahead."

"Deposit the money, then we'll talk."

Click.

Rick ended the call and dialed another number.

It rang five times before it was answered. "What do you want? You got any idea what time it is?"

"How'd you like to make a hundred grand?"

"Okay, okay, but I don't like being woke up in the middle of the night."

"Well, too bad. It's urgent." He laid out his plan. It would take substantial coordination and perfect timing. If only his heart would hold out during the stress of it. "Are you in?"

"Sure thing, boss."

"Good. I'll be in touch."

He snapped the phone shut.

Zoya, where did you go? He'd had someone follow her, but her dogs proved too fast to keep up with on foot. But they'd have to find her.

Before anyone else did.

ZOYA
February 3
Deep Bush, Interior Alaska
4:47 a.m.

Tiny snowflakes fell. But they would get bigger. And soon.

I had to find shelter. But where?

Shivers crept up and down my spine. It was getting colder. And colder. Always colder. I rubbed my arms. If nothing else, I needed to build a fire. But how could I? We'd need to find shelter.

I looked around. Tried to find somewhere to stay. Anywhere out of the wind.

Wait . . . *What's that?*

I called to the dogs, and they turned. A cabin. Out in the middle of nowhere? My brow furrowed. I called the dogs to a stop.

Why would someone build a cabin way out here? Was there someone inside? What if it was the bad guys? Would they harm me? The dogs?

I stood. Staring.

My heart pounded out a consistent rhythm. Each *thwump* echoed in my ears.

What if the murderers saw me? What would they do? Or if it was someone else . . . I didn't want anyone to see me, to know where I was. To know *who* I was.

Get inside, Zoya. You'll freeze if you don't.

I blinked. No one was in there. I just had to be brave.

The dogs barked. But I was too exhausted to stop them. If someone was in that cabin, they'd come outside to see what was going on . . . right? Yeah. And no one came. So it must have been safe.

I went up the creaky steps, knees bonking together. My fingers shook as I grasped the handle-like contraption and pushed the door open.

I looked back at the dogs. Was it safe? What if I went in and someone showed up? Maybe I should just leave. But I couldn't stay out in the cold. The dogs needed to rest.

I sighed and stepped inside.

It was dark. Really dark. I pulled out my flashlight.

One room. One empty room. Well, empty of people. There was furniture . . . A rough table, a chair, and—

My heartbeat quickened.

A fireplace. And logs piled beside it.

Someone must *live here!*

I spun and ran back to the sled. Great! And now whoever lived there would know someone came in . . . I couldn't stay.

I put my hand on the sled. Something stopped me. An urging. Prodding.

Look closer, Zoya.

I took a deep breath and turned.

Best take a closer look. *But just a quick one.* If someone did live there, I most definitely didn't want them finding me in their home.

I tromped back up the stairs.

Deep breath.

My flashlight clicked back on.

Yes, there were logs. And furniture. But when I looked closer, I saw something else. Dust. Everywhere. Covering everything.

No one had been here in a long time. Weeks. Months. Maybe even more.

My shoulders relaxed and I let out a sigh.

We were safe.

CHAPTER THIRTY-TWO

SEAN
February 3
Naltsiine Kennels
6:00 a.m.

Steam covered the bathroom mirror after his shower. Since moving to the cabin, there'd been no more mysterious messages on the mirror. Somehow he had a feeling his father had been involved. His father's reach circled the globe.

He shook his head. Forget it. Other things—more important things—deserved his attention. Sean dressed, purpose and promise growing inside him.

He loved his job. Loved Alaska. Loved the dogs. Loved . . . Anesia.

The thought took him by surprise. When did his feelings go so deep? He'd admired her, yes. Been attracted to her, yes. But love?

He wiped the mirror with a towel and stared at his reflection. A smile stole over his features. What was so wrong with having feelings for a woman?

Not just any woman.

Anesia was amazing. Intelligent. Beautiful. Driven. Talented. Stubborn.

He shook his head. As he prepared to shave, his thoughts shifted to Zoya. She seemed so troubled. Burdened. *Lord, how do we reach her?* Cole had told him a little more of the history between Dan and Marc, Jenna's late husband. Maybe understanding Zoya's dad would help them reach the sweet, hurting young lady.

No adult should have to go through what this teen had endured. The world was an ugly place. Sin and its darkness had control.

Zoya was fighting an inner battle. It was hard enough going through the teen years when everything was stable and happy. But throw in the horrific events of the last few weeks, and fear and doubt could take over. Not to mention all the loss the poor child had suffered.

She had an incredible relationship with her mom and Jenna and Andie, but with the murder, and shooting, the threats were piling up—

Wait a minute. Threats. His feet felt glued in place.

Zoya hadn't acted right the day before. Could someone be trying to scare her? No. She'd tell Anesia or him, right? Would she? Maybe.

But yesterday . . . at the time, he'd attributed her skittishness to everything that had happened. But if they caught the shooter, then why was her fear almost palpable?

Sean went to the kitchen for more coffee. He drummed his fingers on the counter. The thoughts wouldn't leave him be. What if there really was more to all this? Or was he overreacting?

Only one way to find out. He'd check on the dogs, and then he'd talk to Anesia and Zoya.

Mind made up, he threw on his outer gear, grabbed his keys, and headed to the kennel. The dogs barked at him in greeting. A smile split his face even in the bone-chilling cold. He loved the bond he'd built with the beautiful animals.

His smile was short-lived as he reached the gate. Small foot-prints and sled tracks led away from the kennel into the forest beyond. Away from the house. Away from town.

The light snow that had been falling filled up the prints about halfway. That meant it'd been several hours already. His gaze darted around the kennel. Sean's heart sank. One of the litters was missing.

Zoya!

Sean ran across the snow-covered yard to the main house.

He burst through the mudroom door, not bothering to take off his snow-crusted things. "Anesia!"

Heart racing, he bent at the waist to catch his breath. "Anesia!" He straightened. "*Anesia!*"

She came around the corner and barreled into his chest. Fear filled her eyes. "She's gone! They've taken her! Where's Zoya?"

"Whoa. Hold on. Who's taken her?"

Anesia pushed off him and wrung her hands as she paced. "She's been kidnapped. She's not here! I've searched the entire house—"

"Was there a note? Did you get a phone call?" He gripped her shoulders. Could he have prevented this?

"No. No note. No call. She's just gone. I could've sworn I set the alarm last night . . ." Her shoulders shook and then tears spilled down her cheeks. "I need to call the police. I was about to dial when I heard you yelling for me."

"Some of the dogs are missing."

She turned. "What?"

"I found paw tracks, and sled tracks. And the Wildlife Litter is gone."

Her eyes darted around the room. "Sasha! Here, girl."

Sean knew the dog wouldn't appear. She'd be with Zoya—assuming, of course, the girl left of her own free will.

Anesia sprinted from room to room calling the husky. He followed her and caught her in the hallway. "Anesia. I think Zoya ran away."

She stiffened. "Why would she do that?"

"She's been deeply troubled lately. Even more so than in the past few weeks."

Anesia grabbed the phone. "I'm calling the police."

He waited, listening as she gave the police a rundown of the situation. Her voice stayed calm and even until the end of the call. When she thanked the person on the phone, the calm evaporated and her voice broke. She set the receiver in the cradle and stood there, head bowed.

Sean took her by the elbow. "She'll be okay."

She bit her lip and looked up at him.

He held out his hand. "Come on. Let's check her room while we're waiting on the police to arrive."

Anesia took his hand and held on with a vise-like grip. "I can't lose her, Sean. I can't . . ."

"You're not going to. We'll find her." He glanced down at her. Shoulders set. Mouth in a grim line. She'd had to rely on her own strength for so long. Was she giving this over to God? Was he?

They'd reached Zoya's bedroom door, but he tugged Anesia to a stop. She met his eyes.

"Anesia, we need to pray."

She didn't resist as he tugged her close and wrapped his arms around her. "Father, we come to You with heavy hearts. Please protect precious Zoya. We don't know where she is or what's happening, but we know that You do. Father, we beg You right now to keep her safe. She's just a child, and she's been through so much. Keep us calm and relying on Your strength alone. Amen."

For a moment Anesia rested against him. Then she pulled away and headed into her daughter's room. "Everything looks normal. Like she should come bounding out of the bathroom at any minute."

"Why don't we start searching for clues?"

"What kind of clues?"

"Well, why don't you check her desk, maybe the pockets of clothes she's worn the past few days. I'll check the trash can and the bathroom. Can you check her e-mail or Facebook or anything?"

Anesia nodded.

They worked in silence for several minutes. Nothing appeared out of the ordinary to him, but he wasn't a parent, and he definitely didn't understand teen girls' habits.

"Sean"—Anesia called from the closet—"her heavy backpack is gone." Dread covered her features. "She really must've left on her own."

"Well, at least that's some relief. Zoya knows how to take care of herself. We should be thankful she's not in the hands of kidnappers."

"But she's just a kid, Sean. And it's been forty below and colder the past few days." He saw her resilience slip.

Gripping her by the shoulders again, he turned her to face him. "She's a good kid. And you've taught her well. Looks like she was smart enough to take her pack, so she's got some supplies. She's got the dogs. You know Sasha will guard her with her life."

She blinked rapidly. Tears standing ready to fall. Then she set her chin. "You're right. We just have to find her."

"We will."

She sat on her daughter's bed, the rigid set of her frame clearly fighting the weight of her daughter's disappearance. "Why would she leave?" Her voice diminished to a whisper. "I just don't understand . . ."

"Maybe there's a clue here somewhere." Sean smoothed her hair with one hand and leaned down to kiss the top of her head. "Let's keep looking."

He left her alone and headed back to the bathroom. Teen girls spent lots of time in them, didn't they? Well, maybe most teen girls, but Zoya was different. Makeup and jewelry and curling irons didn't seem to hold any appeal to her.

He glanced around the room and eyed the trash can. It was full of tissues. Like she'd been crying a lot or had a cold. But Zoya had been healthy. She must've hidden her grief and hurt and cried all alone in the bathroom.

Sean reached in and dug past all the wadded up Kleenex. At the bottom of the bin was a large M&M bag. He pulled it out and something white slid out.

A crumpled piece of paper.

He unraveled it and read:

> Tell anyone that you saw me and you'll never see your mom again.

"Anesia."

She was beside him in a heartbeat. He held the paper out to her. "I think we know why Zoya ran away."

"What?" She took the piece of paper and read it—then closed her eyes. "No."

"She's trying to protect you."

Anesia leaned against the sink, staring at the note. "Who could have sent this?"

Sean didn't know. But one thing was for certain.

He was going to find out.

ANESIA
6:40 a.m.

It made no sense. Zoya had no reason to run. They'd caught the shooter.

So who could have sent her daughter that threatening note?

The crinkled piece of paper lay in front of her on the kitchen counter. The police were scouring Zoya's room with Sean. Jenna and her crew were on their way over.

Who would write such a note to a kid? And why? To scare her even more? To keep her from talking? But if they caught the person Zoya saw shoot a man, then why would she run away?

Anesia's chest hurt. Like her heart tearing in two. She needed to be out there, looking for her daughter.

Her head snapped up. What if there were more notes?

She took the stairs two at a time and ran into Sergeant Roberts at Zoya's door. "Have you found anything else?"

"No, ma'am. Not yet."

She looked down at her hands, still clutching the note. "Have you wondered if there were more of these?"

"Like I said, we haven't found anything yet, but we won't rule out the possibility."

Sean came out of the room and pulled her into a hug. She melted into his arms. So much for strong, independent Anesia Naltsiine—who never needed a man. She'd been wrong. She needed a man.

This man.

Right here. Right now.

She spoke with her head buried against his chest. "I need to be out there. Looking for her."

"I know. I already talked to them about that. Let's just make sure we haven't missed anything before we head out."

He took a deep breath. "As soon as Cole and Jenna get here, we'll head out." He hesitated. "Cole and I will, that is. The police want you to stay here in case she returns."

She pulled back enough to look into his eyes. "Sean, you know I can't do that. I can't just sit here and do nothing. The waiting would kill me."

Officer Roberts exited Zoya's room and gave her a pointed look. "We need you here in case we find her, or in case she heads home on her own."

"*I* need to find my daughter."

"Ms. Naltsiine, let me be blunt. We could use your coopera-tion. We still haven't ruled out foul play. Too much has happened on your property recently."

Sean held her in a firm grip. As if he knew her mama-bear attitude was about to maul a police officer. "Let's go back down to the kitchen and wait for Cole."

Anesia allowed him to lead her down the stairs, but that didn't mean she had to like her circumstances.

Sean released her and sat on a stool at the bar. "Anesia, Zoya seemed a little out of sorts yesterday. Very skittish. Afraid of every sound. Did you notice anything different?"

She thought back. "No. Not that I can think of. The girls went out to check on the dogs with you. But then you all found the chips and—"

He hopped up. "Wait a minute. Where's the coat she wears out to work with the dogs? Would she have taken it?"

She headed in the direction of the mudroom before she answered. "Maybe not . . . She probably would've worn her heavi-est coat for running the dogs, not her work coat . . ."

There it hung. On the hook above her heavy-duty Carhartt overalls. Anesia reached into the pockets of Zoya's thick work coat. Nothing.

Sean searched the quilted bib overalls. "Anesia, look!" He pulled out another wadded up piece of paper.

Go away. Run. Or you'll never see your mom again.

Anesia crouched onto the floor of the mudroom, overwhelmed by the struggles her daughter faced. "This had to be from yester-day. We washed all the gear the day before." She looked up into Sean's green eyes. The anguish she saw there mirrored her own. "Do you know what this means? She's not out of danger. Someone is still threatening my child . . . and I have no idea where she is!"

He stood there for several seconds. The expression in his eyes changed from hurt and sorrow to a red-hot anger. His jaw clenched and unclenched. He walked out of the mudroom.

Anesia stood up and followed, frightened at the sudden change in him. And by her own anger. "We've got to find her. Before anyone else."

His face was like flint. Cold. Hard. "I'm going to make a few phone calls. Go show Roberts the note."

She raced up the stairs. All that mattered right now was getting Zoya back home.

Safe and sound.

The officer met her at the top of the stairs. She handed him the note.

He took a second to read it and then slammed his hand against the railing. He grimaced and gave her a sideways glance. "Sorry about that." He paced a few steps before he spoke again. "This case is getting weirder by the minute."

Cole, Jenna, and Andie burst through the front door at that moment.

The sergeant yelled down the stairs. "Major Maddox, you need to get on the horn to the FBI pronto. We've got a mess they need to help us sort out."

Jenna ran to her and hugged her tight. "It'll be okay. What've we got?"

"Zoya ran away, apparently to try to keep me safe. We found some notes threatening her."

Andie joined them on the steps and grabbed Anesia's hand. "Auntie, she gave me a weird note too. Made me promise not to tell, but I think I have to break that promise. She told me she had to go on alone. That must be what she was trying to say. That the only way to protect us all was for her to leave!"

CHAPTER THIRTY-THREE

SEAN
February 3
Naltsiine Kennels
7:02 a.m.

"Does this mean you're coming home?" His father sounded pleased with himself.

Sean knew that would be the first question out of the man's mouth. "No. But I need your help. And please don't tell me you can't do it. You're the CEO of CROM. Get Charlie in there and have him get the satellite in place."

"Why can't the local authorities and the FBI handle it?" The voice was a bit too sugary-sweet.

"We don't have time to waste, Father. A little girl's life is in danger. You and I both know you have the technology to help."

"It will cost a small fortune to redirect that satellite—"

"Well then, it's a good thing you have hundreds of small fortunes at your disposal, isn't it?" His temper had gotten the best of him. He couldn't remember ever speaking to his father in sarcasm.

A hearty laugh came over the line. "Wow. Seems you're becoming more like me everyday. Now, I'll forgive you for your comments since I know you're stressed over this situation, but remember in the future who you are addressing."

No time for petty squabbles. Finding Zoya was the only thing that mattered. "Yes, sir. I'm sorry. How soon can you have Charlie contact me?"

"I'll have him down in the sat room in thirty minutes."

"Give him my cell number. Tell him I'll give him our GPS coordinates soon. Then he can look at current images of the area around. He should be able to locate her." He started to hang up.

"Sean!"

"Yes?"

"I hope you find the girl."

When had his father ever shown compassion for anyone else? Ever? "Thanks." Sean hung up. He couldn't believe he'd just asked his father for help when he swore he'd never do that again. But even more surprising was the fact that his father acquiesced without making him promise anything in return.

Could the man have a heart after all?

"Sean?" Anesia stood in the doorway.

"I heard Cole come in." He reached for her, but she hesitated. She held his gaze for several seconds, then moved into his arms. They both needed the contact. "Are we ready to search?"

"Yes. Jenna and Andie will take her plane up. They brought several handheld GPSs and radios so that you all can stay in communication. She'll scout from the air while you and Cole take sleds out."

"And you?" He touched her face.

"I'm supposed to stay here. The FBI will be here soon, and Sergeant Roberts will stay here as well." Her shoulders slumped as she looked out the window. "Please, Sean . . ." Her gaze came back to his. "Find my daughter."

ZOYA
Unknown location, Interior Alaska
7:38 a.m.

Very little light shone through the small window in the cabin. I stared up at the log ceiling. Mom would've noticed I was gone by now. She'd be worried. Frantic. But Sean was there. He would take care of her.

My eyes closed and I sighed. Would they look for me? And what if they found me, then what would I do? I couldn't defend myself for leaving.

But what else could I have done?

I sat up. I hadn't gotten any sleep, not when everything was floating around in my head at once.

Very few furnishings inhabited this place. No couch, only a bed. No kitchen, only a fireplace. No bathroom, or bedrooms. No doors except the one at the front. Although it couldn't really pass as a door . . . more like a giant square with a thing of wood blocking out the wind and snow.

Everything looked historical. Like it was a building from *Little House on the Prairie*. There were many, many bookshelves, overflowing with books of all sorts. Old books.

I snuck closer to peek, then blew dust off the ancient books. An *Almanac* from 1899. *American Dictionary of the English Language* from 1828. Four books titled: *The Birds of America* by Audubon. Books on flowers, plants, and farming. Most tattered and torn . . .

Not a contemporary book whatsoever. Nothing more recent than 1900. How long had this cabin been here? There were many natives who didn't agree with the "new" America. The "new" way people lived. So they stuck to the traditional way of things. No electricity, no bathrooms, no stoves or sinks, no plumbing of any kind, except maybe a well outside. But how did they keep it from freezing?

I stood. Time to stoke the fire.

I looked down to my hands. I was glad no one was here. Didn't want to put anyone else in danger.

A shiver crept up my spine. Why wouldn't this nightmare end? What was God doing to me? Why wasn't He helping me?

You have no faith. Not anymore.

Was that true? Really? Or was it more like Sean said? I'd let my anger get between me and God?

"Don't trust Him . . ."

The tears came.

I didn't know what to think, to believe. What if the killers followed my trail?

"This is all His fault . . ."

Or was it mine? I was the one who decided to run. I was the one who led the killers to this place.

I was the one who pushed God away.

My breath caught on a sob.

I pulled my legs up close to me. Lowered my head onto my knees and hugged them. I couldn't cry . . . but I was.

My body shook with each breath. Just let the sobs come. Get it out . . . But the emotions swirling inside of me wouldn't let go. They had an iron grip.

On me. On my heart.

I fought to feel the pain, the anger, the heat. It was better than not feeling anything. Better than not feeling His presence.

I couldn't even open my eyes. Darkness surrounded me. Everywhere. On every side. Dark . . . Dark . . . Dark. It was like a haunting chant. It wouldn't leave.

"Don't trust Him . . ."

Tears pushed past my eyelids and slid down my cheeks. My heart hammered. Air. I needed air. Spots danced behind my closed eyes.

I couldn't make a sound. But inside . . . I screamed. Let it out. Everything. Everything in me that said I hated Him. Everything in me that said I never wanted Him in my life.

Everything in me that begged for a Savior. For someone to be there. For someone to care about me. For someone to save me.

Help me!

I gasped for air. Little came.

God! Show me You're here! Please!

The darkness closed in. *No!*

I couldn't let go . . . I needed to hold on.

To what?

My throat closed. Chest closed. Mind fogged.

Darkness.

ANESIA
Naltsiine Kennels
8:42 a.m.

Anesia sipped her coffee, playing the role of the worried mom for the two police officers staying in her house. The worried mom who could fall apart at any moment. The worried mom who sat by the phone waiting. The worried mom who did what she was told.

But inside, she was planning.

Sean's presence had comforted her. Her heart soared every time he came near. Hope sprouted once again in her soul—that she could possibly have her own happily-ever-after.

But none of that mattered if she lost Zoya. She'd never forgive herself.

Where is your faith, my child?

Her faith was still there. Just because she needed to *do* something didn't mean she didn't have faith.

She paced back and forth to the window. The others shouldn't have left her here. No Sean to comfort her. No Jenna to kick her in the rear end before she did something foolish. No Zoya.

Zoya . . .

She had to do something. And soon.

She glanced out the window and noticed the clouds packing in. That meant lots more snow. Time to make her move.

Anesia set the coffee cup in the sink. "Sergeant Roberts?"

He appeared in the kitchen. "Yes?"

"Looks like we've got more snow coming. I'm going to head out to the kennel for a few minutes and make sure the dogs have everything they need."

The officer poured himself another cup of coffee. "Do you need some help?"

"No, that's okay. I know you guys are busy. I should be back in just a few minutes." Ouch. That lie didn't taste good on her tongue. But she had to do it. For Zoya.

"All right." He headed back to their computer set-up in the living room. "Take a radio with you. We'll let you know if we hear anything."

"Okay. Thanks." She was already to the mudroom and slinging on her gear. Adding an extra layer against the cold, she bundled up. Who knew how many hours she'd be out?

Anesia shoved a bottle of water and two protein bars in the pockets of her massive coat. She wiggled her fingers into her gloves and headed out the door.

The dogs saw her coming and yapped expectantly.

With deft movements, she unlocked the shed and pulled out her fastest sled. Her movements were quick and steady. Years of practice and training had her ready with a team of dogs in under ninety seconds.

She released the hooks that anchored her sled and the team took off. As the sled whooshed on the fresh powder, Anesia whispered to the wind.

"Hold on, baby girl. I'm coming."

CHAPTER THIRTY-FOUR

SLIM
February 3
Naltsiine Kennels
9:59 a.m.

Great. Two police cruisers sat in front of Anesia's house. What were they doing there? He needed those chips. Now.

He parked in the long driveway and pulled binoculars out of the glove compartment so he could watch through the windows.

Yep. Two cops. Sitting in the living room with computers set up. One talked on a radio.

Something must've gone down.

This would mess up his plan. His buyer already said they couldn't wait. How was he gonna get those chips?

The cell phone on the console bleeped at him. The familiar number flashing with the incoming call.

"Hello?"

"Well, hello, Slim. How are you doing today?"

Great. The guy wanted to make small talk. "Fine. You?"

The man chuckled. "I'm doing very well. Just wondering about you. One of my few employees that I care about."

Yeah, right. "As I recall, you weren't real happy with me last time we talked. Are you willing to up your price?"

"You aren't in any position to negotiate"—The congenial tone turned hard—"I know they found the chips. But I have a plan that will help us both."

He sat up straight in his seat. No. It couldn't be true. The guy was playing him. "What do you mean they found the chips?"

"Exactly what I said. They found them yesterday. Pulled more than fifty chips out of those poor dogs. While you were shopping. The FBI has them."

How did this man know where he'd been? Nausea rolled through his stomach. This guy was bad news. The money and power had seemed so intoxicating, but now he felt sick. How would he get his money now?

"Slim? You still there?" The voice changed back to its original soothing sound. "Like I said, I have a plan. It'll help us both, and you can still get your share."

"I'm listening." Would Ma want him to continue?

"I'm tracking all of the players right now. It seems little Zoya has run away because of the threats, and mommy dearest has gone after her. The police don't realize Anesia has left yet. But you and I do. I want you to kidnap Anesia while everyone else is looking for Zoya. Then we'll ransom her for the chips."

Who did this guy think he was? "I'm not an idiot. There's no way the feds are going to trade one lady of no importance for those chips and you know it."

"Ah, but that's where you're not seeing the full picture. Of course they won't trade her for the chips—they'll certainly switch them out with phonies and then ambush at the hand-off—but I have a man inside. A man who can get us the real chips while everyone is out trying to catch the kidnappers."

He sucked in a breath. "You've had a man inside this whole time?"

"Of course. I like to keep my options open."

COLE

February 3
Miles outside of North Pole, Alaska
11:24 a.m.

"Whoa!" Cole slowed the dogs to a stop and pulled out the crackling radio. "Maddox here. Whatcha got?"

It was Sean. "I lost my GPS in a tumble down a hill a little while ago, so I'm not sure where I'm at, but I found some faint tracks. They may or may not—" Sean's voice broke up as the radio crackled and hissed.

"Sean! I think you're getting out of range. What were your last coordinates?"

No response.

"Sean! Can you hear me?"

Nothing.

Not good.

Maybe he should head north, toward Sean's last known coordinates, and follow his tracks.

Time ran out all too quick in this frozen north. Heavy snow fell now, and light dimmed on the horizon.

The roar of a plane's engines echoed toward him.

Jenna.

Maybe she'd seen something in her wide sweep.

Cole clicked the small handheld radio. She'd be in range for only a little bit. "Jenna, I'm below you at a clearing just north of Pleasant Valley. Have you found anything?"

"Nothing yet, Cole"—Andie's voice came over the com— "but I'm sure we'll find her."

"Can you see Sean? I lost contact with him, but I think he said he saw tracks."

"We saw him a little bit ago. Mom says we'll sweep back that way."

He watched the plane change directions. "Good. We won't have light for long today."

SEAN
11:35 a.m.

There. Barking in the distance. Could it be Zoya?

Sean pushed his dogs as fast as he dared following the call of the dogs ahead. After another hill his sled broke through the edge of the trees. A lone cabin sat in the distance.

And sled tracks led straight to it.

Sean slowed his team as he reached the cabin and set his hooks. The cabin seemed deserted except for a dying trail of smoke from the chimney. He banged on the door.

Nothing.

The barking grew louder. There were definitely dogs inside that cabin. Grabbing the handle, Sean pushed on the door. As it groaned its way open, his eyes adjusted to the darkness of the interior.

A lump in the corner captured his gaze.

Lifeless and gray.

Zoya!

RICK
11:37 a.m.

The hit would take place later that afternoon. Everything was in place.

His chest ached with every breath. Probably his imagination, kicked it into high gear. If he were going to die from a heart attack, it would've happened by now, wouldn't it?

Rick popped another pill into his mouth and swigged water down with it.

His phone rang. He glanced at the caller ID. Good, his man. "Yeah?"

Raspy breathing answered.

"Hello? Olman, is that you?"

"Yeah"—a gurgly wheeze came over the line—"you've been duped, man . . ."

"What do you mean? What's wrong with you?"

"They . . ." A long exhale resounded in his ear.

"Olman!"

Thud.

"Olman!"

Dead air.

Rick's hands shook. He hit END on his phone and glanced at his watch. Not much time.

He'd ordered the hit. But he'd also ordered the hit to prevent the hit. If Olman was dead . . . then one of the pieces was no longer in play.

And Zoya would die.

CHAPTER THIRTY-FIVE

ZOYA _____
11:40 a.m.

Someone stroked my hair.

Mom? Had they found me?

No. It couldn't be.

Was I in heaven? Would I have to stand before God? Look at Him? Talk to Him? Tell Him about my doubts?

Guilt flooded over me. No, it couldn't be Him . . . Why would He still want me after what I had done?

"Shh . . . Sunshine, it's okay. I'm here."

Sean?

My eyes slid open. Sean sat beside me. Heavy coat. Tousled blond hair. Tears running down his cheeks.

Thank You, God. How had he found me?

No, I couldn't let him take me back. Those men would hurt Mom. Kill her. I had to get away. From Sean. From everyone.

"Sean?" His face loomed above mine. In that moment my heart tensed so much I almost couldn't breathe again. I'd missed him. More than he could ever know.

Why had I run away?

My vision fogged.

A gun . . .

I blinked back the images. For some reason, they weren't as scary as usual . . .

"It's okay. I'm here, Sunshine. I'm right here. I found you, it's going to be okay." Sean put a hand to my forehead. Did I have a fever?

No.

Tears ran down my cheeks. The anger . . .

"Shh . . . Zoya, it's okay." Sean pulled me up into his arms.

I let the tears come. One by one. Agonizing torture.

I cried. As the tears fell, my anger puddled at my feet. And then, just like that, it was gone. But it would return. It always did.

"Shh . . . Sunshine, it'll be okay."

How could he say that? I grabbed his arm and pulled myself closer.

For the first time in weeks I felt safe.

But not safe enough.

I couldn't help but think of Jesus, even though I promised not to. He died on the cross. Took my sin. He paid the price for me.

So why hadn't He taken care of me? Or saved my dad? Or kept that man from being murdered?

Sean rubbed my back in a slow, circular pattern. I let myself melt into his gigantic frame.

"Sunshine, talk to me." Sean's gentle whisper made my heart break. Again.

I wanted to talk. But I couldn't.

I wanted to make things right. But I couldn't.

I wanted to trust God.

But I couldn't.

"I feel so lost." I tried to pull myself as close as possible. I couldn't get close enough. Couldn't hide. Couldn't run. Fear, anger, hatred stared me straight in the face.

I didn't want to listen to their demands to come into my heart.

But I did. I let them in. Just like I'd done before.

Nothing made any sense anymore. I wanted to die. To lose my spirit and return to the dust. Never again to return.

But I was there. There with Sean. In a cabin far away from home. In a dungeon far away from God. My Savior. My Friend. My Father.

God . . . please. I don't know how to get back.

"I'll take you home, Zoya. I'll get you home."

My body trembled all over. I didn't know why. I didn't know how to stop it. But I was there. With people who loved me.

God loved me. But did I still love Him?

"I *can't* do it, Sean. I just can't do it."

He squeezed.

"I can't feel God. I don't feel Him by my side." My voice squeaked. Everything in me shook. Everything cried out my fear, that I wanted someone to take away all this pain. Forever.

"I feel lost and alone. I don't know how to get God back. I don't know how to live without Him. Yet I don't want Him to be here if it's going to cause all this pain."

Sean held me. Said nothing. Just held me. As if assuring me. What was he trying to tell me? Why couldn't I get the message?

"Sunshine, God hasn't left you. He's been right by your side the entire time. He doesn't leave us. We can move away from Him, but He never abandons us."

"Then why can't I feel Him? Why isn't He near?"

"He is here. He brought me here, to you. He's helping me know what to say to you. Just because you can't feel Him, it doesn't mean He's not there."

I stared at the floor.

Could that be true?

No.

Yes.

Maybe . . .

"Zoya, 'He will never leave you nor forsake you.' He loves you beyond description. You are His creation."

"Then why? Why is everything . . ." I tried to hold back the tears. It didn't work.

"He never leaves, He never abandons, He never drops you off at someone else's doorstep as if you're being thrown away. He loves you very much, Zoya. He wants you to run into His arms. To love Him. To trust Him."

I felt the rhythm of Sean's chest, up and down. Listened to his heartbeat. Rubbed my fingers in circles against my snow pants.

"God doesn't move away from us, Sunshine. If anyone moves, it's us. We move away. But He's still there. Always. Waiting. Ready to open His arms to us."

His words repeated in my mind. Over and over.

Was it true?

Had God been there all along? And *I* just moved away? Had I not given Him time to show me He was there?

I swallowed back more tears.

No, He—

Yes.

I sobbed. Then sank into Sean's embrace. What had I done?

God, I'm sorry.

I'm so, so sorry.

SEAN
12:17 p.m.

How could he not have known? How could he never have realized how much he could love someone? How deep love could go.

As he sat there, holding Zoya, hearing her pain and despair, it was all he could do to hold back his own tears. This girl, this precious child, she was part of him. As much a part of him as Anesia had become. And all he wanted to do was comfort her. Protect her.

"Zoya, listen to me." Sean placed his hands on either side of her face. "God is here. He's just waiting on you to reach out to

Him. Let go of your fear and your doubt. Let go of the anger. He's there with open arms, Sunshine. Run into them."

"But it's all my fault"—her words choked on the sobs—"I couldn't stop the murder. I couldn't stop the murderers after that. I couldn't protect my mom . . ."

He tapped her nose. "That's not your job."

She looked up at him. The dogs inched closer. One licked her face as she stroked its head. "But why would God want a failure? A kid whose mom and dad weren't even married! Everyone's always looked at me like I'm different. As soon as I was old enough to understand, their words haunted me. And they've always said that my mom distracted my dad. That he could've been the greatest champion ever if he'd never gotten messed up with that 'girl' they called her." She sniffed and wiped her nose on her sleeve. "Why do some people have to be so ugly?"

So much pain, so many wounds for one so young. *God, ease her pain.* "Living in a small town can be like that. But, living in a small town can be wonderful too. Can't it?"

She stared down at her hands.

"I'm willing to bet there have only been a couple of people who've said those things to you. Am I right?"

Zoya scuffed her boot on the floor. "Maybe."

"I've seen how many of those small-town people adore you and your mom. They respect you both, and they cheer you on during a race as if you belong to all of them."

"Yeah." She chewed on her bottom lip and pulled a wiggling dog into her lap.

"So maybe it's about impressing people."

Her head popped up and she looked him in the eyes. Finally.

"Maybe you're just afraid. And you've let that fear take hold. You've driven yourself to prove you're worthy. And you've let one or two people's gossipy comments fester inside you. You've kept it hidden and squashed down, and then the horrific events of late made that festering, nasty infection explode. And the poison spread. So now, you have a choice to make."

Another sniff. "A choice?"

"A choice." Sean tapped her chin. "To hang on to your fear and anger, or to let it all go and forgive. Forgive your mom and dad. They weren't perfect, but they loved you. Forgive whoever made those nasty comments. Those people, those words don't define who you are. Forgive the murderer. It wasn't your fault. Forgive the guy who shot you. Forgive whoever wrote those threatening notes. But most of all, you need to forgive yourself, Zoya. And be the beautiful Sunshine I know you are. You are God's child. And perfectly worthy in His sight."

Zoya's hand reached out and took his hand. "Sean . . ." The words choked, and she dove into his arms again.

He hugged her close, wiggling dog and all. "Shhh . . . it's okay."

He didn't know how long she cried, how long they sat there like that, but finally she nodded against his chest. "You're right. It finally is okay." She sucked in a shuddering breath. "I want to go home now."

"Good."

She sat back and wiped her face. "And I want to tell Mom everything. Then I want to tell Andie, and Auntie Jenna, and Cole, and my Uncle Rick."

He flinched. "Your who?"

"My dad's brother. He came to one of my races recently and talked to Mom. But I'd just gotten one of those notes and passed out."

"Okay then. We'll tell Uncle Rick."

Zoya smiled. The first real smile Sean had seen in a long time. He hugged her close, then stood.

"Come on, Sunshine. It's time to go home."

CHAPTER THIRTY-SIX

SEAN
3:08 p.m.

Dogs yapped in their harnesses as he finished hooking them up. The lead dogs would have to wait until they were fully loaded, otherwise, they'd take off without him. Snowhooks and all. He looked over his shoulder.

Again.

What is it, Lord? Why do I feel so on edge?

If he didn't know better, he'd think someone was out there. Watching . . .

He shook the feeling away and pulled out his radio. It hissed at him again. No signal. Sean pulled out his cell. No signal there either. They'd have to get closer to civilization for him to let everyone know that he'd found Zoya.

If only he could've found the GPS. But after the sled took that crazy tumble, he was thankful he'd made it in one piece. The last information he'd received had been from Charlie when he'd given him the coordinates of this cabin. Once he found Zoya's tracks, he knew he was onto something, but he'd gotten too far away from Cole for the FRS transmissions on their little handheld radios to work.

Now their window of daylight was gone, but at least it had stopped snowing. For the moment.

He didn't relish heading back in the dark, but he was even less inclined to keep everyone worrying. As long as they didn't hit another storm, they'd be fine.

He walked back into the cabin to check on Zoya. "You doing all right?"

Zoya gave him a small smile. "Yeah, I think I'm okay."

"Okay. Then let's get going."

Sean opened the door, then paused. Couldn't hurt to stock up on warmth before the long ride home. They'd doused the fire, but the cabin still held a welcoming warmth—

What was that?

He peered at the woods. Listened. Though the snowfall muffled the sounds, he could swear he heard—

There! A rustling. A flash of color.

Someone *was* out there.

Sean stepped back and slammed the door shut.

"We have a problem. There's someone out there."

Zoya's eyes went wide. "What?"

"I had a feeling I was being watched but couldn't confirm it until now. There's someone out there. Watching the cabin."

Zoya grabbed Sean's hand. "What do we do? I'm scared. This is all my fault . . ."

If only he'd been able to let Cole know where they were! If ever there was a time to have a trained spec-ops man on your side, it was now. Sean had sat behind a desk most of his adult life. How was he supposed to protect his charges from a trained killer?

Hold on. Maybe it was Cole out there watching the cabin and he didn't know they were in there. Sean tried the radio. "Cole? Cole? You out there, man?"

No response.

He tried again. "Cole?"

The radio was silent.

Zoya moved toward him. "Maybe we just need to get on the sleds and go—"

Glass shattered beside Zoya.

"Get down!" Sean threw himself over the girl as another shot ripped through the window and whizzed through the heavy down of his parka. Ferocious barking came from the dogs outside.

Numerous shots flew through the air around them. Sean heard the muffled cries of the teen beneath him, felt her shaking. Then the unmistakable sound of shattering glass came again and a great whoosh, as the old oil lantern exploded into flames on the wood table.

Sean jumped up, grabbed a tattered blanket from the bed, and worked to extinguish the fire, but the flames were spreading with great speed.

He pulled Zoya with him, speaking in what he hoped was a calm but firm voice. "We've got to get out of here."

Another bullet zinged toward the fireplace.

"Stay low. The dogs are ready to go, so as soon as we hit the sleds, we run all out, got it?"

Eyes wide, Zoya nodded. Now or never. Or they'd go up in flames. The smoke thickened. He coughed, then opened the door and dragged Zoya behind him.

A shot hit the frame of the door, not two inches from his face. Then another shot rang out from a different direction. He threw Zoya to the ground and covered them. *Two* shooters?

Bullets seemed to fly over him from every direction. Then just as suddenly as the shooting started, it stopped.

He counted the seconds with his breaths. One. Two. Three . . .

. . . Twenty-nine. Thirty . . .

No more shots. But the heat of the flames behind him began to singe the hair on his neck.

"Go!"

Zoya jumped up with him, and they broke for the sled.

Where was the other shooter? Sean scanned the area around them. He knew which way he needed to go but didn't want to head straight into the path of a bullet. As his glance came back around, he heard Zoya gasp.

A man turned toward the trees and ran.

CHAPTER THIRTY-SEVEN

ANESIA

4:12 p.m.

The darkness wrapped around her like her cozy flannel sheets. Most people hated the dark. But not Anesia. It fascinated her, invited her, calmed her. And right now, she needed all of that. Needed to keep her senses about her as she searched for her daughter.

The faint scent of evergreens mixed with wood smoke floated on the air. If she knew her daughter, Anesia figured Zoya would've headed way out into the bush. Away from anyone and anything.

Because when Zoya went into protect mode, there was no stopping her. The girl was fierce in her affection. If people thought Anesia was a protective mama-bear, they'd have another think coming when Zoya was grown up and had kids of her own. Zoya had protected Andie for so many years, always making sure her friend didn't hurt herself, didn't get too hot, and being an extra set of eyes for Jenna.

She rounded a bend with her sled as she watched the blip on the screen of the handheld GPS. Even though she'd covered a lot of ground, Zoya was probably still miles away.

Anesia settled into the familiarity of the sled. The runners. The dogs. Her grip.

As the wind whipped through her heavy hood and tangled the ends of her hair, she allowed her mind to drift back to Sean.

What she wouldn't give to have normal circumstances again. To be able to pursue her feelings for him. Feelings that hadn't stirred within her chest for years. His arms around her soothed all the aches and pains within her soul. The intensity of the situation heightened her feelings for him.

It had also broken down all the walls she built around her guarded heart. And she'd let him in.

What would it be like to have someone take care of her for a change? Someone she could share the burdens of life with? Someone she could love.

And she did love Sean.

But she didn't want to make the same mistake she'd made in the past. She didn't want to lose him, like she'd lost Dan. Was it worth the risk?

This time would have to be different. Or she probably wouldn't survive. And she had to survive. For Zoya.

Oh, God. Let her be okay.

God hadn't brought them this far to let something happen to her, had He?

Lord, protect her. Please.

A dark figure darted across the snow in front of her and stood between two trees. There wasn't any other place to pass. The dogs barked and yapped, should she slow them down? But if that was someone after her, shouldn't she just keep going?

She couldn't just run over someone, though. She couldn't.

"Whoa." The dogs slowed and then stopped.

The figure pulled his hood back.

She let her breath escape. "Oh, Derek. It's you! Thank goodness . . . wait, what are you doing outsi—"

He pulled a gun out of his pocket and pointed it at her chest. "Get off the sled, Anesia."

"Derek, what are you doing?"

"You just had to find the chips, didn't you?"

"What?" She stared at the young man who'd been her employee for several years. Whom she'd trusted! Now he was standing in front of her, holding a gun? One of her snow machines sat beside him. He'd been waiting to ambush her?

"I'm sorry about this, Anesia. I really am. But you should've never gotten involved. Now get off the sled."

She shoved the GPS in her pocket and held up her hands.

"Gimme the GPS."

Great. He was apparently sharper than she'd given him credit. She threw the GPS at him.

"Get. Off. The. Sled." He reached down and petted Chocolate. Her lead dog. A dog that knew him well. A dog that licked his gloved hand.

She stepped off the sled.

He waved her over with his gun. "Over there, by that tree."

Anesia complied. She had to think. "Are you the one threatening my daughter?"

Derek laughed. "No. But I know who is." He pulled rope out of his pocket. "Don't worry about it. As soon as we get what we want, this will all be over and you can go back to your little girl and your dogs."

Anger blazed to life. Hotter than it ever had before. How *dare* he. And she'd sunk hours upon hours into training him. Sent him to vet classes. Paid for his education. Paid for him to work for her.

Forgive.

No. No way. Not this time. Not ever.

ZOYA
4:24 p.m.

"Sunshine, God hasn't left you. He's been right by your side the entire time. He doesn't leave us. We can move away from Him, but He never abandons us."

Sean's words echoed, repeated. Over and over again.

Was he right? Had I done the leaving?

He was right. I'd doubted, I'd been unfaithful. But what now? God couldn't still love me.

Could he?

I shook away the lies trying to get to me. God still loved me. I knew that . . . somewhere deep, deep down in my heart. Now if only I could accept it.

Home. We were going home. But what if those men came to hurt Mom? What if I put them all in danger again?

I closed my eyes. The wind whipped across my face. My hands squeezed the bar. My lips cracked and I tasted blood. We picked up speed and the wind got colder.

Everything in me begged to get under blankets, go to sleep, and not get up for a month. And yet I wanted to ride like the wind and never stop. Go somewhere far away. Then go home and feel safe again.

"Zoya, 'He will never leave you nor forsake you.' He loves you beyond description. You are His creation . . . He never leaves, He never abandons, He never drops you off at someone else's doorstep as if you're being thrown away. He loves you very much, Zoya. He wants you to run into His arms . . ."

I opened my eyes and watched Sean. He wasn't far ahead. But I still wanted him closer. Those men were still out there . . . My body shuddered. Why couldn't I get rid of this fear?

"God doesn't move away from us, Sunshine. If anyone moves, it's us. We move away. But He's still there. Always. Waiting. Ready to open His arms to us."

I leaned closer to the sled. Shivers ran up and down my spine.

". . . But He's still there . . ."

"Sean?" My voice was muffled, but loud enough for him to hear me.

He turned his head around and looked at me. "Yes?"

"Can we pull over a second?" I pointed to the side of the path.

His gaze locked with mine. Then he nodded and gave a small smile. "Sure thing, Sunshine."

We called to the dogs and pulled over.

I could do this. *Just breathe, Zoya.*

Sean stepped off his sled and sat down on a fallen tree trunk. "Come sit."

I walked over and sat down.

He said nothing.

I said nothing.

What did I ask first?

"I—I need to ask you some questions." I fiddled with my hands, not wanting to look into his big, wise, sympathetic, green eyes.

Again he nodded. "Go ahead."

I tried to swallow back my fears, but the effort proved in vain. I was going to have to just push through it.

"What should I do?" I rubbed my thumb and forefinger together, hoping it would warm them up. Even through the thick gloves the cold still bit at them.

I took a quick glance at his face. Would he understand?

"You need to figure that one out." He sighed and rubbed his temple. "What do you feel like you should do?"

Simple question, punch to my gut.

I didn't even know what I was feeling, exactly. I just wanted whatever the bad feeling was to be gone, to have that sense of peace again. But how did I explain that to Sean?

"I don't know." I shrugged. Why was everything so difficult? Why couldn't I, for once in my life, figure this thing out and fix it? "I feel so lost, Sean. I'm not sure of anything right now." I stared at the ground.

I wanted to take care of this by myself. Why couldn't I?

Snowflakes, millions of them, sat in perfect harmony creating the fantastic beauty of a thick sparkling blanket. If I could see each and every snowflake, define each one's differences . . .

But I couldn't do this. *I couldn't fix things. I couldn't save my mom.*

Only God could.

I sniffed. "I know I was wrong. I let my anger and fear get so strong that I couldn't feel anything, hear anything but them. And I'm sorry." I was sorry. Very sorry.

He smiled. "Then tell Him." He stood and walked over to pet the dogs.

I swallowed. *That's easier said than done.*

Deep breath.

Okay.

God, I'm sorry. Please forgive me. Please forgive me for everything. I sat there, unable to move. No peaceful feeling came. No thunderous "you're forgiven."

It's not working . . .

Or was I still doubting? Still trying to do things my own way? I folded my hands and leaned my elbows on my knees. Closed my eyes.

God? I'm sorry. I give it up. Please take all this. My doubt, my fear, my . . . everything. I don't want to be untrusting anymore. I'm tired of doubting. Please help me.

I held my breath.

God, please . . .

"We should get moving. Are you okay?" Sean walked back over. "We need to get you home. It looks like more snow, and I don't want what light the moon has to offer to be covered."

Couldn't I just have a few more minutes? I sighed. "Let's go then."

We got on the sleds.

Focus . . .

On God.

Focus. And, no matter what my feelings told me, *never* let go.

311

ANDIE
4:50 p.m.

I touched my fingers to the cold glass window of our plane. Searching. And searching. And searching some more.

God, where is she? We hadn't seen any sign of Zoya. But we had to find her. And when we did . . . boy, was she gonna get it. And get it good. Who in their right mind would run off like that? *Sheesh. Girl, I love you to death, but you are a fruit loop.*

I was worried. Frantic. Where had she gone?

The radio whistled and crackled.

"Anything, Jenna?" Cole's voice came over loud and clear. Well, clear for a radio.

"Not yet. But we'll keep looking."

I shook my head and turned back to the window. Where could she be?

"Just be careful, hon."

"Will do." Mom turned the plane in another direction.

I scanned the ground, hoping and praying that by some miracle God would tell us where she was. And that she wasn't in danger.

"Jenna, Cole?" Sean's voice came over the radio.

I leaned in closer.

"I've found Zoya."

I jerked upright. Mom smiled.

Tears slid out from my eyelids and rolled down my cheeks. *Wow, that was a fast reply! Thank You, God!* "You tell her that when we get back to the house she is going to get the lecture of her life!"

Mom smiled and grabbed the radio with one hand. "Where did you find her? Is she okay?"

"Yeah, she's fine. We're on our way back to the house right now."

"Gotcha." Mom smiled again and turned to me. "Praise God."

I smiled in return. *You can say that again.*

We turned back in the direction of the house.

I let out a sigh. *Thanks again, God.* I couldn't wait to get there. And wring Zoya's neck.

— —

Almost an hour later, I hopped out of the plane and ran toward the house. Mom followed not far behind.

Cole must have seen us coming. He met us halfway.

"Zoya?"

When Cole didn't smile, I knew something was wrong.

God, please let her be okay! "What is it?" I folded my hands and held them to my chest. She better not have run off again.

Cole hugged us. Then sighed and rubbed his temple. "Sean and Zoya haven't gotten back yet." He glanced to Mom, then back to me. "And Anesia's gone."

Mom gasped. "What?"

"We can't raise her on the radios."

My jaw dropped. "You've *got* to be joking."

Cole shook his head. "I'm sorry, Einstein. She left hours ago. Sometime this morning. Nobody's heard from her since."

Great. Now I had two necks to wring. And at this point I'd never let go of either one. *Ever.*

CHAPTER THIRTY-EIGHT

SLIM
February 3
5:32 p.m.

"I'm really not a bad guy." He smiled at his former boss.

She didn't look like she believed him.

"Oh, *really*? Then why do you have a gun pointed at me?"

Anesia was a strong lady. He admired her for that. Still, he couldn't help but enjoy the feeling flowing through him. The feeling that grew every time he looked into her fear-filled eyes.

Power.

"Because you have something that we want. And I don't get paid unless I deliver it."

"AMI?"

So the boss lady knew more than he'd thought. "Bingo. I knew you were smart." Just not smart enough to beat him.

She looked down at her bound hands. "How did you get mixed up in this? You're such a good kid, Derek . . . you have such potential. I . . . I thought you were a Christian."

"That's the whole point, Anesia." He wielded the gun, enjoying the feeling of it in his hands. Swung it closer to her face, then to the dogs. "I do have potential, and no offense, but working for

314

you was a dead end." He anchored the dogs, told them to lie down, and crouched down beside them, petting each one. "Don't get me wrong, the job was great. Love your dogs. But I need . . . more."

She gazed at him. Almost motherly. Sympathetic. "Why?"

He chuckled. She wasn't that stupid. "Because money and power rule the world."

"And what does your mother have to say about all this?"

"Leave Ma out of this!" He jumped to his feet.

"But I thought you said she was your best friend?"

"Shut up, Anesia!" He stood in front of her. Inches from her face. His stocky body shook with the anger that seeped through him.

She sank to her knees and nodded.

His pocket vibrated. Finally. He answered his phone. "I've got her."

"Good. I'll arrange for the call and the drop-off." The powerful voice was syrupy sweet. That grated on his nerves. Like the guy had no respect for him.

"When do I get my money?"

"It's being transferred right now as we speak. You'll need to get her to the drop-off point."

"Nuh-uh. No way. You said you had someone to take the fall when they ambushed. I'm not goin' down with this."

"You're right, Slim. I have someone, but you have to get her there."

Heat crept up his neck. "You better not be double-crossing me. You forget that you still need to know how to remove the encryption on the chips. And I'm the only one who can do that."

"Don't worry, Slim. We'll take care of you. Check your phone, if you can. You'll see the money's there. Now just get her to the location."

Derek checked his messages on his iPhone. Sure enough, a text came through from his bank, showing the money was there. He put the phone back up to his ear. "All right. I'll do it."

"Good. Nice working with you, Slim."

The phone call disconnected.

Soon it would all be over. He had his money. Just needed to finish this last part of the job and head out of the country. He smiled. Hadn't gone so bad after all.

"Derek?"

She just wouldn't be quiet. "What do you want?"

"Are you just going to throw your faith away?" A couple of tears perched on the edge of her lashes. As if she'd cry over him. Yeah, right. She was worried about her own hide. Not his.

"Anybody can fake it, Anesia. In fact, I knew a pastor once who did a great job fooling everyone. He's in prison now."

"But you know the truth, Derek. You know it. We've talked about it."

"So what? What has God ever gotten me? That pastor yearned for power and money too. What's wrong with me wanting some of that? But I'm not gonna steal money from the church, or control everyone and everything around me. And I'm not gonna be a fake and say God's behind me. I'm gonna do things my way. And *I* won't end up in prison."

"Derek, the love of money is the root of all evil. I'm sorry you had to know a pastor that did that, but you need to remember we're all sinners—"

"Don't quote Scripture to me, Anesia. And don't try to defend that man. I don't care. Yeah, I know what the Bible says. But I've made my choice. I'm doing things my way. So nobody else can trample on me the rest of my life." His stomach churned. Acid burned up his throat. Enough of this stupid conversation. He grabbed her by the arm. "Get up. It's time you earned *your* keep."

COLE
10:42 p.m.

Cole paced the length of Anesia's house. Foyer to office to kitchen to living room. And back again. Where were they? They should be back by now.

The two officers in the living room tapped away on their computers.

Jenna and Andie were out taking care of the dogs in the kennel.

He hated waiting.

Hated it. More than anythin—

Yelling reached his ears from outside. Cole ran out the door.

"Cole!" Zoya waved her arm in the air as she jumped off the sled.

Sean anchored the two sleds while Zoya ran up to the porch.

Andie and Jenna came running from the kennel.

"Zoya!" Andie squealed.

"Thank God, you're okay!" Jenna grabbed Zoya up in her arms.

Sean turned to Cole. "Are the police still here?"

"Yes."

"Good. There's a lot we need to catch them up on." Sean glanced around. His brow furrowed. "Where's Anesia?"

Zoya disentangled herself from the hugs of Jenna and Andie. "Yeah, where's Mom?"

Cole inhaled the bitter cold air. "Let's go inside." He turned to the door.

Zoya grabbed his arm. "Cole, where's Mom?"

He looked from Jenna's sad face, to Zoya's, then Sean's. "She's not here. We're not sure where she is."

—   —

Cole looked at Sean as Sergeant Roberts scribbled on his note pad.

"And you have no idea where the shooters went?"

Sean shook his head. "No. But Zoya recognized the second shooter as her Uncle. Could he have been protecting Zoya?"

Cole stood. "It doesn't add up." He turned to the officer. "So far, the only link is AMI. So where is Anesia?" The stubborn woman no doubt went out to look for Zoya. Even though she was told to stay put.

Sean leaned forward. "Well, we know she took a sled and a team of dogs out. Just like her to be so stubborn."

Well, at least Sean knew what he was getting into. Smart man.

The landline rang.

Jenna jumped up and grabbed the cordless. "Hello?" She clutched her throat. "What do you want?" Her eyes widened.

Cole yanked the phone from her. "Who is this?"

"We have Anesia. Go to the North Pole monument in the park. Directions and coordinates will be there by midnight. Then bring all the chips you retrieved from the dogs to the drop-off and we'll trade her. Four a.m. Tomorrow. Otherwise, she dies."

Cole waited for something more, hoping, praying for some sound to give him an idea where they were, but the caller hung up. He pulled the phone from his ear as an automated voice came over the line: *"If you'd like to make a call—"*

He set the phone back in its cradle.

Everyone in the room stared at him. "Anesia's been kidnapped. They want to trade her for the chips."

RICK
February 4
3:28 a.m.

The boss knew.

That's why he called and told him to handle the drop-off. Because the man knew he'd be killed or taken to jail when the FBI ambushed. Knew that Rick would have to follow through. Because that was the code.

But Rick wasn't an amateur. The business had held him in a choke hold for too many years. He'd been second in command for a long time. All those wasted years. All that wasted time.

Time was up.

He spotted the kid without too much trouble. The FBI had been set up for hours at the drop-off location. As soon as Rick waltzed in with Anesia, they'd take him. While the others stole the real chips containing the program.

His chest squeezed. Pain radiated toward his shoulder. Rubbing the spot, he attempted a slow breath. Then popped another pill into his mouth.

Leaving the kid and Anesia, he headed back to the drop-off location. His Jeep sat off the road. He pulled out his flashlight and aimed it toward his windshield. Flicking the switch several times, he signaled the man inside. At least, he hoped the guy was still inside.

The beam shut off as he clicked the button and put it back into his pocket.

A shaggy man exited his Jeep, manila envelope in hand. Now if only the ten one-hundred dollar bills he'd given him were incentive enough for the guy to do the job.

Rick walked back toward where the kid held Anesia. He checked his watch. Pulled the pistol out of his pocket.

One step at a time.

He had to finish it.

3:38 a.m.

Slim saw him approaching. A smile split the young guy's face. "Glad you could make it. I'm outta here."

Before the kid made it five yards, Rick lifted the gun, aimed, and pulled the trigger. A clean shot to the back of the head.

Slim dropped to the ground.

Anesia cried out behind the gag in her mouth.

Rick knelt down in front of her. Recognition lit her eyes and she shook her head.

He yanked the gag from her mouth and untied her hands.

"No. Not you. Why'd you kill him?"

His chest tightened even more. Breathing hurt. The pain shot in arrows down his left arm. Up his neck. "To save you."

Snow crunched behind him. He clutched his chest, the pain too much to bear.

"Freeze! FBI!"

CHAPTER THIRTY-NINE

ANESIA
3:45 a.m.

Everything blurred in front of her. Rick collapsed into her arms. She blinked back tears as uniformed agents and officers crowded around her.

"Ma'am? You okay?"

She nodded.

"Are you Anesia Naltsiine?"

Another nod.

Rick's eyes fluttered open, his hand clutching the front of her coat.

Agents pushed forward.

"No!" She held them back.

Rick gasped for air. "Dan . . ."

She clung to him. "Dan? Dan what?"

"Forgive me. Forgive . . ."

Guilt flooded her. She'd held on to her stubbornness and pride too long. Sobs gushed from her, she couldn't see. Couldn't even speak around the emotion pouring out.

Rick slumped back. Two big men pulled him from her arms.

An agent spoke into a cell phone. "She's alive. We'll bring her home."

A female agent gave a gentle prod, encouraging her to stand. "Come on, ma'am. We've got some people who are anxious to see you." The woman kept talking as she led her to a car, but Anesia couldn't hear her past the fog in her brain, couldn't feel anything other than the sobs wracking her body.

She needed Zoya. To feel her baby. Make sure she was okay.

She needed Sean. To feel those strong arms around her.

She needed to go home.

The image of Derek lying in his own blood flashed in her mind. Over and over again. She wanted to throw up. Guilt grew. All she could think about earlier was revenge. Rage had blinded her. Every time that still small voice whispered "forgive" she'd ignored it.

Oh, God! What have I done?

Two more men were dead. Two men who needed forgiveness. Two men who needed the Lord. And she'd been too angry to see it. Closing her eyes, she allowed her thoughts to drift back to Dan. Her first love. Her only love until Sean.

How was Dan mixed up in all this? Why hadn't he ever told her about Rick? Why did he have to die?

Forgive.

They were moving, but she wasn't feeling anything other than her anger. The guilt and pain it caused. Tears poured from her eyes, drenching her face, her shirt, her hands.

Let go, Anesia. Forgive.

Derek's face, then Rick's popped into her mind again. She couldn't take it anymore. She poured her heart out to God. All the guilt and rage. "Help me forgive."

Derek. Rick. The shooter. Dan. Herself. God. Everything burst to the surface. Stubborn and prideful, she'd held tight to her independence. But it'd only hurt her in the end.

As she confessed each thing, tiny weights lifted off her shoulders. As she forgave each name, each face, even her own, she felt the knots in her shoulders and neck release.

Her sobs subsided and an indescribable peace and joy flooded her.

After all these years, she could still see Dan's smile, because Zoya inherited it. And right now, she felt him smiling at her. Urging her to be happy. To move on with her life. And Zoya's.

"Ms. Naltsiine." A tap on her shoulder brought her back from her state of exhaustion. Had she fallen asleep?

"Ma'am, you're home. Let's get you inside." The female agent was beside her again.

The door of the house flew open and Zoya raced down the steps toward her. "Mom!"

Sean followed right behind her, with Cole, Andie, and Jenna bringing up the rear.

Her daughter threw her arms around her shoulders, and Sean wrapped them both in his arms. He whispered into Anesia's hair. "I'm so glad you're okay. I died inside thinking you didn't even know how I felt."

Anesia allowed the laughter to bubble up inside her even as the tears streamed down her cheeks.

She was home.

The agents stood to the side for several moments, then Agent Philips spoke. "I think we need to move inside."

She nodded. And the others traipsed up the steps into her home, everyone talking at once.

When they were seated in the living room, Anesia ensconced between Sean and Zoya, Cole started the questioning. "Did anyone hurt you?"

"No. I'm fine."

He turned to the agent in charge. "What happened? Your call came in before the drop-off was even to take place."

Agent Philips sat on a chair across from Anesia. "Rick Kon' hired a homeless man to deliver an envelope to us before the drop-off. In it, he outlined the plan to use our ambush at the drop-off as a chance for their inside man to steal the real macrochips from us. But even more than that, the mastermind—who we haven't found yet—blew the facility at precisely four a.m. Mr. Kon' saved ten of our agents tonight. And we caught the mole."

"And AMI?" Cole stood stiff.

"Secure."

"Thank God." Cole paced in front of them. "What happened to Rick?"

"He was DOA at the hospital. Heart attack."

Anesia wanted to cry. Long and hard. She'd only just met the man, but he'd been a link to Dan.

Sean wrapped an arm around her shoulders and squeezed. She looked up at him. Those deep green eyes. Staring back at her. Full of adoration and love.

"My dogs!" She sat up straight. "We left a sled and a team out in the middle of nowhere."

Two officers headed to the door. "Do you know the location?"

She rattled off her last known coordinates. "That's where Derek stopped me."

"Derek?" Jenna looked at her in horror. "Derek, your employee?"

"Yes. Apparently it was his idea to implant the chips in my dogs."

Zoya shivered next to her. "He was so nice. And to think he was here. All the time. How long had he been doing this?"

Sergeant Roberts stepped up to answer. "Quite a while. According to what we know, they stole the program in small increments. Then hid it on the chips and implanted them in the dogs."

A knock sounded at the door. The sergeant answered it. Agent Philips walked into the living room. "Major Maddox, I have that evidence you were looking for."

Cole greeted the man and took the brown paper bag he held out. He dumped the contents into his hand.

A shiny little black box.

SEAN
9:00 a.m.

Even his most frenzied days at CROM couldn't compare with the craziness he'd been through in the past eight hours.

Now, sitting here in the bank with Anesia, all he wanted was a nap. Exhaustion, deep and powerful, seeped into every cell of his body. Cole had said he would go to the bank with Anesia, but she requested Sean accompany her. His heart soared at her desire to have him with her, but now he was too bone tired to think straight.

The black box they'd recovered from evidence had, indeed, belonged to Marc. Inside they'd found several small pieces of paper. One was a note for Jenna. From the look on her face as she read it, Sean was willing to bet it healed some bruised portions of Jenna's heart. Another note informed Anesia that Marc had left her a safety deposit box—one that contained something from Dan. The last piece of paper, which looked like it had been scribbled in a hurried hand, was written to Cole, telling him what he needed would be in Anesia's safety deposit box.

Now, here he and Anesia were, sitting in the bank, waiting for Anesia's ID and account number to be verified against the bank's security records. For access to the box. For the end to this whole, crazy situation.

Then . . . Sean hoped for a new beginning.

Anesia fidgeted beside him. She looked up and, when she found him watching her, she smiled. "Sorry. I'm just ready for this all to be over."

"Me too."

"Sean, I haven't thanked you properly for all you've done to help us through this crazy time. You've had to put up with a lot."

"I'm glad I was here." He took her hand in his and squeezed. "I wouldn't have it any other way." Those long lashes of hers distracted him. It seemed everything she did distracted him. "Anesia?"

"Mm-hm?"

"I want to ask you someth—"

"Ms. Naltsiine, we are ready for you. Please follow me." The tall woman was all business.

Anesia stood and he trailed her as the woman led them down a corridor. She opened a door to a room, and Sean could see the safe deposit box sitting on a table inside.

"This room will be yours for as long as you need it." The lady waited until they entered, then closed the door behind them.

Anesia took the key in her hand and approached the box. "Well, here goes."

Sean stepped up. "Anesia, wait. Before you open that box, I want to finish."

She turned to him. "Okay."

"I know the time isn't appropriate, but I can't hold it in any longer. I love you." His heart beat the rhythm of the three words.

"Really?"

"Yes. I do."

She giggled. "You love me?"

"Yes. And your daughter." He pulled her into his arms. "Oh, and the dogs, too."

She pulled back. "I'm not sure what to say. I haven't done this in so long . . ."

"Shhh." He held her hands in front of him. "I'm not going to push. And I will respect your boundaries."

"I think you misunderstood, Sean." She released his hands and walked around the table. "I *do* love you, but I'm going to need some time." Her eyes pooled with tears. "Time to say good-bye."

"I understand." And he did. "I'll wait for you, Anesia. However long it takes."

"And you'll keep working at the kennel?"

"You couldn't stop me if you tried."

Her smile lit up her face.

"I'm in this for the long haul, Anesia. With you, Zoya, and however many dozens of dogs—"

She came back around the table and hugged him tight. Then she pulled back again.

Man, oh man, he wanted to kiss her. But something held him back. He caught her hand, turned her to face him, looked into her eyes. "However long it takes, I'll wait. Until you tell me."

She held his gaze. "Tell you?"

He took her hands in his. "When you're ready. For me. For us." His fingers tightened on hers. "But when you say that, you'd better be prepared."

A small smile lifted her lips. "Oh? For what?"

He lifted her hand, placed it over his heart. "For a kiss you'll never forget."

Pink tinged her cheeks, but she didn't pull away. Instead, she lifted her other hand and placed it over his. "I promise. I will tell you." Her smile grew. "And I will, most definitely, be prepared. But you'd better be ready, too."

He let his fingers caress her cheek. "Yeah?"

"Yeah. Because, Sean Connolly, I plan to kiss you back."

9:18 a.m.

Sean stood by the door while Anesia unlocked the box and opened the lid. She pulled out an envelope first. Lifted the flap with her fingers and peered inside. "Sean, look."

He came to her side and saw another tiny disk. A macro SD card. How astonishing technology was nowadays to be able to store large amounts of information on such a tiny piece of hardware.

"There's a note." Anesia unfolded the paper and read:

Anesia,

I'm sorry to throw this at you, but my time is short. I'm afraid I won't be around much longer. Please make sure Jenna and Andie are taken care of. You'll find account information in the box. One for you, and one for Jenna.

Please find a Major Cole Maddox and give him this disk. Tell him it has to do with encryption. He'll know what that means and what to do with it.

You've been a wonderful friend all these years. I'm sorry for all the pain I've caused. Forgive me.

Marc

She stared down at the paper. "I had no idea. He must've known. And prepared . . ." She choked. "Accounts? What does he mean?"

Sean stood beside her for support but knew she needed to process all the information.

She pulled out a small cardboard box. Packing tape held it shut. Another note was taped to the top. Sean read over Anesia's shoulder.

Anesia,

Dan asked me to hold onto this for you. He wanted me to give it to you if anything ever happened to him. I'm sorry to say that I forgot about it. I had it stashed in one of my safety deposit boxes.

As you know by now, things got out of control for me. If you're reading this, then I'm also gone. Please forgive me.

Marc

She ran her hand over the box and sniffed. "I think I'll take this home to open. Cole needs the disk."

"There's one more thing in there, Anesia."

She blinked back tears and reached in for a large manila envelope. The brass clasp opened with ease. As she pulled out a stack of papers, she gasped. "Sean, look at this!"

He perused a few lines then glanced at the bottom. "Good night, Anesia! That's a hefty sum."

"Ahh, so the truth comes out. You just love me for my money."

He pulled her into his arms and laughed with her. "I'm worth way more than that. I don't need your money. I just need you."

CHAPTER FORTY

ZOYA

February 26
Junior North American Championships
11:44 a.m.

The championship.

I couldn't believe it. I had *actually* made it to the Junior North American Championships. Finally. After all those dreams, all those days of hoping, praying . . .

I was about to race in the biggest race of my life yet.

Sean whistled and cheered along with Mom, Auntie Jenna, Andie, and Cole.

Thank You, God. For everything.

God was there. He was with me. All the time.

And I loved it.

I took a moment to think of how I had been blessed: Sean, soon to be my dad. The promise of a whole new life.

I sighed.

God was a great Giver.

I didn't deserve His love, His kindness. And yet there I was. Standing in the midst of them.

My eyes closed. I could feel the slight breeze whipping across my face.

I wanted to stay in God's love forever. Never wanted to leave, never wanted to let go of Him again . . .

My thoughts were cut short as the starter sounded. The Painkiller Litter once again took off running at full speed.

Oh, how I loved racing.

As we rode down the trail, I realized I had been blessed with more than I could ever imagine.

As I closed my eyes, my heart cried out. Cried out to my Savior. My best friend for all eternity.

I love You, God. Thank You for loving me.

I cried, the tears sliding down my cheeks and freezing, making my mask stick to my face. But for once my tears fell from joy. The joy of forgiveness. The joy of love.

The joy of everlasting life.

"I press on so that I may lay hold of that for which also I was laid hold of by Christ Jesus. Brethren, I do not regard myself as having laid hold of it yet; but one thing I do: forgetting what lies behind and reaching forward to what lies ahead, I press on toward the goal to win the prize of the upward call of God in Christ Jesus."

In reality, life really was like one big race.

I knew it would be hard. But I ran it with God by my side. His love in my heart. His strength upholding me.

With everything in me, I raced toward the finish line.

And I was determined to win.

ANESIA
11:53 a.m.

Cheers from the fans cascaded over Anesia like a warm blanket as Zoya passed the marker at the midway turnaround.

Her daughter. Precious girl. Running her race with a smile on her face as her body turned with the sled.

Thoughts skittered through Anesia's brain as she jumped, cheered, and waved her thirteen-year-old on. *Go, Rainbow. Fly.*

"Go, Zoya!" Sean's deep voice rumbled next to her.

Pride surged and joined with the bubbling of joy in her heart. God was so good. To bring them through such difficult circumstances and bless them with joy.

Dashing back to her truck, she shot a smile to Sean.

What a man. As they climbed into her 4x4, her insides buzzed with butterflies every time she thought of him. She wanted to take things slow, think things through, but who was she kidding? She knew.

He was the one.

In the last few weeks, she'd finally forgiven, finally let go of her past. Now? Anesia looked forward to her future. A future that no longer stretched out in front of her like a barren landscape. No longer desperately alone.

A future as bright and vibrant as the Alaskan fireweed.

As they bounced along the dirt road taking them back to the finish line, Anesia reached over and squeezed Sean's hand.

"What's that for?" He winked.

"Just a promise."

"A promise of what?"

"Oh, you'll see."

The parking area came into view and she focused on the racing crowd ahead. Zoya would be coming in just a few moments. Unable to contain the laughter that poured out, Anesia grabbed Sean's hand again and they ran to the crowd.

Cheers once again washed over her. Time stood still—only for a moment, but it was long enough for an old dream to resurface. Closing her eyes, she leaned into Sean, grateful for his strength, his warmth. As he wrapped an arm around her shoulders, she realized the dream was different now. And oh, so beautiful.

Whistles and yells grew in their intensity. Anesia opened her eyes. A smile split her lips as Zoya and her dogs barreled toward them. Her daughter crossed the finish line and raised her fist in the air in answer to the roaring crowd.

Sean lifted Anesia off her feet and spun her around. "That's my Sunshine!"

Breathless when her feet hit the ground, Anesia melted into him. He loved her. He loved her daughter. Loved her dogs. This man was so—

"Mom?" Zoya stood there, hands on her hips. She whipped off her goggles and glared at Sean. "Well? Aren't you going to kiss her? I just won the Championship!" Giggling, she threw herself into Anesia and Sean's arms.

When they untangled from their group hug, Anesia winked at her matchmaker daughter, then turned and slid her arms around the man she loved. She smiled up at him.

He studied her face for a moment, then his eyes widened. "Are you . . . ?"

She nodded. "Zoya's right, Sean. I'm ready for that ki—"

She didn't get to finish, but then, she didn't exactly care. Not when his lips on hers told her everything she needed to know. Promised her not just today, but tomorrow. And the day after that.

And forever.

Amen.

Dear Readers,

We had the awesome privilege to live in Alaska for several years. Part of that time was spent in the Aleutian Islands living among the native Aleut (al-ee-oot) people. They are precious to us. We maintain a deep love for Alaska and a respect for all the different native peoples of Alaska and hope that our heart is shown in attempting to capture the beauty of the Ahtna-Athabaskan.

There are only about twenty people left in the world who actually speak Ahtna, so a huge thanks goes out to Dr. John Smelcer for his work on the Ahtna dictionary, which we were able to use for the Land of the Midnight Sun series. The Ahtna Heritage Foundation and elders were also key in helping us.

There is a list of Ahtna words with pronunciations and definitions at the beginning of this book. We know several native people who are doing what Jenna, Andie, Anesia, and Zoya are doing by trying to learn more of their native language and pass it on. In writing about them, we hope to do our part to help preserve another beautiful piece of Alaskan and American History. Our characters in this series are from the North Pole, Alaska, area. The Ahtna are not originally from this area but from a region farther south.

We'd like to thank you for reading *Race Against Time*. As enjoyable as it was to write, it was equally a doozy. Tackling anger, forgiveness, and PTSD in teens were all challenging. PTSD is tough and manifests itself in so many different ways. Add in our imagined defense weapon, the Ahtna language, sprint racing, and all those dogs—and our hands were full juggling all the pieces to the puzzle.

Sprint racing is so incredible. Hundreds of hours were spent in research. A lot of people helped with that and with the facts in this book. But the Callis Family deserves a trophy and medals of honor for putting up with all our questions. We are so thankful for their help and expertise. During the writing of this book, some of the rules changed within the world of sprint racing. We tried to make sure that we got it correct, but any mistakes are clearly our own. If you'd like to see pictures of some dogs and videos of our sled rides, go to http://kimberleyandkaylawoodhouse.com and go to the All About Alaska page. To find out more and see pictures of racing and sled dog trucks, etc., go to http://sleddogcentral.com and click on the photo gallery.

While we had wonderful sources with the North Pole Police Department, FBI, Army, and other military, please keep in mind that this is a work of fiction, and some artistic license was taken to preserve the integrity of top secret intelligence and procedurals of law enforcement officials. AMI and the AMI ops facility beneath Fort Greeley are completely of our own imaginations.

Oh, and about law enforcement in Alaska . . . if you've ever watched the shows about the state troopers or pilots in Alaska, or even *Deadliest Catch*, you understand that things in Alaska are different. The risks, the terrain, the amount of sunlight (or lack thereof) are all different. In short, Alaska is an amazing place and it fascinates people. We hope we were able to capture a tiny taste of its magnificence and give you a yearning to visit.

As we worked on this book, our respect and admiration for all law enforcement and military grew. We'd like to challenge you to encourage, support, and pray for all these men and women.

More than anything, we hope you were able to come away from *Race Against Time* with the reality that God loves you. More than you could ever imagine. His love and forgiveness know no bounds. This life on earth will never be easy, but His joy is always there for the taking. So grab on, friends. And hold on for dear life as you run your race.

> Therefore, since we have so great a cloud of witnesses surrounding us, let us also lay aside every encumbrance and the sin which so easily entangles us, and let us run with endurance the race that is set before us, fixing our eyes on Jesus, the author and perfecter of faith, who for the joy set before Him endured the cross, despising the shame, and has sat down at the right hand of the throne of God. For consider Him who has endured such hostility by sinners against Himself, so that you will not grow weary and lose heart. (Hebrews 12:1–3)

As always, we love to hear from our readers. So please drop us a note or e-mail.

Kim and Kayla